The Shakespeare Diaries

J. P. Wearing

a fictional autobiography

SANTA
MONICA
PRESS

Copyright ©2007 by J.P. Wearing

All rights reserved.

This book may not be reproduced in whole or in part or in any form or format without the written permission of the publisher.

Published by: Santa Monica Press LLC
P.O. Box 1076
Santa Monica, CA 90406-1076
1-800-784-9553
www.santamonicapress.com
books@santamonicapress.com

Printed in the United States

Santa Monica Press books are available at special quantity discounts when purchased in bulk by corporations, organizations, or groups. Please call our Special Sales department at 1-800-784-9553.

ISBN-13 978-1-59580-022-0
ISBN-10 1-59580-022-0

Library of Congress Cataloging-in-Publication Data

Wearing, J. P.
  The Shakespeare diaries : a fictional autobiography / J.P. Wearing.
    p. cm.
  Includes bibliographical references.
  ISBN-13: 978-1-59580-022-0
  ISBN-10: 1-59580-022-0
  1. Shakespeare, William, 1564-1616—Fiction. 2. Diary fiction. I. Title.

PR6123.E224S53 2007
823'.92—dc22

2006102339

Cover and interior design and production by cooldogdesign

Contents

Preface 5
1582 7
1583 13
1584 15
1585 17
1586 21
1587 23
1588 29
1589 37
1590 43
1591 47
1592 61
1593 77
1594 91
1595 105
1596 111
1597 127
1598 145
1599 163
1600 189
1601 207
1602 231
1603 249
1604 277
1605 297
1606 313
1607 333
1608 347
1609 359
1610 365
1611 373
1612 379
1613 383
1614 389
1615 393
1616 395
Postmortem 397
Notes 399

Preface

To the great variety of readers

For more than twenty years I taught Shakespeare courses at the University of Arizona, and, in the midst of endlessly fascinating and rewarding discussions about Shakespeare's plays, students would frequently ask me some question or other about the man, his life, his experiences, his thoughts, and his opinions. Initially, I greeted these unanswerable questions with the lame response: "We don't know." Then one day, quite spontaneously, I replied jokingly: "I don't know; but when I get home I'll dig out his diaries, consult them, and let you have the answer next time." This response soon became my stock answer to such questions and something of a running joke with my classes (although occasionally a student would entertain serious skepticism about my sense of humor).

Over time that recurring pursuit of answers to the unanswerable became the inspiration for this work. I thought: What if Shakespeare's diaries did exist? What would they be like? What would they contain? What might they tell us about the man, his life, his work, and his times?

The outcome, after several years' worth of musings and research, is the current work of "faction," a blend of fact and fiction: each fact and event is historically accurate, and presented from a contemporary point of view; however, the facts are woven into a fictional narrative. The result is a fictional autobiography: what Shakespeare himself might have penned had he indeed kept a diary. Thus the diaries include virtually every known fact about Shakespeare, details of many of his theatrical and social contemporaries, allusions to numerous contemporary events, as well as "Shakespeare's views" on his own plays and those of other dramatists, people, events, and the like.

Moreover, the diaries employ only those words that were available in the Elizabethan and Jacobean vocabulary—Shakespeare's vocabulary. In addition, many fragments and snatches of lines and phrases from Shakespeare's plays and poems are incorporated as part of the narrative, although not necessarily as direct quotations.

Naturally, there is much in the diaries—events, facts, allusions—that needs further explanation and elucidation, and consequently I have provided such information. An overview of Shakespeare's activities and historical events precedes each year of diary entries. Brief explanatory clarifications within a diary entry are provided in square brackets: [. . .]. The endnotes offer much fuller factual material, references to the plays, citations of sources, and additional fascinating details that the curious reader may explore further.

I trust my former students will find their quest for information is now fulfilled, for herein lie the answers to such previous imponderables as "What did Shakespeare and Ben Jonson talk about when they had a drink together?" "What did Queen Elizabeth actually say to Shakespeare (if anything)?" "Was he happily married?" "What was he thinking about when he wrote Hamlet?" Perchance my students, and the present gentle reader, will find *The Shakespeare Diaries* is not entirely "an improbable fiction."

—*J. P. Wearing*

❧ *A restless seventeen-year-old Shakespeare wishes for more fulfillment in his life. During the summer, he woos an initially reluctant Anne Hathaway, who becomes pregnant. An unwilling Shakespeare is forced into marriage, and incurs his parents' displeasure. His hopes of an exciting future disappear.* ❧

[SUMMER]

Satisfaction. I crave satisfaction. Though for many a year I have been a home-keeping youth, plain of wit, I crave some satisfaction. For I have within me what I fain would set down for mine remembrance, and what, mayhap, other folk might read one day or another. I believe I might be a poet such as we were taught in school; mayhap I might be celebrated like Ovid. God-a-mercy, the hours I have passed with his book that dear mother gave me; there's no tardiness in my nature! But more to the matter at hand—my cause. Yester afternoon, father not requiring my labour, the day being clear and warmed by the summer's sun, I journeyed across the cornfields to Wilmcote. The hedgerows were afire, a blaze of native hues; in every bush birds chanted sweet melodious songs; green leaves quivered with the wind; bees drank in every open flower. After some time, tho' all was pleasing to mine eyne, I grew aweary with the heat and determined to return home by way of Shottery.[1] I had crossed the brook and was some distance from the village, when I heard a voice call my name from behind some tree or hedge, tho' which I knew not. I looked about me, yet seeing nothing. Again came the call, & this time I saw some silken, shining strands of hair which a breeze lifted from the trunk of an oak. I darted forth & found Anne [Hathaway] all smiles.

We sat & talked, & talked as never before, & ere I was aware some two or three hours had passed. How might it be that someone I have known many a long year might be some other person, with little semblance to the person I had imagined? I' fecks, the Anne of yore is now a stranger to me. A new woman hath sprung forth, and devoutly I dote upon her, desire to see her, be with her, caress her. In truth, her image was so wondrous rare that I loved it in an instant.

I live in hope, for when we parted I asked Anne when next I might walk & talk with her. Anne said, "Well, sweet Will, ye know father died a twelvemonth come this September, and now I may come & go as I please.[2] So, if ye ask me, pleasantly, I will indeed walk with ye & talk with ye." And I did. I am trembling fearful the day will never come.

[LATE SUMMER]

Time is the nurse and breeder of all good! Anne sent word she fain would see me, &, surfeited with desire, I hastened to Shottery as fast as any young man's legs might carry him. I remarked nothing of my journey thither, for my heart, lungs, and loins were afire, & Anne was all my thought. How swiftly my flames were quenched, for Anne would not let me near her. One moment she would be coy and smiling, the next she scorned me and all my sex. I said, "Will you rent our new-found love asunder thus in scorning me?" Woo her as I might, she did reproach and upbraid me; she was a tiger, I a dove. I said there was no pursuing her in this vein. She said, "Men's smoothing words do naught but bewitch fair maidens' hearts. Oh, how I do hate all men." But, as quickly as she uttered those words, she said, "but not you." I said, "'Tis death to me to be at enmity with ye, dearest Anne." Much else passed between us, but ere I came away, she relented somewhat, & told me I might see her again. The path of love ne'er did run smooth. Needs must I speak with Dick [Quiney], for, surely of any man, he may comprehend the ways of women.[3]

To Dick Quiney, to seek his advice and counsel about Anne. I told him all my story. He listened closely, & then spoke earnestly. "Dear Will, search your heart & mind fervently. Before you pursue this course, you needs must know whether you love Anne, or whether all this you profess is but the hot blood of summer's lust. And you must consider your father & family, & what folk might say, & so forth. And, mark ye this, when you take her hand in marriage, it must be in true constancy." He spoke much to this effect and concluded, if I did truly love Anne, I must be patient & bide my time, for women will use their wiles, as 'tis but their nature to ply men so.

Despite the burning fever of my heart, I have been patient, & I have won a heaven on earth by wooing Anne. Said she, "Clear thy cloudy countenance," and was all most loving kindness. She led me on, and I have tasted those joys, the sweetest delights only woman can give to man. She yielded up her virginity, and, a thirsty man at the well, I drank deep & slaked my thirst. We meet again tomorrow.

> Those lips that love's hand did make
> Breathed the sound that said "I hate"
> To me languishing for her sake.
> When she saw my woeful state
> In her heart did mercy come,
> Chiding that tongue that sweet
> Was used to give breath gentle doom,
> And taught it anew to greet:
> "I hate" she changed to an end
> That followed like gentle day
> Follows night like that fiend
> From heaven is flown away.
>   "I hate" from hate away she threw,
>   And saved my life, said "not you."[4]

Once more with Anne; I burnt with desire. As we parted, Anne was serious, and asked me if I loved her truly—if my intentions be honourable, if they incline to marriage. I knew not what to say, for these be new sensations, & I ne'er loved e'er this. Yet I smiled & said she should surely know what lies in my heart. "Thou hast metamorphosed me," I said, "and made me lose all count of time." She frowned and smiled, saying she knew not what I meant. Then we parted, and I do believe I have deceived with a lie indirect.

Beshrew me, the heavens, all hung with black, have ordained my doom. To me this day came Anne with heavy news—she is with child. She said we are contracted, needs must marry, needs must speak with my father as soon as may be—"I am impatient of all tarriance," quoth she. I know not what to think; my mind is awhirl. Yet I did importune Anne greatly, took my pleasure; in sooth, I would be honest.

I have told father & mother; they were not well pleased. Father spoke much, & asked why I might not be like Dick Quiney, who has a fine wife, is respected in the town, aids & comforts his father, & much more. He swore he wished he had Dick for his son. "It grieves me sorely when now I think of many a time when I danced thee on my knee and sang thee asleep. And now 'tis come to this." Mother was sorrowful, though not greatly, & asked why I had chosen a woman so much more advanced in years than myself. "And, dear Will," she said, "a hasty marriage seldom proveth well." After some time, father, being quietened, said that it must be God's will and that we must accept matters as they are. "There's small choice in rotten apples," he said, and told me to speak to Anne that she might bring her relatives or friends to speak with father that our marriage can be arranged.

[NOVEMBER]

Today Anne came to my father's house, accompanied by two of her father's friends.[5] Deep chat about our marriage, for which the Bishop must issue a licence, & I know not what else. Vexation almost stopped my father's breath, so brimful with annoyance & anger was he. "Was ever a match clapped up so suddenly," he shouted. Mother smoothed and managed the business. Anne's friends go to Worcester for the licence. After, when all was quiet, Mother said to me, "Leastways, dear Will, Anne be not an irksome brawling scold."

27 NOVEMBER

I muse whether my wedded life will be like Dick Quiney's. Today his daughter was baptized and named after Dick's wife,[6] and both are filled with joyful happiness. Perchance all will be transformed when Anne & I marry, and the child is born. I pray by'r Lady it will be a son.[7]

[DECEMBER]

Key-cold my mind; endless days to repent and rue me. I had not thought to marry thus, and now the wages of fleeting pleasure are mine. Yet I confess I went to it lustily; Anne pleased me and I pleased her. We had no thought in the hay for what may chance afterwards, and I cannot tell o'er what hath befallen us since. So are we married, and I am the coney snapped tight in the snare. I needs must work for father, and we are beholden to him for lodging and more besides. Each and every day he makes me sensible that I stand debted to him & mother. Will I ever be free from this? When I was a child, I dreamed such dreams. I do recall, how old I was I know not, when I sat on my father's knee in the Guild Hall and watched, enraptured, some players enact some bombast stuff, but to my childish ears most magical. I thought to join the actors. What freedom, what lives.[8] But then, with Anne, I tasted consuming passion for that first time—Anne, who grows daily with child. Now am I confined, condemned to Stratford. Needs must it suffice, needs must I like it well. Thus goes the world.

> ⸘ *Shakespeare's first child, Susanna, is born, and provides him with some consolation. However, he continues to dream of life outside Stratford and a career onstage.* ⸙

[APRIL]

*A*nne is great with child and would be delivered of it. Mother tends her by the hour. I lack ambition & care little for this life, this petty pace.

26 MAY

Last summer, long since passed, is naught but a dream—those pleasures as fleeting as the morning's dew warmed by the sun. Some joy yet remains, for our Susanna is baptized this day in Trinity Church.[1] She is a comely child, more like her mother than me. Curiously, on me she smiles, but frowns at Anne; why I know not. Peradventure we three can jostle together, but I fear Anne is too old for me. She hath no other ambition than to settle here, with me in father's trade. Yet I would not. She knows I dream of fanciful adventures, for dissemble I cannot—I would be an actor like the players who pass through the town every once in a while. Essex's men, Strange's men, Worcester's: their very names excite me, my mind, my imagination. God a mercy, that I might be like them, to enact a part, or one day pen a play. But a wife and child is all my lot, my burden, & I must bide my time.

[NOVEMBER]

Married nigh on a year. A puling child, and a wife who takes on Puritan ways. Father gives me but little rest. I think "I am I, howe'er I was begot"; but there is only the certain knowledge of the truth of these petty, servile days. Of an evening, I look into the fire & dream of tales I might tell the world, tales I might set upon a stage. Shall I be naught but a dreamer? How long shall I be patient?

Dire news. Mother's cousin is taken for plotting against the queen's life, and he is to be tried in London.[2] Mother believes he is innocent, but she fears the worst will come to pass.

[CHRISTMAS]

I had thought to write, but of what, some enigma, some riddle? I have been merrier and do believe this life would vex a very saint.

❦ A touring company of actors, including Ned Alleyn (later a leading actor) visits Stratford. Alleyn tells Shakespeare about London and the life of an actor. Shakespeare's ambition is whetted further, but he is still constrained by his humdrum life in Stratford. Anne becomes pregnant again. ❦

1 JANUARY

As we feared, cousin Arden hath been executed, though his wife is spared and some priest who had spoke against him [Arden]. Mother weeps, is full of heart-sore sighs, and will not be comforted.

8 MARCH

In the twinkling of an eye, my dreary daily round was all changed. Yesterday came to town Worcester's Men. My excitement and joy were unbounded, and I can hardly retell what they enacted. They were eight men in all, though one was a youth some two years or so younger than me—Ned Alleyn.[1] He hath a pleasing yet commanding voice, eyes like rivets, and carries himself well when he acts; I noted all eyes were fixed on him until he left off speaking. To rule and sway an audience like him is now all my desire. Oh, that I might. Their play finished, I lingered so that I might chance to talk with one of them. To my delight, nay trembling ecstasy, I saw Ned Alleyn, who smiled and walked straight towards me. "I saw you enraptured," said he. Assuredly, I was. So we fell atalking for some while; he told me of the actor's life which he loves, though it be hard work. I ventured to tell him my dreams—to act and mayhap pen a play. He said if I could write I should, because many new plays are wanted. He told me tales of his life and his adventures about the countryside and in London. He was scarce a stripling ere he became an actor. His father, keeper of an inn in London, died when Ned was but four years of age. Then his brother, John, kept the inn, presented plays, & thus Ned learned his craft, enacting girls & women, as boy actors do in their prenticeship. Sithence, he hath played all manner of parts. He told me of how some eight people were crushed to death when scaffolds collapsed at a place in London they call the Bear Garden.[2] Some thousand people were watching the bear and dogs in high battle together, when the gallery shook at its foundation and fell flat to the ground. This and much else. How I could have talked all a long night with him, but he took his leave & departed with the others. Can my future lie that way? I have ambition enough, but will it suffice? How can this be accomplished with wife, child, & more besides. If there be nothing new but that which hath been before, what can be life's purpose?

[MAY]

Anne says I needs must be more of a husband to her. She said, "And may it be you have quite forgot a husband's office?" That could not be gainsaid. We have been more kindly one to another.

[NOVEMBER]

Nigh on two years married. Anne with child. My ambition faint & sickly. What muse can I invoke to stave off raven-black despair, the midwife to my woe?

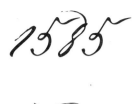

Anne gives birth to twins, Hamnet and Judith, much to Shakespeare's delight. He discovers that writing plays is troublesome; more troublesome still is the whipping and temporary imprisonment by Sir William Lucy that Shakespeare receives for poaching on Lucy's estate.

3 FEBRUARY

Nothing writ for many a long month, spite of my trials and assays. I cannot work for father and write, and what with Anne wanting me to be more of a husband. Well, last May I was husband well enough, soon after Ned Alleyn was here. Yesterday Vicar [Richard] Barton baptized our twins—our heavenly benison worth all worldly tribulations & far above gold. Such wondrous creatures they are, I can never regret those times when Anne comes to me and rouses me. And this time we are blessed with a boy child. We name the children Hamnet and Judith, after their god parents who share our joys and delight.[1] Thus am I ever rooted here, whiles London and the players remain afar off. I have determined to read some history—Hall, Holinshed—for I recall that Ned said history is a storehouse wherein lie good plays. The plot is ready laid out, so it is but the characters that must be fleshed out. I need not dare greatly—show but the how and the why, motives & such. I must find a way to buy Hall, so that I might find what inspiration may lie therein—perchance the War of the Roses would suit & be dramatic, for all our present lies there.[2]

APRIL

From London Dick [Field] hath sent me a letter with his joy & blessings for our children.[3] Dick fares well, & ere long he will be a prentice no more. But that we are friends, I might be jealous & envy his success— & he hath toiled hard & long. As God's my life, I wish that I were in London with him, & not here, save for my dearest children. Alas, there is no virtue like necessity.

[SUMMER]

History is dreary stuff, tho' there be incidents in these Wars of the Roses that seize the imagination, that breathe fire to illumine all. Joan La Pucelle is such a one, but mayhap she is too strong and robust a creature for a boy to act. Yet might she command the stage in a scene or two.[4] I have a fancy for a garden scene where roses be plucked—red on one side, white by t'other—symbols of much.[5] Of roses I know somewhat, and fields when wheat is green, and when hawthorn buds appear.

Hamnet [Sadler] and I have been in parlous trouble, tho' there was sport in the making. We were poaching rabbit near Charlecote, and mayhap we were on Lucy's land.[6] I know not, but Lucy and his keepers happened upon us, seized us, and had us whipped like hounds. Then Lucy took us to a farm house at Daisy Hill, and for a day or more we were locked in some foul-smelling stable there until Lucy thought to set us free. Father is angered mightily & sore troubled because he is [an] alderman. I know not whether he is more ashamed by our whipping or because we were caught, but he will not show his face at the council. I had thought to write a ballad or some such thing against Lucy—on him, his wife, asses, horns, and deer—but I must play the obedient son and dutiful father for the time being.

[AUTUMN]

Father is less troubled, & I have tried to please him. Anne & I are friendly enough. The other day she said, "I am affected in all as yourself. Whatever cause there may be betwixt us twain, the bitter clamour of two eager tongues cannot arbitrate. So let be." I had no thought she might think thus; but hers was a worthy thought. Our bonny children grow apace.

1586

The year is marked by the arrest and imprisonment of Mary, Queen of Scots by Queen Elizabeth, which causes Shakespeare and his family much sorrow. Shakespeare makes little progress in his efforts to become a playwright.

[FEBRUARY]

Hamnet & Judith are a year old, & I rejoice heartily in their health and strength. Anne & I have been married more than three years—so long, oh Lord, oh so long. I had not thought it would be so.

[AUGUST]

Fear is everywhere; we speak to hardly a soul. Queen Mary is arrested; tho' it hath been long in coming, we thought it might be so eventually.[1] Some folk say there is a plot against our queen, Elizabeth, but all the world knows the true reason. I pity the poor creature, & wonder how long she will live now, tho' people say Elizabeth has a terror of killing a queen, lest it show others the way and the means to kill her. We keep to ourselves and bide close to home. The little I have written is paltry stuff that even Ned Alleyn could not transform it in the speaking.

6 SEPTEMBER

Father hath been deprived of his alderman's gown for his long absence from the council's meetings & such. He keeps himself unto himself & says little. He is bitter, for by his face straightway may men know his heart.

OCTOBER

Chiding autumn, pelting river, contagious fogs, rheumatic diseases. Would I were not here, this petty place, creeping from day to day. My soul withers away fast with the daily round. There's but little comfort, & that my children give.

❦ *At the beginning of the year, Shakespeare finally ventures forth to London and lodges with printer friend and native Stratfordian, Richard Field. His hopes come to nothing, and are overshadowed by the execution of Queen Mary. He witnesses the funeral of Sir Philip Sidney, and, after three or four fruitless months, Shakespeare returns home. Two months of despair are overturned when Shakespeare encounters John Heminges (later a close friend and colleague) and his touring company of actors. Shakespeare follows Heminges to London, and quickly meets such notable figures as Richard Burbage, Christopher Marlowe, Tom Nashe, and others. Shakespeare sees Marlowe's plays performed, and records both his favorable and adverse opinions of Marlowe's work. In November he finds himself next to a pregnant woman who is accidentally shot and killed during the performance of Marlowe's* Tamburlaine. ❦

JANUARY

Spite of Anne's pleas and father's threats, I have dared venture to London. I could remain no longer in Stratford, an' if I did my mind, my very soul & spirit would die. There is much I must do ere I die, & death sends no missive of its intent, & is a greater power than we can contradict. London quite o'erwhelms my senses—coaches, carts, throngs of all manner of folk, the noises, the smells, the bustle where'er I go. I have not seen such finery, such magnificent apparel which the better sort wear. Merchants with bags of money hastening about their business, porters sweating 'neath heavy burdens. And the hordes of prentices, boys, maidens, dogs, & I know not what. Farewell tranquil Stratford. 'Tis fortunate Dick [Field] lets me lodge with him till I might settle somewhere in some fashion. He hath proved to be a fine printer, and works hard. I think he casts his eyes upon his master's wife, leastways should his master die, when he could get both wife and business. Should ever I write a book, Dick says he himself would set it up and sell it in St. Paul's Churchyard. So my ambition works, & perchance I may fashion some play or other from all the history I have read these months past. I shall seek out Ned Alleyn, for he did assure me of his aid if ever I came to London.

Later—Ned is no longer with Worcester's Men but with the Admiral's, and they are gone into the country. Such is fate; I am cast down for the nonce, for I know not what to do. I thank the stars Dick is close at hand.

9 FEBRUARY

What a day was yesterday. As I have long apprehended, Mary was executed at Fotheringay Castle where she was imprisoned these many months. Alas for her poor soul, tho' now her troubles and pains are past care. I fear children yet unborn shall feel this day as sharp to them as a thorn; but we shall see and know our friends in heaven. All day the church bells rang, and in the evening bonfires were lit everywhere. Will there be peace now? Some folk say James[1] was pleased enough to let his mother die, since he neither loved nor cared for her. And should Elizabeth die without an heir, as she seems like to do, he may be our next king. Such are the ways of the mighty.

16 FEBRUARY

This month is as cruel and harsh as ever it might be. Today was the funeral of Sir Philip Sidney, who was cut down so young in battle at Zutphen.[2] All London was there to watch the hundreds joined in his funeral procession. I wonder why he fought and for what cause? Those who knew him say he wrote such wondrous poetry, tho' I can find no book of his to read. Dick Field says none is published and may never be. So Sidney is with the worms, his bones covered with dust by that churl death, and all comes to naught—'tis our common woe. Fat tripe finely broiled for supper.

MARCH

A star is in the moon, which some folk declare is an evil omen. For all I know, they may be right. As for me, I drift, like a twig on the Avon, but whither I know not. I lack advancement; my ambition wanes. Should I return to Stratford, Anne, my dear children?

[EARLY SUMMER]

These last two months have been so drear I scarce can conceive how life itself may be endured. Anne was glad enough for my return, as was I to see my dear children. Hamnet, that little abstract that doth contain the large, is a cherub who ne'er ceases smiling all the live long day; I could hold him until the day of judgment. Yet I do nothing, from which nothing springs. Working with father is ever tedious, though he seems happy enow for my help.

[C. 15 JUNE]

So swift a change I might not comprehend. Two days since, Elizabeth's Men were here [Stratford] and did perform *Felix and Philiomena,* a pastoral (as they term it).[3] I thought little of the piece and was emboldened to say as much to one of the actors I accosted at the Angel [Inn], where it chanced we both supped ale.[4] This player thought me impertinent, and said if I thought I could write better then I should. We argued for some while; indeed I thought we might come to blows. But we became more friendly when he told me he was bred and brought up in Droitwich, and was by name John Heminges.[5] Then he told me more of his work &, to boot, that one of their number was killed but two days before. "Aye, it was a bad business," he said. "The two fellows argued over I know not what, but the upshot was one of them was wounded in the throat and died. So our company hath need of an actor."[6] Thus it is settled, and my hell is turned into a heaven. I am to join them as a hired man to do whatever may befall, *and to write*. I shall begin with *Felix,* and make it anew to show what I can do. I have six months to prove my worth. I dread what moan Anne will make, & Father too. Parting from my dear boy will be hard.

[JUNE]

Such a fierce contentious argument with Anne, father, & mother that if I told it o'er 'twould not be believed nor credited. It sufficeth but to say they laid no credence upon my promising fortune with the actors, nor did they offer me their love. Welladay, I must try my fortune or nothing be, an' if I fail—but that I shall not, save an' if some higher power prevent me.

[AUTUMN]

In London. I sojourned but two days with Dick Field, & now have lodgings in Shoreditch convenient to the Curtain [Theatre] and the Theatre. Burbage and Tarlton live hard by, and already I know them, and Nashe, and met wild Marlowe at the tavern.[7] Nashe and Marlowe were together at Cambridge [University], & they have been fast friends ever since. Ned Alleyn is to play [Marlowe's] Tamburlaine soon, and I shall go to observe Marlowe's craft and what manner of play he writes, which should prove goodly instruction.

10 NOVEMBER

Today at the Curtain—Marlowe's *Tamburlaine* [*Part I*], in truth I should say Ned Alleyn's Tamburlaine, for without Ned 'twould be a poor thing. Ned held sovereign sway over all and translated Marlowe's words with powerful magnificence. Lord, how he declaimed "I hold the Fates bound fast in iron chains, / And with my hand turn Fortune's wheel about; / And sooner shall the sun fall from his sphere / Than Tamburlaine be slain or overcome."[8] Yet what weak stuff is "I long to see thee back return from thence." Better to pen naught than that. Marlowe is enamoured with lines that in their repetition hypnotise the audience, vide— "And ride in triumph through Persepolis." Yet his style is little suited to my purpose. A sweet boy, who did enact Zenocrate, spoke lovingly, "As looks the sun through Nilus' flowing stream, / Or when the morning holds him in her arms, / So looks my lordly love, fair Tamburlaine." Marlowe is half in love with sensation, scenes that shock, processions— as when two moors tugged the conquered Bajazeth in a cage, wherein he and Zabina brained themselves to death. That was naught but horror for its own self. For all that, the groundlings, those penny stinkards as Marlowe calls them, cheered and roared. Next week there is to be more, for Marlowe hath writ a second part—another torrent of words I'll be certain.

16 NOVEMBER

Today the second part of *Tamburlaine* at the Curtain. All was marred by an untoward circumstance, most wretched ill-fortune. The play was all but concluded: Tamburlaine's victim, the governor of Babylon, was hung on his city's walls that he might be shot, when one of the players slipped and a gun, charged by accident, was fired and killed a woman great with child, and another child. They stood but next to me, and the child fell at my feet. I scarce knew what to do in the confusion. The play was stopped whiles some folk cried out and shouted, but then they began aplaying once more. I picked up the poor mite, but to no avail. How like art life is. I am so sore distracted I remember little of Marlowe's piece; much as before, he feasts on sensation, and the play is feebler than the first, for he seeks to profit merely by his success. In brief, this second part is but revenge, war, death, and cruelty. "We all are glutted with the Christians' blood," said one, and in truth we were glutted wholly. Yet Marlowe uses the stage with sure craft, viz—one [character] was discovered behind an arras, others appeared on the city walls, and processions to capture the eye, as when Tamburlaine was drawn in his chariots by kings and saith, "Holla, ye pamper'd jades of Asia! / What, can ye draw but twenty miles a day." Ned Alleyn was ever a fine figure, and in honeyed tones he chanted "to entertain divine Zenocrate" like some sorcerer. Yet the greater part of the play was but sensation. I must learn further what this theatre might encompass.

Shakespeare's first play, The Two Gentlemen of Verona, *begins to take shape, though Shakespeare is far from satisfied with the results; Marlowe declares it "simpering stuff," and urges Shakespeare to write more like Marlowe himself. August provides the highlight of the year as the Spanish Armada is defeated, and Shakespeare turns to collaborating with Nashe, Marlowe, and Robert Greene, and writes sections of* Henry VI Part 1. *The envious Greene reveals his enmity for Shakespeare who, in turn, holds no affection for Greene. Shakespeare is gratified when* Two Gentlemen *is staged in the autumn, but is displeased by the antics of the clown Will Kempe who can never stick to his lines. Shakespeare sees Queen Elizabeth in a procession.*

[SPRING]

How many a time & oft have the sights, the sounds of this great city seduced me, beguiling my tedious days. I have wandered in Finsbury Fields and watched its windmills, lingered in alleys, ambled by stables, inns, & brothels, dallied by the gardens of the better sort. And though I fain would not tarry by Bedlam, I have seen the poor wretches therein and heard their piteous cries and moans. All the while, I have struggled mightily to amend *Felix* [*and Philiomena*] that I might fulfill my boast to [John] Heminges that I can write better stuff. Yet I am humbled, for the task is not so easy as, childlike, I had thought it. Something have I made of the love talk of the young suitors—this to please the multitude that relish puns and such. And there's merit enow in my clown [Launce] such that Kempe[1] might desire the part—his companion is a dog that pisses inordinately & causes trouble, though I know not how this may be encompassed, whether this shall be a dog or an actor dressed up. But my difficulties lie all in the plot; many a time & oft I find no rhyme nor reason why these characters do what they do. I wonder whether Kit [Marlowe] be troubled thus? Only today I wrote of Robin Hood & Friar Tuck in a forest, which was but tricksy fantasy.[2] Will the throngs howl, or applaud such business? Perchance I should direct my mind to other matters to spur me on. I might read *Romeus* again,[3] for 'tis a good story, though the verse wants improvement. This life is not easeful, and where lies fame, I know not.

APRIL

I had not thought play-making such toilsome labour. My trade, my profession I would say, is fiction, fantasy, illusion; yet many a time & oft I cannot conjure thoughts or words, but stare vacantly at the quill before me. I must persevere.

1 JUNE

I have moiled and toiled long &, at last, the thing is finished. I call it *The Two Noble Men of Verona*. I do believe it hath some merit, though I confess I lack modesty. I shall venture to show it to [James] Burbage and trust my stars be auspicious. Beef and mustard for supper.

2 JUNE

Full of perturbation, I have accost Burbage, who says he will look o'er [*The Two Gentlemen of Verona*]. He encouraged me thus: "Ruminate upon other pieces ye might write Will, for players hath need of fresh stuff every day." Yet I confess, when I perused the thing this morn, there was much I can scarce read o'er. So it falls out the players must make my ill stuff well.

3 JUNE

Kit [Marlowe] looked o'er my copy [of *The Two Gentlemen of Verona*] yester eve in the Mitre, and pronounced it the worst simpering stuff he had ever read. I told him he pens but blood, meat, and sensation, & there is a place for finer matter such as resides within my play. He scowled and cursed me for a fool. "If this be finer matter," he said, "I have the finest arse in all of Christendom." He asked me if I smoked tobacco or cared to lie with boys. "What know ye, Will, of wanton wild slips, fencing, swearing, quarrelling, drabbing, those taints of liberty?" I knew not what to say—such things I have ne'er heard ere this, and I know not if he spoke sooth or desired but to shock me. Kit drank more sack and began to curse all manner of things; in sooth I believe he is sorely troubled—by what I know not. Mayhap beneath the bluster of his wrath he is kindlier than he seems, but his rash fierce blaze of riot cannot last, for violent fires soon burn out themselves. Truth to tell, he hath some affection for me.

20 JUNE

My wait is over. [James] Burbage says if I cut and amend *Verona* according to his direction, it shall be given before Hallowmass [1 November]. I was so joyed I forgot to ask him how much he will reward my labours. I dare be sworn he is an honest man, & I confess my pleasure lies more in my play than the coin I earn thereby. I have determined to go home tomorrow with my news, and for love of my children, whom I miss grievously.

25 JULY

How tedious long can a month with Anne be; by times we lead a frampold life together. Yet she loves me, she says, and questions why I return to London, and why I write plays. Said she, "You swore to me when you did give me that wedding ring that you would love & honour me till the hour of your death." All true enow, & no answer could I make. Hamnet is the dearest boy in all the world who grows slowly, yet babbles and gurgles his delight at me. Stratford is verdant, peaceful, and I had forgot how sweet-smelling the air is after the stenches of London. But return there I must. *Verona* is writ out anew, & thus my business calls me to embrace th'occasion to depart.

3 AUGUST

London. Tumult and turmoil—everywhere ababble with the Spanish threat. Some folk say the Spaniards have shipped already and have landed in the far west. Others say our ships have whipped the Spaniard dogs.[4] I know not what to think, but everywhere there is fear and excitement. I tremble with perturbation lest they triumph o'er us.

9 AUGUST

The Spanish Armada is defeated; today the streets are full of wild throngs, cheering, shouting, laughing, yea weeping for joy. I wandered the streets & thoroughfares, and there was not a man or woman I met but did salute me with fair words & good cheer. At the tavern, all the world was in drink, tho' I had money enough but for one pottle.

17 AUGUST

Today the Lord Leicester,[5] more handsome than fine, as proud as a peacock, rode in triumph into the city from his camp at Tilbury. So many gentlemen did accompany him that it seemed he were the king. The crowds cheered and cheered, running after him, and throwing their caps high in the air. How might this be the very subject of a play, except it be not history yet and we can have but one monarch o'er us. I wonder what would have come to pass had we not been victorious.

20 AUGUST

Today to the pulpit outside St. Paul's [Cathedral]. There a huge throng was gathered, and we heard the proclamation that the Spanish Armada was defeated. Afterwards there was great celebration, as there hath been this two weeks past when first we heard the glad tidings. Twice I have seen men and women coupling together beast-backed in an alley, though they paid me no heed, such was their lust as they went to it. As I turned to wend home, I encountered Tom Nashe (his clothes worn, his hair long & wild). "Let us see what physic a tavern may afford," said Tom, and together we went to the Bel Savage Inn and drank ale. After some while of talking on the Armada, Tom observed how much people like history and despise foreigners, as this latest victory proved. Then, looking full hard at me, he raised one of his long skinny fingers, and said he knew of my ambition to be a poet [dramatist], and he had a proposition for me. It seems Tom and one Robert Greene,[6] whom I have heard mentioned but never yet met, have drafted out scenes for a history of Henry VI and the wars against the French. I told him that some years since [1585], I had also thought on a play on the French, and that I had read Hall. This pleased Tom. Marlowe is also of their party, yet how Tom did not say. The upshot of our talk is that I am to assist Nashe write his scenes, and perchance add some lines of mine own. I was overjoyed, though I said it was strange he should importune me, the merest novice. But he said he was kindly disposed towards me, and that he needed the help and someone on whom he might rely more than Greene and Marlowe, much though he loves them. So we meet on the morrow and begin; mayhap the world's my oyster!

21 AUGUST

Nashe hath shown me his beginning part of the Henry VI play, and was desirous to know what I thought of it. Novice that I am, I guarded my tongue, e'en though I could see right readily there was much to improve. But Tom approved my suggestion that a funeral procession in the beginning would hold the audience, and that "civil broils" and their consequences should be the theme. I had almost wrote "our" theme, for already I work on my part. I asked Tom how effectual he thought the lad to play Joan Pucelle [Joan of Arc] might be. He thinks armour will help and if Joan's scene be humourous. I have taken a liking to Talbot, tho' not his fight with Pucelle, as that is man against woman.[7] Nashe also had with him some other scenes, one being Marlowe's—least ways words like Scythian, thrall, and tyranny sound like Kit's.[8] I am to add two scenes after Marlowe's, but I fear how evident my hand will be, how abrupt the changes. My words sound a different key.

27 AUGUST

Last night I saw another eclipse of the moon—an auspicious occasion? A ninny awed by a deal of skimble-skamble [nonsensical] stuff might think so. Such I profess not to be. Two scenes [of *Henry VI Part 1*] I have done. The first, where the two factions pick red or white roses in the Temple Garden [2.4], hath some merit—much on roses, colour, blood and the like, and some legalities. I had thought to pun on Richard Beauchamp Earl of Warwick, but 'tis as well I resisted the impish notion.[9] The other scene at the Tower with Mortimer [2.5] is but convenient. Yet I do no more than patching up, & I must devise better ways to tell history if I am to seize the oyster.

1 SEPTEMBER

The thing [*Henry VI Part 1*] is finished, but what violent divisions there were and are between us, much like the play itself. Yester afternoon four of us met in Marlowe's room—Kit, Tom Nashe, Robert Greene, me. Some folk might call Greene handsome, & he is well-made enough. He has an unkembed red beard, and, kept close around him, a goose turd green cloak. Greene I know now penned the French parts, or least ways most of them, some with Kit. But I dislike them because Pucelle is not of a piece, and provoketh mirth which she ought not to do. Kit hath scribbled here and there, tho' he hath little interest; he hath his own plays he cares for more. Greene opined my Talbot scenes are weak sentimental fustian, and was venomous about how I have made them [Talbot and his son] noble and self-sacrificing. Greene is a bitter man, and true affection galls him. He sneered at my rhymes and couplets, and said they served no purpose, are mere prettiness and ornamentation. Nor would he listen when I explained how the vital love between Talbot and his son lay in the sonnet they spoke between them.[10] Greene lacks all art and sensible feeling. In truth, I think him a mad-headed ape; a weasel hath not such a deal of spleen as he is tossed withal. I would have said much, but being the novice without a play upon the stage, I said little and bit my tongue. I did not tell Greene about *Verona* lest that provoke him more. 'Tis as well I did not reveal my small jest when I send Sir William Lucy as a messenger to York and Somerset.[11] Tom Nashe tried to quiet Greene, but he would not be reasoned with; he is the most impenetrable cur that ever kept with men. Well, the thing *is* finished and who knows whether it will be enacted. I must spare less money for food.

3 SEPTEMBER

Today they buried Richard Tarlton, that dear sweet comedian, touched with human gentleness and love.[12] Gone are his squint, his flat nose, his jigs. I saw him play once, and how the crowd roared. And the more they roared, the more he jested with them. His mind and words were quick silver. A fellow of infinite jesting; worse epitaphs there are.

4 SEPTEMBER

The Earl of Leicester, patron of players, died today. It was but days ago that he rode in triumph through the streets of the city. In the dark and backward abysm of my mind, I recall going as a young boy with father to the Earl's castle at Kenilworth, when the queen was there, and seeing some kind of water pageant with a dolphin, and many fireworks.[13] Now the man is dead, & many speak more openly against him than they dared before, yet they temper their words, for 'tis said the queen is sick full of grief at his passing.

[OCTOBER]

[James] Burbage hath presented *Verona*, for which I am three pounds the richer. Kempe thralled the crowd with Launce, tho' he did so much extempore I scarce could recognise mine own words. For his dog [Crab], there was a child not six or seven years grown, which pleased the multitude well enough, tho' they liked less my puns, and groaned or feigned groaning aplenty. Speed drew forth much laughter as well. The better sort took note of the romance, and approved Valentine's friendship. Yet I think it a much poorer thing than I can do, than I believe I shall do.

17 NOVEMBER

Today is the queen's accession day. Everywhere people are joyous and glad, not least for our latest victory against the Spaniard. And St. Elizabeth's Day [19 November] is to be a holiday too.

26 NOVEMBER

Today I was in the street when Her Majesty passed by me as she and her grand procession made their progress to [St.] Paul's for a service of thanksgiving for our deliverance from the Spanish. Her chariot, bedeck'd with a resplendent canopy, was drawn by two white horses, and, as she went, there were loud shouts, cheers, and huzzas. Though I could not see nor hear them, I hear tell there were pageants and ballads given for her as she went along. A fine spectacle for our monarch triumphant. And in the deep recess of my memory, I recall the day when I was but two years old or so, & father took me to see the Queen as she passed by on the road from Charlecote to Banbury.[14] 'Tis passing strange to see her again these years later.

❧ *The pillory and political pamphlets provide a counterpoint to Shakespeare's theatrical work. He presses on with history plays, though now without collaborators. Shakespeare's steady work contrasts with the wild antics of Marlowe, who is imprisoned briefly, and who still believes Shakespeare is on the wrong track. Marlowe manages to seduce Shakespeare after a drunken evening together.* ❧

[JANUARY]

Tom Nashe hath shown *Henry* [*VI Part 1*] to [James] Burbage and to Henslowe.[1] Neither says yea or nay. Tom is full of hope, but I doubt success, for the piece hath too many hands in't &, as too many cooks spoil a pie, so is this play marred.

1 FEBRUARY

Today I was returning to the Theatre when, hard by the Cross Keys at Leadenhall, I saw two soldiers in the pillory erected there. A withered crone, standing by & watching, told me that they had been placed there for three hours or more. One soldier had his ear nailed, t'other his tongue—this their punishment for abusing their captains, and speaking ill of them.[2] Thus is fear engendered, order maintained, but it is surely a practice more worthy of heathens than Christian folk.

9 FEBRUARY

With Nashe to Paul's Cross to hear one Richard Bancroft preach a sermon on the episcopacy. He defended the bishops and their judgments. After the sermon was done, Nashe gave me a pamphlet with this curious title "Pappe with an hatchet. Alias, A figge for my god sonne. Or, cracke me this nut. Or, A countrie cuffe, that is, a sound boxe of the eare, for the idiot Martin [Marprelate] to hold his peace, seeing the patch will take no warning."[3] I asked Tom what such a title signified, but he smiled merely, and said I should but read the piece. I do believe Nashe is caught up in this noisome business, for it is the kind of stuff he doth savour.

5 MARCH

News from Dick Quiney that his son Thomas is christened. I am saddened that I could not share Dick's joy with him and Elizabeth.[4] Yet am I well pleased for their sake, & hope the boy will thrive. Dick wrote the child will prove a weeping philosopher when he grows old, which is as strange a thing as e'er I heard. And now am I blessed with fond remembrance of mine own dear cherubs. This evening I have the toothache.

[MARCH]

With Tom Nashe & Marlowe, and we talked of plays. They said that, though they be fast friends with him, they cared not that Greene should write with them again. I desired to say that I cared not to be pestered with the popinjay—but mum's the word. I said it mattered but little to me, though I must work & earn all that I can. I said that we might continue Henry, for there is, as I have read in Hall, much fine stuff in the Wars of the Roses. But they care no longer for history—Kit calls it dull matter except for the killing. Nashe says he is ever busy with his pamphlets and other such matters. Yet they urge me on to do the thing, and so I shall, for I am as vigilant as a cat to steal cream. After, we drank more than a pottle or two of wine. After an hour or more, Tom took his leave, and Kit

& I fell atalking between ourselves. He told me how his affection for me o'erswayed his reason, and he burned with the itch of consuming desire. In brief, he said he would have me use him as I would use a wench. "'Twill be all the same to you, Will," said Kit, "but for me greatest pleasure." In my stupor I gave little heed; I pray he be not diseased. I swear I'll ne'er be drunk again whilst I live, but in honest, civil, godly company.

History is the easier way, for my path is laid before me. Still the play [*Henry VI Part 2*] must needs seize the imagination of the multitude. This Henry [VI] is weak, but pious, & he is a king who labours for his realm. In the king lies order, whiles others would bring chaos through usurpation. I might make much of a ruthless queen [Margaret], and also a rebel [Cade]—nobles against the commons. The truth be that two stars cannot keep their motion in one sphere.

4 APRIL

I hear that the wife [Mildred] of Lord Burghley[5] hath died. They say she was the learnedest woman of her time, even above Her Majesty.

[MAY]

To Dick Field in Blackfriars, who was mightily pleased with himself, for he hath published the first book from his own press. 'Tis called *The Arte of English Poesie,* and in sooth 'tis a fine piece of work.[6] In spite of my pleadings, Dick would not take money for the copy. He said 'twas all his pleasure that he might give this first fruit of his labours to his right good friend & countryman.

[JUNE]

This Henry play but plods in my brain, & I must needs fashion the beginning aright, for then all else will follow. I have devised one scene will make the groundlings watch—Gloucester's wife [Eleanor] will ascend aloft whilst witches sink beneath the platform.[7] To my mind 'tis not much, but 'twill suffice for the nonce.

18 SEPTEMBER

Marlowe is cast into Newgate [prison] with Tom Watson. I thought that Kit would find himself in grievous trouble ere long, and now it hath come to pass. Marlowe is ever quick to take offence, I fear, & he courts violence, & in the consequence a man hath died.[8] Mayhap some good thing will come tomorrow.

3 OCTOBER

Marlowe is released, tho' not Tom Watson. Kit called at my lodging yester even, and we betook us to the Falcon on the Stews in Southwark. We drank heartily together and partook a good repast of fowl & fish. Kit said but little of his sojourn in Newgate, though I fain would have learned more. He said, on leaving, he will look o'er *Henry* [*VI Part 2*].

[OCTOBER]

Kit [Marlowe] thinks the multitude cries out for blood and sensation, & I must give it to them if my play [*Henry VI Part 2*] is to be worth the seeing. Kit said, "If this were my play, Will, I would write such scenes as these—the grieving Queen carries in Suffolk's head, Gloucester suffocates in bed, the heads of executed lords stuck on poles and made to kiss one with another. That's the stuff to excite folk, Will."[9] I do believe such excess will make folk surfeit, tho' peradventure Kit knows the multitude aright. I told him that what he would work me to, I have some aim.

[C. 6 NOVEMBER]

Our play [*Henry VI Part 1*] was enacted yester afternoon by Lord Strange's men at Cross Keys Inn in Gracious [Gracechurch] Street—this despite the order that playing should cease.[10] I am full of vexation at what I witnessed. Whiles Ned Alleyn and his Talbot brought my eyes to tears when he mourned his son, the rest was mingle-mangled, and held the multitude poorly. Pucelle was coarsely done and much laughed at. I' fecks, I had rather be set quick in the earth, and bowled to death with turnips, than see my work treated thus. Me an attendant lord to swell a progress.

14 NOVEMBER

The Privy Council is all against us and we must submit our books.[11]

22 NOVEMBER

George [Peele],[12] whom Tom Nashe calls the Atlas of poetry, showed me his play book that he names *The Old Wives' Tale*. It is a wondrous, fantastical gallimaufry of fairy tales and myths, with knights, conjurors, and princesses. There are plays within plays within plays, which make the mind whirl, but in joyous delight, and what seems to be real is only so for a while, and then vanishes. I have ideas now where I too shall play with plays, with reality. For mine remembrance: "A merry winter's tale would drive away the time trimly"; "as good a fellow as ever trod upon neat's leather."[13]

20 DECEMBER

Tom Nashe hath buried his mother,[14] and mourns her passing as dearly as he might mourn anyone. He said, "I have too grieved a heart to take a tedious leave of her." Yet he says he will sell her silver spoons and pewter candlesticks for bread and cheese to eat, of which he hath the greater need. I think on mine own family—father, mother, Anne, & the children—& I have determined not to pass Christmastide apart from them. Tomorrow with all speed to Stratford.

❧ *Shakespeare now labors on the third part of the Henry VI plays, which inspires him to think of writing about the Machiavellian Richard III. His friendships with Marlowe and Nashe continue to develop, although Shakespeare does not always agree with their advice about writing plays. In November an amusing fracas takes place at the Theatre.* ☙

[JANUARY]

Stratford. This chronicle [*Henry VI Part 3*] almost exceeds my powers, for many events must be compassed about in little. Henry is a small king—good, pious, religious—his queen, Margaret, is strong—a tiger's heart in a woman wrapped.[1] And all is family fighting family. 'Tis brother shall fight against brother, father against son. Power and evil before country, order, and family. Yet before mine own family come plays, & I must return to London, or lose all. What cannot be eschewed must be embraced.

13 FEBRUARY

Yester afternoon Tom Watson received the Queen's pardon, and is freed from prison. How he endured months of Newgate misery is more than I can comprehend or fathom. Marlowe rejoiced to see him, and hung much about Tom's neck. Mayhap they're bumboys together.[2] All to Nag's Head with Nashe. Drank heavy all night, with much foolery, if I could but remember it. Sick today with ague, & the little food I have partaken I have vomited forth.

[MARCH]

Still I labour on *Henry* [*VI Part 3*], and wonder how 'twill be accomplished. Today I pieced out the Battle of Towton [1461] to some effect, in particular a scene where sons & fathers find each other in the midst of battle. Common folk suffer most, & it is said forty thousand were slaughtered at Towton. And there lies my difficulty, for on our stage we can place but three or four or so actors, who must encompass many moe.

10 APRIL

From Kit [Marlowe], news of the death of Walsingham.[3] Kit told me a little of the secret errands & business he hath done these past several years—he hath been Walsingham's agent or some such. "Other men might be afeard, Will," quoth Kit, "but, though I am privy to many a dark secret, I fear no man. Besides, were I to tell the truth and shame the devil, there are many tales I might relate, of those nobles—boys & men—who have found sweet delight with me. And I could tell of hours filled up with riots, banquets, sports, & such like. But I am no fleering telltale." If Kit's tale be credible, Walsingham had a large growth in his stones [testicles], and died because his physician had tried to remove it. Yet I have heard Catholic gossip that he had an odious stench, and wine poured from his nose and mouth. I know not what might be believed, & I care little for complots & the like. We talked somewhat of my play [*Henry VI Part 3*] and Kit, as is his wont, said the first scene must be bloody and brimful of sensation. Perchance we might employ Suffolk's head once more.[4] Margaret shall be man-like, Henry weak and woman-like, which is disorder. I would the thing were finished.

[SUMMER]

I dwell long upon Richard's ambition: "I'll make my heaven to dream upon the crown." I do believe I am half in love with this Machiavel. "I can smile and murder while I smile."⁵ A play upon this Richard [*Richard III*] would be worth the writing, for he is the evil villain incarnate that will fascinate all who see him. It needs must be an excellent play, set down with as much modesty as cunning.

15 SEPTEMBER

Tom Russell is a week married.⁶ Once more, for that I am in London, I have not shared in the joys of such a good-hearted, generous friend. Well, that's as must be, if I am to make my fortune.

FEAST OF ST. MATTHEW [21 SEPTEMBER]

Today there was an affray by prentices against the students in Lincoln's Inn, which the magistrates quelled & crushed as sudden as it began. I know not if the cause of th'affray be just, tho' I marvel how much alike to history it all be—naught but disorder. But what be that adage? "In time the savage bull doth bear the yoke." All have yokes to bear.

OCTOBER

Nashe would have me read Greene's *Friar Bacon* [*and Friar Bungay*]. Lord, how marvellous self-conceited Greene is, for at the end he writes "made by Robert Greene, Master of Arts." Well, he is a poor master, for the speeches are plain and unadorned, and he employs the same words time without number—mercy, jolly, dump, frolic. There is little enough interest in his scenes, which serve no purpose that I can discern. The conjuring parts are better, whereby other characters appear & tell their story—thus Greene needs to pen less—a happy device. The confusions are righted in a twinkle; 'tis convenient, and the groundlings pay no heed to such trickery.

There is naught for me to learn from this "master," tho' I would not wrangle with Nashe on this matter. Kit [Marlowe] says he is fascinated by conjurors, wizards, and such stuff, and means to write his book on them [*Dr. Faustus*]. Kit is bloody sensations, Greene is stage sensations.

10 NOVEMBER

To St. Mary's [Aldermanbury] with John Heminges to see his daughter baptized. The child was christened Alice, & she is bonny enough with lusty lungs. Much joy in feasting & drinking with John & his family.

16 NOVEMBER

What a commotion broke forth at the Theatre today. Widow [Margaret] Brayne and Robert Miles came to blows with [James] Burbage & his sons over money the widow, a strong buxom woman, was taking at the galleries. She avouched the money was but her right and due portion, tho' Burbage would have none of that. Dick [Burbage] beat Miles about the head with a broomstick.[7] I laughed heartily but took a care not to let them see me amused with their foolery.

※ *With Richard Burbage by his side offering helpful advice, Shakespeare makes good progress on* Richard III. *However, that advance is surpassed when yet another drunken evening with Marlowe results in Shakespeare meeting the Earl of Southampton, later to be Shakespeare's friend and patron. Shakespeare writes the first of many sonnets for Southampton, as well as* Love's Labour's Lost, *and their relationship grows more intimate. Such happy moments are punctuated by war on the continent (there is always the fear of being impressed to fight in the army) and bloody executions, the latter much revelled in by Marlowe. Much of this violence is captured in* Titus Andronicus, *which Shakespeare is now fashioning under Marlowe's influence and that of Kyd's* The Spanish Tragedy. *The year ends with a performance of* Richard III *for Queen Elizabeth.* ※

[JANUARY]

This Richard [*Richard III*] hath possessed my mind; his evil appetite for power thralls me. Twice or thrice Dick Burbage hath sat with me to learn how my play fares, & we have talked o'er how he will play the role. I am but a novice, yet Dick listens courteously, and gives a gentle hint here or there. I' faith, Dick knows the man already, how he will prove a villain, how he is subtle, false, & treacherous. "You know, Will," Dick said one evening at the Mitre, "I recall that line from t'other play—'I am myself alone'[1]—& I do believe that is the very essence of this instrument of ill you have fashioned." I laughed heartily, & said he should write the play for me because in sooth those very words are always in my mind when I think on Richard. "Indeed, Dick, in the first scene you speak three speeches solus to show Richard is alone—he is outside looking in, observing all." Dick thought this a goodly device. Much other chat with Dick, by which I profit greatly, for I am a prentice still, & 'tis well to be humble. I' fecks, I have much ado to know myself.

3 FEBRUARY

'Tis Lent, and again meat is forbidden to us, tho' those that observe the edict are not so numerous. It will trouble me not a whit, for I have money little enough. Bread, cheese, ale, or a mess of potage must needs suffice. I do believe my breath stinks with eating toasted cheese, & 'tis fortunate none but myself sighs upon my midnight pillow.

[FEBRUARY]

I have read wondrous adventures in *The Travails of an Englishman*—men eaten by sea horses, elephants killing negroes, scaley alligators, all which befell in the new world. That is stuff enough for a play with fancy and imagination.[2] All this is a world away from Richard the third on which I labour yet. Dick [Burbage] talks with me about it once in a while, & I cannot envisage Richard without seeing Dick in my mind's eye. He doth excel above all other actors, save Ned Alleyn, & if my play triumph, 'twill be all Dick's doing.

10 MARCH

Dick Field hath given me *Orlando Furioso* which he hath printed. It is translated by Sir John Harington, and Dick says Sir John told him the Queen told him to translate it so that thereby he would keep himself from trouble at Court.[3] What more he meant, I know not.

[MARCH]

I have fretted & vexed myself in extensio with this play [*Richard III*], which is as much the tragedy of Richard as 'tis the chronicle of his rise, of his decline, & of his age. Howsomever, all that was swept from my mind & cares by what passed some two or three days ago. Kit [Marlowe], myself, & several other fellows were eating & drinking at the Bel Savage Inn. There was deep chat & plenty of ale, & the night drew on apace. Kit was in good humour, and hung on the arms of one or two he would favour, & he was exceeding pleasant with me—why we both know. At a late hour, when the clock gave all their cue to depart their several ways, Kit said to me he knew a person of high degree with whom he was on friendly terms & who, so Kit thought, would be pleased if we visited him at that very hour, late tho' 'twas. "The truth is," said Kit, "he knows a little of your works, & hath admired mine, & he is an adventuresome fellow, for all that he is a lord." I assented, though with fear and perturbation. I recall but little of what ensued, for my mind was awhirl, and, in sooth, I had drunk more than a quantity of ale. In brief, the lord we sought out was Henry Wriothesley, or Harry as he bade us call him.[4] He is a handsome man with beauty many women might envy, & wears his hair very long. His eyes are somewhat blue, his nose & fingers long, and his mouth delicate. We talked but a short while, yet he was interested in my plays, & I told him of my ambition to be a poet, if fortune would but smile upon me. "Then, Will Shakespeare," said he, "you must & you shall write poetry. Indeed, I should be obliged if you would write poems—sonnets or some such—for me." I told him I had vainly attempted some sonnets, but they were poor, bare, mean stuff that I would not have his lordship read. Harry said, "I see that thou art not for the fashion of these times, where none will sweat but for promotion." Yet at his command I would strive to write poesy of more crescent note, worthy of his lordship's expectation. Then after some time, I departed for my room, Kit remaining behind. So now I have a lordly command & charge which I *will* fulfill, for I feel that way lies my destiny.

[MID-MARCH]

How my mind is divided since I met the Lord Southampton, or the rather, Harry, as he would have me call him. My endeavour is to piece out the Richard play [*Richard III*] which needs must be writ—as more tragedy than chronicle, for I do perceive the king [Richard] shall come to know himself. Mine own other self desires nothing more than to pen poetry for Harry, & indeed I have by me some several sonnets which I will fashion into worthy offerings. My labour goes hard to accomplish the perfection I seek after, & perchance it may ne'er be achieved. I needs must strive or fail in th'attempt.

I have shown Harry a handful of sonnets over which I toiled long & hard. We drank some canary wine, & I read to him this:

> Who will believe my verse in time to come
> If it were filled with your most high deserts?
> Though yet, heaven knows, it is but as a tomb
> Which hides your life and shows not half your parts.
> If I could write the beauty of your eyes,
> And in fresh numbers number all your graces,
> The age to come would say "This poet lies;
> Such heavenly touches ne'er touched earthly faces."
> So should my papers, yellowed with their age,
> Be scorned, like old men of less truth than tongue,
> And your true rights be termed a poet's rage
> And stretchèd metre of an antique song.
>   But were some child of yours alive that time,
>   You should live twice, in it and in my rhyme. [Sonnet 17]

When I had done, Harry laughed & said I flattered him mightily, and he thought not yet on children. "I have no intent to turn husband yet," said he. Then he read o'er my hopeful remainder which he declared he believed to be some of the finest poems he had seen. I told him he prized them too highly. "Nay, Will," said Harry, "be not so humble and modest, e'en tho' nothing so becomes a man as modest stillness and humility. I have heard some account of your work upon the stage, & now

I see these poems before me. I doubt not you may write e'en finer poetry, as you say, but the worth of these may not be gainsaid. Indeed, I shall not hear one word said against them. And, by your leave, I will keep them by me for a while that I may peruse them when I have leisure or idle hours." I told him they were his & he might do with them as he pleased. We talked some hour or more together, & I do confess I am surprised that a lord doth consort with me, tho' that may be but his youthful ways.

7 MAY

Today Harry [Southampton] gave me Florio's *Second Fruites*, and therein is one of my sonnets for all the world to see, but none to know.[5] Harry laughing said, "Why, you were humble enough when you gave it to me, & why should you care when I and Master Florio know the poesy is thine?" Perforce I must agree, and yet for vanity's sake 'twould be pleasant to see W.S. there. We drank claret.

23 MAY

All the prattle is of some twenty or more Spanish ships that lie off Cornwall, and Sir W. Ralegh[6] has gone to meet them. Will wars never cease, what with this and the troubles in Brittany? I am embroiled with the like commotions in this Richard play [*Richard III*]! This evening I wrote a scene wherein Queens Elizabeth and Margaret mourn together & are joined in grief [4.4], & I am pleased withal.

31 MAY

What parlous wretched days be these. One thousand soldiers have been slain at Rouen, tho' I think they be mostly French. There's nothing in the streets but talk of this bloodshed. And by my art I profit from such bloodshed, for history such as I encompass in my plays is ever thus—bloody, tho' bold & resolute.

[JUNE]

Now dicing, cards, and bowls are forbid, and all are commanded to take up the bow to defend against attacks, if they come. Well, I might put my hand to it, but there are more profitable pastimes. Some several days past I came by these notions.[7] Whether, in regard to marriage, the parents' choice shall be considered before the children's affections. Thus—a man may bestow his goods where he will, so may he bestow his children as he thinketh best. Children are goods. Yet should a match imposed by parents upon their children, where the child loves not the intended in matrimony, be obeyed? Surely a young, lusty maiden ought not, to satisfy another's pleasure, marry with an infirm old man? How should I command my own children when they are grown? Should I command them? Parents, children, marriage, obedience—such matters be the ready stuff for a play if I might finish Richard, which ends with [the Battle of] Bosworth. There shall R[ichard] see his guilt, and so despairs. "I am I. I am a murderer." "An if I die, no soul will pity me."[8] Dick Burbage hath read much of what I hath writ, & says there is meat aplenty in the piece. I needs must keep my mind & thoughts on't, & accomplish all. There is little time for sonnets, tho' my heart lies that way. I fain would please Harry more. When I met with Kit [Marlowe] t'other day, smilingly, he asked me how the world fared between Harry & myself. I told him "well enough," but said little else. When Kit smiled, he looked in that instant like Richard [III].

16 JULY

As I happened by Cheap[side] today, a multitude was stirred up by some men who preached from a cart.[9] One [Hacket] said he was Christ Jesu and the Emperor of Europe, or some such foolery—I heard but little because of the din which grew fearsome. After some time, the preachers were pulled down from the cart and taken away. How like a scene from a play it all appeared, & I marvel how little 'tis that doth separate life from fiction.

17 JULY

Today came a messenger with a letter from Harry [Southampton], who hath given me a commission for a play to be acted when Her Majesty goes a progress to Titchfield. I am commanded to observe that the play shall be done out of doors, & that it should lack not wit and punning, for the young lords delight in such. I am to include allusions to such diurnal events as may pass in France or Spain, comic figures, for it is to be light and to delight, &, in fine, such stuff as shall please courtly folk, for only such is to be the audience. To boot, Harry wants some japes upon his tutor Florio, or mayhap some part he could enact. And if I can jest at Ralegh in some, nay, any fashion, Harry would be well pleased & gratified. I have in hand a brief work which I might enlarge I think, tho' whate'er I do I think it should be such as with prudence it might be used again. For, tho' there is profit in this business, more may be gained later. I would not waste so much labour for a mere occasion, even for Harry and the Queen.[10] But this might, like a tide at flood, lead on to moe fortune.

28 JULY

At Cheap[side] today. There thronged vasty crowds of folk to see the Christ man [William Hacket] hanged.[11] He cursed much, and then he called upon the Almighty saying, "Save me, O God my father." I marvelled that he was so much divided from himself & fair judgment. After he was quartered, his heart was held up for all to see. Kit [Marlowe], with me, was mightily jocund; he said that little learning died with that hanging. Then he blasphemed up and down, tho' I felt sick at heart & stomach, & was like to vomit. Later we went to the Bunch of Grapes for ale, tho' Kit would prate about the execution. He chided me for my "February face, so full of frost, of storm, of cloudiness," & bid me be more of a madcap. "'Twere good you do so much, for charity's sake," said Kit. I declare it is well nigh impossible to understand & comprehend the man, tho' he can, when he choose, be friendly & affectionate enough. Verily, after we had drunk deep, he would have me take him to my bed again, but I had nor strength nor inclination to do it, urge me mightily tho' he did.

31 JULY

So the Christ tale is completed. One of Hacket's accomplices hath died in Bridewell and t'other is set free.[12] "Strange are the ways of the Lord," said Kit laughing. One fly be squashed whiles another goes free.

3 SEPTEMBER

Love's Labour was played yester afternoon, & was right good. Her Majesty laughed heartily at the wit and puns, even those upon France where my Lord Essex is, on whose absence she grieves. Florio was spirited enow to personate Holofernes, tho' Tom Nashe was sullen when he did perceive that Moth did present him. Before our performance came Master Banks' dancing horse, called Morocco, on which I swiftly wrote a line—a pert device for the nonce. Master Banks departed today for Shrewsbury, as we do to town. So I am well pleased and somewhat richer, though the piece is as yet but a passing thing. The plot is a matter of small consequence, and the characters but shadows. The fantasy of it all was palpable when the mask was played. Too much artifice, methinks.[13]

[SEPTEMBER]

Kit [Marlowe] hath shown me his play he calls Edward the second. His lines are plain—the fire and flash are gone. There are but two scenes worth their salt—when Edward looks inward upon himself at Killingworth, and when he toys with the crown and thinks on abdication. I do believe that Marlowe thought to write about Edward and Gaveston and their practices together, but his mind turned cowardly at the last. So his characters are weakly—where is the flesh & blood? I observed to Kit that, perchance, Edward & Mortimer might talk on kingship, and God, and power, and such, to which he rejoined (quite angry) that I had best write such a play. Well, I have written too many that way, yet I foresee one I might write [*Richard II*].

[OCTOBER]

With Harry [Southampton], and we gave wanton dalliance too much rein, leaving off but to eat and drink. He told me of the war in France, of how my lord Essex's brother hath been shot in the head, of how Essex desires to revenge him, and of the siege of Rouen. To hear of these deeds recounted stirs the imagination, but I'd as lief never venture there—'tis enough mine own fictions hold up the mirror to such events. Such other things as we said and did, I may not set down where idle errant eyes may chance. After, we enjoyed the honey-heavy dew of slumber with no figures nor no fantasies which busy care draws in the brains of men.

3 NOVEMBER

Kit and Kyd[14] took me to Tyburn today to see the traitor O'Rourke hanged.[15] I protested such stuff was poison to my stomach, and i' fecks, I have seen too many wretches suffer so; but they would have me go. To the end, O'Rourke would not repent him, and was a rebel even unto death. 'Ods life, how people cheered when he was cut in pieces, & most when his heart was cut out, and the executioner held it aloft and, finally, when his head was lopped off. Later Kit said it was not for nothing he had impressed me to the execution, for he would have me see how the spectacle did please the multitude, most particularly when the body was dismembered. I told him this I knew. "Why, then," says he, "it were well a play should contain such as we had seen," and I allowed as much, even if it were unpleasurable to me. "Why, then," says he again, "you are just the man for e'en such a task." I should have suspected ere this the plot Kit was devising for me. So again I am cozened to work o'er another's play. Kit, Kyd, and Peele have drawn up the action and call it "Titus' Complaint," after some ballad Kyd hath read. Their plot hath some twelve or thirteen deaths, rape, hands cut off, tongues cut out, and I know not what mayhem beside. All this I am to leave as they have pictured, but I am to give it verse and character. I despair of such work, but I am in need of it until I am established among my fellows. I am but green as yet, and they say that modest doubt is called the beacon of the wise.

20 NOVEMBER

That pious, charitable man, Sir Christopher Hatton died today.[16] 'Tis said the queen herself administered broths and cordials to him whiles he lay sick, for he was a great favourite of her majesty. What I shall remember is that he tried Queen Mary of Scots and many a Catholic. But, as comes to pass with all men, cormorant devouring time doth join him with worms, and thus are the mighty & the lowly ever joined in death, tho' they think not so beforehand.

21 NOVEMBER

In ruminating upon this Titus piece, I recalled that in Ovid the rape of Philomel is much like Lavinia's in Titus, and so I shall fashion the two alike.[17] Kyd hath given me his *Jeronimo*[18] to peruse, and says therein is incident enow for this play. Murder and revenge abound, and the people have seen it before and much approved it. Kyd says it *is* violence and bloodshed they must *see*.

10 DECEMBER

To Tyburn again today where seven Catholics were executed. Then I went to Holborn where died a priest taken whiles saying mass for one of Harry's [Southampton's] tutors.[19] All this in Christ Jesu's name, they say. In *Titus* I write of Rome—the Catholics' world is real, mine not, yet both are suffused with death and mutilation. I try to render truly Titus' anguish, despair, and madness, tho' the bloody sensation o'erwhelms all. I am nigh admiration for the extremities of the blackamoor [Aaron], who is greatly hardened in his crimes of nature and ne'er repents. He is lustful, is evil incarnate—evil which none may overcome—& seems to triumph—& I am reminded of Richard three.[20]

13 DECEMBER

Tom Nashe showed me Greene's *Second Part of Conny-Catching* which is, so says the book, a warning to the honest-minded yeoman about the art of cosening and card play.[21] Then there is the art of crossbiting where strumpets and their men entice a young man into a house, and there pick his pocket, or the woman sends for her husband and would send the young man to Bridewell, and declare he had raped her. I have seen as much myself in Turnbull Street, & indeed it might be stuff to flesh out a play at some time or another. Of Greene I think but little, for he ne'er likes me, & is a serpent's egg, which, hatched, grows mischievous.

14 DECEMBER

I have thought much on Tom's *Jeronimo*[22]—he renders Jeronimo better than I my Titus, save Titus cannot be called all *mine*. Tom hath fashioned a wondrous & quaint device in Jeronimo's lines:
> Haply you think, but bootless are your thoughts,
> That this is fabulously counterfeit,
> And that we do as all tragedians do:
> To die today, for fashioning our scene,
> The death of Ajax, or some Roman peer,
> And in a minute starting up again,
> Revive to please tomorrow's audience [4.4.76–82].

Through all the play, Revenge and a Ghost sit and watch all else. Later Jeronimo enacts his own play wherein he revenges himself and kills his enemies. Other characters on stage watch this, & applaud the "actors" in this play within the play for "acting," and yet where assuredly death is real. And Jeronimo doth remind *all* those that watch, *all* audiences, that this is but a fashioned scene, a fiction. 'Tis all the cleverest stuff I e'er have read, and I see how we players counterfeit, & dramatists to boot.

16 DECEMBER

Today Sir Christopher Hatton was buried in St. Paul's church with that lamentation which is the right of the dead. I was amidst a mighty crowd, which stood all silent. Before his coffin walked some hundred or more poor folk dressed in caps and gowns given to them for the purpose. Then followed afterwards some three or four hundred lords, gentlemen, guards, and the like. This scene spread out before us like a play. A procession is a powerful spectacle, a device to seize upon, as Marlowe oft hath told me. And i'faith, I confess he's right.

20 DECEMBER

I have done what I can with *Titus*, but all is excess, & it be not a play I fain would pen. Kyd says despair not, and 'twill be acted ere long.

29 DECEMBER

I fain would have returned home this yule, and had I done so I had missed a wondrous sight, for my *Richard* [*III*] was enacted for Her Majesty at Whitehall. [Richard] Burbage was magnificent [as Richard III]. When once he took off his own clothes and put on Richard's, like Proteus, he became Richard, and remained Richard until he was clothed in his own garments once more. How he spoke the words; they scarce seemed those words I had written, for he transformed them, made 'em something rich and rare and wondrous. And ever did he animate his speech with action. But he sawed not the air like common players, nor strutted, nor bellowed like them. As I stood at the back of the platform listening, I was transported backward to Bosworth Field & all the rest—I might have been there, verily I was there, not here. It was a thing not to be missed e'en for the whole world. When all was done, my Lord Ferdinando [Lord Strange] addressed Her Majesty, making a low bow, and declared the play did enact his family's loving loyalty to her gracious majesty,[23] and he trusted she were well pleased. At which she smiled somewhat, & spoke but a little. It is said H.M. stuffs cloths in her mouth to keep her cheeks plumpy, but I could not tell if that be true or no. Then all, and myself, did stand before her, and bowed low. After which we were taken to a room hard by a kitchen, and given much to eat and drink. I am brimful of pleasure & pride that I must chastise myself lest I forget all due humility, and fall thereby. Modesty must ever be my beacon.

❦ *Shakespeare's* The Comedy of Errors *contrasts sharply with Marlowe's latest effort,* The Jew of Malta, *though the latter sets Shakespeare thinking about making a Jew the focus of one of his own plays (*The Merchant of Venice*). Shakespeare finds that he is the subject of some subtle allusions in Kyd's* Arden of Feversham *and that he and Southampton share the same mistress, Aemilia Lanyer (who marries an entirely different man later in the year). Therein lie the germs of his next comedy,* The Taming of the Shrew. *Disorder in London prompts Shakespeare to make a long summer visit to Stratford where he delights in the company of his son, Hamnet. As the year ends, Shakespeare is denigrated in Robert Greene's* Groats-worth of Wit, *for which the printer Henry Chettle makes amends in his* Kind-Harts Dream. ❦

[JANUARY]

Marlowe has read *Richard* [*III*], and is enamoured of my villain, though he thinks the play be a sprawling piece. I told him I knew that, and that [Richard] Burbage had been fine, nay, magnificent when we played it before the queen this December past. Yet *Richard* might be amended if occasion warrant. Kit said I should employ the unities (tho' he himself pays them no heed, and well might he follow his own advice, I trow). I cannot conceive how a chronicle might be written after that fashion. Kit is to give me his book of Plautus' *Menaechmi*, as I told him I could read the Latin. Tom [Nashe], who was with us, said if I read Plautus I should read *Supposes*[1] for the hint it might provide. So shall I read both, and perchance pen a comedy with unities, if such be to my fancy, for I will dance to mine own tune.

19 JANUARY

The news is that the Lord Essex hath returned and is at Court with Her Majesty. Mayhap she is now better pleased than when we performed for her at Christmas. I marvel she has never taken a husband, tho' 'tis said she would not suffer any man to be her equal. But sure she must have tasted carnal pleasures.

4 FEBRUARY

Read *Delia* by Samuel Daniel.[2] The book is sonnets in a sequence writ upon a lady who lives by the Avon. 'Tis worthy of emulation, & that I might write in like fashion might please my Harry [Southampton] more.

7 FEBRUARY

More on conny-catching is printed by Greene, tho' methinks there is enow already.[3]

15 FEBRUARY

Folk may be more simple than may be conceived, for they spread rumours of some invasion at the ports, but where no one knows. I demanded of one fellow what he knew; he could say only that so & such had told him. Then he said another man had told him all the Romish priests have fled to Lancashire, & her majesty will die this year, & other like foolishness. Yet tens & thousands will believe one long-tongued babbling gossip, whose oaths are no stronger than the word of a tapster, and both are the confirmer of false reckonings.

18 FEBRUARY

My seething brain apprehends new joy, for on the morrow Ned Alleyn is to lead Lord Strange's men in several plays at Henslowe's Rose on Bankside. Ned says he is wooing Henslowe's [step-] daughter Joan [Woodward], tho' I believe he woos Henslowe & his theatre in equal measure! Many plays are in hand—mine, Kit's, Kyd's, even Greene's wretched *Friar Bacon* [*and Friar Bungay*], which is not worth nor pen nor ink. I had thought to improve mine own work, but it must suffice, for my mind is on new stuff [*The Comedy of Errors*] that I must write. I have cast mine eye o'er Plautus and in his prologue lies all the tale, as thus:

Nunc ille geminus, qui Syracusis habet,
hodie in Epidamnum veniet cum servo suo
hunc quaeritatum geminum germanum suom.[4]

I would not be his slavish imitator, but I think all the confusions in Plautus' comedy might be made twofold: two pairs of twins, twin brothers, twin slaves. The greater the perplexity, the greater the laughter? I believe I know somewhat of twins—those my dear children.

21 FEBRUARY

Today at the Rose was enacted Peele's *Muly Mollocco* [*The Battle of Alcazar*]. Tho' the play held my mind but a little, Ned Alleyn who personated Muly, a usurper, was as good as any actor might be. Howsoever, the play was long, tedious, and tiresome, though I did not tell George that. Ned hath played also Orlando in Greene's piece [*Orlando Furioso*] which Greene should account his good fortune, for naught else in this world might help it. And yet 'twas done before at Court,[5] tho' why, I know not. Greene scowled when I told him that. Said he, "I observe you are no fawning greyhound would proffer me a candy deal of courtesy." I replied, "I believe you have the mind that suits with this your outward character." Bought cheese—2½d a pound.

26 FEBRUARY

With Marlowe to the Rose where his *Jew* [*of Malta*] was given today.[6] Sans Alleyn as Barabas the Jew the play would be naught, tho' I did not tell Kit this, for that would be a rude, sharp-toothed unkindness. Yet Kit hath given the crowds much that they delight in hissing and condemning, but then applaud roundly. They rose to Machiavel as prologue, though they little understand what Machiavel was. And they curse the Jew, e'en tho' Kit hath rendered Barabas as less than evil incarnate, leastways when the hypocrite Christians work against him. Much be blasphemy, & Kit, who believes not in God, delights to see the many-headed Hydra enraged by his words. He delighted too in my astonishment when I heard "Till Titus and Vespasian conquer'd us" [Act 2], which he did add but yesterday because of my play that is to come. He thought it a merry jest. The platform was strewn with corpses, though the best device was Barabas' death through a trap in the upper stage from whence he fell into a cauldron, all the while cursing the Christians and Turks. In brief, 'twas a play that is caviar to the general, but far from perfection. Yet this *Jew* hath made me think on what might be written about Christians and Jews.

2 MARCH

My three plays on Henry VI that have long lain by me are to be enacted. The first is played tomorrow, and if the multitude take a liking to it, the other two will be put forward. I trust the groundlings be not fickle, for my fortune rests upon their favour, which will make or mar me. Yet I fear how all will fadge [turn out].

3 MARCH

With so many of our men impressed and engaged to fight in France,[7] *Henry* hath delighted the multitude that thronged the Rose to see it yesterday afternoon. Henslowe is much pleased at the money it hath brought in,[8] and assured me I should see some profit too—this though the company hath paid me already for the writing of it. I rejoice that fortune hath smiled upon me & rewarded my diligence. Now I can stand before father, mother, Anne, & all the rest, & know my success hath justified leaving them & coming to London.

13 MARCH

I despair. Tomorrow Dick [Burbage] is to be Kyd's Jeronimo, and 'tis to be a month or more afore he be my Titus. So I fear the people will see how better Kyd's drama be.[9] Dick thinks he is young for Jeronimo, and for Titus, and is afeard he'll not fare as well as did Ned when he played the Jew.[10] Yet have I told Dick that he and Ned are alike as actors, both without compare. I must begin anew to frame and make fit my comedy [*The Comedy of Errors*].

14 MARCH

As I thought & believed 'twould be so, *Jeronimo* hath been a triumph, and Dick a wonder, a veritable Titan. Will he do the like for Titus? I can but wait & hope, but all my thought is "then did the sun on dunghill shine."

[APRIL]

I have read o'er Plautus again, and this sentence hath lodged in my brain: "nimia mira mihi quidem hodie exorta sunt miris modis: alii me negant eum esse qui sum, atque excludant foras."[11] There's the rub of it all, & of my play [*The Comedy of Errors*]. Twins and identity. Am I I? I am I. Why, these are my own very words come back to me.[12] Thus can both comedy and tragedy be alike, & they differ in this only: one *be* a comedy, & the other be a tragedy. So might I place into this comedy those sentences I put not into *Richard* [*III*]—viz:

> He is deformèd, crooked, old and sere,
> Ill-faced, worse bodied, shapeless everywhere;
> Vicious, ungentle, foolish, blunt, unkind,
> Stigmatical in making, worse in mind.
> [*The Comedy of Errors*, 4.2.19–22]

Richard described so be a villain, but a suitor described thus in this comedy causeth laughter.

6 APRIL

Today I had no particular purpose and, after I had walked about for close upon an hour, I found myself at [St.] Paul's and purchased *Arden of Feversham* at the north door.[13] I recalled Kyd had made mention of the play, tho' he said it was not by him, though he laughed on saying that. Now I do suspect the play be his, for two desperately ruffianly murderers in it are called Black Will and Shakebag. Kyd puns on my name, and makes me a murderer for all the world to see, tho' I believe 'tis done but for a japes.

7 APRIL

Certes 'tis Kyd that hath writ *Arden*, though the tale be taken from Holinshed.[14] Kyd jests that I am Arden,[15] Black Will, *and* Shakebag, and thus, in his play, I kill myself! The wife, Alice, Kyd would have be mine own Anne, though Alice is vicious and cruel, and I cannot think my Anne unfaithful, nor would she murder me! Black Will and Shakebag act at the behest of one Richard Greene, who can be but Robert Greene whom Kyd knows I like not—yea, I despise him as he despiseth me. Yet *Arden* is tedious long, tho' there be an effective scene—Alice cannot wash away the blood of her murdered husband.[16] Lines to remember—"Chief actors to Arden's overthrow," "then all our labour's lost," "a raven for a dove," "Then rides he straight to London; there, forsooth, he revels it among such filthy ones as counsels him to make away his wife."[17]

11 APRIL

Today *Titus [Andronicus]* was presented at the Rose. In a trice, all my fears were vanquished, for the groundlings devoured the blood—lord how enamoured were they of the butchery, just as when they see the bowels on Tyburn's hill. Dick [Burbage] was mightily triumphant, and so are we wealthier in gold, but not in art.[18] I must cast aside such base stuff.

23 APRIL

How out of love am I with this time of my nativity. Today I lay abed with Aemilia,[19] gazing on that delicate mole upon her neck, when she told me how she had made wanton with Harry [Southampton] some evenings past. I knew not what to say for, though she hath been my secret mistress, I have suspected that there is some vicious mole of nature within her, that she shared her pleasurable delights with other men. But I cast my doubts from that thought. And why should I condemn so fair a creature when I am not blameless? I might give Harry chastisement for this abuse, save that I love him & hold his friendship close. This instead must suffice:

> That thou hast her, it is not all my grief,
> And yet it may be said I loved her dearly;
> That she hath thee is of my wailing chief,
> A loss in love that touches me more nearly.
> Loving offenders, thus I will excuse ye:
> Thou dost love her because thou know'st I love her,
> And for my sake even so doth she abuse me,
> Suff'ring my friend for my sake to approve her.
> If I lose thee, my loss is my love's gain,
> And, losing her, my friend hath found that loss;
> Both find each other, and I lose both twain,
> And both for my sake lay on me this cross.
> But here's the joy: my friend and I are one.
> Sweet flatt'ry! Then she loves but me alone! [Sonnet 42]

[MAY]

I see little to mark in *Supposes*. 'Tis a gentle comedy, tho' much longer than need be. It is much like Lily,[20] many words to small purpose. Yet Gascoigne's argument touches on the nature of what I do in my farce of errors, where nothing that is so is so. "But understand, this our suppose is nothing else but a mistaking or imagination of one thing for another. For you shall see the master supposed for the servant, the servant for the master: the freeman for a slave, and the bondslave for a freeman: the stranger for a well-known friend, and the familiar for a stranger" [Prologue]. This is the very midsummer madness of my characters, and all is like the parts of a clock. By art mechanical must I contrive all the errors, till all can be set aright when all are in the same place. And so it ends.

8 MAY

Thousands moe men are to be ordered to fight in France to aid the French king [Henri IV] 'gainst the Spaniard & the Catholics. 'Tis said our cause be just, & doubtless 'tis, but what numbers will die for't, and how many wives & children will the dead leave behind? I am glad I am not called upon, e'en tho' the cause be just. Thus are let slip the dogs of war.

9 MAY

Marlowe hath been bound to keep the peace for threatening the constable of Holywell Street. Kit continueth a violent man, yet, when he chooseth, he is good company. He leads himself and his many boys astray, and takes delight in mere disorder. He is a wanton spirit &, I fear, like to die afore his time if he amend not his ways as swift as may be. I should be aggrieved to lose his friendship.

26 MAY

Today with John Heminges and his wife Rebecca to St. Mary's Church Aldermanbury where they baptized their baby, Mary. She is a weak and sickly child, and John was not much cheered. I offered them some small comfort, but John & Rebecca felt no joy, fearing the worst to come.[21] 'Twas not a joyous day. Bought Suffolk cheese & salt butter, 6d.

[27 MAY]

Jeronimo [*The Spanish Tragedy*] & *Arden* [*of Feversham*] give a hint of how next I may write, tho' my comedy shall be upon a husband who tames his shrewish wife. All the action shall be observed by a Warwickshire man who looks down from the gallery,[22] e'en tho' the chief action shall be set in Italy. The boy who plays the wife [Kate] must needs be pert, sharp. And my theme shall be how love may be transformed or some such, worthy perchance of Ovid,[23] which I must read all o'er. Sundry and divers allusions to [Gascoigne's] *Supposes*.[24] While husbands will applaud an obedient huswife, what of the women?

1 JUNE

Harry [Southampton] sent word for me to see him, & to be not tardy. I took some sonnets with me, for he expressly commanded I should read some two or three to him. This in particular he commended smilingly:

> How can my Muse want subject to invent,
> While thou dost breathe, that pour'st into my verse
> Thine own sweet argument, too excellent
> For every vulgar paper to rehearse?
> O, give thyself the thanks, if aught in me
> Worthy perusal stand against thy sight;
> For who's so dumb that cannot write to thee
> When thou thyself dost give invention light?

> Be thou the tenth Muse, ten times more in worth
> Than those old nine which rhymers invocate;
> And he that calls on thee, let him bring forth
> Eternal numbers to outlive long date.
>   If my slight Muse do please these curious days,
>   The pain be mine, but thine shall be the praise.
> [Sonnet 38]

Then I dared Harry's worst objections, and gave him my poem upon Aemilia,[25] which he read, & then said, "Dear Will, 'tis no matter, & surely we shall not quarrel over a woman. Besides there are others who have lain in the heat of her luxurious bed, tasted of that delicious fruit, and smelled her fragrant rose. I doubt not that all will see that as plain as may be ere the year be out." I forbore to ask him what he meant by that; I can see yet without spectacles. Then, while we drank a rare claret & ate figs, he told me all the gossip. Ralegh is confined in his Durham House [London] because he hath married one of Her Majesty's ladies [in waiting].[26] Burleigh's son[27] did arrest him. Harry says my lord Essex is cock o' hoop in ecstasy, tho' he detesteth Cecil. Harry, who loves Essex, was joyed for his sake. Much more gossip after the same fashion. So the noble & mighty love & hate, & are mean & spiteful in no less degree than common ordinary folk. Though this should not astonish me, I am surprised withal. I took my leave late in the dull watch o' th' night.

SATURDAY [10 JUNE]

At the Rose today I played Osrick, this but a small part in *A Knack to Know a Knave*—Ned Alleyn the King [Edgar], & Will Kempe the Clown, whose merriments drew plaudits from the multitude. Amongst the groundlings, that some call the penny stinkards, were many prentices who were oft rowdy & rude. But for all that, the crowds were pleased mightily with my small jest on *Titus*, for which I had license, as it was not set down.[28]

12 JUNE

Some prentices, perchance some of those at our play this Saturday past, did riot yesterday in Southwark. 'Tis said they do not care for strangers taking away their work. Whate'er be the reason, there was a mighty affray with the [Knight] Marshal's Men, who cudgelled the prentices much about the pate. When they would not be subdued, the Lord Mayor & his men rode in to quell them & set all in order. These be parlous violent days.

24 JUNE

The prentice riots have caused much disorder, & our theatre is to be shut till Michaelmas [29 September]. All are commanded to keep indoors at night & carry no weapons. I know not how much money we lose thereby, though I have 23 angels [gold coins] put by. Mayhap Harry [Southampton] might give me moe, tho' I detest the asking, and I must earn more by my pen. E'en though the prentices complaints were legitimate, they have caused us much trouble & difficulty. Well, it is the way of the world, we cannot all be masters, & not every path may be smooth or easy trod.

29 JUNE

How like unto books is life. I heard yesterday of two people executed at Smithfield for murdering the wife's husband—'twas as strange a tale as e'er I might tell.[29] I shall leave London on the morrow, and return to my wife—and to my beloved children that they may know I love them dearly. So shall I be away from such sights, and death, and the plague. To breathe sweet country air again in summer's halcyon days will be all my delight.

[JULY]

Home! How wondrous are my dear children, who have grown apace. Anne is all smiles, & I rejoice to see father & mother. Many are the joys here that I never may find in London. Yet I must write ever & anon. I have a mind to pen another chronicle, for the multitude savour histories, & the action is ready laid out before me. There's much ado with the reign of Richard the second, Bolingbroke, Henry five—I must read o'er Holinshed once more. I have *K. John* by me which may new-fire my imagination.[30] Well, all this & my dear family be enow for the nonce.

All summer long my beloved Hamnet & I have walked by the river, & apprehended such jollity & wonders that my heart is full of unstained love, & my soul o'erflows with joy. Such happiness is beyond earthly pleasures. The boy babbles with the zest of youth, and all delights his eye. One day we walked out as far as Tiddington and sat on the river's bank. While we took our rest, an ancient fisherman stopped and talked awhile; he pointed across to some willows by the water's edge and asked me, "Do ye know what those be?" I told him they were willows. "Ah, indeed they be, but they be also where Kate Hamlett drowned a good few years back.[31] Some folk say she slipped and fell, but there be others who say her death was doubtful." Then he went on his way. Hamnet said, "Father, did that man say my name just now?" I told him what the man had said, and said Hamnet, "Oh, Hamlett and Hamnet do both sound alike, don't they?" After that, we returned home, and together in the garden we set the dibble in the earth to plant gillyvors, marigolds, sweet lavender, & marjoram. And I pray the Lord that we may watch them grow & Hamnet be spared for years & years to come. Without him I might despair eternally, tho' many folk might say 'tis foolish fondness to be thus affected.

AUGUST

I was surprised withal to receive a missive from Tom Nashe with much news. His book is already entered, and he looks to send it soon.[32] Ralegh and his wife are sent to the Tower,[33] a strange conjunction of news. Contagion rageth across London, so it is well I am here, and plague hath taken off poor Simon Jewell.[34] I trust Tom will be spared.

21 AUGUST

Today father & I went to value the goods of Henry Field—a good man I knew when I was young.[35] Dick, here since the burial, is o'ercome with grief—I told him we shall be happier when we are back in London, though who knows if that be true, for the plague rages on. 'Tis all too true, excessive grief is the enemy to the living. We spent several hours together in quiet conversation.

[C. 15 SEPTEMBER][36]

Nashe hath sent me his *Pierce*, and with it news of wretched Greene's death, tho' he be Tom's friend not mine.[37] Tom says a month past they feasted together on pickled herrings and Rhenish wine, after the which Greene fell grievous sick. I marvel he could repent his dissolute, swearing, unseemly ways as Tom writes he did—the death's head must have been well nigh for that. I doubt not he died o' the French pox [syphilis], tho' I care not, and cared not for him. There's a divinity that shaped his end.

[C. 20 SEPTEMBER]

Nashe's *Pierce Penniless* is brimful of thoughts, such as these—"Plays be no extreme, but a rare exercise of virtue," "the subject of them is borrowed out of our English chronicles." (Much of this have I done.) "How would it have joyed brave Talbot (the terror of the French) to think that after he had lain two hundred years in his tomb, he should triumph again on the stage, and have his bones new embalmed with the tears of ten thousand spectators at least (at several times), who, in the tragedian that represents his person, imagine they behold him fresh bleeding." (Here doth Tom greatly flatter me, for methinks Talbot was all Ned Alleyn's doing; yet I might well believe ten thousand hath seen *Harey* [*Henry VI Part 1*]. But Talbot's scenes were all my fancy; modesty becomes a man in all things.) "What a glorious thing it is to have Henry the Fifth represented on the stage." (A pregnant suggestion—and Tom knows I think on Richard II and what follows.) "In plays, all cosenages, all cunning drifts over-gilded with outward holiness, all stratagems of war, all the cankerworms that breed on the rust of peace, are most lively anatomiz'd; they show the ill success of treason, the fall of hasty climbers, the wretched end of usurpers, the misery of civil dissention, and how just God is evermore in punishing of murther." I do confess such is truly the purpose of plays and of playing. [King] John is brought down, yet Bolingbroke triumphs. And bless Tom for his praise of Alleyn, Tarlton, and Knell.[38] Tom is much vexed with what Harvey hath written.[39]

25 SEPTEMBER

Father hath been named a recusant, as are George Bardolfe and William Fluellen.[40] Father hath not been to church these several months, but he says that he goes not to church for fear of process for debt.[41] More he will not say, & I am afeard there is more to this troublesome matter. I know not what to do, for father is a stubborn man. Perchance 'tis none other than some debt.

30 SEPTEMBER

I hear poor Kit [Marlowe] is much distracted and sick with grief that his Amyntas is dead. I knew Tom [Watson] somewhat, & all I have left are his *Tears* which I shall read o'er in fond remembrance.[42]

11 OCTOBER[43]

Today I heard a proclamation—there are to be no festivities this Lord Mayor's day [29 October] because the plague increases. I fear I was foolish to return to the city—yet work lies here.

19 OCTOBER

Aemilia married yesterday, and secures thereby a father for her child.[44] I' fecks I wish her well, bear her no ill will, & wish her joy o' the worm.

> My love is as a fever, longing still
> For that which longer nurseth the disease,
> Feeding on that which doth preserve the ill,
> Th'uncertain sickly appetite to please.
> My reason, the physician to my love,
> Angry that his prescriptions are not kept,
> Hath left me, and I desperate now approve
> Desire is death, which physic did except.
> Past cure I am, now reason is past care,
> And frantic-mad with evermore unrest;
> My thoughts and my discourse as madmen's are,
> At random from the truth, vainly expressed:
>> For I have sworn thee fair, and thought thee bright,
>> Who art as black as hell, as dark as night.[45]

I have laid hands on Greene's book, & it is full of the bitterness with which he died. And there, in the midst of his hatred, I find myself—"for there is an upstart Crow, beautified with our feathers, that with his *Tygers hart wrapt in a Players hyde*, supposes he is as well able to bombast out a blanke verse as the best of you: and being an absolute *Johannes fac totum*, is in his owne conceit the only Shakescene in the countrey."[46] I know not whether to curse him for his drunken libels, or rejoice that his words may make my name known to all. I knew him a notorious liar and a pestilent complete knave. Welladay, he hath received his just reward.

22 OCTOBER

Alleyn married Joan today which hath made Ned double joyous.[47] He looks to find ever larger fortune and fame, and I wish him well. Ned treated us to a fine wedding banquet, tho' a delicate stomach is my reward.

Now *K. John* is finished, I must think on other matters, tho' 'tis hard sith this plague lies all about us.[48]

24 NOVEMBER

Ned [Alleyn] has begun as he means to continue. He builds a house on Bankside, and it promises to be fair and as grand as can be.[49] Like a careless heir, he spares no expense to satisfy his desires. Well, all joy to him.

10 DECEMBER

Two days past, I read *Kind-Harts Dreame* wherein [Henry] Chettle, a portly, amiable gentleman given to huff & puff, makes some amends for his hand in Greene's wretched *Groats-worth*. I told Chettle what I took amiss, and now he praises my uprightness. Well enough. He still dislikes Marlowe, and for what I can well guess.[50] Today was foggy, raw, and dull.

14 DECEMBER

Some days I hear or see things which almost pass understanding, & unless I saw them myself I might not credit it. Today a woman called Anne [Burnell] was whipped through the streets of the city because she had declared that she was the King of Spain's daughter. A long time ago, a witch in Nottinghamshire had said that some marks this Anne bore about her body showed she was the King's daughter. In sooth, the woman was but a butcher's daughter in Eastcheap. I marvel folk may believe such foolery, & yet they do.

22 DECEMBER

For once in a while, good news. In a week, and spite of the past plague, we are to play at the Rose. I am to furnish or burnish two or three plays—Kit as well.[51]

❦ *The plague threatens everyone, prompting Shakespeare to think of writing better work than he has produced so far before it is too late. He and Marlowe, abetted by Southampton, wager who will write the better poem: Shakespeare wins with* Venus and Adonis. *Marlowe is unable to complete his own effort,* Hero and Leander, *when his nefarious activities, possibly as a government agent, lead to his murder in Deptford. Marlowe's roommate, Tom Kyd, is imprisoned, tortured, and suffers horribly (he dies the following year). Shakespeare visits Bath where his fellow actors are performing, and he outlines some of his works in progress. He also visits Southampton at his country house in Titchfield, presents him with a copy of* Venus and Adonis, *and promises him another poem. By year's end, Shakespeare is abuzz with new projects—*A Midsummer Night's Dream, Romeo and Juliet, *and* Richard II. ❦

1 JANUARY

Today Kit's Jew was given.[1] Ned [Alleyn] ever triumphant as Barabas—to his great pleasure, the penny stinkards hissed him lustily, which incited him all the greater to his business.

4 JANUARY

I care little for my prentice stuff, but I must furnish a comedy haste-post-haste, & *Errors* hath been chosen.[2] I have amended it as best I can,

& truth to tell, as much as I care to. 'Tis better than before, but still prentice stuff for all that.

6 JANUARY

The groundlings devoured my Titus as they do Kit's Jew. They care not if the action be improbable so that there be butchery aplenty. 'Tis only Dick [Burbage as Titus] can make the play supportable for me now, but he deserves something more worthy from my pen.[3]

16 JANUARY

Our Henry mishmash [*Henry VI Part 1*] was this afternoon. Ned's dying Talbot was all I cared for.[4] I must not make moan for money is wanted. A play unperformed is not worth the candle, & I *am* set before the public.

26 JANUARY

A second mishmash this afternoon—Kit's mayhem on the murder of the Paris Hugenots—blood upon blood, which incensed & incited the multitudes that cheered to the very heavens when Guise was slain. Religion and the French always stir 'em up. Yet the piece is not entire; 'tis but bits and pieces that want flesh. And how Kit hath saucily stolen my words, tho' I care not.[5] Care is no cure, but rather corrosive. Indeed, now I think upon't, I am flattered, for wholesome berries ripen best when neighboured by fruit of baser quality.

2 FEBRUARY

Damnation—the plague hath shut us up.[6] Tho' I should be grateful for what good fortune I have, more would have been right welcome. Such are the winds fate blows in our face when some ill planet reigns.

And I am a feather for each wind that blows; at the least I have my health, a providential benediction.

19 FEBRUARY

Parliament hath assembled, and all talk is of the Spanish, how they mean to invade us, and how we shall defend us.[7] I am aweary of such rumour, and must put my mind to fancy, whimsy, comedy—something not at all of this world, yet a mirror of it. Nature and supernature, reality and myth, men and fairies, lords and workaday folk. Something for the groundlings, gentry, & nobility alike.

[FEBRUARY]

Today I read *The Knight's Tale*,[8] & later these mine own words came to mind:
>Our wooing doth not end like an old play;
>Jack hath not Jill. These ladies' courtesy
>Might well have made our sport a comedy.[9]

Both works have set my mind awhirl for a comedy upon love & marriage [*A Midsummer Night's Dream*]. Love is fantasy and fleeting; we know it and we know it not, tho' all men, and women, pursue it. My characters shall be real and unreal—workaday mechanicals like the folk at home, & nobles from myths. Names—Theseus, Hippolyta, Bottom, Snout, Flute, Pyramus and Thisbe, Oberon, Titania, country fairies (Robin Goodfellow, Puck, and such). I fancy I shall play Theseus (the lord of all), and speak of imagination, fancy, poets, and such.[10] Would the play were as swiftly written as these thoughts cram & blaze in my seething brain.

SUNDAY [25 FEBRUARY]

This winter hath been lean, hungry, miserable, and cold. With the theatres closed, I scarce know where to turn, for my plays find no audience

& without which there is no money. To my joy & relief, last night an answer presented itself as clear as day. As we three lay together drinking, Kit [Marlowe] proposed a wager—we two shall compose a poem upon a mythic tale, and his poem that first is published shall be the victor, to whom t'other shall give five pounds. At this Harry [Southampton] said he would give five pounds more, and would permit, moreover, a dedication addressed to him that might bring fame & fortune to one of us. Harry did ordain that the dedication cannot show forth the love we both bear him. "Do not presume too much upon my love," he said. Ten pounds is a fortune to me now, and I agreed right quickly. Then we turned to what tales should be fit for our poems. I said, as I like him best, that Ovid suited me and that one book on love could well furnish my poem. Kit said he had thought already on Hero and Leander, and I think Kit already hath begun verses upon that theme. No hap, we agreed. So I shall turn to Venus and Adonis because Apollo and Hyacinthus is too like what Kit will write (as I guess), and Pygmalion and Galatea is stuff for a play.[11]

24 MARCH

Tom Nashe is gleeful at the arrest of the Welshman Penry for his Marprelate pamphlets.[12] He can scarce contain his joy, e'en tho' the wretch may die. Ralegh hath won a monstrous large subsidy in Parliament by his speech, if it might be collected.[13] For mine own part, I declare such stuff leaves me not much moved, for I am little more than a speck, one of thousands who but toil for daily bread. He needs must work who the devil drives.

TUESDAY [3 APRIL]

Venus [and Adonis] is accomplished, tho' not as well fashioned as I hoped, for I wrote for money. I went & showed *Venus* to Dick [Field], & asked him, because he is excellent in his trade, if he would publish it for me. "Well, dear Will," said he, "you know well I will do all I can to assist such a good friend as yourself. It is true my usual work lies not with such a poem as you have written—theology and classical works are more my business. But that is no matter, and you have a dedication to his lordship [Southampton] which is something to reckon with." I told Dick that Harry had seen already the dedication & approved of it, though I told him not that Harry had given me five pounds (as promised). Dick said, "That is well, & I think we must give some thought to the selling. I know Master Harrison who has a shop at Paul's, & I believe he would be the very man to sell your poem, for it is indeed more in his line & scope." I told Dick I would trust to his good judgment, for truth to tell, I know but little of such affairs. "And one more thing, Will. I would be obliged to you in the highest degree if you would look o'er my printing for you. Whiles we exercise great care, your perusal of the printing before the book is bound would prevent mistakes." I assured Dick I would look o'er the printing eagerly, for I would not want to offend his lordship (meaning Harry) with my carelessness by presenting him with a book that was not perfection itself. And so we agreed terms &, light of heart, I left Dick. Of Marlowe I hear and see nothing.[14]

SUNDAY [6 MAY]

Joan [Alleyn] hath had a letter of Ned. The company was at Chelmsford and far away from our woes.[15] Kit [Marlowe] woke me this morning, tho' what the time o' day was, I know not. He was greatly troubled—a libellous poem against foreigners is set upon the wall of the Dutch Churchyard and, he thinks, bears his name, though 'tis not him that did devise the slander.[16] I calmed him and said the business would pass, but he would hear none of it. Kit was wild, desperate, furious, and drunk even at that hour. I fear for him, for he is like to commit some ill-considered act, & then the authorities may do with him as they please. But how am I guilty when he will not embrace my counsel?

7 MAY

Kit here again, the morning little worn, & he as wild as ever he hath been. He flies to Scadbury to avert trouble; "I'll be hanged else, Will," he said. But still he writes his poem [*Hero and Leander*] for he wants better employment.[17] As he departed, he said, "I fear one woe doth tread upon another's heel."

10 MAY

As I passed by the Guildhall today (though no particular purpose had led me there), I heard a proclamation read which offered one hundred crowns for information on the author of the Dutch Churchyard libels. Now I do believe Kit's fear hath some foundation. Some heavy business is in hand, though what it might be, I cannot conceive. I trust Kit lies safe at Scadbury.

13 MAY

Tom Kyd was arrested yesterday and thrown in Bridewell. None may see him, and I fear hellish trouble brewing. I was turned from Harry's [Southampton's] door when I sought his aid.

Later—Harry came to my closet late tonight so disguised I scarce could recognise him. He is troubled and o'erflows with fury at Marlowe, whom now he despises for consorting with Ralegh and his circle of confederates. He said nothing can be done for Kyd or Kit, 'tis all government business that goes deep, he knows not where."It is a business of some heat, Will; more I cannot, nay, may not tell ye." He thinks both may yet live, but he seemed to despair. Harry stayed a short time, long enough for but a glass of canary [wine]. He brooded, said little else, & showed me none of the affection he was wont to do. He departed in ill temper. I can do nothing; I fear everything.

21 MAY

As Harry [Southampton] had prophesied, Marlowe hath been arrested.[18] I grow ever more fearful, and will leave for home tomorrow early. Naught else can be done here, & Harry will not importune any help to put Kit in his place again. I long for the sweet refreshment of home & children.

21 JUNE

[Stratford] Yester noon the christening of Anthony's [Nash] son, whom they have named Thomas, & now there be two T.N.s in my life. This latest, however, is a fair cherub, tho' a bawling brat at the font. T'will give me great joy to see him achieve his manhood.[19] We passed all the afternoon afeasting and drinking, for which my head is sorely troubled today.

1 JULY

From t'other Tom Nashe these news, & my heart is grievous heavy at what hath befallen Kit Marlowe. Tom hath written—"Parlous sad news, Will. Poor wild Kit was stabbed and killed at the Bull [Inn] in Deptford by a low companion.[20] 'Tis said they quarrelled over the reckoning, but it may be over a rival of their lewd lustful love. There may be deeper treachery in all this. Kyd remains yet in Bridewell, though he hath not been seen by any friend. Peradventure he is tortured (I doubt it not), hath confessed to I know not what, and hath Kit been murdered in consequence? But he is gone nonetheless. I heard tell of an inquest, and the man Frizer (that stabbed Kit) is gone free.[21] The authorities have executed the 'Marprelate' Penry [on 29 May] which I saw, though few others, since little notice was given for fear of multitudes. He was hanged at a place called St. Thomas à Watering some two miles from the city on the Kent Road, which is passing strange. Penry was kept quiet before he swung. The plague increases, and the summer fairs are banned."

Nashe hath sent also his book, which is crammed with jests, japes, rapine, and torture. His traveller Jack cavorts through France and Italy wherein lies much humour and satire, tho' oft there is scarce any action, for Tom will ever discourse and digress. The executions therein are bloody and gruesome, yet have I seen them likewise myself. But the whole book is novelty, and I shall tell him to print, tho' he says he needs a lordly patron. Harry [Southampton] could be such a one, and i' faith they were men of the same college.[22]

17 JULY

This letter from Kyd, which I showed to Anne, who wept piteously thereat: "Will—Be not angry nor vexed with me, for I have suffered much at those hands (you will know whose I mean) in Bridewell and elsewhere. I offer you these words, and hope you might forgive me. After the authorities arrested me, they kept me close locked up and mostly in darkness. Some little rotten food and dank water. What can be done to a man's body and mind with their instruments of torture, I can scarce describe. When I was taken, they found some of Marlowe's atheistical writings among mine own, for you know we had shared lodgings together. 'Twas with great difficulty and much disputation, and what all else I know not, that I declared the waste and idle papers were not mine but Kit's. I said too these papers I had delivered up unasked. The authorities declared that I must then be the author of the libels against foreigners at the Dutch Church, though I know naught about them. So again they charged me with his [Marlowe's] papers and beliefs. Time over time I cried out no. I said also I despised him, and thought him cruel, intemperate, and irreligious. This you know is but half a truth, for the fact is we did quarrel only once in a while. What else I said in pain I know not nor can call to remembrance, though I fear those words sent poor Kit to his death, whereof you surely know. Though I suffered nigh on a month, my conscience continues in dis-ease for what hath passed. I have entreated Sir John Puckering's aid for preferment since I needs must eat and sleep. Whether or no I can write again, the Lord only knows. Think no evil of me that was ever thine—Tom."²³ Thus goes the world for poor Tom; he who suffers alone suffers most in the mind.

5 AUGUST

John Heminges writes with news of their [Strange's Men] travels and travails. He wishes us to meet when they get to Bath to see and talk over what work or works I may have in hand. The fellows of the company are anxious for something that is new for when the theatres may open again. So I shall journey to Bath, and thereafter seek out Harry [Southampton] that I might show him my latest offering for him.

14 AUGUST

> How heavy do I journey on the way
> When what I seek, my weary travel's end,
> Doth teach that ease and that repose to say
> "Thus far the miles are measured from thy friend."
> The best that bears me, tired with my woe,
> Plods dully on, to bear that weight in me,
> As if by some instinct the wretch did know
> His rider loved not speed being made from thee.
> The bloody spur cannot provoke him on
> That sometimes anger thrusts into his hide,
> Which heavily he answers with a groan
> More sharp to me than spurring to his side;
>   For that same groan doth put this in my mind:
>   My grief lies onward and my joy behind. [Sonnet 50]

I had thought Bath to be a grander place than it is, & I satisfied my eyes with naught of fame but the Roman reliques, the springs, and baths. Whate'er else might be of renown in the city, I perceived it not. 'Twas good fellowship with the company last night, and I had quite forgot what good, kind fellows they are. Each and every one was eager to learn what parts I have writ down for them. I showed them [*King*] *John*, and then my midsummer play [*A Midsummer Night's Dream*] that is nigh complete, tho' it may be enlarged or compressed to suit whate'er the occasion might be. Will [Kempe] was much delighted with that part I have named Bottom. He says he can make much of it, tho' I fear he would make far more than is writ down for him. But I said nothing. Tho' the two other plays be little more than my idle fancy yet, 'twould seem the fellows would have them. The one is to be a tragedy of love [*Romeo and Juliet*] that is the reverse or shadow of the midsummer play. T'other, which will be swifter in the writing, shall be a tragedy upon King Richard 2nd, where from more may spring if wanted. Tomorrow I leave, tremulous, for Titchfield. My way lies through Warminster & Salisbury where I hope for fair rest.

20 AUGUST

Joy and terror—I find myself in Place House [Titchfield] and beloved Harry [Southampton] all smiles and affection. As before, the house dazzles my senses. I stood before the Gatehouse, tall, crenellated, gargoyles leering, and wondered whether I dared to set foot inside. 'Twas an old abbey once, but now a mansion. Harry told me all its history, but I most call to remembrance the stories of the Henry kings who have sojourned here, the one I have writ of already, and t'other would furnish much stuff for a play.[24] After we had supped privily together, I presented Harry with a copy of *Venus and Adonis*, which he accepted graciously & lovingly. What else passed between us may not be set down on paper.

22 AUGUST

Harry [Southampton] hath again opened his purse and heart that I may write another pamphlet for him. I told him of Lucrece, which he thinks would be worthy of my art. I showed him these lines, whereat he laughed and bathed his lips upon my cheek with a whispered, "pray come hither":

But Will is deaf and hears no heedful friends:

> Only he hath an eye to gaze on Beauty,
> And dotes on what he looks, 'gainst law or duty.
>
> I have debated even in my soul
> What wrong, what shame, what sorrow I shall breed;
> But nothing can affection's course control
> Or stop the headlong fury of his speed.
> Know repentant tears ensue the deed,
> Reproach, disdain, and deadly enmity;
> Yet strive I to embrace mine infamy
> [*The Rape of Lucrece*, lines 495–505]

I told him none would know what in truth lies behind them, for truth should be silent betimes. Yet my purpose in this poem be thus: "What win I if I gain the thing I seek?" "What momentary joy breeds months of pain; / This hot desire converts to cold disdain." "The sweets we wish for turn to loathèd sours / Even in the moment that we call them ours" [*Lucrece*, 211, 690–91, 867–68]. I muse that words be but mirrors sprung from the same fancy, as thus:

> O comfort-killing Night, image of hell
> O hateful, vaporous, and foggy night [*Lucrece*, 764, 771]
> O grim-looked night, O night with hue so black,
> O night, which ever art when day is not!
> [*A Midsummer Night's Dream*, 5.1.168–70]

Yet one way lies death, t'other mirth. With such ease one may become the other. And so tomorrow is one day more of joy; thereafter shall I despair, repair home, and the world will divide me from his bosom. Methinks Anne will feel guessingly my hidden joy.

10 SEPTEMBER

Sithence my return home, Anne & I have been ill at ease one with the other, tho' she will not say what I know lies in her heart—to wit, my pleasure with others, & the lack thereof with her. Well, moody silence perhaps is better; other words or deeds we could regret. Dear Hamnet, & the girls, are my joy, my consolation.

15 SEPTEMBER

Tom Russell's brother is dead and gone.²⁵ Anne is all gloom. Midsummer [*A Midsummer Night's Dream*] hath more form & model, and *Lucrece* shapes well. I have a mind to read the *Tragicall History of Romeus & Juliet* by Brooke, which I have thought long to do, & to emulate, nay far surpass, in limning out that tale. Indeed, an honest tale speeds best being plainly told.

28 SEPTEMBER

John Heminges hath sent news that their company is now called Derby's.²⁶ He would know which of my works go forward, for the fellows are anxious for novelty when they return to London. I shall write to him of the play on Romeo and the chronicle. I have heard also from Henslowe that, if it be not interdicted, Sussex's company would act for him at his Rose [Theatre] come Christmastide. Henslowe wants Titus and Richard [III] if Heminges will release them. This I wrote also to John, telling him I have need of the money and would publish *Titus* if I could. Thus must I write hard these next two months, and mayhap I will return to London in December, tho' I know Anne will berattle and berate me mercilessly for such Yuletide leaving-taking. I must abide her scolding: we needs must have money—'tis scarce a divided duty.

[OCTOBER]

John [Heminges] hath sent to me a manuscript, a play upon Richard that hath passed among several hands.²⁷ He muses whether I have a mind to augment or to finish it, or to render it fit for playing. Well, it is plain stuff, and I have no desire to expend my muse on another's scaffold. What this play lacks—true interest, lively personages, beautified language, villainy; what is good—some humour, though 'tis laboured in the main, for a leaden hand hath worked this. Yet there are scenes that might prove worthy enow at another time—Richard dividing his kingdom for his favourites, a prettified courtier of foppery fashion, ghosts that visit Woodstock and presage death.[28] Thus have I writ to John what I purpose instead—mine own chronicle (from Holinshed) of the last years & fall of Richard in which is the stuff of tragedy. Richard is as a player, brimful of pride and rhetoric, believing he is the deputy elect of the Lord. He fails in his duty to the realm & is usurped. I see a scene where Bolingbroke and Richard both do grasp the crown,[29] but I wonder whether the authorities will permit of a scene wherein the king be deposed? This play on Richard [*Richard II*] might be the first of several to conclude with the glories & triumphs of Harry fifth in France. Those be chronicles to espouse.

[NOVEMBER]

Brooke's argument in little be this: "Love hath inflamed twayne by sodayn sight. [. . .] She drinkes a drinke that seemes to reve her breath. [. . .] When she awakes, her selfe (alas) she sleath."[30] Herein lies all that my play need encompass, and folk know the tale well enow. One scene, & I know not why, I cannot put from my head—when Romeus is banished he falls on the ground and rageth, at which the Friar saith: "Art thou quoth he a man? Thy shape saith so thou art: Thy crying and thy weping eyes, denote a womans hart, For manly reason is quite from thy mynd outchased" [Brooke, lines 1353–55].[31] I know not whether to laugh or weep, for it is that shadow difference twixt comedy & tragedy. Mayhap all tragedies should have comedy within them?

29 DECEMBER

At Anne's entreaty I dwelled at home this Christmas, yet all the while thinking how I must needs be in London. Now I am returned here [London], and gone is her chiding, but so too the smiling faces of my dear children. Journeying in sleet and snow hath left me numb with agues, and I need dear repose for limbs with travel tired. I had little time enow to talk with the men about tomorrow, yet they know the play well enough and make it briefer.[32]

30 DECEMBER

Richard [III] was enacted well enough, though he [unknown actor] was no Dick [Burbage]—he lacked Dick's voice & those his eyes. I must give thanks my work is played; a play is nothing unless it be before an audience. Then it lives, breathes, & has its being.

❧ *The year in which* The Rape of Lucrece *is published begins quietly, although Shakespeare is concerned by the false rumors of Queen Elizabeth's death. Shakespeare witnesses the trial (and later the execution) of the Jewish Dr. Lopez on trumped up charges, an event that crystalizes Shakespeare's ideas for* The Merchant of Venice. *More pleasant is the performance of parts of* A Midsummer Night's Dream *for the marriage of the Countess of Southampton at Titchfield. To his concern, the Countess asks Shakespeare to urge her son to marry, and later in the year the Chamberlain's Men (the company of actors Shakespeare has joined) stages* Romeo and Juliet *before Queen Elizabeth in an attempt to overcome the queen's opposition to Southampton's proposed marriage. Her Majesty is not amused, and tells Shakespeare so. The year is rounded out by a riotous performance of* The Comedy of Errors *at the Inns of Court.* ❧

15 JANUARY

So little of note, 'tis scarce worth the parchment. My lodgings cold, my food poor, only ale worth the drinking. I scribble poesy [sonnets?] and ponder the love tragedy [*Romeo and Juliet*].

24 JANUARY

Before so little, now much. *Titus* was given this afternoon. Lord, how they [audience] rise to it, the blood and what not. For me 'tis but bombast, and money. I am advanced much since I wrote such stuff, those were my salad days.[1] They say the Queen's physician is taken for trying to poison Her Majesty (a wild tale, methinks).[2] As he is a Jew it will go hard for him, for these Christians (thus they call themselves) lust after the sight & smell of blood.

3 FEBRUARY

Though a prohibition 'gainst playing hath been issued, Kit's *Jew* is to be performed tomorrow.[3] It will remind me of much that passed between us, and how, tho' wild & riotous he was, I am bereft his company and companionship. What might he have done had he lived the Lord alone knows, & I doubt they keep company together.

5 FEBRUARY

Though Kit's *Jew* should have been stayed, it was performed yesterday. The multitude hated and hooted the Jew [Barabas] mightily. What I thought strange is now clear—they hate the Jew on the stage and thus the Jew in the Tower.[4] I ponder whether Essex was the instrument in having Kit's play performed, and thereby incite the popular voice against Dr. Lopez. How easy 'tis for players like ourselves to be used and abused. Can our practice ride so easy on the green minds, the foolish honesty, of the multitude? If that be true, then am I fearful of what may ensue when some particular play of mine might be performed & inflame the crowd. What might the authorities do then?

6 FEBRUARY

I have never been to Stationers' Hall, which lies close by [St.] Paul's in Paternoster Row. Thus today, because I was something curious, I went with John Danter to register *Titus*, but there was little enough to learn of the business. I pray it be profitable.[5] There are matters of small import in it I must needs amend.

9 FEBRUARY

Yester afternoon, not long after I had dined on naught but bran & ale, a wild rumour roared through the city that Elizabeth our queen was dead. Her body had been carried, so it was said, in the dead still of night and lies at Greenwich. Sundry folk prate on this e'en now, though I heard a proclamation that the news was false. Some folk scurry about & demand that the Queen show herself unto her people. 'Tis all a sign of our uncertain times—the Queen hath not given us an heir of her loins, & there is general fear of who will be king if she dies, & die she must one day. I pray the next king be not a Catholic for that would turn all the world on its head as in Bloody Mary's time, with the burning of heretics, the changing of beliefs, & what not.[6] Religious folk will forever poke their noses into the lives & business of other folk, & all to no true purpose. I trust we have not seen the best of our time.

28 FEBRUARY

As a fly on the wall I crept into the Guildhall where today the authorities arraigned Doctor Lopez.[7] 'Twas clear the Jew was lost at the outset and his blood sought. He rested composed, as well as any man might, thinking death no hazard, knowing the executioner is nigh at hand. I observed him and all present closely, for I fancy such proceedings might furnish a drama withal. What I remember most is this: when one party is in ascendancy it bays for the blood of all others. At one time Protestants feared, now Catholics quake, and Jews always. Damned errors in religion are blessed and approved with a text. Religion and politics, fie!

20 MARCH

[John] Danter to me today. Early he had gone to the Stationers' [Company] to consult the register, and did note that Tom Millington hath registered a play called [*The First Part of*] *the Contention betwixt the Two Houses of York and Lancaster*.[8] Was this my work, he asked, to which

I replied I did not know. Later I found out Tom, who said some actors had given him the play, but he had it not about him for they had yet to perfect it. If the play be mine, 'tis stolen, and I know not what to do for the loss. I am told the law affords me no protection, even after all my labours. And yet it goes hard with a thief or e'en a poor beggar.

30 MARCH

The great storms of this month have continued, and many trees have been uprooted, buildings blown down. Where is April with its sweet showers that portend the warm months of summer? As swiftly as I write that, my mind springs to the Avon & walking along its banks with dear Hamnet. To hear the hedge-sparrow, the cuckoos, & all their young. Well, that shall be soon, I trow.

5 APRIL

Tomorrow at the Rose I am to play Perillus, for they lack a man and know I can con the lines, which are but few, as fast as any man can.[9]

6 APRIL

My Perillus was all the little it required. The play ends happily, Leir restored, and so forth, but to my mind the play should be tragic. After his frank heart gives all, Leir should suffer monster ingratitude, lose his wits, be restored for the moment, but at the last lose all, e'en his life. 'Tis most affecting, that e'en tho' Leir be a king, the play is in its heart about father and children, friends, enemies, the stuff of life day in and out, tho' I protest I have no heartless, serpent-tooth'd children. Perchance I might turn to this tale when my work elsewhere is done.

11 APRIL

No sweet showers of April, naught but down-pouring rain all day and night, blown by a sharp north wind. Surely summer may not be far behind. It cannot come too soon.

20 APRIL

Today with Gus [Phillips], and much news. They [Strange's Men] are greatly distressed, for their patron is dead.[10] Gus and his fellows believe he hath been poisoned, for he was strangely sick for eleven days with much vomiting. Gus said that they scarce know what to do, but think to go to Winchester to play. Thereat I told him I thought I could bring them some joy midst all these travails. Some days past Harry [Southampton] had written me of the marriage of his mother to Sir Thomas Heneage, and begged me for some piece for the celebrations to come. At first I had thought of some epithalamion which I might deliver, for, after [*The Rape of*] *Lucrece*, poesy feeds mine ambition. Howsoever, I have the dream play [*A Midsummer Night's Dream*] much in hand, and I could amend it, if the company like of my notion. Gus was o'erwhelmed with joy, and went to gather up our friends. Later with much ale at the Bunch of Grapes, we all devised what might be performed and how, and I can amend whate'er might be necessary. So tomorrow I write to Harry with this proposal which I trust shall come to pass and increase all our joy.

3 MAY

Titchfield and Harry again, tho' I scarce saw him, for we were busy each in our own way. The wedding celebrations yester afternoon passed in high style with great festivity.[11] We gave parts of the dream play [*A Midsummer Night's Dream*] to the great delight of the assembled throng. I had amended much of the lovers' scenes where they be at cross-purposes each with the other, and also those with the small fairies, for which we had no boys to play.[12] Bottom and his rude companions caused much mirth, but most in *Pyramus* [5.1]. Our courtly audience delighted to see the stage court, and so I believe my intent here succeeded—it was them and yet not them, real and yet fantasy. They laughed so heartily at Pyramus they were brought to tears, at which I thought how quick those tears could spring from grief, and grief indeed is what the comic Pyramus has! 'Tis but circumstance that yields joy or grief. I muse much on the Romeo play that is like unto this other play, but wherein lies no joy. Tomorrow I leave this pastoral idyll and all else for the noise and confusion of the town. But I am to join the company as an actor, and furnish such plays as I am able and as are wanted. I am joyed to be with Ned Alleyn, and he is most warm and affectionate, and hath many plans.[13]

4 MAY

As I was about to betake my leave of Titchfield, to my wonderment the Countess accosted me. In brief, she said she would have Harry [Southampton] marry, and entreated me to urge him to that course. I told her I doubted I might thus persuade him. She said, "Your play [*A Midsummer Night's Dream*] shows him the way; I pray you urge him." Then, in departing she said, "Some rise by sin, and some by virtue fall. Forget not that, William Shakespeare." I took my leave in much perplexity, and I wonder what she knows of our friendship.

7 MAY

Today with Dick [Field] to show him [*The Rape of*] *Lucrece*, and ask him to print it. Dick said he would gladly print it, but, as he had said last year over *Venus* [*and Adonis*], my poem is not in his line of work these days. So together we went to see [John] Harrison and ask him to publish it. Harrison said, "Most assuredly, Master Shakespeare, I would be right gladdened and honoured to publish this poem, for you know t'other hath pleased greatly and sold well. There are but two things I would ask, if Master Field here is agreeable. First, that you assign *Venus* to me, & second that Master Field be the printer once more, for his work is truly amongst the best in all of London." We had some little discussion of this matter, but there was no dissension or rancour, & all was settled on the best of terms. Dick thinks 'twill be a month or so before the poem will be printed & ready.[14]

5 JUNE

I am the lowest, most dejected of creatures, for we perform with all our hearts for little reward. The crowds absent themselves, when, in my vanity, I thought they would clamour for our plays. The truth is, I fear, the plays have been too much acted, & the multitude wants novelties. *Titus* was but half-hearted.[15]

7 JUNE

Though I care not for them [executions], I went to Tyburn where the Jewish doctor [Lopez] had his appointed day, as did two of his fellows. He comported himself with exceeding dignity, & I marvelled at his rare composure. On the gallows, in fewness and truth he declared he loved the Queen, & then he said he loved her as well as Christ Jesu, whereat those that stood by laughed right heartily because he was a Jew. I fain believe he purposed well, and some folk said he was a converted Christian. Then, before the horrors of execution ensued, I turned away and came home. I have dwelled much upon the matter & the fate of the Jew whose sole fault, I believe, is his religion. It is hard to be a stranger in a foreign land, an alien to the hearts of all around. Lopez was *in* England, but not *of* England. There lies the rub, but all men must endure their going hence, e'en as their coming hither.

9 JUNE

This afternoon *Hamlet* was played, & was as poorly received by what few folk there were, as our other plays have been. Yet there is stuff in the piece that I might mend a little and make finer.

11 JUNE

My shrew play this afternoon, and as with all else, it was scarce worth our time nor our labours. Perchance the multitude is fickle; but I think the fault lies more with us, for we set not before the public such works as it desires to see, for all that my words express my purpose.

15 JUNE

Today I hastened to [John] Harrison's shop at Paul's for copies of my pamphlet of [*The Rape of*] *Lucrece*, which Dick Field hath printed most fair and handsome. Harry's [Southampton's] copy I have dispatched with tremulous, true hope that's swift and flies with swallow's wings. I pray my dedication to such a gentleman of blood and breeding seem not too familiar, tho' I was rapt in writing it.[16] In truth, my affection is more than word can wield the matter. Harrison told me he had sold a dozen or more copies that very morning, which bodes fair for my poem. Now I begin to think I would write poems only, & cast aside plays, which have done me little good of late.

22 JUNE

I had foreseen this day for some while. Our company hath divided in twain, for it could not encompass all the ambitions bound up therein. So we go to Shoreditch, and the poor remainder to the Bankside. I shall sorely miss Ned Alleyn, yet I fear I could not write well for Henslowe with whom Ned's fortunes now all lie.[17]

[JULY]

More labour on *Romeo*, which I needs must set down ere long. Dick Burbage hath provided good counsel, and we have talked much on how I will amend Brooke's poem, so my way lies clearer. Romeo is fortune's fool, a doting mallard, and Mercutio his bawdy friend. Time is ever present;

it rides at the back of the lovers, a winged chariot. The Prince [Escalus] brings concord to the feud, ending all social discord and dismay through his authority. Juliet is sweet, yet as wise as she is beautiful, circumspect, and wily, which young Gough can accomplish right readily.[18]

15 AUGUST

We laid Tom Kyd to rest today, another cold and wet afternoon like many another this summer, and suited to the poor dear man. I had not seen him much in those days since he was imprisoned & tortured. I pray those torturers suffer, & their pernicious souls rot half a grain a day in hell for the pain and misery Tom endured. What he confessed was but to save himself, & tho' he betrayed Marlowe, Marlowe betrayed him. I believe truly he could have writ much that might have been applauded. Yet no more—the silence eternal hath descended, and brave day hath sunk in hideous night. Requiescat.

1 SEPTEMBER

I have endured an arduous, storm-beaten journey here to Marlborough, and all for very little. I' faith I can scarce recall why we came, save for to see [*King*] *John* enacted. Strangely, I could recall but little of the play, for my mind is fixed on Richard [II] which is a better work.[19] If the weather prove kinder I may rest here a day or two, for the country hereabouts is fair & pleasant, and I long to walk along the hillsides.

12 SEPTEMBER

Once more returned to London, & today I saw Ned Alleyn as magnificent, as fine as ever: he makes Tamburlaine his own.[20] On the stage he commands as few men can, save Dick [Burbage]; his mien and voice mesmerise the multitudes. 'Tis pity he's not one of our number, tho' I wish him & his company joy & all prosperity (that our own may follow).

29 SEPTEMBER

Magdalen Phillips, Gus's daughter, was baptized at noon today in St. Saviour's, Southwark. Gus was all tears & smiles, the babe as quiet as a lamb, unlike most of her testy tribe. We ate an excellent repast afterwards, tho' I drank too much canary wine.

30 SEPTEMBER

Today Ned Alleyn played Faust, whom he was so like 'twas beyond belief. Devils and terrors *live* through him.[21] I care not for the scenes of mere trickery, for Faust would cast aside such frippery, leastways Faust in my hands would, and he would challenge the entire universe. Yet the play makes its mark as talent wasted, & poor dear Kit [Marlowe] hath lain buried more than a year. He wasted time and now doth death waste him. But there's many another dramatist who is not worth the dust the wind blows in his face.

1 OCTOBER

Father hath sent news of a terrible fire and destruction at home, though, thanked be God, all are safe.[22] I should see Anne and my children more, for we know not the hour of our death, and all be taken away. Yet father says I am not wanted now the danger is passed, & truly I am loath to depart from London.

6 OCTOBER

I am forlorn, oppressed with melancholy. Today Harry [Southampton] becomes a man, and I wish I might clip him in my arms, & have him play wantonly with me, me with him. When I see him, noble thing, my rapt heart dances more than ever it did when I wooed Anne. But there is no place for me where he lies today, & I stand upon the farthest earth removed from him. I wish him joy & happiness e'en tho' we are worlds away, some other where.[23]

10 OCTOBER

Harry [Southampton] here today—he stormed and raged for some long while, for he perceives he is reviled in a book that hath been published lately by Henry Willobie.[24] I told him I knew naught of it. When he was more peaceable, we sat and read o'er parts wherein he sees offence. I' fecks, I believe he hath some cause, for the suitor in despair in the tale is named "H.W.," Harry's very letters. 'Twould seem I am also addressed therein & am "W.S." whom the author doth call an old player [canto 44]. This "W.S." advises "H.W." on his rejection by Avisa, telling him "She is no Saynt, She is no Nonne, I think in tyme she may be wonne" [canto 47]. These words sound like mine own, and surely 'tis someone that knows Harry and my plays.[25] He thinks 'tis one Matthew Roydon who loves Ralegh and hates my Lord Essex and Harry. Said Harry, "If it be Roydon, then he is naught but a knave, beggar, coward, pander, & the son of a mongrel bitch." I told Harry that it is curious strange that the wife of my good friend Tom Russell is cousin to Henry Willobie, but Willobie abides in Wiltshire, and sure cannot know us. How hath Willobie seen these plays? But he might have read my [*The Rape of*] *Lucrece*.[26] Thus, it seems to me "H.W." is this Henry Willobie and "W.S." might be me. Thus, Willobie alludeth to me because he thinks me popular in some fashion or other. Harry was then something calmer, yet he believes those in town still think "H.W." be him and smirk at him. He said, "All the world knows of my troubles with Lord Burghley and his lordship's thwarted desires."[27] I soothed him awhile before he left, and dissuaded him from any ill intent to Willobie. It is strange how this fiction hath become reality. Harry an "H.W." hath visited his "W.S." to aid him as a suitor and thus, all unknowing, this *Avisa* is true! How like to Romeo and Juliet are Harry and his Elizabeth.[28] They love each other, yet family & friends are all against them.

5 NOVEMBER

This morning I saw [Francis] Langley in Gracious Street where we idled the time in chat on this & that. The Lord Mayor is, says Langley, against his new theatre and wants all our playing suppressed.[29] He said he knows not what the authorities intend, but they are a meddlesome lot who care not for us & our plays. It is ever thus.

17 NOVEMBER

Our Queen hath been on her throne for thirty years this day, for which there is much rejoicing. Many folk have scarce known another monarch, tho' it is a great sadness she cannot endure for many more years. What troublesome unseasonable times will ensue when she does die? I dare not think thereon.

28 NOVEMBER

Her grace, Harry's mother [Countess of Southampton] hath been to me with a stratagem to aid Harry and to divert Her Majesty's anger, since Harry would not marry the Lady [Elizabeth] Vere. Her grace, by means of Harry, hath heard of my play on Romeo and Juliet and of their death because their families opposed their love. She thinks therein lies some moral instruction for Her Majesty, and 'twould soften Her Majesty's objection to Harry's love for Mistress [Elizabeth] Vernon. Thus might the pair marry. I told her the play wants some touches and amendment, but that it might be done soon enough at her convenience, & if the company would agree. She asked if £10 and some materials for our clothing would persuade them. I am to meet with all the fellows tomorrow.

29 NOVEMBER

We are agreed to perform *Romeo* at the Savoy Palace[30] this 7th of December. In some manner we will hint at Harry's likeness in Romeo and Mistress Vernon's in Juliet. I am to play Escalus, Dick [Burbage]

Romeo, and young [Robert] Gough Juliet. Will Kempe—Clown and Peter, and I trust he will say little more than is written down. John Heminges—Lord Capulet, George Bryan the Friar Lawrence, Tom Pope to be Mercutio. Will Sly[31] will be Tybalt, with Gus Phillips Benvolio. What remains, the hired men will enact, as needs be. I worry somewhat, for our stage is to be naught but two or three platforms with hangings or curtains—no balcony or bedroom aloft, which quite spoils the effect of some scenes. Yet I hope we may please & fair success ensue.

8 DECEMBER

What a night we had of it yester eve. Tho' we were prepared well, yet were all our company tremulous, for Her Majesty did but glower all through the play [*Romeo and Juliet*]. Many a time and oft she paid us no heed, but called instead for wine, and sucked on her blackened teeth. She wrinkled her face and scowled oft. Afterward, she called for me to come forth. Said she, "We know what you do Master Shakespeare, in this play of yours that you call *Romeo and Juliet*. We know what my Lady Countess of Southampton intends by this. A play may not persuade such as ourself where high policy is concerned, though dolts would doubtless think otherwise. You do not think a high and mighty prince a dolt, Master Shakespeare?" I bowed low and muttered about not wishing to cause any offence, and we poor players did but do what was commanded of us by others. "That's as may be," she said, "yet we think you wot well what was *meant*. And we may tell you roundly, Master Shakespeare, that when you can catch a weasel asleep, then may you piss in its ear." So saying, she stormed from the hall. My lady countess knew not what to say, but fretted and fussed, and rid herself of me and the company as swiftly as we could pack up our belongings. We are £10 the richer, though regal wrath hath no price.

21 DECEMBER

Kit's old plays are admired e'en now by the multitude.[32] *Tamburlaine* grates: it is but rant and more rant; *Faust* can stir my spirit upon occasion, as when the necromancer's soul is called for, and by that moment I was moved withal, but naught else.

INNOCENTS DAY [28 DECEMBER]

If Her Majesty entertained any anger towards our company because of our *Romeo* at the Savoy, we did not see it these last two nights. I' faith we were treated most handsomely with food and drink after we had given our plays.[33] Yet all the talk at the palace was of the execution in France.[34] I do believe the French excel us in the savagery which the condemned must endure in their extreme torment. But what wretch can be so foolish as to kill a king?

30 DECEMBER

What shall I write of two evenings past [28 December]? Our company was commanded to perform at Gray's Inn [in the Inns of Court], for the which I had prepared o'er and amended the *Comedy of Errors*—such a piece seemed to be required. It was well past nine o' the clock, or nearer ten, before there was room upon their stage for us to begin. Beforehand there was such a jostling of gentlemen and a tumult for what they called the prince of state and his retinue. This prince is called the Prince of Purpoole, whom they place on a throne and, with his retinue, he is monarch of such dancing and revelling as there may be these twelve days of Christmastide. Such was the boisterous multitude that watched our play, wherein they did partake more freely than I fain desired. Yet were we well paid for our labours. Some jested that our comedy well suited a night of errors such as it had been. I have been sick with an ague yesterday & today, & must keep to my bed.

※ *Although a court performance of* A Midsummer Night's Dream *pleases Queen Elizabeth, Shakespeare achieves little during the first half of the year. Ralegh sets sail in search of gold overseas, and priests are executed at home. The middle months are marked by a Spanish incursion in Cornwall and by unrest from apprentices in London. The latter event threatens to close the theatres and Shakespeare's livelihood. He already feels anxious that he is insufficiently productive.* ※

15 JANUARY

A day for birth and marriage. We baptized John Heminges' girl (a fair child) at noon. That was no sooner done than I trotted two miles or more to Shoreditch to hear Francis Langley plight his earnest troth to his worthy bride. Afterward a goodly feast & wine aplenty.[1] While we drank, I was surprised withal when Langley did accost me & said, "There's beggary in the love that can be reckoned." "Forsooth, that may not be gainsaid," was all my reply. There are worse ways to pass a deep midwinter day.

20 JANUARY

We are commanded to perform my dream play [*A Midsummer Night's Dream*] at Court afore Her Majesty six days hence. John Heminges said the command is issued directly from the queen herself and that there is to be a court wedding before we play. John said I am commanded especially to enact Theseus.² I asked John the reason, & he said he knew not, tho' I have ever played Theseus in performances past.

27 JANUARY

We gave the dream play [*A Midsummer Night's Dream*] yester eve to a pleasant, courtly audience. Afterwards, Her Majesty called me forward, and spoke to me in a most mild and obliging manner: "Prince Escalus, or is it Master Shakespeare? You see now when it is fit and proper to present one of your plays for a wedding before *your* prince. Know ye this now?" I bowed low and said but "majesty." Whether or not she smiled, I know not, for when I glanced up she had departed. I saw only the back of her auburn wig as my knees knocked together. Afterwards, the other fellows desired to know what H.M. had said, & which I told them. Kempe said, "I believe the queen means to teach you a lesson, Will, & mayhap one day she might give you a box about the ears right soundly." Everyone laughed, & then we set to the repast laid out before us. Indeed, the mighty are not to be offended, & I must dare do only what becomes a humble subject.

10 FEBRUARY

Today when I sallied forth for bread, cheese, & wine, all the word was that Sir Walter Ralegh and his ship have set forth from Plymouth in search of gold. And here we struggle for our own meagre coin. Yet in such adventures as Ralegh's may lie a tale to be told—ships at sea seeking gold and fortunes, and all their success rests on their safe return. That, with a tale or two of love, might well suffice.³

15 FEBRUARY

'Twill be no penance to eat no flesh this Lent, for where is the money?⁴ And I know not what else I may do to gain more. Well, as 'tis said, the Lord will provide, and I pray devoutly He may.

22 FEBRUARY

Today the authorities hanged another Jesuit priest [Robert Southwell] at Tyburn. I know not why I went to watch, for truly I abhor executions; but I felt drawn strangely to Tyburn Hill. One man, that stood by me at the hanging, said the priest had been in prison and tortured for three or more years. Before he was hanged, the priest prayed for Her Majesty, and then gave himself up unto our Lord. Today the gathered multitude was quiet, I might say prayerful, not as when they hanged the Jew Lopez. Verily, there is no sure foundation set on blood, no certain life achieved by others' death.

14 APRIL

Tom Nashe hath lent me [Sir Philip] Sidney's *Defence of Poesie*, wherein he hath marked passages, he says, for my instruction. I note these hereafter as worthy of consideration, though I would not heed them if thereby the drama should fail:

For where the stage should alway represent but one place, the uttermost time is presupposed in it, should be both by Aristotle's precept, and common reason, but one day; there is both many days and places, inartificially imagined. But if it be so in *Gorboduc*,[5] how much more in all the rest, have Asia of the one side, and Africa of the other, and so many other under kingdoms, that the player when he comes in, must ever begin with telling where he is, or else the tale will not be conceived. Now shall you have three ladies walk together to gather flowers, and then we must believe the stage to be a garden.

While in the meantime two armies file in, represented with four swords & bucklers.

But they will say, how then shall we set forth a story, which contains both many places, and many times?

Again, many things may be told which cannot be showed: if they know the difference betwixt reporting and representing.

How all their plays be neither right tragedies, nor right comedies, mingling kings and clowns, not because the matter so carrieth it, but thrust in the clown by the head and shoulders to play a part in majestical matters, with neither decency nor discretion.

Delight hath a joy in it either permanent or present. Laughter hath only a scornful tickling.

[There are no further entries until 5 July.]

5 JULY

I returned to the city this morning amidst much news of prentices causing turmoil and disorder. Men must not walk too late, for we are commanded to be home each day by sunset.[6] What will become of all these wild eruptions, I know not, but I am afeard worse may ensue—from either the prentices or the authorities, or peradventure both.

24 JULY

This is the sorriest world in which I live in. Hanged today [on Tower Hill] were five prentices that had been unruly. Is there no better way? Had they no cause? Disorder must cease, but the law must surely be tempered with mercy, which blesses him that receives it & him that giveth it. But the law, vulture-like, gripes at our guts.

5 AUGUST

This evening at the Bunch of Grapes, I fell into chat with a Cornish sailor who told me of some Spaniards burning down Penzance several days past, & other such matters. I know not if this be true, for we had drunk much ale.[7] He spoke in marked accents which I observed close, for I have heard it little ere now. News from home that this long wet summer, like the one past, hath destroyed the crops nearly. I fear the price of corn, and there will be famine surely. I pray father will lay in as much corn as he can, if only for the sake of my dear children. And, doubtless, never-resting time will lead this summer on to hideous winter, and confound us.

15 SEPTEMBER

With John [Heminges], Gus [Phillips] and Dick [Burbage] this even. John says the mayor would have our theatres shut down because of the prentices & their riots.[8] This disquiets me, as I told them, for how am I to write and then be paid for my labour if there be no theatres. They said to fear not, & the time will pass. Said John, "This comes to pass from time to time, & 'tis true the Puritans and the mayor desire to be rid of us entirely. But the queen, the court, & assuredly the common folk, all favour us & delight in our wares. So we must bide our time & say little. All will be well, you mark my words. So, dear Will, live a little, comfort a little, and cheer thyself a little." In sooth, I did find comfort in John's words.

27 SEPTEMBER

Hamnet [Sadler] writes that his house and that of Adrian Quiney hath been destroyed utterly by a huge fire. Wood Street blazed from end to end by his account.[9] All this is hard to believe without the true avouch of mine own eyes. Yet I have heard it said that it hath rained corn in Wakefield this summer.[10] I pray everyone may find swift relief.

1 NOVEMBER

At the Mermaid this afternoon, where I saw Sir Walter Ralegh.[11] To me came Anthony Munday,[12] who had with him the play on Edward III that we had sought to contrive together some long time past. He asked me if I would look o'er my scenes and amend them (if I chose), for he would seek to have the weak thing published, if I and the others [collaborators?] have not objections. 'Twas quickly done, for I care little for the piece, and it hath scarce been acted for all I know. Yet there is a line or two I noted that have some savour and I could employ again.[13] Munday sat awhile, and we drank and ate. When he was to leave, I recalled on the sudden that I had still his play, the which he had forgot also.[14] He thanked me kindly and told me that, if I would but return it on the morrow, he would show me his *Zelauto*, wherein I would find some hints for my Jew play that we had talked on earlier.[15] Munday is an amiable, pleasing fellow.

28 NOVEMBER

Today *Harry the V* was played at the Rose.[16] The groundlings took delight in the piece, tho' for my part, I do believe I can write a more perfect chronicle of King Harry's glories & victories, such as will make our theatre shake with plaudits. I am sorry now, for my sloth hath allowed another to write such a paltry play ere mine own be writ. 'Tis true, celerity is ne'er more admired than by the negligent. Yet if there be nothing new but that which hath been told before, how is my brain beguiled, labouring for invention. But labour I must.

10 DECEMBER

Yester night Dick Burbage, John Heminges, Gus Phillips, & myself went to Sir Edward Hoby's house in Cannon Row to read much of *Richard II*.[17] Sir Robert Cecil was present also. We thought it prudent to omit the scene of Richard's deposition, lest we might offend.

15 DECEMBER

We buried Helen, James's daughter today.[18] All bleak, solemn, & sad, like this foul season.

1596

Men are impressed left and right to be sent with the Earl of Essex to fight on the continent where Essex is triumphant over the Spanish at Cadiz. A long discussion with Tom Nashe about The Merchant of Venice *convinces Shakespeare of his success with the play. The Burbages fail to fulfill their hopes in taking over the Blackfriars Theatre—the failure kills James, the father. Meanwhile, Shakespeare ventures into the provinces, visiting Plymouth and Faversham, the latter having given its name to the play* Arden of Feversham. *But the year is most notable for the blackest event in Shakespeare's life, the death of his beloved son, Hamnet, an event that haunts him forever. It takes him months before he can concentrate on writing plays about Henry IV and Henry V. The year ends with a successful court performance of* Henry IV Part 1; *a character named Oldcastle (later renamed Falstaff), as played by Kempe, becomes a favorite of Queen Elizabeth.*

3 JANUARY

Such a time as we have had, I can scarce draw breath. First we were at Court, then by cart we journeyed into Rutland, where Sir John Harington paid us handsomely for *Titus*, though I could have wished a better play was chosen. Dick Burbage said he saw Anthony Bacon's page-boy there, for such is he called, though he is naught but a bum-boy. Though why he should be there and not in London with his lord and master, I know not either. We play again at Court three days hence. Our good fortune hath been the mild weather; I might believe it Spring if it were not January.[1]

4 FEBRUARY

Dick's father [James Burbage] hath bought the Blackfriars for some £600, so says Dick. This building he desires to convert into a theatre indoors with seats for all, which will cost him a goodly penny, I think.² For me, 'twill be a mighty opportunity, if I can but write plays swiftly enow. For the moment, I will bide my time and see how this adventure works.

19 FEBRUARY

The dream play [*A Midsummer Night's Dream*] hath fast become naught but a wedding play—the which I detest heartily; much of my intent and purpose therein is lost when we play it thus. Nonetheless, there is money in't, & so I must be thankful.³ With good hap, it may be an earnest of greater honour. Better this than no play, no performances.

21 MARCH

With Tom Nashe this even to the Dagger in Holborn, a disreputable place that I like not, yet which Tom enjoys as a libertine in a field of feasts.⁴ He had returned from Deptford, whence he had been on as strange an errand as ever I heard, to wit—to see Mistress Bull well and truly buried, as Tom did say. He rejoiced in her death and burial, and that she lies close by where Kit Marlowe is consumed with worms.⁵ Well, I care not for that, but talk of Kit recalled his Jew play [*The Jew of Malta*] to mind, & wherein I may catch a hint or two for mine own purposes.⁶ Nashe & I ate pies, and drank long into the night.

GOOD FRIDAY [9 APRIL]

I have heard it rumoured some 6,000 men are wanted to go with the Lord Essex to Calais. I stay close, at home, & trust my present fears prove less than my horrible imaginings.⁷

1596   113

12 APRIL

Yester morn [Easter day], while we were at communion, all the churches in the city were closed up so that the Lord Mayor and his men might impress a thousand men to be sent to Calais. Where I was, one man in five was taken and marched away, & then at noon the doors were opened up, & those of us not impressed were set free. I was sore afeard, but was let alone.[8]

[MAY]

I have heard a few tales that Ralegh hath been impressing men round about London to serve with him on an expedition to Cadiz. As soon as the men are impressed, they run away—no fools they. Therein lies a notion I might employ perchance in some comedy.[9]

A long debatement with Tom Nashe on my Jew play [*The Merchant of Venice*], which I had desired him to read before I amend it. I attended to his deep insight, for he is full of worldly drifts and ever raises just objection—more than I can perceive. Thus his voice sets the seal on what I needs must do. Tom likes the play *in toto*, and saw my two plots—the casket-choosing and the pound of flesh—will be well known by many folk. Yet have I given them a new lustre, he says. In answer to my question, he said he knew not whether it should be called the Jew of Venice or the Merchant thereof. 'Tis a vexed question, for the Jew [Shylock] interests me more than the merchant [Antonio]; certes, in the writing, I have grown to admire the character more than I had thought. The Jew appeareth in but five scenes, yet his presence o'erpowers all, seizes the imagination. But, I told Tom, I think on what an audience might, must feel when it sees this play. Tom said he knew that they would hiss and jeer at the Jew, much as they had when the wretched Lopez was executed some while past. "Will, for them, he is a man who is the abstract of all faults." This is all too true, I fear. I asked him if he could perceive I had taken my aim at the Christians in the play, and how the audience might admit of that. Here Tom proved most sharp in wit. The Christians are, said he, on the surface (which phrase he repeated) an amiable band, and it is they who triumph in love and fortune when the play concludes. "For there you have shrouded them in a remote, magical, mystical kingdom [Belmont], far away from the cares of the world, where there is love, moonlight and magic. There, we forget Venice and the Jew." I said, "Yes indeed this is so, for I purpose to write a comedy, and must arrange matters after this fashion. The finality is the multitude must forget the Jew e'en tho' his daughter is there in that scene." Then Tom said, "But look at what they are in reality—full of sentiment, foolishness, greed, hypocrisy, bigotry, legalisms, revenge, hatred, and I know not what. Why, Antonio risks all his goods and fortune at sea, mere foolishness and not prudence; yet he would risk more for his spendthrift friend [Bassanio], a profligate and fortune hunter. For him Antonio signs a bond that no wise man would sign, and that with his avowed enemy [Shylock]. Those two, Antonio & Bassanio, are the dearest partners in foolishness. I marvel at what may be the cement of their love!" Here Tom was nigh unto apoplexy. And, he added, Antonio expects not to fulfill this bond; but a wise man of commerce would consider most carefully that such a possibility might arise.

Then I enquired of him his opinion of my lady of Belmont, the wondrous Portia. "Indeed," said Tom, "she is wondrous, and like unto a fairy princess in her magical, remote domain, and yet she disdains and despises all her suitors in such a fashion as we can see she be prejudice itself—she likes not their countries, their habits, their costumes, their race. She is brimful of Christian charity." This last Tom said with leaden irony. "And this is the lady you have preach Christian mercy to the Jew in your trial scene."[10] Tom saw I was smiling, and realised I agreed with him. I asked him if my expedient of placing Portia in disguise imported aught to him. "Well, 'tis a common enough device. You have a boy playing a clever woman, yet he appears best as a young man. This is simple enough. But here in your scene, the boy playing a woman is disguised as a learned doctor of law. Thus *she*, your Portia, is false, and when she expounds upon the law she must be false too." I urged Tom on. "Let me see. She extols mercy, the effect of which is to undo the letter of the law. Yet, when Shylock demands the letter of the law, she applies it not, though she *seems* to so do. She says he may take the pound of flesh but no blood, but all the world knows that flesh compriseth blood too—thus Shylock is tricked by deceit. And then they would deprive him of all." I told him he had perceived my intent, and the Christians had not given Shylock the mercy that Portia would have him practice. Even when Antonio lessens the penalty, he does but follow custom, and so his "mercy" is but common practice.[11]

The evening of our conversation grew long, but I wanted Tom to tell me some little more of his opinion of Shylock. Tom said the best scene was when Shylock talked to Solanio and Salerio about being a Jew, and that he was most affected by this speech: "If you prick us, do we not bleed? If you tickle us, do we not laugh? If you poison us, do we not die? And if you wrong us, shall we not revenge?" [*Merchant of Venice*, 3.1.56–58]. What was remarkable was that Tom had this speech by heart, and was so greatly moved as he spoke that I could imagine he became Shylock. "His wife arouses my pity too," he said.[12] Then Tom, as he made to take his leave, said, "Shylock thought he was just like any other man, but he is a Jew, they Christians. He believes the Old Testament, they the New. He believes the law is the same for all, yet it is not. He is *in* Venice yet not *of* Venice, he is an outsider whom they would not have but for his money, which they take anyway. Thus you shall call your play *The Merchant of Venice,* for indeed Antonio is *of* Venice."

So our chat ended, and I was pleased Tom had divined all my purpose. Now I needs must write o'er the casket scenes whereby my idea of the exterior belying the interior is made palpable.

1 JUNE

Plymouth. 'Tis the first time I have ventured thus far into this part of the country, & a long, hard journey I have had of it. Here I witnessed the fleet of such mass and expense set sail in the face of fortune, danger, and death. And what they purpose against the Spaniard, I know not for certain, save they strive to be great and to gain great wealth. Yet surpassing all, I came here to say farewell to Harry [Southampton] who sails with the Lord Essex. John goes with them.[13] This was my fond, foolish dream, & why I entertained it, I know not. I have not seen Harry, nor could I, because he & all else have been busy with preparation. I sent him word from the inn—Lord of my love to whom in vassalage my duty is strong knit—but received only "not now Will" in return. In sooth, I am foolish like a young green girl, though my heart sinks down, oppressed with melancholy until I am assured of his return. I needs must return to London haste-post-haste.

8 JULY

Sir Robert Cecil hath been appointed Her Majesty's first secretary [on 5 July] in the absence of the Lord Essex. Were Harry [Southampton] here, he would tell me this should be the root and cause of much discontentment and dissension. Welladay, he is not, & doubtless is brimful with adventures, & I pray he return safe.

11 JULY

With Gus Phillips at St. Saviour's [Southwark] to witness the baptism of his girl child (bonny enow) they have named Rebecca. We made a goodly feast afterwards. Gus was as proud and jocund as could be, though he had said a boy would be best. The kindly man deserves all the joy & happiness this world may bring him.

19 JULY

Early this morning I was awakened by great clamours beneath my window. I asked a man who was passing by what all this noise should portend. He said there is news that Essex hath made a great victory at Cadiz, and that a great Spanish treasure ship is taken. It is called the St. Andrew. As I had at that very moment my Jew play before me ready for amendment, I added the ship's name therein—'twill garner popular applause when the play is acted [*The Merchant of Venice*, 1.1.27]. Alas,

Romeo [and Juliet] proved not so with the crowd this afternoon, for the Curtain [Theatre] was so meanly attended I could count each and every man there present. All men else were in the streets rejoicing at the victory, and lighting bonfires.

23 JULY

No longer are we the Lord Chamberlain's Men; our patron hath died, tho' his son is to become our patron in his stead.¹⁴ Yet is all this for naught, because our plays are inhibited because the plague grows apace. We are to leave town awhile, and seek what fortune may bring elsewhere.

31 JULY

Today our company bobbed down the Thames, tho' I wished our scarfed bark were bigger. We moved swiftly with the tide awhiles until the river broadened and ran slow. For some time, our boat hugged the shore of what is called the Isle of Sheppey before we turned southward and made towards the pebbled shore. We moored in the Swale until the tide was high again, and then put into Faversham where we cast our anchor.¹⁵

Though I had not thought to travel with the company this summertide, it was this visit to Faversham that compelled me so to do. This is the very town where the murder took place that was captured in our fiction [*Arden of Feversham*].¹⁶ I swiftly sought out a venerable old man who lived at that time, and he took much delight in recounting his tale and in revealing unto me the places where it all had passed. It seemeth Thomas Arden was the mayor of the town and thrived in his endeavours. He married one Alice Mirfyn, the stepdaughter of Sir Edward North, the clerk to the Parliament. This Alice became ardent amorously attached to her stepfather's steward, Thomas Mosby, and together they plotted the death of her husband. On the evening of 15 February 1551, Thomas Arden was murdered by two villains procured for the purpose by Alice & Mosby. Arden was murdered in his own parlour in the house to the outer gateway to Faversham Abbey. The culprits were finally brought to trial and condemned. Alice was burned to death at Canterbury, whiles they hanged Mosby at Smithfield [London], and their accomplices were hanged in chains in Faversham. All this, in Faversham, this old man had seen and heard, & I thanked him heartily for his tale. Together we drank fine ale which they brew from the hops that grow hard by. He said that if I liked the ale, I should eat their apples which are the finest in all Christendom. Apples and ale goeth not together, I said. "Ah, right 'un are," he said. Then after a time he said, "yet there be oysters aplenty—you shouldst eat those." And this we did. If the apples be as good as the oysters, the town is well blessed.

1 AUGUST

Faversham. Today we presented *Romeo [and Juliet]* which I had abridged and amended a little. Dick [Burbage] was fine as ever [as Romeo], with young Bob Gough a most sweetly pert Juliet. We played in a large hall that hath been lime-washed, & so is called the White House, which the folk here use as their Guildhall. They say that our queen was entertained rarely there some twenty years ago.[17] One way & another I am well pleased with this visit; we return to the city on the morrow.

SATURDAY [7 AUGUST]

Tomorrow there is to be great celebrating for the Lord Essex's triumph over the Spanish at Cadiz. Howsomever, the celebration will lack my presence for, within this last hour, I received word that my dearest Hamnet is grievous sick, and I ride for home as fast as horses may carry me. I trust I be not too late.

9 AUGUST

Hamnet is parlous weak, & he lies so still I might think him dead. When he opened his eyes for a moment, he saw me and tried to smile.

I sit by his bed, uttering what prayers I can, but I fear all too wretchedly they will not be answered. I repent me much I returned not home long ere this; I am alone the villain of the earth.

12 AUGUST

His smile was but brief, as brief as his life, a weak candle snuffed out by the merest breath of death.[18] Now he goes before us, like so many babes before parents, before their time. Was it meant to be ever thus? Proud, scornful death conquers all, reduces all to dust wherein worms dwell. Father & mother have been a comfort through all; Anne sits & weeps quietly.

Am I guiltless in my child's death? I am ashamed that death has power to shake my manhood. With what strong a bond the child was bound to the father, & the father unto his child. Would I could beat cold death aside & retrieve my dear child. Death lies on him like an untimely frost upon my sweetest flower of all the field. Life is as a whisper in the ears of death.

1 SEPTEMBER

Tho' my heart says otherwise, I must, I know, shake off my grief for my beloved Hamnet & all that he might have become in this world. Forget him I never shall, nor ever could, and his spirit will abide with me for evermore. But I must rejoin my company and the world, e'en tho' the time be unagreeable to such business. Anne is sad, resigned.

12 SEPTEMBER

Bristol. 'Tis good to be rejoined with my fellow players who are acquainted with my cause of grief, and assuage it. They do all that men can.[19]

14 SEPTEMBER

Dick Burbage is as ever most effective & affecting as Richard II; as he took leave of his queen [5.1] tears quite o'erwhelmed my eyes. Bob Gough was plaintive when he said "must we be divided? must we part?" and "whither he goes, thither let me go" [5.1.81, 85]. Methought I heard my dear Hamnet in those lines. Later Dick came and sat with me in my room, and said that now he had traversed Richard, he would fain reveal another side to kingship, and personate Henry IV if I would but write the piece. I told him I have thought on Henry, but that the play would be different from Richard II—less poesy, some humour, & I would seek to show a king with his troublesome son whom he loves despite of all. "Henry," I said, "will not interest the crowds as much as his wayward son, Hal. To boot, if more history be called for, I have in mind Henry V's glorious battle at Agincourt with such rousing speeches that will make the rabblement roar." I told Dick my play would improve upon that weak, sickly *Harry the V* played last year.[20] Dick laughed & said indeed that might be accomplished most readily.

16 SEPTEMBER

[Dick] Burbage and I came nigh unto to blows tonight; wilful, he plays Shylock for laughter, and panders to the lowest sort. Tho' he says he sees the red-haired Jew is abused, yet he feels no pity for him. "And what of those hypocrites, those Christians," I cried. "Will," he replied, "ye have been guided by your own true affections, I know; but, for all that, Shylock is a Jew." I despair, and believe I have failed in what I have written. Mayhap evil is all folk see in Jews. Gough was a sweet Portia merely.

17 SEPTEMBER

More deep chat with Dick [Burbage] about his Shylock. He now discerns, I think, more of my import, for we read o'er the Jew's scenes; but when next we enact *Merchant* 'tis better he assume Bassanio—tho'

Dick says Bassanio is but another Romeo, and offers little he has not already assayed. Tom Pope says he can play Shylock, tho' I did not tell Dick this, & I fear Tom be too much a comedian and no better for Shylock than is Dick. Mayhap the fault is all mine, for the Jew will ever be evil to the English, & 'tis all to do with money.

21 OCTOBER

Yester afternoon I was summoned to the College of Arms. The Garter King-of-Arms[21] hath approved and granted the coat of arms I had solicited for father. Thus I dare avouch he will be well pleased in his old age that this honour hath come to pass at the last, as our motto states.[22] I' fecks, it is little enow and a comfort for him. I would that Hamnet had lived to see it come to pass.

17 NOVEMBER

Tomorrow the dream play [*A Midsummer Night's Dream*] once more is to be a wedding play.[23] Of this I am now become heartily sick and angry, for, tho' the piece be of love and marriage, it hath more to do with imagination, illusion, realities, and the fictions this world encompasseth. I fear 'tis chosen merely because it hath manifold weddings. Yet am I in a goodly company, for Spenser hath shown me a poem he hath writ for this same occasion. Much of it is pastoral poesy merely, tho' it enchants sweetly; what remains most in the mind is "Sweet Thames run softly, till I end my song."[24]

19 NOVEMBER

A few days past I was talking with Tom Pope about what I had in mind for the new chronicle [on Henry IV or V]. He said that he believed a play he had in his possession might take my imagination, or leastways it might prove a prick or spur. So he gave me a much soiled copy of a something entitled *The Famous Victories of Henry V*, and said he had some idea that Tarlton had writ it.²⁵ The piece is the merest gallimaufry of comic and serious scenes, which lack all style, discernment, and development. It treats of the reigns of both Henries [IV and V], and stretches across the years, yet little but broad daubs of history and characters are there. Howsomever, within each scene lies some germen I might seize upon, possess, and make my own. I' faith, I might make two, nay three works out of this scarecrow, of this slightest scaffold. After I had perused this piece some hour or so, Tom returned and asked me how I liked it. "Well enough," I replied, "tho' 'tis but scant." "Aye, it is that," said Tom. "But you see that much could be made of the comedy scenes with Hal, and of the character called [Sir John] Oldcastle." I replied that indeed such was already on my mind. Thereat Tom's eye glinted and gleamed. Would I, he said, think on him when working o'er Oldcastle, for he would dearly like to play the party. I told him that the role might well be his, and I might suit it accordingly. I asked him if [Will] Kempe or John Heminges knew aught of all this. Tom said nay.²⁶

20 NOVEMBER

Boils and plagues plaster him; why could not Tom Pope keep matters to himself? Hardly had he left my closet afore first John Heminges and then Will Kempe came acalling. Both declared they too had read the Famous Victories play, and would fain play this character Oldcastle if I would but suit the role for them. Yet I have scarcely thought on what to do, and Oldcastle in that piece is but a scant part, tho' indeed I might make much of it. I needs must consult Holinshed and Daniel,²⁷ and ponder what might be possible—tho' the fortunes of kingship, which is to say Henry IV and Prince Hal are of more import than whate'er this Oldcastle might have been (or might be in my hands).

21 NOVEMBER

Lord, how the words for this new piece [*Henry IV Part 1*] fly from my quill—my hand can scarce keep apace with my whirling thoughts.

The thrust of the thing now is clear to me, which is to make compare those men that are around Prince Hal. Thus Hal and Hotspur must be differing sons, but of an age.[28] Harry IV and Hal—the father contra son, one old, one young, duty against disorder. Harry IV and Oldcastle [Falstaff] shall both be like fathers to Hal. Oldcastle and Hotspur are the coward and the honourable noble. Oldcastle is riotous, unlawful, liar, coward, fool, glutton, braggart, lecher, parasite. Pope shall have his fun forsooth. Yet shall Oldcastle provoke laughter and joy, leastways until Hal finds the path he must take, which he shall. Oldcastle is the madcap lord of misrule who leads Hal astray until Hal learns what becomes a monarch. Today I have taken naught but ale & pepper-gingerbread, & it needs must be that which stirs my brain

22 NOVEMBER

Two acts of Harry [*Henry IV Part 1*] are complete, and yet I find there is so much the more to pen that I perceive more plays will yet be born of this chronicle. I have shown what is done to Dick [Burbage], and he sees he may make much of his role as Hal, and he is much enamoured with the robbery at Gadshill. He said he had done little in the comic way, and 'twill be fresh stuff for him. Dick said Harry would suit Gus Phillips well, for he can be grave & stately well enough. The vexed question is who shall play Oldcastle. I told Dick that all three—Pope, Kempe, and Heminges—do try to seize upon the role. Dick fears Kempe would be too riotous, for 'tis one thing to portray riotousness and another to be riotous in the portrayal. I am of the same mind, though I know not how the matter shall be settled and keep all our company in harmony and good spirits. "They might," said Dick, "all three play Oldcastle by turns, whilst at other times playing Oldcastle's compatriots in crime." "And there, Dick, thou hast hit upon our salvation, if you can stomach Kempe once in awhile," I said. Leastways, we may tell Kempe he might play it by turns.

23 NOVEMBER

With Gus Phillips this even. He read o'er to me what I have written thus far for Harry IV [*Henry IV Part 1*]. The moment he intoned Harry's lines I knew, as did he, that he is Harry—"so shaken as we are, so wan with care" [1.1.1]. And then again with "but be sure / I will from henceforth rather be myself, / Mighty and to be feared" [1.3.4–6]. Gus seemed to grow and transform his very self, as I have seen him do so oft. Together we looked o'er what else is done, and Gus said, "Why here's Will Sly to the word." Yes, indeed, I replied, for when I conceived Hotspur I thought all the while of Sly. "'Tis a fine opportunity for Will," Gus said, to which I jested, "I know ye play not favourites, dear Gus."[29] "Nay, good Will, never. I trust I ne'er must confess myself wondrous malicious or be accused of folly. But I trust [Henry] Condell shall have Northumberland, for we would go together well." I told him 'twas as good as settled. Then we set forth to the Boar's Head, there to meet and to sup ale with Dick [Burbage], since he needs must sense what I depict.[30] We drank more than a few deep draughts.

25 NOVEMBER

James Burbage is frustrate in his plan for our Blackfriars theatre. Numerous folk have petitioned the [Privy] council, amongst whom is our own Lord Hunsdon and Dick Field, who I can scarce believe would so betray us. Dick Burbage told me they complain that there will be great annoyance and trouble to the nobility and gentle folk by reason of the gathering together of all manner of vagrant and lewd persons that, under colour of resorting to our plays, will work mischief. And besides, because the playhouse is near the Church, the noise of our drums and trumpets will disturb both the ministers and parishioners in time of divine service, and such. So the adventure comes all to naught, & Burbage hath wasted hundreds of pounds. Dick Burbage says his father is sick with grief at the loss, & Dick fears for him because he hath placed all his hopes on this Blackfriars. "Will," Dick said, "I told father wise men ne'er sit and wail their loss, but cheerly seek how to redress their harms.

But he received it as poor counsel, and, in truth, I scarce believed the words myself." I knew not what else I might say.

29 NOVEMBER

My mind hath been maimed with Harry [*Henry IV Part 1*]; the words flow no longer, my ink quite dry. To boot, I have now this writ against me craving sureties, whereof [Francis] Langley says he knows naught, save he hath sought sureties against Wayte and Gardiner some while ago.[31]

30 NOVEMBER

With Will Sly this even that he might look o'er his scene with Glendower [*Henry IV Part 1*, 3.1.] "'Tis a long and goodly scene," he said "and 'twill give more occasion than did Tybalt." I agreed with him, tho' I think the scene more desultory than he does. We had chat o'er the Welsh in it; I know but little and Sly none. I like much the lilt of the speech, and think 'tis affecting, tho' it be prohibited.[32] Mayhap some one doth know enough for our purpose. After Sly had departed, I fell to thinking how much this play discourses upon fathers & their sons, & I thought of mine own lost, dear son Hamnet, & the father I might have been unto him.

4 DECEMBER

Today, after noon, came Gabriel Spencer greatly troubled, for yesterday, he said, he and one [James] Feake were arguing violently in the house of Richard East, a barber. Gabriel said naught on the cause of the argument, nor why this happened in the barber's house. Whate'er the cause or reason, Gabriel struck Feake a mortal blow in the eye.[33] Gabriel appealed to me for aid in his sore distress, saying he hath wanted employment some several months, & would have me speak for him with my fellows. I said there would surely be such parts as he hath played before when we play at Court this month's end.³⁴ When Gabriel had departed, I pondered why he hath not been arrested by the authorities, tho' that is none of my business.

20 DECEMBER

Rain, rain, and more rain; it raineth every day and night. Some folk even tell of the earth moving in Kent. Our goodly band is well nigh ready for the Court. We shall give my Harry play [*Henry IV Part 1*] and some two or three others.

27 DECEMBER

Yester even, at Court, the new Harry play [*Henry IV Part 1*].³⁵ Methinks 'twas performed lively enough, tho' the court took most delight in those scenes of Oldcastle. Tom Pope is overjoyed because his Oldcastle was called for again at play's end. As now seems her custom, Her Majesty called me forth. "Master Shakespeare," said she, " we have taken much delight in this play that touches on our forebears, and 'tis well we see that rebels and rebellion are made frustrate. We have a mind to see this chronicle again, tho' think you not Master Kempe might personate him you call Oldcastle? Master Kempe jests very prettily and is a witty wag." I bowed low and mumbled my assent with a "majesty," though my thought was "better a witty fool than Kempe's foolish wit." Thus is the play called for come January. I pray Kempe will con his part well, though I fear him extempore. It appeareth he is destined to be Oldcastle.

1597

The year begins with another successful performance of Henry IV Part 1, but a controversy over the name of the character called Oldcastle forces Shakespeare to rename him. Plagued by pirate editions of such plays as Romeo and Juliet, *Shakespeare learns there is little he can do about the situation. He is also obliged to please Queen Elizabeth with a reincarnation of Falstaff in* The Merry Wives of Windsor. *In April the Burbage brothers hint at their plans for the future as the lease on the Theatre expires.* Merry Wives *is a triumph at the palace of Whitehall; also present is the irascible Ben Jonson, and Shakespeare has his first encounter with this soon-to-be-friend and colleague. Subsequently, they engage in numerous debates on the art of writing plays. Jonson is later in trouble with the authorities for his hand in writing the play,* The Isle of Dogs, *and is imprisoned. His co-author Tom Nashe manages to flee London, but is never heard of again. During the summer Shakespeare and his fellow actors travel to Dover, Bristol, and Bath. At year's end, Shakespeare remains at work on* Henry IV Part 2.

2 JANUARY

We presented Harry [*Henry IV Part 1*] once more last evening. Will Kempe played Oldcastle as Her Majesty had commanded. Lord how she roared through her blackened teeth at Kempe's antics, though all the while I scarce recognised what I had set down, so much was extempore. I had lief the town crier spoke my words than Kempe give them utterance. Again was I called for by the Queen. "Good Master

Shakespeare, you have given us great pleasure in this work of your hand, and we like well this character Oldcastle. It would gratify us greatly to see more of him in another play." My ever-ready mumbled "majesty." "Indeed you shall write more, though, if you look to our advice, you were best to call him by some other name. My Lord Cobham appeareth much displeased this evening. Know you not his forebear was an Oldcastle?"[1] I explained quickly that I had but taken the name from another play and intended no offence. "Indeed, you should not intend offence, Master Shakespeare. Write this new play, but vex not my Lord Cobham further." So write I must, though my thoughts rest on what else of Henry IV's reign and the growth of Hal I might write. Fathers and sons are more to my mind than Oldcastle, or whate'er I shall call him. Yet now Lord Cobham is angered, I fear.

5 JANUARY

News from father—uncle Henry hath died and is buried already.[2] He was a hard man, resentful, bullheaded, and bloody minded. So, all is past now, and what with all the recent rains I could not have travelled thither, as father knows well. Besides, I would not have gone on any account.

7 JANUARY

Romeo was played last night at Court, though why it was called for I know not; Her Majesty took such violent dislike of it before.[3] Yet last night she did not glower, and seemed much affected. I played Escalus as before, & all the company personated their roles with spirit.

10 JANUARY

As I feared, and as the Queen had said, offence hath been taken at Oldcastle. This day from the Lord Chamberlain came a letter wherein is stated that offence is taken by worthy personages descended from Oldcastle's title and also by many others who hold him in honourable memory. So all is clear that 'tis the Lord Chamberlain himself & his family who are much offended, and I did all but in error & ignorance! When next we play Harry [*Henry IV Part I*], Oldcastle must be christened anew. Some name from my histories must suffice.⁴ *Later*—and now Harry [Southampton], the master-mistress of my passion, writes of his delight that I used the name of Harvey in my play, as 'tis the name of his mother's lover, whom she would marry. (Harry, tho', is disquieted and prays they will not marry.) He would be pleased if Harvey took some offence, and asks, "Know ye that the Earl of Bedford's given name is William Russell."⁵ So Harry may be pleased or no, yet these names must be changed, for I seek but a peaceable life!

26 JANUARY

News—Lord Cobham's daughter Elizabeth hath died while she laboured with child.⁶ That family haunteth me every & which way, tho' I intend no harm. Doubtless Oldcastle & myself will be blamed once more. All this pother over names hath left me full of vexation to which only Kate might minister consolation.⁷

2 FEBRUARY

Today with Dick Burbage to lay his father to rest, who was a violent, rough man, and not over-honest; yet Dick loved him well enough, and Cuthbert too.⁸ Afterwards we did chat and drank long. Dick believes the business about the Blackfriars [Theatre] is what killed his father, for, ever sithence that petition November last, his father had lost all heart & interest in the least thing. I doubt it not, for a man's ambition, like salt, gives savour to this life. Weather cold.

9 FEBRUARY

I have read with profit Bacon's *Essays*, & find them brimful of wisdom, sound counsel, & fine phrase.⁹ I dare say it will prove a popular work.

15 FEBRUARY

Father sends news that aunt Margaret is dead and buried. Mayhap she could not live without her husband, tho' many could have.[10] I liked her more than uncle Henry; she was kindly & worthy my prayers, he was a kind of nothing. Kate consoled me this evening.

20 FEBRUARY

Tom Nashe today showed me what Danter hath done to my *Romeo*. Tho' it looks much like unto my play, Danter's book is all a mangled gallimaufry. I asked Nashe what power is in me to stop it. Naught or little, said he, unless I please to bring forth my own copy, which the company might not allow.[11] Dearly I desire to berate Danter, a friend ere this, but I needs must write the Falstaff play [*The Merry Wives of Windsor*] Her Majesty hath commanded (tho' I desire to proceed apace with Harry [*Henry IV Part 2*]). Besides, why should I spend my choler when no good will come of it? I have an itch of Kate, which I pray be not the pox.

6 MARCH

Lord Cobham, stricken with grief at his daughter's death, died yesterday.[12] I pray Oldcastle-Falstaff be not thought on now, lest more trouble be cast upon my head. Oh, what's in a name!

18 MARCH

Today came to me my Lord Hunsdon, newly created Lord Chamberlain after Lord Cobham, and our company is now to be called the Lord Chamberlain's his men. His Lordship asked of me what I have set down of the play that Her Majesty hath commanded. I told him I had done but little, for my mind is still on Henry [*Henry IV Part 2*], yet I had not forgot H.M.'s command to see more Oldcastle, or rather Falstaff as I call him now. His lordship then said he desired in a great way to please

H.M. who, besides making him Lord Chamberlain, is to create him a knight of the Garter. He would present, therefore, before H.M. this play with Oldcastle-Falstaff at the Garter Feast that shall be held at Whitehall Palace on St. George's day that is to come. Could it be ready & prepared by then, he asked. Before I could think, I heard myself say "aye," and "we are born to do as befits us," & saw myself bow low. "Then 'tis settled," said he, "and spare no expense for the great occasion, for we must honour Her Majesty right thoroughly." And then he departed. Ye gods & heavens, what foolishness have I said & promised, and the performance is set for my birthday.[13] No more Harry—I must set that aside, and this Falstaff play must be all my care.

19 MARCH

I spent all day with Will Kempe from dinner [lunch] until bed. I told Will what a parlous pickle I had gotten myself and all our fellows into. And, since Her Majesty must have Will and Falstaff, I yielded myself up to Kempe's hands (with what dislike I did not tell Kempe). I told him I had penned but a few points that perchance might be made into more. Love, comedy, and confusion is what's wanted. If Kempe might prick my imagination, something might body forth & be made much of. Well, Kempe smiled mightily, and a torrent of notions issued forth—disguises, concealment from irate husbands, hiding in a basket of linen, place—the Garter Inn, scene—around Windsor, & much more I cannot recall. I scribbled down all as swift as quill could fly. To my amazement, and some delight, there was something of a poor scaffold, a scarecrow I can dress, if not invest with great life, & save mine own labours to boot. I thanked Kempe with some warmth. "'Tis no matter," said Kempe. "Ye may not care much for my method, for mayhap 'tis a madcap method, yet there is method in my madcapness, and, on the day, we shall be as right as the rain." So we drank ale a while longer, & I believe I like the man somewhat the better.

26 MARCH

Now a week spent with Kempe, and I fear I have had more than sufficient of his company. More of his conversation would infect my brain. Yet together we have fashioned this play on Falstaff and Windsor [*Merry Wives*] which may answer. Much of what is plot, so called, is Kempe's doing, but I have sewn it together with what words I can. What I truly call my own I set down now, lest I forget too readily what in the piece be mine. I) prattle on the coat of arms and Sir Thomas Lucy, tho' 'tis a jest only I know.[14] II) I own and acknowledge the Welsh parson [Sir Hugh Evans] is mine, tho' his Welsh is but a travesty, not as in the first Harry [*Henry IV Part 1*]; yet am I endeared to the tongue. III) the gesture to Kit's memory; I had the poem by me and thought of Kit.[15] IV) the lesson on Latin [4.1] culled from my schoolboy days, wherein I take much delight, leastways in the memory thereof. V) Falstaff dressed in a buck's head [5.5], tho' that I have stole from the dream play [*A Midsummer Night's Dream*], which the wary shall know if they do but listen.[16] As for the rest, Kempe may make as merry with it as he chooses, as I doubt not he will do.

14 APRIL

Yester even to the Boar's Head, with Dick & Cuthbert Burbage. Tho' the Boar's Head doth remind me of the Harry play [*Henry IV Part 2*], Dick & Cuthbert had not asked me there to prate on that. Said Dick, "What concerns us now is what to do," as if I knew what he meant. Cuthbert broke in to tell me what had passed. Their father James, dead but these two or three months, had a lease for the Theatre with one Giles Allen for one and twenty years, the which are now passed.[17] Their father had tried to buy a new lease, and even offered Allen £24 per annum, which was £10 more than before. But Allen would not agree beyond five years more because he desired to put the playhouse to his own purposes. "Today," said Cuthbert, "is the very day of expiration. E'en tho' father built the Theatre, 'tis no longer ours to use." I asked what was to be done. Cuthbert said, though Allen might yet agree to terms, he had plans, but for the present our company might have use of the Curtain. Dick said that it is a fair place, and he cares not where we go so long as we may perform and bring in money. I told them I would likewise be happy, and desired only that my plays were heard and seen. "I've plays aplenty that just want penning," I said. "Aye," said Dick, "that's true enough, tho' Will Kempe says thy brain runneth dry." "Blast Kempe," I said. "That thing [*The Merry Wives of Windsor*] fulfills a command merely, and his lordship gave me precious little time to think what might be best. And as you know, I care not for Kempe's antics, and my heart was not in the thing. I pray it goes well on George's day." Well, we chatted on further, tho' I was angered and drank wine deep. Sore head and cough today.

Later—Blast Kempe yet more. He presents *his* list of characters and actors—himself, Falstaff; Burbage, Fenton; [Robert] Gough, Mistress Ford; Dick's prentice Nick, Mistress Quickly;[18] And whatever else I will!! "They are but suggestions, Will," said he. And I care not, tho' I do confess I am full of anger.

24 APRIL

Whitehall was resplendent for the Garter Feast yesterday, and I might have rejoiced in it greatly, but for the *Merry Wives* that bore my name. Never have I seen Kempe act so wild & boisterous, so stuffed with his own importance. Tom Pope would have personated Falstaff better to my mind. But Her Majesty needs must have Falstaff, & Kempe as Falstaff. Lord, how she and all her courtiers laughed. I was called for, as is the custom. "We are right well pleased Master Shakespeare," quoth she. "Ye shall be rewarded most handsomely, as shall Master Kempe. Forget not this Falstaff." I mumbled my reply. His Lordship [Hunsdon] pranced to me in gay excitement, all smiles, & said I had done exceeding well, would be rewarded, and so forth. Yet what ensued was far more remarkable. From behind me I heard, "So you are Shakespeare," the voice gruff and blunt. I turned and saw a middling-sized man, his thin copper face marked by the pox, eyes deep set and somewhat far apart, nose prominent. Before I replied, he repeated his words, blunt again. I told him I was, whereupon he assailed the play [*Merry Wives*] with mighty vituperation & most volubly. It wanted characters, plot, sense, and much else besides. "And what's its point?" he asked, "where is the satire? Why, almost any man alive could pen such trash." Then his scolding grew again. I thought I would be angered, but, for some reason, I know not why, I laughed, and told him he was correct, and that the piece was not worthy of many a man who could improve upon it. And, indeed, almost "any man" (I meant Kempe) had penned much of it. At this he was astonished, for verily he had expected an angry reply. Then I told him how the whole thing had come to pass, that the *Merry Wives* was commanded merely, that Kempe had provided the action mostly, and that I had patched it up swiftly. "And you saw how well pleased Her Majesty and the Court was," I said. "Then is the Court an ass," said he.

After that there was naught else to do but go and drink ale and chat. It was only at the Feathers Inn in Cheapside that I thought to ask his name—Ben Jonson, sans the "h" he was quick to say,[19] a quondam bricklayer, erstwhile soldier, & actor of little account. Since this February past he hath been with Pembroke's Men at Langley's Swan, tho' Jonson was unkind in his opinion of the company.[20] "What we need is *plays*, something that hath bite to it. I' fecks I would write myself, tho' not after your fashion Shakespeare." I told him he should seek out Tom Nashe, for I thought together they might do well. Jonson was pleased. Then most strangely, since we had but a three hour acquaintance, he added, "I am given much to venery, and I mean not hunting." Then he departed, but I am certain we shall meet again.

4 MAY

Stratford. Anne is pleased, she says, to see me. The girls grow apace—Susanna becomes 14 this very month, Judith 12, as would have my beloved Hamnet had he lived. Tho' Judith reminds me of my son dearly, she is not the same; yet the fault lies not with her. But I please all three (and father and mother) in buying New Place, the grandest house there could be, with rooms and fireplaces aplenty. And what a fine garden we shall have. Anne cares not for the murder, but I told her *she* need fear not. "Nay, indeed," quoth she, "for ye are but here rarely." Then her anger died, & we set to devising the how and the what, for we shall occupy the house before too many months are out.[21]

10 MAY

London once more. Anne was all tears when I departed, though happy and proud enough of the new home, once the chattels are there. Well, there is little else I might do, as I needs must be here in town for our plays, and neither do I lust for her. Such are our fortunes; i' fecks, I believe a fairer fortune than I have seen lies before me. This afternoon I spent at the Bunch of Grapes with Tom Nashe; 'tis a long time since we had met & talked. I told him of this new man Jonson and how he did accost me at the *Merry Wives* at Whitehall. Forewarned is forearmed. Tom said he had a mind to meet so forthright a man, and perchance they might well devise a new piece together. After some while we went over to the Mitre & found Jonson sitting there deep in thought. Ale and chat. Tom & Jonson became fast friends on the instant, so I departed, musing on what might become of this new amity.

24 MAY

At Windsor for the installation, this day, of his lordship [Hunsdon] as a Knight of the Garter, as well as other knights. Yesterday was a grand procession that began somewhat after four o'clock in the afternoon. First, Sir Henry Lee & his company rode through the town, his men in blue coats and badges. Next after them rode the Lord Mountjoy,[22] his men in blue coats, a plume of purple estridge feathers in every man's hat, and his gentlemen with chains of gold. Immediately after them, came his Lordship [Hunsdon] with us marching along. We made a brave company, us, his gentlemen, the servants, and retainers, with our blue coats faced with orange taffeta, and orange feathers in our hats, and many with chains of gold. And besides, there was a great number of other knights and gentlemen who accompanied his lordship. Then, last, following our company, Lord Thomas, with a like troop in blue coats faced with sea-green taffeta and feathers of the same hue, and also many chains of gold. 'Twas a goodly show, & why I know not, but I did feel pride swell within my breast. It was late when our company returned to the city, bed & rest.

2 JUNE

Yester even, as I would go to the Mitre, I saw Sir Walter Ralegh riding abroad with Her Majesty. So is he restored to his place at the Court. Such are the changes of fickle fortune, & I am happy my lowly station keeps me safe from harm. Ever blessed is the humble suitor.

3 JUNE

At the Rose this afternoon, Ned Alleyn in *Frederick and Basilea*, a play noteworthy only because I cannot recall its import.[23] Ned played as fine as ever, tho' it did not seem his heart was in the piece. Ale with him afterwards and, i' faith, he spoke of leaving off playing. I asked him, in God's name, why an actor of his power would think such a thought. Ned replied he was tired of the many parts which he had played o'er too many times. "Will, there are times, now, when I can no longer discern what is life and what be the stage. Why, only the other day I was enacting Faustus, and I thought I saw a devil on the stage. So strong was this illusion that it seemed the rabble saw it too."[24] He continued after this fashion for mayhap a hour, and he was much disquieted. After I had left Ned, I returned to my closet to muse on my own dilatory sloth. There lies the Harry play [*Henry IV Part 2*], which is still no more than jumbled scribbles. Where now is mine ambition to finish it? Shall I become another Ned & cease my work? Yet I think I lost the taste for the thing because of Falstaff that Her Majesty would have more of. Falstaff is but a part, a fragment of the whole I must present. I needs must ponder anew, for my muse wants some subject to devise, some argument, some invention.

1597 ❧ 137

10 JUNE

Fair words from Harry [Southampton], whom I have scarce seen or heard from these many months. He goes with the Lord Essex on an expedition against the Spanish.²⁵ I wonder why Harry wrote now; mayhap because of the dangers he will face. I wish him God speed & safe return.

> That god forbid that made me first your slave
> I should in thought control your times of pleasure,
> Or at your hand th'account of hours to crave,
> Being your vassal bound to stay your leisure.
> O, let me suffer, being at your beck,
> Th'imprisoned absence of your liberty,
> And, patience-tame to sufferance, bide each check
> Without accusing you of injury.
> Be where you list, your charter is so strong
> That you yourself may privilege your time
> To what you will; to you it doth belong
> Yourself to pardon of self-doing crime.
>   I am to wait, though waiting so be hell,
>   Not blame your pleasure, be it ill or well. [Sonnet 58]

12 JUNE

This evening with Jonson at the Mitre. He railed much as he had before. 'Tis some odd, sour humour that pricks him to this fashion—and he wanted to know if I had done with Falstaff. Jonson and Tom Nashe work together on a play, tho' Jonson said but little on't. I muse why I stay to be baited with one that wants his wits betimes.

1 JULY

We are to play at Sir Robert Cecil's house before him, the Lord Essex, and Sir Walter Ralegh. My Richard II play hath been asked for, though why in particular, I know not, but go we shall.²⁶

14 JULY

News from father that Fulke Underhill hath murdered his father [William], at which I am astonished & vexed mightily, for this confounds in a degree the purchase of the house [New Place] that I made from the father. I fear it doth presage some ill event, & our legal woes will be the more protracted. I expect Anne will be all tears.

15 JULY

To Shoreditch with the Burbages [Richard and Cuthbert] to bury Cuthbert's poor mite.[27] Both brothers wept grievously as Cuthbert's hopes were laid in the ground.

29 JULY

What a day was yesterday. Early in the afternoon, the Players at the Swan [Pembroke's Men] performed a play entitled *The Isle of Dogs*—this being the very piece that hath made Jonson and Nashe confederates. Before the play was ended, in marched a troop of guards that arrested Gabriel Spencer, Robert Shaw, and Jonson, the others having made good their escape. All three are committed to the Marshalsea. Later I heard from several folk that the Privy Council did consider *The Isle* to be full of seditious and slanderous matter, and that all playing is to be stayed at Her Majesty's pleasure. That night, Nashe, wrapped close in his cloak with a hat pulled half over his face to avoid discovery, crept into my closet. He said, "Will, I must commune with you of such things that want no ear but yours." He spoke of how those in authority talk of great disorders, the chaos that ensueth, and lewd matters in the theatres, that they, meaning the theatres, be the resort of idle apprentices, masterless men, vagrants, coseners, whores and whoremongers, thieves, and all manner of evil people. Nashe believes that Topcliffe[28] was the cause of all the trouble, for the man would prank up himself in authority upon the least occasion. Tom was greatly troubled because his lodgings have been searched & his papers removed, tho' he rejoiced he was not therein when they ransacked his room. Well, now he hath fled to Yarmouth, tho' I could have wished he had not told me this, for then I would not know where he is, and have no cause to betray him if I am questioned. Now the theatres are closed, and we lose our livelihood. The other fellows will take to the road to do what they may, but I have resolved to go home first for awhile, and perchance will seek them out later.[29]

[AUGUST]

Stratford—'Ods my life & lungs, the air is so sweet & fresh I wonder how I breathe in London. Anne is happy now I am home once more, & my daughters grow fine and bonny. Yet, where'er I go, I am minded of how dearest Hamnet and I walked together. But I must work and flesh out the second Harry play [*Henry IV Part 2*] ere I rejoin the men at Dover, which gives me little enough time. Notandum:—amend *Love's Labour's*—Heminges says we must present a comedy for the court festivities at Christmas.[30] And I must look o'er the second Richard play [*Richard II*] ere it be published, tho' I think little need be amended there.[31]

[AUGUST]

After the tedious process of my travel, with limbs tired and exceeding weary for dear repose, I have come to Dover, to join my hearty good fellows. I marvel that, as I have oft heard people say, the cliffs of France can be seen afar off across the sea. Carcasses of many a tall Spanish ship, the hulks of that Armada, lie scattered still on the beach, rotting with the waves. Also strange to see were some men and women clinging to the chalky sides of the cliffs to gather up herbs, tho' they make a poor living.[32] Poverty is the father of unnumberable infirmities. The town is pleasant, indifferent large, the air salt sharp and fresh to the nose. We sojourn here but a day or two before we journey on to Bath, & Bristol, then we return to the city.

[SEPTEMBER]

These last several days we have passed in Bath and then Bristol. His lordship [Hunsdon] keeps a fine house in Bath, for the sake of taking the waters for his health, as do many of the nobility that visit the town. Bristol is a fair enough city, though it hath, of late, fallen upon hard times for want of good harvests. I saw many a poor beggar going about the city. For all that, we played at the Guildhall, and received thirty shillings from the Mayor for our pains. Tho' I might, if I wished, journey home, I shall return to London with the other fellows.

25 SEPTEMBER

The King of Spain is dead, though I know not whereof he died.[33] There will be few Englishmen will mourn his death, what with his marriage to Bloody Mary, the Armada, and such. He was a cruel tyrant to Protestants—yea, the demon of the south. I have heard tell that he said he would burn his own son at the stake if he were condemned to death for heresy. Well, he will answer to the Lord now for all his sins, and God rot him.

8 OCTOBER

Ben [Jonson] with me this morning. A long deep chat. He was gaunt, for he was released from the Marshalsea but this very day. He told me the order for his release, and that of Robert Shaw and Gabriel Spencer, had come the third of the month, but they were detained all this while. "They have given me a harsh, rough time, Will," he said. "I made them all the more angry and vicious because I would admit nothing. Twice they tried to trick me by placing informers in my cell, but I swift smelled out the bastards for what they were, two damned villains that would catch advantage of me." Ben believes [Richard] Topcliffe contrived the whole investigation, for 'twas he showed Ben the rack and hot irons. He spoke more of the vile food and so forth, yet Ben is not the man to yield in such conditions. Then we spoke of plays & such:

Ben has many ideas for plays, but will not give more offence, leastways not for the moment. Though I have borne many a blunt upbraiding and bitter scoff from him in times past, I am heartily sorry that Ben hath been abused and hath suffered thus.

11 OCTOBER

Today I went to the Rose where they gave Kyd's *Tragedy*.[34] Ned Alleyn possessed not his fire of yore as mad Hieronymo, and I doubt not he will leave the stage as he hath said, for his passion hath left him.

21 OCTOBER

In the street this morning, I saw [Andrew] Wise. Quoth he, "I have not seen you long; how goes the world?" And then he told me he was well pleased to have registered my book of Richard [*Richard III*] on the day before. I told him I had not the time yet to amend it, & that I thought it not complete if it be the book used this summer past. He said it was no great concern, for all the world would recall how Burbage had played Richard to great applause. Well, I know my rank & rate; the actor is ever prized the higher.[35]

24 OCTOBER

Parliament assembled today, and I had thought to see the procession to the Parliament house. Yet the crowd which pressed about the streets was so thick I could see nothing and I came away. Later I learned from a man that had been there that, as the queen and the nobles passed by, several people (he knew not how many) had been crushed to death as the way was cleared before the queen. In little, that is the way of this world—like ears of corn in the wind, the lowly bend before the high & mighty.

30 OCTOBER

At the Bunch of Grapes this afternoon I drank ale with a west countryman who said there is news that the Spanish will invade again down there. Thus there is much mustering of forces. This last intelligence gave me a notion for the Henry play and its beginning [*Henry IV Part 2*]. There shall be a Prologue named Rumour, who shall spread false report & hope of the rebels' victory, and all shall be dashed when the true news is revealed. Thus shall the audience be put in mind of what passed in the other play [*Henry IV Part 1*]. As a jest, I shall enact Rumour.

15 NOVEMBER

Parliament debates once more the subsidies for the defence of the realm, or should I write Her Majesty's realm. I suppose we shall be assessed, tho' in truth I did not pay the last reckoning.[36]

1 DECEMBER

Jonson gave me news that the wretch Gardiner is dead.[37] Well, let him rot thoroughly for, e'en though he was but a small thorn in my side, yet was he a monstrous slanderer of heaven and earth, and was full evil to others. Ben said Gardiner was a man of such an evil mind and conversation that he would deny what he had but just spoke, and that he was the subtlest knave in the whole county. And 'tis curious strange that, as Ben would have it, Gardiner's funeral is to be prepared by Camden. But true it must be since Ben & Camden are fast friends.[38] Ben told me also that he had shown the plot of a play he means to write to Henslowe's company. Henslowe is to give him twenty shillings, & Ben hath promised that he will make all complete come Christmas.[39]

[DECEMBER]

Another long dreary journey and for little reward, save I can see how my amendments to *Love's Labour's* may succeed.[40] So shall we yet have time until we perform it for the queen. The countryside hereabouts is ill-fitted for this winter weather, though it must be a fair sight to behold in springtime.

22 DECEMBER

Jonson went to Gardiner's funeral today; I would not have gone for a wilderness of monkeys. Bought a half gallon of sweet wine, 2 shillings.

27 DECEMBER

Yester eve we performed *Love's Labour's Lost* (amended) for Her Majesty, and she and her courtiers did seem mightily pleased withal. We were given food and drink aplenty afterward, though Her Majesty asked not for me as she hath done on like occasion. Mayhap she took offence that I played the king? Others—Berowne-[Dick] Burbage, Longaville-[Gus] Phillips, Dumain-[George] Bryan, Armado-Kempe (blast him), Holofernes-Heminges (fine), Dull-Cowley,[41] Costard-Tom Pope, Rosaline-Sam Gilburne (as sweet a girl as he is a boy).

❦ *Shakespeare's fellow actors are rather unhappy with* Henry IV Part 2 *because Shakespeare has trimmed down the role of Falstaff. However, Shakespeare does convince them to perform Jonson's* Every Man in his Humour, *despite his own reservations about the piece and Jonson himself. Southampton marries secretly in order to avoid Queen Elizabeth's anger, while Shakespeare allows himself to succumb to the sexual blandishments of male admirer. Once more Jonson finds himself in jail, this time for killing a man; Shakespeare witnesses Jonson's trial where he gains an acquittal by pleading benefit of clergy. More congenial is a chance conversation with a stranger to whom Shakespeare tells the plot and ideas of* Much Ado About Nothing. *The stranger's reactions convince Shakespeare his play is a winner. In December, there is mystery and conspiracy as the Burbages and Shakespeare's company decide to dismantle the Theatre, take it across the River Thames, and build a new theatre, the Globe.* ❦

30 JANUARY

I passed several pleasing hours today with Dick Quiney, a good friend in whom I repose my trust in matters of heavy consequence. He is in good health & spirits, & says he will look about for some land that I might buy.[1] We spoke on that for some while, and I would fain help him in his affairs if I might.

15 FEBRUARY

Last evening at my Lord of Essex's house, we did perform *Romeo* [*and Juliet*] and *Love's Labour's* to the great delight and pleasure of the company there assembled, though the ladies wept grievously at Juliet in her tomb. We were not done until after the chimes at midnight. To my joy Harry [Southampton] spoke with me privily before we played. He told me he hath been much in and out of favour with Her Majesty, which troubles him greatly, though he hath leave to travel (he sailed for France on today's tide). I think he is much in love; though he said naught of it, I believe he would marry if he could. Well, I wish him all joy, e'en tho' 'twill mean we shall see one another but rarely.

> How like a winter hath my absence been
> From thee, the pleasure of the fleeting year!
> What freezings have I felt, what dark days seen—
> What old December's bareness everywhere!
> And yet this time removed was summer's time,
> The teeming autumn, big with rich increase,
> Bearing the wanton burden of the prime,
> Like widowed wombs after their lords' decease.
> Yet this abundant issue seemed to me
> But hope of orphans and unfathered fruit;
> For summer and his pleasures wait on thee,
> And, thou away, the very birds are mute;
>> Or if they sing, 'tis with so dull a cheer
>> That leaves look pale, dreading the winter's near.
> [Sonnet 97]

25 FEBRUARY

The first Harry [play] is to be printed; [Andrew] Wise registered it today. I needs must complete the second part whiles the first remains in the public mind. 'Tis mine own sloth that so hinders my pen, & that will not do. I want that tenth Muse worth more than the nine rhymers invocate.

26 FEBRUARY

I have bought Kit's *Hero*.² What a flood, a tide of remembrance it hath invoked of that dear, wild, passionate man. What he might have become! I fear the same may be said of me if I work not harder & write this play [*Henry IV Part 2*].

10 MARCH

Today, for the first time, I see my name on a page bearing the title of one of my plays. I should be proud, but an oaf hath marred the printing.³ Yet am I a poet new inspired, and I am resolved to complete Harry [*Henry IV Part 2*] before a week be passed.

18 MARCH

This poet's life is naught but toil, trouble, and tumult, & yet, vexed as I am, I must forbear and work with my fellows. After months of moiling labour, I have completed my second Harry play [*Henry IV Part 2*]; it is the thing I wanted. At the still centre I have placed what was its very essence—"Uneasy lies the head that wears the crown" [3.1.31], for thus does Henry understand what kingship is. He usurped Richard [II] and faced civil unrest, as Richard had foretold. His allies, dissatisfied with their share, rebelled & thus must Henry reestablish the order he disrupted. But Hal, his son, is a riotous, disordered youth who cleaves not to his father, & takes up with the riotous lord of misrule Oldcastle (or rather Falstaff, as now I must name him). All I wrote was to lead to the scene [4.5] where father and penitent son become as one, yet just before, while his father sleeps, Hal takes the crown and places it on his own head—an act of usurpation, though he intends it not.

All this I crafted carefully, and this morning we all forgathered, and I read the play. I could see there was great dissatisfaction, though I read through all. Dick Burbage and Heminges both said it was fine enough, but would need to be pruned, for I had in places favoured the rebels too much, and 'twould not pass for approval.⁴ But this was mild to the chorus of disapproval that Falstaff's role was too little and that the whole play wanted humour. In this was Kempe the leader (I needed no prophet for that) and his reasons were all for himself, though Pope did second him and said folk want more Falstaff and we must think on that and the money 'twill bring us. And no doubt they are right. The upshot of this is that near half of my labour is wasted and in its stead Kempe, Pope, and I will work together on the scenes of low life in Eastcheap and such. Howsoever, I will revenge me on Kempe, for I shall enlarge the part of Mistress Quickly for Pope and give him a fine opportunity and take from Kempe in the people's eyes. And there may be other parts where I may do the like. Yet there is a greater revenge on Kempe that I kept back—Falstaff shall not be in the play on Harry V, and what little of that I have penned already is easily blotted out.⁵

15 APRIL

This morning I read the ballad on Tiverton,⁶ which recalled Stratford's woes and my friends and kindred there. Some poor woman, who would make pancakes, began the blaze that consumed the greater part of the town. Them that be feeble in mind believe it was a just punishment from God for the unmercifulness of the rich and their small regard of the poor, who were seen to perish daily in the streets for want of relief. Mayhap they are in the right, and sure the rich ought to succour the poor, for 'tis but ungentle fortune hath placed them in their sties. Yet what species of god would inflict such punishment? That is a thought I dare not pursue and must erase from all remembrance. And 'tis not the stuff to trick out a play.

29 MAY

With [Francis] Langley at the Bunch of Grapes. Langley morose and sullen, for he hath been ordered not to proceed any further with his suit against the actors who did leave him and took up with Henslowe. But he lacks a licence for the Swan, as he did confess, and none want to work for him after the *Isle of Dogs* business for fear of imprisonment.⁷ Then more unprofitable chat; I care not greatly for the man.

[2 JULY]

Rumours abound that the Queen boxed the Lord Essex's ears for turning his back upon her. Thereupon he threatened Her Majesty with his sword, a sin against the obedience which he owed his queen. Now he hath withdrawn from the Court. They say 'tis all much ado about the disorders in Ireland and what should be done.⁸ 'Tis a merry thought to think on the Queen boxing the ears of his lordship!

15 JULY

Of what followeth, I have endeavoured to bring to mine remembrance all that passed, for the import thereof. I recall 'twas in April a year past, yea upon my birthday that I met Jonson when *Merry Wives* was enacted at Whitehall. Then he charged me somewhat too roundly that the play had no point and lacked satire with which did I fain agree. Since then we have talked mightily together of many matters and much of playmaking. From his discourse, it seemeth Ben had within him a great fire for plays and would write, nay I had thought, was writing such dramas as would stir the imagination, set the crowds aroaring. He seemed all the while brimful of passion and choler. After some time, I enquired of him what he had set down, and if I might peruse whate'er it might be. Yet he fobbed me off with this excuse and that, saying the time was not yet ripe for such. So I determined there to let the matter rest, tho' our discussions continued apace.

Then some four or five weeks past, Heminges did inform me that Ben had placed a play into his hands for our company to perform. I mused why Ben had not told me of this, but let it pass, for, when I thought on't further, I did surmise 'twas the wiser course for my fellows to judge Ben's play. Mayhap, I thought, Ben sees us twain as rivals only, though in a friendly fashion. Some several days passed, and Heminges came to me again. He asked me if Ben had shown me this play entitled *Every Man In his Humour*, which he had not. "Well," said John, "I do not know what to tell ye, for I and some of the fellows think it be a sorry work, and not worth the performing. Yet we would not offend Master Jonson, for we know ye and he be thick together." I said we were not so close as mine own judgment might be beclouded and eclipsed. John said he was gladdened thereat, and asked would I read the play for myself. So I did, whereat I was not greatly heartened, for I did see why my fellows did not desire to act it. Yet, upon deeper thought, it seemed there might be something that could be pieced together, and that mayhap it was the style of the play, or I know not what, that was amiss.

It was several more days before I encountered Ben at the Mitre, where I boarded him about his play. From the first his eyes blazed, his mouth quivered and worked, and choler smouldered deep beneath. Yet we did chat long and hard for two and three hours without a blow struck (which I feared). I asked him if he had seen or read my *Comedy of Errors* or *Two Men of Verona*, to which he said no, tho' he had heard something of them. I told him his *Every Man* was like unto those plays. Ben dismissed my words, and said if his play was like any other 'twas [George] Chapman's *Humourous Day's Mirth*.[9] I told him in sooth that I had not seen Chapman's play, but that his *Every Man* lacked a deal of plot, unlike mine. "And what is plot?" was all his reply, tho' I knew he had not considered his words, for he knows plot can be all. Before I said aught else, he told me roundly that I was but a thief of plots or of history, and all my plots did but sprawl and toss about, and wanted form and art and invention (and I know not what else). Thereafter we ne'er touched upon his work again, for he did naught but tell me his theories of what drama ought to be—viz. there be the unities of which Aristotle spake, wherein there is one action within one day within one place— viz. every man and character is composed of a humour, on the which he again discoursed so that my brain reeled and whirled. Then again on "art" and how I lacked this. I did endeavour to tell him I wrote as I found and could not be confined within the cell of his theorem. Much more was said beside to poor purpose and little remembrance.

Howsoever, I comprehend there might be some merit in his *Every Man*, and did admit that our company could amend its style to suit his work. Ben admitted his words might be set down better, and 'twould enlarge the jest were the play set not in Italy but in London. Yet he would fain have us present it as 'tis, and so it is to pass, for I told my fellows, as we lack any novelty, we might yet perform Ben's work. I am to play Lorenzo senior.[10]

19 JULY

A petition is out from the Vestry [of St. Saviour's, Southwark] to close down the playhouses in our parish.[11] What's to be done I know not, tho' Heminges seemeth not troubled for, says John, 'tis a matter oft mentioned but ne'er acted upon.

22 JULY

I met John Heminges in the street. He had been to the Stationers' Hall with our James Roberts so that my Jew play cannot be printed by others. John said it [publication] must be stayed for 'tis still popular, and we must not lose money by it. I care not, for I see little money from these books.[12]

4 AUGUST

The Lord Burleigh died this forenoon, which will please the Lord Essex, though the rumour is that Essex still finds no favour and will not attend the queen at court. Some folk say Burleigh was a sweet and well-mannered man, and in truth he hath served England and the queen well. Yet would I not have been his enemy for a thousand pound. 'Tis said the queen is grievous sick at his passing; she marks her own mortality in his death.[13] That's true enough, for all must die—man that is born of flesh—but the death of the queen will be of greater moment than aught else in this realm.

22 AUGUST

At Oxford, on my road home. I supped ale at the Blue Boar [Inn] this evening, & there was much talk of the news from Ireland; they say some 2,000 men or more were slain at Blackwater. 'Tis but a matter of time before the fort there must surrender.[14] But it is home and Stratford for me, at least a fortnight or more.

12 SEPTEMBER

Upon my return [to London] I have heard news to marvel and wonder at. From Harry [Southampton] came a letter to tell me that he hath married Mistress Vernon in secret, the lady being with child, and the queen much angered. Harry & I have scarce known each other these passing months, but he writes this news to me, and his kindness has stretched thus far. Well, I wish him joy, happiness, & whate'er he would wish himself. Methinks I shall seek out Kate.

> Being your slave, what should I do but tend
> Upon the hours and times of your desire?
> I have no precious time at all to spend,
> Nor services to do, till you require.
> Nor dare I chide the world-without-end hour
> Whilst I, my sovereign, watch the clock for you,
> Nor think the bitterness of absence sour
> When you have bid your servant once adieu.
> Nor dare I question with my jealous thought
> Where you may be, or your affairs suppose,
> But like a sad slave stay and think of naught
> Save where you are how happy you make those.
> So true a fool is love that, in your will
> Though you do anything, he thinks no ill. [Sonnet 57]

16 SEPTEMBER

This afternoon we gave Ben's *Every Man [in his Humour]* at the Curtain, and tho' the crowd did not thunder & roar, yet was there goodly approbation. So I am satisfied and gratified, since I persuaded the company 'twas worth performing. Ben is heartily cheered, & says he hath more plays yet to pen. Leastways he seemed not angered with the world, as he hath betimes.

20 SEPTEMBER

We played *Every Man* once more, me Lorenzo senior again, for this is as much as I care to enact these days. I fain would write but plays or poesy. After the play, as I went for food and ale, Tobie Matthew[15] fell awalking with me in the street, though the reason for this was a mystery. I have not seen him since long past, & then in the company of Harry [Southampton], the Lord Essex, and Sir Francis Bacon. His looks show he be Bacon's catamite, for he is still a smooth-faced youth and somewhat womanish. Matthew told me he had seen Jonson's play and enjoyed it, though he could see where it wants improvement and amendment. Then he extolled the virtues of mine own works that he professed to seeing, to being enamoured with them. After, he made compare of me with Bacon—our incomparable abilities of mind and sprouting invention, our elegant felicity of expression, our ravishing way with words. "Master Shakespeare," quoth he, "your words are a very fantastical banquet with so many strange delights." Then he spoke of how the strains of poets' wit beguile soft & human minds, and much more thus of a flattering and insinuating kind. By now we had happened upon an inn, and I asked him if he would take a cup of wine with me, to which he readily acceded. So we drank and fell to chatting the while, and 'twas then his purpose unfolded. He admires me so like Bacon that he would have me use him as my bum-boy as well, for he sought some kind of union of the mind through the body. I confess his flattering whiles seduced me, and later I fulfilled what he desired. Mayhap I should repent me such unallowable pleasures, and perchance I may be cut off even in the blossoms of my sin. But I fear the sweet hour I spent with Tobie might make me seek him out betimes.

22 SEPTEMBER

What shall I write now of Jonson? Today he duelled with Gabriel Spencer in Hoxton Fields, wounded him fatally. Now Ben lies in Newgate, imprisoned for manslaughter. Poor Gab, for he was a good actor and much loved of Henslowe.[16] Marlowe's evil star must have reigned over Ben, for 'twas in Hog Lane that Kit killed a man, & Gab had lodgings in Hog Lane.[17] Yet might it be but the mere coincidence, for doth our fortune lie all in the stars?

24 SEPTEMBER

To St Leonard's Church [Shoreditch] where we buried Gabriel Spencer this forenoon. 'Tis but in death we find a man's worth, when he is no more. Vermiculi triumphi [worms victorious].

1 OCTOBER

"Well, you're a made man now, all right" said Tom Nashe this evening when he walked into the Mitre to drink ale with me. I told him I knew not what he meant. So then he stood, opened a book he was carrying, and declaimed for all the world to hear: "As Plautus and Seneca are accounted the best for comedy and tragedy among the Latins, so Shakespeare among the English is the most excellent in both kinds for the stage. For comedy, witness his *Gentlemen of Verona*, his *Errors*, his *Love's Labour's Lost*, his *Loves Labours Won*, his *Midsummer Night's Dream*, and his *Merchant of Venice*. For tragedy his *Richard the 2nd*, *Richard the 3rd*, *Henry the 4th*, *King John*, *Titus Andronicus*, and his *Romeo and Juliet*. As Epius Stolo said, that the Muses would speak with Plautus' tongue, if they would speak Latin, so I say that the Muses would speak Shakespeare's fine filed phrase, if they would speak English." When Tom had done, he showed me the book, *Palladis Tamia*, writ by one Francis Meres.[18] "Well," I said to Tom, "'tis fine to hear such praise, though as you know I ne'er had a hand in this *Love's Labours Won*. I' faith I've never heard of such a play; perchance this Meres is confused or his memory faulty, or some other wrote it." I sat awhile and read here and there. "Why, Tom, I perceive now why you show me this book, so that I might see these fine words: 'As Actaeon was worried of his own hounds: so is Tom Nashe of his *Isle of Dogs*. Yet God forbid that so brave a wit should so basely perish; thine are but paper dogs, neither is thy banishment like Ovid's, eternally to converse with the barbarous Getes. Therefore comfort thyself sweet Tom with Cicero's glorious return to Rome.'" Tom coughed and smiled a little. Then I said, "And behold, Tom, this Meres puts you down as amongst the best for comedy. Here is your name straight after mine!" "Indeed," said Tom, "yet hath he placed [Robert] Greene afore ye!" Tom laughed loudly at this. "Ay," I said, "but here am I also amongst the best for tragedy with [Thomas] Kyd before me in which there is no disgrace. And Jonson is here too." Then I came across my friend and fellow countryman, Michael Drayton. "Now, Tom, here is fine discernment: 'Michael Drayton a man of virtuous disposition, honest conversation, and well governed carriage, which is almost miraculous among good wits in these declining and corrupt times, when there is nothing but roguery in villainous man.' And Meres hath taken my very words!"[19] We passed some time thus which made the evening pleasant enough, & I do confess to no little pride that my work is extolled for all the world to see.

6 OCTOBER

This forenoon I walked to the Old Bailey where Ben Jonson was arraigned for murdering Gabriel Spencer some two weeks or more past. I feared greatly for Ben as there was little contention as to what had passed between him & Spencer. Ben said the two of them had been drinking for some while when they got to talking of the Admiral's Men and of the Lord

Chamberlain's. Each held the other was the better company of actors, Ben being stoutly for us, the Chamberlain's. After more argument, they both became heated and challenged t'other to a duel. Ben claimed Spencer had the advantage of youth and a sword some ten or twelve inches longer than his own, and, besides, Spencer wounded him in his arm. Spencer received a fatal wound on his right side some six inches deep and an inch wide. Then came for me a moment of true wonder and amazement. Ben told the judge Gabriel's final words were "the hurt is not so deep as a well, nor so wide as a church door; but 'tis enough, 'twill serve." Verily I almost swooned and fell down at these my own words.[20] That a man might remember them at his moment of death caused my head to turn and whirl. I must have remained thus dazed for some while, for next I heard the judge asking Ben if there were any words further he wished to say before he pronounced the sentence of death. In a trice Ben pleaded the benefit of clergy, and so a Bible was brought forth for him to read the neck-verse in Latin, which the judge made him translate also.[21] So Ben was saved from Tyburn's halter, but he was still to be branded with a "T" so he shall not 'scape Tyburn again. And all his goods are confiscate. He left the Bailey smiling, and I had thought to see him today, but he is not come.

7 OCTOBER

Jonson was here today, but briefly. He returns to his trade (he hath been a mortar treader, tho' he cares not for it), for he have great want of money after being in prison.[22] He has nothing put by and no play writ. I offered him a crown or two, but he refused, and that none too pleasantly. In sooth, he is a difficult man, though he hath been in prison and must be excused I suppose—yet hot-tempered, and a murderer. Such is the spirit of the time.

25 OCTOBER

With marvellous great fortune this forenoon I came upon Dick Quiney walking in Thames Street. He had writ me a letter, which I had by me, and thus was I able to assuage his troubles with the loan of some money. He was pressed about with several matters and hastened on his business, though we would fain have passed more time together.[23] How unlike Jonson Dick was, for he heaped his thanks upon me.

28 OCTOBER

More rumours abound—two thousand or more men are to be impressed and sent to Ireland, from where I doubt but few poor souls may return. This war in Ireland is a foolish business, & peradventure will ne'er be won.

8 NOVEMBER

This even I was wandering idly down alleyways and streets, caring little where I strayed. I thought on whether I should suffer Jonson, or mayhap Tom Nashe, to read what I finished writing this morn. After some hour or so thus, I turned into a tavern for food and wine. As I waited for some mutton stew to be set before me, I fell into conversation with a delicate gentleman who wrote oft in his tables. His name was John Chamberlain,[24] & a palpable gossip because, for no cause or reason, he began to tell me of all manner of doings at Court & elsewhere. "Sir Edward Coke, you know," he said, "did yesterday marry the Lady Hatton to the great admiration of all men."[25] I asked him why. "Why? Indeed, you well may ask why. For in truth, Lady Hatton, who is but twenty years of age, hath received many large and likely offers for her hand in marriage; yet she declines herself to a man of Coke's quality. I dare be bound there is much mystery withal." Thus I enquired of him what such a mystery might be. "Indeed it must be so, for his first wife is but some several weeks dead. For the second, the banns of marriage were not published, & such ceremony as took place was not in church. Your third mystery is that the marriage should have been conducted afore noon, yet 'twas done at night." "Indeed," I said, "'twas not done in a straightforward manner." "Indeed, not," said Chamberlain. "And there are those that opine the lady is with child, but that Sir Edward be not the father. Yea, that the true father be one of the lady's former servants, on whose lips she tendered her passionate service." I said, "'Tis but a common, workaday occurrence; yet it is the more reprehensible in the high and mighty. Still, they are fast married." While this Chamberlain nodded, and supped on some wine, my remembrance fleeted to that warm summer so many years ago, nearly twenty years past, when Anne and myself were much like unto this Attorney General and his lady. Save our outward trappings, where lies the difference? And our human nature is, in our thirsty base instinct, all but the same.

"I have in mind I have seen you before," Chamberlain said, rousing me from my musing. "Indeed you may have, sir," I replied, "for I am an actor with the Lord Chamberlain's Men, and I am the writer of some several dramatic works." "Indeed, and now I recall. You must be Master Shakespeare and your plays, such as I have witnessed, have given much pleasure. Might it be that some new work engages you?" I told him that, by curious chance, I had that very morning completed my newest play, which I call *Much Ado About Nothing*. "Do you mean, by that," he said, "nothing or noting?" I smiled, and replied that he had caught my whole plan and purpose straightaway for by "nothing" I mean nothing and noting.[26] "Indeed, Master Shakespeare. And yet am I not amazed by this, for in your work, such as I have seen, you have always a ready and quick wit. May I be so bold as to ask you to relate this newest work, if I may be privy to it?" And thus I told him: "As is oft my practise, the stories I tell are such as have been told before many a time and oft, and, like the marriage of the Attorney General, common amongst many folk. One tale tells of Claudio who rejects his bride, Hero, because he is deceived that she hath been unchaste. The deceiver is a villain, self-proclaimed, called Don John. His machination is exposed by a Constable, one Dogberry and his watch [Verges], though they are but low comedians. T'other tale tells of two others, Beatrice and Benedick, who ne'er meet but there's a skirmish of wit between them [1.1.55]. And yet beneath this battle lies true love, and by friendly deceptions they are tricked. All ends well for all." "I mean no offence," he said, "but this plot you describe is but a commonplace one." I agreed, and said such was the case with most of our fictions; the trick lies in clothing the old in new garments, so to speak, so that all appears fresher than before. In this play I desire, I told him, to point to what is appearance, what reality, and towards that end I employ some several devices— masks, disguises, deceit, eavesdropping, looks, words, wit, all "seeming truth" [2.2.41] of all variety that might be employed. "Well," he said, "this is indeed of great interest, though as you say, it will be the final outward garment that will lend the inner truth. And who shall be the players? Is that settled upon?" I told him that was not so, for as I had said, the ink was but fresh upon the page this morning, and I had yet to show the play to my fellows. "But surely, when you write, you have someone in your mind's eye?" I told him that such was oft the case because our company hath been together these several years, and each man hath a line in the way of acting that suiteth him more properly. "Dick Burbage is like to be Claudio, tho' Benedick would suit him as well. If Burbage be not Benedick, then Tom Pope might enact the role, for tho' Tom would be a fine Dogberry, 'tis likely Will Kempe will seize upon Dogberry, for Verges is not sufficient enow for him. So our Dick Cowley will be Verges, I think." "Ah, ah," he broke in, "I have seen Kempe as Falstaff, tho' methinks he did enact Falstaff too low at times, yet did the groundlings love him." "Indeed, forsooth." Then I told him, "As for the rest, I see Gus Phillips as the villain Don John (tho' in the flesh Gus is gentle enough). What boys we have are fine enough, yea pert enow for the ladies, if their voices be not broken when we come to act the play." "Well, master Shakespeare," said Chamberlain, "I may remark I have passed a most interesting hour with you, and I am much informed on your plays. You may look for me when this *Ado* of yours comes to the stage. I wish you joy & a long life." And so he left me to my mutton stew which had now become chill and greasy. Yet, in telling him all, I have decided I have no need to show the thing to Ben or to Tom; it is as ready & prepared as may be.

3 DECEMBER

Today the Coroner's inquest on Gabriel Spencer, & I know not why I went to listen, save I knew him & Jonson. Again I heard how Ben had killed him in a paltry argument. And they would mention how Spencer had killed James Feake close on two years ago.[27] Mayhap this was to say some providence divine o'errules us. Before the inquest much gossip on the poor condition of our soldiers in Ireland, and all the desperate events there. Not for a thousand pounds would I set one foot in that benighted land, though there be many men seek fame, fortune and glory there.

10 DECEMBER

Bitter cold weather; the frosts are so great even the Thames itself has frozen over at London Bridge. 'Tis a brave soul that might walk upon the ice. But I munn think on *Much Ado*, for we are to give it at Court come January. I muse whether Dick's [Burbage] mind be on this and t'other plays we are to perform. Of late he and Cuthbert have been strange and quiet as though fearful of shadows of some untimely-parted ghosts. I know not what this might portend.

12 DECEMBER

Now is the mystery made plain. Yesterday Cuthbert Burbage called several of us together at Heminges' house where were assembled some others I knew not. My fellows were Cuthbert & Dick Burbage, Heminges, Phillips, Pope, and Kempe. Cuthbert named the others. There was William Smith, a friend of the Burbages, who hailed from Waltham Cross; one Peter Street, a master carpenter. Finally three from Heminges' parish, Nicholas Brend, Thomas Savage, and William Leveson.[28] Cuthbert stated the case plainly. "All of you know that Giles Allen will not sign a lease for the Theatre, tho' I have tried patiently with him for these many months past. I offered new terms and a hundred pounds more, but, when I met Allen at the George Inn in Shoreditch, I knew he did not mean well, nor was he acting in good faith. He would not accept Dick as a surety, &, in brief, we quarrelled, & there'll be no reconcilement. Thus, Dick and myself have spoken with William Smith here who is willing to provide some portion of money required for a new venture—videlicet, to tear down the Theatre, as our old lease provides & build another. This will carpenter Street and his men do for us. They will carry the timbers across the river [Thames] to Southwark and there rebuild our theatre." Cuthbert ceased, and Nicholas Brend spoke. "My father died this past September leaving me all he possessed, which includes some land on the Bankside, the which I am willing to lease unto you. I have spoke with Cuthbert & Dick on the matter, & the terms we agreed were a lease upon the land for thirty-one years for £14 10s per annum. If all here agree to this compact we can sign & ratify the documents after Christmas, for I shall have other business to conduct before then."

At this Kempe broke in. "Ay, this is well & good, Cuthbert. But what I want to know is why you want us here," he said, pointing to myself and our fellow actors. Cuthbert laughed. "Why, Will, we want your money. For you see, while Master Smith may provide so much, it sufficeth not. Indeed, it is maybe half of what is wanted. And you know we have had some hard times these several years past." "Ay," murmured Kempe, "that's true enough." "Well," said Cuthbert, "our idea comes to this. If you, Will, along with John, Gus, Tom, and Will Shakespeare here could find money enough to equal what we, myself, Dick, & Master Smith provide, then should we all be partnered in this venture." At this my own mind began to whirl for, of a sudden, I could foresee what might become of this adventure, though I thought there yet might be dangers unknowable. So while the others were nodding agreement and talking amongst themselves, I said "Ay, Cuthbert, this hath the mark of a grand plan. Yet, how will this idea work?" "I knew, Will, that you would ask that, but I beg you trust me that all will be made plain and simple. We shall all become sharers. Dick and I will have half, while you five shall have the other half. Your share, Will, shall thus be one tenth. You shall provide one tenth of what is needed, and shall gain one tenth of the profit. Masters Leveson and Savage here have agreed to be your trustees, if you will have them, and I think you may. Thus, as I think ye will know Will, you and your four fellows may bequeath your share to your own heirs when, God in heaven forbid it be not soon, you shall die." I saw swiftly that Cuthbert had thought mightily about all this, and had determined the best course for himself and his brother, and for us all. And here was the chance for my fortune to be made, if we prosper. "Well," I said, "I doubt not, Cuthbert, that you have thought on this compact, and know all these men to be honourable. For my part, I am agreed and will provide my portion." At a clap, the others agreed as well, and thus was the matter settled. I tremble now at what the future might be; yet might it be glorious too, with money to boot.

18 DECEMBER

E'en though it is bitter cold in my closet, a thaw hath begun.

29 DECEMBER

Yesterday a heavy snow fell all round about. At the appointed hour, late in the night that we might be not dogged with company and our devices known, I went to aid Dick & Cuthbert at the Theatre. The carpenter Street and some ten or twelve men were there already breaking & tearing down the timbers. These they stacked on carts which carried them away to a wharf Street hath by the river. Tho' the river be frozen again, the ice could not support the weight of the carts (which they had thought at first to do). So they will await another time, and take the carts over to Southwark another way. In the midst of their labours, one of Giles Allen's agents, Henry Johnson, appeared and asked what we did. Cuthbert told him the timbers were in need of repair (this in the dead of night!). Whether or no he believed Cuthbert, Johnson went away. It seems it will be a long, hard task.

1599

While Shakespeare's growing fame is recorded in verse by other poets, the plan to build the Globe is executed and fulfilled by mid-year; Julius Caesar *is the triumphant first production there. Earlier, Shakespeare had scored successes with* Much Ado *and* Henry V, *the latter ending in a paean to the popular Essex even though he is a growing threat to the queen. In March Kempe's departure from the company leaves Shakespeare far from unhappy. The debates on drama between Shakespeare and Jonson grow more furious, and Jonson takes offence at parts of* Henry V. *Meanwhile, Shakespeare is uneasy at more extensive government censorship, and amends some plays accordingly. In September, the unauthorized return of Essex from his unsuccessful campaign in Ireland results in him being placed under house arrest. Jonson takes revenge on Shakespeare by satirizing him (and others) in his* Every Man Out of his Humour *that, surprisingly, Jonson wants Shakespeare's company to stage. Shakespeare answers Jonson and his dramatic theories by writing* As You Like It, *which gives Shakespeare's brother, Edmund, his big acting opportunity as Rosalind, a performance later much appreciated by the queen.*

16 JANUARY

Today with Ben Jonson to Westminster Abbey where Edmund Spenser was interred; he died three days ago [13 January]. Ben said it was for lack of bread he died, but other folk say he had but want of money, and yet Spenser had refused some twenty pieces of gold from my

Lord Essex. Leastways his grace hath borne the funeral expense (though his mind must be on the matter of Ireland for which he prepares daily, though Ireland may well be, as folk say, a cause forlorn that can but diminish his lordship's fortune & stature). Spenser's hearse was attended by several poets who threw their mournful elegies and poems (& the pens that wrote them) into his tomb, which is hard by that of Chaucer. As Ben & I made our way to the Mitre afterwards for food and drink, I called to mind what Barnfield had wrote but this year past & spoke the words to Ben:

"Live Spenser ever, in thy *Fairy Queen*:
Whose like (for deep conceit) was never seen.
Crowned mayst thou be, unto thy more renown,
(As King of Poets) with a laurel crown."[1]

Ben said those were, indeed, sweet words, and jested that I might have penned them myself. I told him they were, in sooth, fine, & I would not be ashamed entirely to call them mine own. At this Ben laughed, & said he did believe I could recall the lines because of what Barnfield had writ upon me. I feigned ignorance & innocence, this but a stratagem to see if Ben could recite what I knew he meant and that he did. "Why, sweet Will, none can forget his praises of ye:

And *Shakespeare* thou, whose honey-flowing vein,
(Pleasing the world) thy praises doth obtain.
Whose *Venus*, and whose *Lucrece* (sweet, and chaste)
Thy name in fame's immortal booke have placed.
Live ever you, at least in fame live ever:
Well may the body die, but fame dies never."

"Ben," I said, "I am right glad your memory can recall such fine phrases, tho' by my modesty, I swear I seek not after such praise. I am mindful that opinion's but a fool that makes us scan the outward habit for the inward man. And ye wot well that Master Barnfield doth praise [Samuel] Daniel and gentle Michael Drayton. Recall:

And Drayton, whose well-written tragedies,
And sweet epistles, soar thy fame to the skies,
Thy learned name, is equal to the rest;

Whose stately numbers are so well addressed."

Ben agreed, & by now we had reached the Mitre, where we passed two or more hours musing on Spenser & the rest of our tribe. Whether 'twas the wine or the lateness of the hour I know not, but I lay down in bed quite knit in a sorrow-wreathen knot.

20 JANUARY

Late this eve, so that it be in secret, carpenter [Peter] Street and his men moved the timbers of the Theatre (that they took down some several days ago) over to the Bankside, where our new playhouse is to be built. I tremble that Dick & Cuthbert Burbage be so bold & full of high resolve, but we are all in the business together and thrive we must. I have fixed upon my next two plays. One [*Henry V*] shall conclude the chronicle of the English kings upon which I determined a long time past. For the other [*Julius Caesar*] I look to Roman history which hath interested me, and wherein human ambition may be seen, yet more remote so that mayhap events and actions be more elevated. Perchance the time is ripe for such a tragedy that be no mere history.

[FEBRUARY]

E'en though I do believe 'tis better to be neither a borrower nor a lender, yet policy must betimes sit above a still and quiet conscience. Thus have I sent ten pounds for Jonson's relief.[2]

21 FEBRUARY

Yester night at the Court at Richmond we played *Much Ado* to much approbation.[3] The wit-match between Benedick & Beatrice pleased greatly the queen and those nobles & other guests there assembled. Dick [Burbage] was called forth by Her Majesty and praised, tho' I was not asked for (as in times past), whereat I trouble not, for my part is but to bow low & mumble. Today we gathered to sign the tripartite lease for the new playhouse.[4] Though I have forebodings at such a mighty enterprise, yet doth it stir my soul to thoughts of greatness. [Peter] Street and his men have begun to erect the timbers, though the ground is hard with frost and they may do little work for some while. I read Plutarch's lives of famous Romans,[5] and 'tis fertile ground for one play I have in mind. Julius Caesar and his ambition catch the imagination—his assassination is a scene made ready for our stage. After his death, the struggle of those rivals who would lead and succeed him be the very heart and soul of conflict, of drama. Yet I must see these Romans as men afore all else.

27 FEBRUARY

To St. Mary's, Aldermanbury, where Henry Condell's daughter was baptized. The girl, but a wee, weakling thing, they named for Henry's wife, Elizabeth. John [Heminges] was jocund with Henry for, said he, conceiving matters before their due time.[6] I laughed, though I remembered one summer's day so many years ago when Anne & I went to it blithe and merry together ("Shall I compare thee to a summer's day"— Lord, what a green unlettered child o' th' time was I then). Henry & his Elizabeth are happy together, & hang the one upon the other as Anne & I have never done—leastways, rarely. Food and ale aplenty.

1 MARCH

Yester even at the Mermaid with Tom [Nashe], Ben [Jonson], & Dick [Burbage] where we chatted long on the business of our profession. As ever, Ben would preach and have us to write plays after his own style, the which he urged the more he drank. I told him his way was well enough for him, but I must write after my own fashion, and that I had our company to write for and to think on. Dick said, "Will has a fair point, Ben, for here we are abuilding our new playhouse in which all have their part. Folk relish what Will hath done and I have acted, so it stands to common reason we must needs give them what they like." "Well," replied Ben, "they like my plays well enough too." "Indeed, that is so," I said, "and there is room enow for all our handiwork. Consider, only the other day, Tom Dekker allowed me to read some part of a new play he is writing which he calls *The Shoemakers' Holiday*."[7] "Why, consumption catch him," snarled Ben, "that man is naught but a dresser-up of plays. Like a jackdaw he does but steal and thieve." "If that be the case, Ben," I said, "then Tom Dekker and I are two of a sort, for is it not true that my plots, well all but one or two, are ta'en from the work of others' hands? Even now I am writing a play about Henry V and still another on Julius Caesar. So I must be a thief too. I fish in my neighbour's pond." "You do a deal more than Dekker, even though I care not greatly for some of your work. Why, the play you mention, this *Shoemakers' Holiday*—he has but stole that from Tom Deloney.[8] The man is but a milk sop, and the catalogue of his endowments is as brief as my farts." "Nay, Ben. As ever you are too harsh," I said. "Tom Dekker is kindliness itself and detests all harm unto others, even unto animals. He never has any money, for he will give it all away." Ben scowled, but said nothing. "Well, Ben, Dekker's play is, I think, all very well and good. 'Tis not like yours, for he is not you. Nor yet is it like mine. He peoples his stage with gentle folk whom the audience may applaud. And as for stealing, well, the truth is, I could not think how to begin my play on Julius Caesar, but reading Tom's play gave me an idea. So, before bringing on Caesar & the other senators and nobles, I have writ a scene about lowly folk who ply their craft daily, who see humour in life, and who rejoice in the triumphs of their great leaders. These lowly folk be cobblers, Ben, for which I thank Dekker."[9] "Things cobbled don't last," Ben said &, roaring, almost broke his heart with extreme laughter at his jest. "Well, for all that," said Dick, "I want to hear Will tell more of these plays, for we will need fresh matter when the new theatre is complete, & likely before that, for we still have our bread to earn. What parts do you have for me, Will?" "I think, Dick," I said, "you shall be Mark Antony in the one and Henry in the other. I have some fine speeches in mind for them both. Indeed, I warrant you, it hath been passing strange to me that both plays be much alike. I have been thinking on kingship and politics, as mayhap we all have, since our queen hath no heir direct (nor will she ever now) and will not name an heir, though many think it will be James of Scotland." "There's always the fine Earl of Essex," quipped Tom, "yet whether he is in favour or out is a question devoutly to be pondered." "Well, Tom," I said, "you have, with thy sharp wit, placed thy finger on my very thoughts and what I may put in the plays. For Henry doth owe his kingship to his father, he that deposed Richard II. And you remember the troubles Henry IV had, which Richard foretold, for those that helped him ascend the throne were not satisfied with their portion and lot. This I will show in *Henry V* too, for Henry deals swift & harsh with traitors that confederate with France [*Henry V*, 2.2]." "Well, in that he is right," said Dick, "for swiftness is all in such matters." "Ay," I said, "but as I think, & as I read in Holinshed & such, Henry, tho' brave & so on, is turned a thoughtful king, now his wayward days are done. He thinks on kingship and remembers Richard II, and atones for his misdeeds [4.1.216ff]. Henry would make good amends for all the past, would give all for England, would reclaim parts of France. Henry inspires his followers (and, Dick, this you will savour) through fine speeches that ring upon the air—leastways, I trust they will, & will be remembered so." "So," said Ben, "this is to be naught but hollowness, piled up anaphora and such, that you take so much to your bosom." I laughed. "Why, Ben, I had not thought you listened so closely to my paltry words, stolen from others, tho' you are in the right. But no, the Henry I put upon the stage shall be a known patriot, a sound lover of his country."[10] "Ay," said Dick, "we need such stuff as that in the midst of all our troubles in Ireland, where so many go to find their graves." "In sooth, Dick," I said, "such had crossed my mind. I think the groundlings will approve the comic scenes because in them are the common sort of folk as were in *Henry IV*—Pistol, Nym, Bardolph, Mistress Quickly, and, for Kempe, Falstaff, tho' he be a knight." "Well," said Nashe, "I see you ply and play Falstaff for all he is worth, leastways for all Kempe will play him. Nay, frown not, Will. No one here condemns thee, for Falstaff and Kempe are what people want, even Her Majesty." I remained silent, tho' somewhat angry, for, if I could, I would not have Falstaff or Kempe, yet what Nashe said was all too true. For awhile, all were quiet—mayhap thinking on Kempe, Falstaff, Essex, or I know not what. We commanded more ale and wine.

'Twas Dick broke our reveries. "Well, Will, what of this other play on Julius Caesar? You say you write on him together with Henry? It would be a fine thing if both plays were in readiness for the new playhouse, tho' we shall still want novelties whiles we remain at the Curtain." So I told them about the Julius Caesar play, and how like some of it was to Henry V—of those rivals who are jealous of Caesar and who would have his place—tho' there is the noble Brutus, a man of conscience. I said, "Much is like our own history, for the question is who should rule—a tyrant such as Caesar has become just before his death, or others such as Cassius or Brutus who cleave to other views. You remember such was the debate in *Richard II*." Dick, at least, nodded his head. I looked at him & said, "And there is Antony who, leastways on the outside, is very like Henry V—fine, good speeches, and he is loved by the plebeians.[11] Yet who makes the fairest show means most deceit—Antony is a cynic for he thinks naught of holding sway by any device, trick or practice. Mayhap that is like Henry who fights because his bishops interpret Salic law as Henry desires [1.2]. Then, too, both men win memorable battles, at Agincourt and Philippi, and return to rule in triumph."[12] Ben quaffed down some ale & snorted, "And which pond have ye fished & robbed for this mighty work?" I laughed. "Ben, ye will be ever quarrelsome, tho' thou shalt not anger me, for ye know well, as I have said once this evening, I care not where the seed comes from. It so hap I have read Sir Thomas North's translation of Plutarch's *Lives*, and have taken, stole you may call it, what I need—indeed, there be so much in North that needs little amending for our stage." "So, then," said Ben, "you're to give us an English play and a Roman play that are so alike they might well be as one." Again I laughed. "Ben, you love to taunt, fleer, sneer, and flout me in the teeth with your scorns, and why I do remain friends with ye, I know not. But, no, they are to be quite unlike each other. I know ye would have me present some still thing that doth conform to your unities, or whatever ye call them." Ben scowled. "Scowl all you want, Ben, but I write as I feel. The Caesar play will be quite ordinary, which is an irony because it is in Roman time. Yet the Roman additions to our costumes will suffice, and folk will believe they are in Rome. For *Henry V* I have in mind another notion, the one I used in part in *Romeo*

& Juliet. Before each act there shall be a Chorus which shall invoke the audience's imagination and then carry folk away to France or another part of England. This Chorus shall also provide aught else needful to know." Ben groaned and said, "The good Lord spare us from such Choruses. But, doubtless, it will be you that shall be the Chorus."[13] "Of course, Ben, of course, for you know I have not the fine art of acting as does Dick here. Yet can I address well the multitude, those your penny stinkards. But your delight shall be I will play only a poet in *Julius Caesar*—I shall be Cinna the poet that is mistook for another Cinna, and is murdered by the rabblement!" "They shall be such sinners for murdering Cinnas," quipped Tom. All laughed, and shortly after I came home, knowing now what I shall do, for all Ben's sneering.

12 MARCH

The news is that the Lord Essex hath received his commission from the queen to go forth into Ireland. Harry [Southampton] goes with him, & I fear for his safety; how like winter his absence will seem. And what of the thousands upon thousands of soldiers that go with them, and the multitudes on horseback? I doubt our cause be just because we fight the Irish in their own land.

15 MARCH

Kempe hath quit our company, and tho' there be others that be sorry, I cannot say so. Oft he made wanton with my words & those parts I had writ for him. Yet, take him all in all, he was not a thing too bad for report, and in sooth he was popular with the multitude. What he does now or where he goes, I know not. Well, enough of Kempe, though I must amend *Henry V*, which may be accomplished briefly—Falstaff shall die, & Falstaff's death shall be but reported to others [2.1, 2.3]; the scene shall sound a comic note, & he shall come no more to make 'em laugh. And so farewell Falstaff, farewell Kempe!

27 MARCH

Today the Lord Essex and Harry [Southampton] left London to quell & conclude Tyrone's rebellion in Ireland. Lord, what a magnificent sight it was to behold. Essex, on horseback, along with Harry, and all his men, departed about two o'clock from Walsingham House, and then they rode through Cheapside and thence to Islington. Everywhere the people pressed to see Essex; they cried "God save your worship," and "God preserve your honour," and gave loud huzzas—some folk followed him for miles. Later I spoke to a man who had followed Essex through Islington where, he told me, an amazing thunderstorm burst forth, with hail and lightning, which some in the crowd took as an evil omen. Yet, said the man, Essex smiled bravely on those followers cheering him. "If any man in all of England can right our wrongs & redress our grievances, the Earl be that man," he said. This set my mind to thinking of how it is the common folk hold Essex in their hearts, how he opens the eyes of expectation, & how like my Henry V he is—popular, inspiring all manner of folk—thus I might add some lines to my play [*Henry V*] which recall to mind this joyous day. Then might the hearts of the multitude be gladdened, & not least, the play be popular to boot. Cheer Essex, cheer my handiwork.[14]

11 APRIL

Condell's joy hath turned to grief, a grief so great that no supporter but the huge firm earth can hold it up.[15] Death & time are ever at our backs in this world of decay. This adage Henry knows well enow, but 'tis no consolation now his darling child is gone and he is left darkling. There cannot be a pinch in death more sharp than this is.

12 APRIL

Today I was up early, for I had not slept one wink, thinking on Henry's grief. I saw Dick Burbage who told me *Henry V* is to be preferred while we yet remain at the Curtain. This is but small trouble—I shall make amendment to my prologue that shall suit.[16]

26 APRIL

My baptismal day proved a good omen. This afternoon we played *Henry V* at the Curtain, and early in the day came news that the Lord Essex, after a dangerous rough crossing of the sea to Ireland, had landed safely in Dublin some 12 days ago. Thus it seemed expectation did sit in the air as the multitude gathered to watch our entertainment. Before we began, I could hear the whole playhouse abuzz with excitement, and I caught Essex's name many times. I rejoiced that I had thought to laud his lordship's triumphal departure. I was right pleased with my choruses—I spoke my best, and it seemed that in sooth the auditors were transported across the sea to the fields of France. Yet was my role but small compared with what Dick [Burbage] did achieve. His Henry was glorious beyond compare, and how the crowd, roaring and cheering all the while, loved him—the more so when he did rouse the soldiers before Agincourt. That proved a mighty speech indeed. But the loudest plaudits of all came when I spoke of Essex in the fifth chorus [lines 30–34]; I thought the crowd would ne'er cease. Sam Gilburne was a pretty Katherine. One moment there was when I thought we might falter and stumble, and this I might well have foretold—when Mistress Quickly said "Falstaff he is dead" [2.3.5]. The crowd became as silent as a churchyard at midnight, and then a voice called out "Poor wretch, poor Falstaff," which was greeted with a universal "aye, aye" and the like. Some men began to weep when she said "'a babbled of green fields" [2.3.16]. Yet the moment passed when Quickly said Falstaff had not spoken against women, & had "talked of the whore of Babylon" [2.3.34]—at which some laughed.

After we had sent the audience on its way, happy in our English triumphs, I went to the Bunch of Grapes for ale and food. There, though I had not expected to see them, I found Nashe & Jonson. I braced myself for whatever jests and gibes they had prepared, for I had seen them amongst the groundlings. Ben began, "A stage, a stage, my kingdom for a stage. Where are those princes that would be seen swelling to become beholden monarchs."[17] I laughed for 'twas a good jest, and I could see Ben's eyes twinkle, which showed he was in good spirits. "I see, Ben," I said, "thou hast, like an attentive schoolboy, listened closely to my words, though the ordering of their going forth thou hast mangled right royally. Yet I trust they did teach thee much this afternoon." "They taught me Essex is like to return from Ireland and be our monarch." "Nay, Ben," I said anxiously, "do not say that, for these are not the best of times for a man to speak of his mind freely, even if there be a measure of truth in your words." Ben said, "Well, there's many folk that were at the theatre this afternoon who may desire Essex as their king, though I know you mentioned him but to draw forth loud huzzas, plaudits, and such like." "So you think me but a cynic?" I asked. "Well, I dunno," said Ben, " but peradventure thou art full of false modesty. I mean that Epilogue ('twas a sonnet, was it not?) with its 'all-unable pen' and its 'bending author.' I' faith, I thought you would bend so low as to touch the stage, &, to boot, with hands outstretched." Again I laughed. "Ben, your observation is most acute, for that epilogue is a sonnet, and a sonnet is art, and by that I mean to remind the multitude of the fiction they have witnessed. And yet my play is true, well, as true as any history may be. And as for the rest, it is but the style to be modest and to supplicate for applause."[18]

At this moment, Tom broke in and said, "I see you found your affection again for the Welsh—Fluellen was his name?" I replied, "You know I hold the Welsh in warm regard, but you did surely note that on this occasion there was a Scotsman and an Irishman, as well as a Welshman [3.2], as well as plenty of English." "Then," said Tom, "is our realm safe from all our enemies, though some of the Irish do seem to be fighting the Lord Essex and his men." "I write of better times," I said. "And, if you please, now let us drink and eat, for you will but weary me if you continue thus—jesting or no." "All in good time," said Ben, his eyes narrowing, "after you have told me what you mean by that quarrelsome creation, Corporal Nym." "Well, Ben," I replied, "I would think you might see the humour of him, for is not Nym after the kind of characters you write?"[19] "I see that well enough, Will," Ben said somewhat grim, "and I am hoist with mine own petard. Ay, indeed. Well, we shall wait and see what the future may bring, eh?" "Now, Ben, have good cheer. 'Tis all in good sport. Let's fall to and eat and drink." Yet I did not say to Ben that, like Nym, he is quarrelsome, given to fighting (what of Gabriel Spencer?), choleric, & he hath been a soldier. In truth, were I like Ben, I'd throw myself away. To bed long past midnight.

11 MAY

Today I chanced upon Tom Dekker in the street. He was much pleased that Edward Pearce, with whom he is friendly, hath been made Master of the Children of Paul's, for Tom thinks Pearce will seek more plays from Tom. The old Master still lives, but is sorely sick.[20]

16 MAY

They say Sir Thomas Sackville, that wrote *Gorboduc*, is made the Lord Treasurer. I recall the play only a little, but remember 'twas he that told Mary her doom.[21] Our playhouse is now all but complete, and will be a wondrous place, I do believe. Ben Jonson says it is but forced out of a marsh and flanked by ditches, which is true enow, tho' I think he says that from envy. I confess Maiden Lane, where it stands, is a long straggling place, and there are ditches and such. Howsoe'er, folk may reach our Globe over the [London] bridge and need take a waterman [ferry] only if they so desire. As Dick said, "If they can get hither easy, they will come more often." Cuthbert Burbage thinks to call it the Globe & have some emblem with Hercules holding up the world.[22] It is a fine conceit, tho' there is little in a name. Cuthbert hath consulted with an astrologer to discover a date propitious for our first performance. If all goes well with our preparations, this shall be the 12th day of June, and my *Julius Caesar* the first play. This is well enow, for the piece is, like the playhouse, all but complete. For a jest, I have writ in another Poet for me to enact. He is to come in to tell Brutus and Cassius to be friends, which he says in jigging doggerel [4.3.124–38]. The jest is that such is the Gospel for Barnaby Bright, which the multitude may recall, leastways some folk may.[23]

1 JUNE

This day the Bishop [of London] set forth an order that satires shall be prohibited. What hath occasioned this decree, I know not, yet it seems such things come to pass time & again. Tho' he wore a brow of distraction, Jonson says he is untroubled, though he hath greater cause than I. I heard from Tom Nashe that all his satires are banned and are to be burned.

5 JUNE

Yesterday some dozen books or more were burned at the Stationers' Hall; the Archbishop [of Canterbury] did order it. Marlowe's *Amores* was amongst them, but I know not if Nashe's books were burned. What troubleth me is one book burned was on Henry IV which had offended Her Majesty because it was dedicated to Essex.[24] Tho' I have not read it, Nashe says parts of it recall my *Richard II*, and that Her Majesty must fear Essex will usurp her. Whatever may be, I have removed the choruses and such from *Henry V* so there shall be no note of Essex.[25] I fear not for my *Julius Caesar*, for it is a Roman play, e'en if its politics lie close to home. I must be ever mindful the authorities are close at hand, and we must not give offense if we are to coin money—and not be thrown into prison.

7 JUNE

There be affairs that surpass my comprehending, question them tho' I may. Yesterday, John Day stabbed Henry Porter with a rapier near his heart and killed him.[26] Why they quarrelled I know not, though quarrel they did. Poets are in constant trouble: poor Kit Marlowe was murdered, Ben [Jonson] killed Gab Spencer, and contention & argument abound. Yet sure there is room for all, work aplenty for all, if the plague not kill us, or the city close not down the playhouses. So for what reason must they fight? Ben would say 'tis their humour, some strange infection that hath befallen them, or some such, & I do believe he may be right.

12 JUNE

The flag flew, the trumpet blew, the sun shone bright and fair, our playhouse, our Globe, opened and all the world—*totus mundus!*—was there today to see our company. What a press and noise of people there was, I could scarce believe it—so many folk did crowd in, we were an half hour late in beginning our performance. Yet all this augured well, as Cuthbert Burbage had foretold it would, and we did not have to beware the Ides of June [13th]. The multitude was rapt withal by my play [*Julius Caesar*]—by times they cheered Caesar, then Brutus, then Mark Antony, as I had devised! John Heminges made a haughty, regal Caesar—I had not thought he could be the tyrant, yet he was. His murder caused much sensation, for I think John had about him some two or three bladders of pig's blood, when one would suffice—so the blood flowed freely, and indeed the conspirators bathed deep in Caesar's blood. Gus [Phillips] was a sinewy Cassius—he did insinuate like a snake, artful and crafty. Tom Pope as Casca, Will Sly as Octavius, both good and commendable. Yet much fell to Dick [Burbage] as Brutus, so noble and right—his nature too noble for this world—his suicide made me weep, for I felt most truly "this was the noblest Roman of them all" [5.5.68]. It scarce behooves me to write of Dick, for all his roles become him. Henry [Condell] *was,* as I have not seen him before in his roles, Mark Antony. And Lord how the crowd rose to his speech before the plebeians [3.2.72ff]. I do believe most thoroughly the groundlings thought *they* were the Roman plebeians, that Antony spoke to them. This is as our dramatic art should be—those that see and listen become as one with those who act before them. A glorious day—triumph!!

30 JUNE

I fell into chat at the Bell Inn with a man lately returned from Ireland and who was full of news. Harry [Southampton] was made and then un-made Essex's General of the Horse, why the man knew not, but said rumour had it the Queen is highly displeased with everything Essex hath done or, the rather, hath not done. Some rebels have been killed, he said, but in the main, affairs go badly and worse, and Tyrone and his men have the upper hand with our armies.

2 JULY

Today in the street I accosted Jaggard, and informed him right soundly I was vexed and much offended with him. He smiled & asked why I charged him thus coldly. I told him he knew well why, and thrust his book, his *Passionate Pilgrim*, into his face. I said, "I gave you no permission to publish any poems by me, and most herein are not mine either. Indeed, I wonder how you came by those sonnets, for they pass only amongst my friends. I believe you would profit from my name, and you are naught but a base scoundrel." I had thought to offer him some blows, but then I stayed my hand as I thought on Henry Porter's death last month [6 June]. Jaggard would say nothing, but smiled his oily smile, and, his heart crammed with arrogancy and pride, he walked away.[27] I stood in the street for some while, cholerful, & thinking what more I might do. But there is no remedy, save keeping mine own work close about me, if I can.

12 JULY

Rumours that yesterday John Hayward was questioned closely by the [Privy] Council, and that the queen would have him racked. All the talk is what he wrote about the deposition of Richard [II], and Hayward's dedication to Lord Essex. Again fear runs in my veins lest my plays might cause offence. Yet those I have writ of late can surely cause no offence. Essex I have removed from *Henry V*, and *Julius Caesar* is but a Roman play. Yet I feel I live cheek by jowl with Hayward, for I shall be powerless if those in authority come seeking me.

[LATE JULY]

At the Rose, where I saw Dekker's *The Shoemakers' Holiday*, which I liked well enow when Tom showed his play to me these several weeks past.[28] And parts I liked well enow on the stage. Yet for all that, I could at times scarce follow the knotty-pated plot. This I think Tom must know, for he cares only for his characters, which are more kin to common folk than most creatures which populate our playhouse stages. Thus he writes scenes for his characters to be in and to show themselves. I like well his Simon Eyre who heaps up his abuse, yet makes the multitude laugh: "Away, you Islington whitepot! hence, you hopper arse, you barley-pudding full of maggots! you broil'd carbonado!"[29] That's rare stuff! For the rest, the play is but two stories of lovers thwarted and then set to right. Upon this love thwarted have I writ too, but 'tis *how* 'tis done that is all.

1 AUGUST

Today there is a great alarum about the city. Some say there is another Spanish armada of above 100 vessels which make towards the Isle of Wight. There is news also that affairs go from bad to worse in Ireland. Men desert on every side, and soldiers have been executed as an example to others. I've seen men creep the streets hereabouts looking upon every side, afeard of their own shadows, and I suspect they have deserted. Poor wretches, I cannot blame them, nor would I find myself in their boots.

6 AUGUST

This afternoon I bought a book of epigrams which satisfied my vanity, for therein is a sonnet after my own fashion.[30] Its author, Weever, I have seen only in company with Jonson. He is a curious man—small, and given greatly to tobacco. This evening news that a Spanish armada is at Southampton & the Isle of Wight. The gates of the city are closed, & everywhere there is consternation & fear. They say 6,000 men are to be mustered. I marvel that I care little of this, tho' why I know not, e'en tho' I should; 'tis a strange drowsiness possesses me.

12 AUGUST

To St. Mary's, Aldermanbury, for the baptism of John's [Heminges] boy. He is a fair, bonny child, though puling. They named him John. Afterwards I ate and drank aplenty, & was joyed, for these are the few hours when, for all the world, it seemeth I have a family about me—e'en tho' 'tis not mine own. No more on that.

23 AUGUST

The Spanish threaten no more, there are no more musters, and no good news from Ireland. Tomorrow I go home for two weeks whiles I may.

[AUGUST/SEPTEMBER]

I have been confined by several domestic and particular affairs, tho' I have made a happy conclusion of all. Anne is well satisfied, all her moans be gone, and she is disposed to mirth. I have spent joyous, blessed hours with Edmund,[31] who is now like a son to me, as much as any one might be sithence dear Hamnet died. His constant desire is to be an actor, for which the blame lies all at my door, for I have told him many a tale of my life in London and he thinks it wondrous. His entreaties I cannot gainsay, for I know the yoke of his existence here at home, & thus I have told him he may journey with me when I return to the city &, for the nonce, lodge with me until he may settle somewhere.

17 SEPTEMBER

[London.] The Lord Essex hath made a treaty with Tyrone in Ireland, & there is to be a truce. The rumour is the Queen is vexed greatly, though why we cannot tell, save that she desired Essex to triumph o'er the Irish, and not conclude a compact.

21 SEPTEMBER

Julius Caesar was presented again this afternoon. The crowd was large and boisterous, though it was full of good intent when Caesar was murdered & when Antony addressed the plebeians.[32] The authorities trouble us not, and all seems well, because *Caesar* is a Roman play. I think my next play should be a comedy [*As You Like It*], for comedies be less vexatious and troublesome. Besides, now that Bob[33] is one of our number, I should write him a part. Though he is somewhat dwarfish, yet is he delicate, sophisticate, and full of thought. As much unlike the wretched, peevish Kempe as day is from night. If Bob prove worthy, we shall fare well together.

30 SEPTEMBER

The news is Essex (and so Harry [Southampton]) is returned and the queen sorely displeased.[34] I hear nothing from Harry, that nothing he so plentifully gives me; yet, I should not expect much these days, for our paths lie far asunder. But, for old time sake, I would I had word of how he fares.

> That time of year thou mayst in me behold
> When yellow leaves, or none, or few, do hang
> Upon those boughs which shake against the cold,
> Bare ruined choirs where late the sweet birds sang.
> In me thou seest the twilight of such day
> As after sunset fadeth in the west,
> Which by and by black night doth take away,

Death's second self, that seals up all in rest.
In me thou seest the glowing of such fire
That on the ashes of his youth doth lie,
As the deathbed whereon it must expire,
Consumed with that which it was nourished by.
    This thou perceiv'st, which makes thy love more strong,
    To love that well which thou must leave ere long.
    [Sonnet 73]

11 OCTOBER

I saw Harry [Southampton] with several nobles & gallants in the gallery [of the Globe] this afternoon. He was merry, but gave me no sign either way. I wondered to see Harry at the playhouse while the Lord Essex lies imprisoned in York House, disgraced for his failings in Ireland, his insults to Her Majesty.

[C. 16 OCTOBER]

At the Rose, whence I went only at [Michael] Drayton's entreaty, though why he should entreat me I know not, save we have been friends long past. Perchance no more. The play was *Sir John Oldcastle*,[35] and a poor paltry thing it was, though the penny stinkards, that many-headed hydra, did applaud heartily. *Oldcastle* lacks plot and characters, and its language is but weakly. 'Tis naught but a slap at me and my Falstaff (that was called Oldcastle). This new Oldcastle is a noble knight and such, and I suspect some in authority did encourage it to keep down my plays. This Oldcastle is "virtuous, wise, and honourable" [1.2], which he may have been, but he is a dull thing here. I should have not remained once I heard the Prologue,[36] yet the more fool me, for I did— only to hear the palpable hits at me.[37] As chance would have it, Drayton was outside the Rose as I departed, & I had not the heart to refuse him when he asked me to share some food & drink with him, tho' I guessed what converse might follow. He desired my opinion of *Sir John*, which

I evaded with a bombast circumstance—which he espied right quickly. "'Tis no use, dear Will, for you to be kind, for the truth is I write such stuff out of want of money. I take no pride in my handiwork, but craft what Henslowe desires. He is not a bad fellow; 'tis his way to take us to that tavern in Fish Street, spend some few shillings on good cheer as he calls it. Why, sometimes he'll pay a pound before I write a word. But, when all is said & done, I shall never become rich whiles I pen stuff for him." I sorrowed to see Michael so disconsolate and full of discontent, and could offer poor, empty words of hope. I knew not what to say, and 'twas no time for sportive humour to lighten his care and melancholy.

3 NOVEMBER

All day the skies looked grimly & threatened present blusters. John Heminges to me yester eve, looking as crest-fallen as a dried pear, and inwardly troubled. For awhile we drank canary [wine] and ate dry cake, no words passing, save on the weather. So perforce I was obliged to ask John why it was he visited me. He thrust a large sheaf of papers at me— a new play by Ben Jonson called *Every Man Out of his Humour*. John said, "You know, Will, because once his other play [*Every Man In his Humour*] did prove popular with the multitude of spectators, our company promised Ben we would take another play from him. Of course, we hoped, yea, we expected it would prove like the first." I nodded and said, "Well, though the play was not all it might have been, yet it humoured the crowds, and you recall I urged that we put it on the stage." "Well," said John, "you may now well regret that you did, for several of us that have read this *Every Man Out of his Humour* believe there are places in it where Ben, most bitter, mean & contumeliously, attacks you, whom I had thought were his fast friend. Y'are indeed abused by this putter-on." I said nothing. "Will, what we want you to do is read the piece o'er, and if you like it not, all the rest of us are agreed that we should break our promise, give the thing back to Ben, and tell him to look elsewhere. For mine own part, I think there is not in the world matter enough to alter it, to make it good."

So we drank some more wine, John left, & I read the play. I know not whether to be angry, sad, or indifferent, for, whatever else might be in the play, I find that it is a wretched exemplar. It is naught else but an expostulation of Ben's theory of humours in a succession of scenes that lack all else wherewith a play is dressed—plot, action, characters, ideas, & I know not what. It is as far from what I conceive a play as being as I am from the moon. To boot, I think John is correct, namely that Ben directs his bitter gibes at me and my plays, and I do believe it is because he took offence at Corporal Nym.[38] Ben hath put me in the play, and called me Sogliardo whom he calls an "essential clown" and "so enamoured of the name of a gentleman that he will have it, though he buys it." And in the midst of the play [3.1], he makes light with, nay fleers at father's coat of arms and motto.[39] I believe too he flies at my *Shrew* when his two characters [Cordatus and Mitis] do interrupt and make comment on the play presented before them. And then the gibes direct at my plays.[40] I believe it is all contempt because his characters repair to the Mitre on occasion, as we two have done oft. Perchance Ben wants us to recall poor Kit Marlowe, his squabble, and murder over the reckoning [5.4]. I could be sorely angered, but I will not plume up Ben's will, nor rise to his gibes, for that will gratify him and his perverse humour.[41] Besides, we want novelty in our new playhouse, and this I shall tell John and the rest. Ben shall not have the pleasure of my anger which I shall keep concealed, but I shall not forget. Yet will I not perform in it.[42]

15 NOVEMBER

As You Like It, for thus have I called the comedy, is well nigh done, and 'twill be a counter to Jonson, for he would have plays written only as he likes 'em. Faith, I had much in mind an answer to his *Every Man Out of his Humour*, wherein precious little happens but all is humours, humours, humours. Well, little enough happens in *As You Like It*, yet it shall entertain and delight because my characters are like people, leastways real enough for the nonce. They are not some fantastical creation drawn to suit but mine own mind. Much is old stuff that I have amended a little here and there[43]—a familiar tale—an evil court, a Duke banished to the country, disguises, lovers, and weddings that set all aright. What will give delight are the songs neighbour Morley hath set to music.[44] My delight is there is no Kempe to botch my words, and for a jest I shall play a clown called Will [5.1]. Bob Armin likes already what he hath read of Touchstone, and hath no thought to meddle and amend. My other delight is that the fellows have agreed to give my brother his chance. The wondrous thing is Edmund's voice is marvellous dexterous; one moment a woman's voice, the next minute a man's, and thus is he suited perfectly to play Rosalind/Ganymede. Yet is he timorous with apprehension lest he should fail. To this end we will rehearse together so he shall be secure when he plays with Dick [Burbage] who enacts Orlando. Sweet Sam [Gilburne]—to be Celia—is to aid as well. One fear, my only one, is this comedy might become naught but another play to celebrate weddings—as did happen to *Midsummer* [*Night's Dream*].

17 NOVEMBER

John [Heminges] to me somewhat before six this evening. He had looked o'er *As You Like It* and much approved of it, for, he said, it will suit well for a performance at Court this Christmastide, even though Jaques is melancholic. I said that was true enow, but I had fashioned him, meaning Jaques, after Jonson's manner. Then John said that no offence could be taken with my play, which is as well these days. I asked him whether he had remarked my hit at the book burning,[45] but John said if that was a hit at book burning & the bishops it was weak & unnoticeable. "But I did remark," he said, "the motto of our playhouse, and that folk will like."[46] I told him there was a jest there too, for when Jaques concludes with "sans teeth, sans eyes, sans taste, sans everything" [2.7.166], I shall be carried on by [Dick] Burbage who is to play Orlando and me old Adam. "Well, Will, I suppose if you must," he said, "though I see little humour in't. But I see dead Kit Marlowe is still on your mind."[47] "Indeed," I said. "But I remember Kit with sweet affection, not bile like Jonson."[48] "Well, Will," John said, "that's if Ben meant to recall poor Kit. Dwell not on Ben, and I entreat you to scan this thing no further. Take your part in *Out of Humour*, for it will be given at Court and we shall need all our best men. I' fecks, we must not stint our necessary actions. And, if I mistake not, your play will suit the better, and gain the plaudits and mayhap revenge." I told John I needed no flattery, and he knew I should be persuaded and perform in Ben's play, for we are a company united, whiles others may come and go.

Then we talked on other matters and on our families, which turned the talk to Edmund [Shakespeare]. I told John how Edmund was thankful for the opportunity we had thrown his way, & how well Edmund was in rehearsing Rosalind. "The thing most remarkable," I said, " is his voice—a woman's one moment, a man's the next, so that his illusion as Rosalind or Ganymede is all the more complete. Young Sam [Gilburne], who is to be Celia, as you know, plays very prettily alongside Edmund. 'Tis most delightful." John nodded his approval, then feigned some disdain that he was to be Duke Senior. "Nay, John, though the Duke be a milk-water character, yet is he, like yourself, full of wisdom and applies correction to the melancholic Jaques." What we said thereafter I cannot recall, save we repaired to the Mitre for wine, where we did not find Ben, & passed a peaceable evening.

1 DECEMBER

The news is the Privy Council hath damned the murmurs abroad that support the Lord Essex. He lies sick abed, but I doubt not common folk love him as their champion. Lord Mountjoy, they say, is to be sent to Ireland in his stead, and all Essex's servants are to be dismissed.

2 DECEMBER

With Ned Alleyn at the Bull Inn, much drink. Ned told me that his father-in-law [Philip Henslowe] hath persuaded him to act again. Because our company fares well, Henslowe suffers at the Rose, and money is all. So Ned & Henslowe have plans afoot. Ned today bought a lease of some land in Finsbury,[49] where he and Henslowe will build their theatre, which they think to call the Fortune. Ned said he holds our Globe in great admiration, and so he will have Master [Peter] Street build this Fortune like the Globe, though finer if that may be accomplished. I thought Ned was morose when he said he needs must act again, though I told him the two finest actors were himself and [Dick] Burbage. Mayhap Ned would have been the happier in our company,[50] & how I would have dearly loved to write plays for him, for him & Dick together—a fine sight to have beheld.

9 DECEMBER

Though he hath vexed me of late, I could not deny Jonson when he asked me to see his son baptized & share his joy. Ben will put his yard [penis] where his venery takes him; yet today he was a happy father.[51]

15 DECEMBER

All about the city are pamphlets calling Essex the champion of the Protestant faith and proclaiming his innocence. Many folk want the queen to show him clemency. There have been writings on the palace walls that vilify her and secretary Cecil. For myself, I say little or nothing, for though I might know who my friends are, these are parlous, dangerous times, and a guarded tongue will save many a man; 'tis the yammerer that will swing from the yardarm. Besides we are busy with the plays we must give at Court this Christmastide. *As You Like It* fares well, and Edmund [Shakespeare] pleases all our company. Jonson scowls and says his play [*Every Man Out*] will be a triumph if we would but exert ourselves in its favour. Some of the fellows have told him the fault lies not with us, so he may conclude from that where lies the error. I play Mitis, one who comments on what passes o'er the stage. Ben calls Mitis a "person of no action" and therefore no character. With that I cannot disagree, tho' he would have me take angry note.

20 DECEMBER

Yesterday there were reports of Lord Essex's death, and bells tolled throughout the city. Some said preachers prayed for him. The reports were false. I muse what all this portends.

23 DECEMBER

A boisterous gale today—trees toppled, roofs blown quite away. I heard that a boat turned over in the Thames and nineteen poor souls were lost.

27 DECEMBER

Yesterday at Court we gave Jonson's play [*Every Man Out of his Humour*] which was received, as I feared, but poorly. I perceived Her Majesty fell asleep on occasion, and though the courtiers laughed betimes, they stifled yawns behind their hands betimes. The queen did not call Ben forth at the end, but strode out of the chamber.[52] So Ben is served as he deserves, but I said naught to him afterwards.

1600

Shakespeare learns his fame has spread to Cambridge University, while Jonson broods because he has been mocked in As You Like It. *Remarkably, Will Kempe dances the nearly 100 miles from London to Norwich, creating a "wonder." While Jonson engages other dramatists argumentatively, Shakespeare sets about writing* Hamlet, *a perplexing, difficult, and at times almost autobiographical task, leaving him little time for controlling the publication of his plays or for acting. Essex, meanwhile, has obtained his release and retires from court. Shakespeare worries that Southampton's friendship with Essex will turn out disastrously. In September Shakespeare shows an early draft of* Hamlet *to Richard Burbage in order to elicit his valuable opinion, and the play eventually takes shape.*

4 JANUARY

This day at the Bunch of Grapes I supped with Dekker and Nashe, & with them was Tom Heywood, whom I have scarce seen before.[1] Dekker was well pleased with his play given at Court, and he said Her Majesty had spoken kindly to him when they had finished.[2] Heywood proved a pleasant enough fellow; he acts and, as he said, writes plays, and patches up many another. He hath been with [Philip] Henslowe these two years past, and hath worked hard for him. Tom Nashe was full of himself & his doings. He & Heywood went to Cambridge last week for old times' sake, and saw there some play or other acted by students. Nashe said they had much good company, though there was some jest at my *Venus*. I laughed, & said I was pleased my fame was bruited about that venerable university. "Why, Tom," I said, "there's money in a poem that is read."³ To which Heywood said, "and in plays that be acted. I flatter ye not, Master Shakespeare, that I keep your plays in my mind when I pen mine." More talk & ale followed and flowed. Heywood seems an honest fellow.

7 JANUARY

As You Like It was performed last evening in the Great Hall at Richmond Palace before Her Majesty who was delighted, it seems, for she paid us much attention and called me forth at the end. She had words of praise, most particularly for Jaques whose melancholy was to her liking and, I opine, her mood. To my great joy, she praised Rosalind, not knowing it was Edmund [Shakespeare] played her, though this I could not tell her. She said, "We trust, Master Shakespeare, you will give us another play wherein we may see that actor, the Lord sparing us for the same." Edmund was overjoyed and much moved when I told him this as we ate & drank afterwards. Jonson was grim, broiling o'er some offence he perceived. Why he came with us I know not. He chastised me for mocking him as Jaques; I told him that he should remember *Every Man Out*, and hold no grudges. Besides, if the boot should fit his foot, he ought not to complain. I fain would not bandy words with him because of my joy at Edmund's triumph. Let Ben sulk and skulk as he may. In all of this I have forgot [Thomas] Morley's music for my songs; these pleased the Court well, & Her Majesty called for two of them to be sung again. Which done, she called for them again afore she was satisfied.

9 JANUARY

At the Bull Inn, I saw Master Peter Street whom I had not seen since he finished our playhouse [Globe]. Yesterday, he, Henslowe, and Alleyn signed the contract for the new theatre [Fortune], which, as Ned had told me, is to be as like our Globe as may be, and no expense spared.

Street is greatly contented, and I told him *we* shall be contented to see Henslowe north of the Thames, & have the Bankside to ourselves. Kate called upon me in the evening. I had not seen her in many a week, & had no desire for her company. She cared little and took her leave after but a few minutes, just as the clock struck nine. Is it not strange that performance should so outlive desire?

15 JANUARY

This evening as we drank ale together, Jonson told me of the infamous Lucy Morgan, or, as she is called, "Black Luce." All the world knows she is a notorious and lewd woman, full of evil conversation, and many a bawd hath learned her tricks from Lucy. She hath kept a bawdy house in St. John Street in Clerkenwell that Ben knows well because of his venery, as he says. What lewdness & lasciviousness he hath conducted there, Ben did not say; i' faith, there was much in his story he omitted, methinks, though I well believe he thinks himself well shaped for sportive tricks. Quoth he, "I might give you an inkling of such ensuing evils I have enjoyed there, but I know ye are not a merry gamester." Then he told me that today the Court of Aldermen committed Black Luce to Bridewell, though she is not to be whipped & carted through the streets because in better times she had been a gentlewoman to the queen and had played for her. Whether that be true or not, I know not. Perchance some part of this tale might piece out a play, though it suits Ben more than me.[4]

11 FEBRUARY

God's blood, I know not why I arose so early, but peradventure it was to see Kempe as foolish as ever I have known him, or so it seemed. Some little time before seven this morning, I made my way towards the Lord Mayor's house where a goodly throng had forgathered to see Kempe dance from that place all the way to Norwich. With Kempe were Thomas Sly (who was to be Kempe's taborer), a servant (one

William Bee), and a man called George Sprat, there to see that Kempe fulfilled his pledge (a wise provision). Kempe saw me and waved, and I smiled a wan reply. Anon, Sly struck up his tabor, and off went Kempe. I followed for awhile, and along the way many folk gave him sixpences, blessed him, and wished him Godspeed. On they went past Whitechapel and thence to Mile End, where I left the crowd, there being little sport in seeing more of Kempe and his morris dance.[5]

6 MARCH

This afternoon, for our Lord Hunsdon, we performed *Oldcastle* [*Henry IV Part 1*] at Somerset House which his lordship's guest, one Ludovic Verreyken, a Flemish ambassador, had requested in particular. His lordship & guest expressed their great contentment, but would have seen Kempe as Oldcastle or Falstaff. Gus Phillips reminded his lordship that Kempe was dancing his morris to Norwich and that, for all that, Kempe was no longer of our company. This his lordship had forgotten; his health fails him betimes. I muse whether Kempe is, in sooth, dancing yet.

20 MARCH

Kempe is returned and made richer by his dance. The Mayor of Norwich gave him five pounds, which is a deal more than any one of his jigs was ever worth, though in his conceit Kempe thinks not so. He thinks to earn moe money by writing the tale of what he calls his "wonder," which his followers and well-wishers might buy. What a brave world that hath in it such creatures!

EASTER DAY [23 MARCH]

A bitter cold day, & I scarce keep warm. Snow lies everywhere. They say Lord Essex is removed to his own house, though he remains a prisoner—belike until the queen dies.

30 MARCH

Today two churchwardens from St. Saviour's [Southwark] came to the playhouse and spoke with Cuthbert Burbage and John Heminges. John said they talked of tithes, and how the poor are always with us and need money, and so forth. Well, we needs must, I suppose, though many folk in the church have not been friends with us, and would have the theatres closed and plucked down. John thinks the tithes buy us good opinion. I thought, but did not tell him, of other items they might buy; but John is forsooth a kindlier man than I am.

4 APRIL

Bitterly cold, & yet more snow. My brain is numb, though for other reasons than this hoar-laden winter weather. I needs must write another play, but on what I know not. Nothing comes—an inky cloak quite subdues my mind—and I would fain not write any more history in these delicate times.

8 APRIL

At the Mitre this evening, with Ben [Jonson], Dick [Burbage], John Heminges, and Bob Armin. Ben was in fine fettle, for his *Every Man Out* is to be printed and, as he told us with some vehemence, "containeth more than hath been publickly spoken or acted."[6] John & I glanced at each other; we refrained from telling him why so much was excised for our performance. I thought to admonish Ben for his gibes at me, but thought better on't because we have been the more friendly of late. So we drank ale, ate bread and a good mutton stew. After some time, I asked Ben what new work he had in mind. He said he knew not, nor cared much. He thought that Marston might take another hit at him for what he, Ben, had set down in *Every Man Out*.[7] Dick laughed and said he remembered that scene, for it was the one in which someone [Puntarvolo] said, "Your Mitre is your best house," and here we were.

Ben continued, saying if such were the case, if Marston tried a hit at him, he would be ready, & would deliver such blows that Marston would scarce recover. "But Ben," I said, "I had thought you & John have been fast friends betimes." Ben replied that was as may be, but Marston writes such bombast that something must needs be done. I said, "Ye are arrogant ever, Ben. You want us all to write as you do, and that may not be. Besides, I warrant some folk like what he writes. Why, look at that play he wrote last year, *Antonio and Mellida*, that was caviar to the general, it pleased the million."[8] Ben said that Marston's play was but revenge stuff and did but slake the popular thirst, as did Kyd's *Spanish Tragedy*. "Well," I said, "the multitudes be our masters, for they be the ones that pay our labours, chide them how ye may. Besides, there were scenes well digested in *The Spanish Tragedy*, and poor Tom Kyd was to be much commended. And now, Ben, whether you like it or no, I must give you my thanks, for I know now what I shall write next, or leastways, the direction I shall take presently." So saying I left hurriedly, for I fain would seek out Kyd's old play to read again. Alas, I found it not in my closet and must needs find another.

9 APRIL

Good fortune came my way this morning when least I sought it. I had just stepped into the street to buy bread and cheese, when I happened upon John Marston who greeted me cheerily. I said that his ears should have been aflame last evening, for we had told pretty tales of him at the Mitre—though I mentioned not Jonson's ire at his name and so forth. However, Marston remarked, "And I warrant, if he were in your midst, Ben Jonson did waste no time in words upon me. Did he call me Carlo Buffone, or mayhap Clove?" I said, i' faith, Jonson's words had not been fair ones, yet I added that, for myself, I had spoke well of his, meaning Marston's, *Antonio and Mellida*. "Master Shakespeare, you flatter me right soundly. That is indeed praise from Caesar." I jested that I trusted I looked not like John Heminges, good man though he be. We laughed and chatted on this and that awhile. As I was about to go on my way, I chanced to mention I could not find my copy of Kyd's *Spanish Tragedy*, and Marston swiftly offered me his. So we went to his rooms, which are furnished most tidily. Marston found the play, and furnished me with some other volumes, for which I thanked him right heartily. As I was taking my leave, he said, "I suppose you could perceive, in my play, that I was not unfamiliar with *The Spanish Tragedy*. Indeed, Master Shakespeare, there is another play, that I think was his, from which I took a hint and more." He then told me that when, last year, Henslowe had paid him for a play for the Admiral's Men,[9] Henslowe had given him also a copy of a play called *Hamlet* that had been acted a great while since and that might be worked anew. This caused me some amazement, & I told Marston our company had presented such a play some five or six years ago,[10] and, as I recalled, the two plays were alike in some respects. "Well, indeed," said Marston, "I have no need of the play, though, as I said, I did take a hint or two for my drama.[11] So if you wish it you shall have it, though the copy should be returned to Henslowe when you have done." I thanked him for his kindnesses and departed. I think I see my way more clear now I have these two plays before me.

21 APRIL

I hear Harry [Southampton] returns this day to Ireland, tho' he must do so with a heavy heart for Lord Essex remains yet a prisoner.[12]

1 MAY

I have read again the old *Hamlet* and *Spanish Tragedy*, and I had hoped thereby to goad my thoughts to a path I might take. Yet each time I take up my quill no words follow. I am transfixed, my mind a dark backward and abysm. All I think on is son and father and family, the very quintessence of those plays and perchance what I would as lief write. Yet my poor dear Hamnet's name and face stare at me from the very bowels of the grave & haunt me. I sit, for hours together it seems, thinking on him, weeping betimes. What might have been had he not been so untimely ripped from me, and aye, from Anne—such thought is more than flesh can withstand, & yet a bootless inquisition.

2 MAY

What is popular on our stage? Revenge, murder, ghosts, madness, incest, sensation. What is in these plays? Family, fathers, sons, mothers, lovers. How might these be encompassed around? As I wrote that, as plain as day after darkest night, I thought on Pyramus and Thisbe [*A Midsummer Night's Dream*], and now I see where lies my way. There, comic though it be, is a tragic love story contained within a play in a play. Art and artifice, reality and illusion, that be the very stuff of my plays—yea the theatre itself is fashioned thus. So shall it be again with *Hamlet*, for that is now to be *my* story—a revenge play, all that groundlings desire, for without them we are nothing. Yet at the heart of the matter will lie the theatre, a play within a play that shall raise manifold notions of illusion and so forth. For what lies in those words above but the quintessence of our being, philosophy, and such. Lord, how my spirits & soul soar now this path lies clear before me. 'Twas ever thus as one day draweth upon another.

3 MAY

Though my way be clear, I cannot write. The frosts every night and morn have frozen my mind. Yet it [*Hamlet*] will come, that I sense in my bones. It shall be all my business.

4 MAY

Nothing. Nothing will come of nothing. Beshrew me, how I am racked nightly by fears and dreams—Hamnet came to me last night, a piteous sight. Yet as he vanished, he smiled. I know he is dead, worm-eaten, but I would fain know if we shall e'er meet again. Is death mere change—one essence for another? What is our being? If we live and have our being, then what is death? Words, words, words, and no matter. This prating will not do, e'en tho' Hamnet was all my essence. Drink and oblivion.

[JUNE]

Marston hath delivered a blow to Jonson. The Children of Paul's have played a piece called *Jack Drum's Entertainment* wherein Ben is a cuckold named Brabant [senior]. I expect Jonson will return the gibe, though wherein lies the meaning, I know not. Our little world is naught but dry musty fictions.

8 JUNE

Some three days ago the Lord Essex was brought to trial, at which the world is all abuzz.[13] I spoke to a man in the street, who said he was a blacksmith, and he called Essex a "strange eruption to our state. And, ye know, good wombs have borne bad sons." Again I thought on these unsettled and unsettling times—Essex imprisoned in his house until the queen shall do with him what she will, & there hath been the deaths of hundreds, nay thousands of men in Ireland, & Spain is ever at our backs. And all to what purpose, what end? Such is the stuff of my play [*Hamlet*]—Denmark unsettled, a king kills his brother and marries his brother's wife. The old king's son who alone mourns his father and wonders how the world can countenance his uncle's actions. Threatening enemies. Yet I do not think nor fear the authorities will see this *Hamlet* play as history, for it is not of the English throne I write. It is only that life and art are as one betimes. At the Mermaid I overheard a man talking who said that he had heard Essex at his trial was a pitiful sight to behold now he is stripped of honour and offices. He said many folk had wept for Essex, tho' whether this be true I know not, for he spoke with another & I dared not question him. There is naught I can do for the fallen creature, for all that Harry [Southampton] cleaves to Essex.

9 JUNE

Vexed though I am with this *Hamlet* play, I am resolved to write what I can merely—let what words come as they will. Then I can amend and fashion 'em, for if I do but think only on't, nothing will come, though the memory of my dear Hamnet be as ever green as is my grief. And forsooth that is the hindrance which I pray must pass.

24 JUNE

Deep chat with John Heminges on this latest order to restrain our playhouses.[14] The good news, which may cheer the spirits of our company, is there shall be but two playhouses—our own Globe and the new Fortune, which Ned Alleyn and Henslowe build. Yet it is decreed we shall perform but two days in a week so that great numbers of people shall not be "idle, riotous, or dissolute" by seeing our plays. Yet they may be idle, dissolute, or riotous in many another fashion! And we are to be stayed in Lent or time of pestilence as before. John assuaged my fears, as he hath done oftentimes before, and said the inhibition will not endure long. He said, "Unless we fear that apes can tutor us, 'tis in our power to be masters of our fortune." But he was sad that the Curtain is to be plucked down because he hath oft played there, and because it may be needed in times to come.[15] Mayhap I should return to Stratford for some weeks, but dear Hamnet would consume all my thoughts, because of this play [*Hamlet*]. So I will write words of cheer to Anne.

3 JULY

After the performance this afternoon, John Heminges sought me out. With him was a handsome young nobleman, a foreigner, who had seen our play and wished to look about the Globe which he admired greatly.[16] The youth questioned me with much discernment on our acting and on the manner of writing a play. Would that all our spectators possessed such discretion.

6 JULY

Supper at the Mermaid where all the talk was of Sir Edward Baynham and three others. The other evening they had supper at the Mermaid, then drank riotously until the morn's early hours, after which they left and assaulted the watch. Now they cool their heels in prison and have been fined. Master Johnson [the host] is fearful lest the authorities seek him out, though he need not trouble himself, for he is a stout, honourable fellow—the which I told him. A fine beef stew and wine.

10 JULY

Today, much upon the stroke of noon, there was an eclipse of the sun. Peradventure some folk will say it portends some event, some catastrophe.

13 JULY

Today Dr. John Hayward was committed to the Tower for the seditions in his book on Henry IV. His fate is bound up with the Lord Essex, & fortune's face shines not on him. So would I not be the good doctor, & I am pleased withal that mine own plays have not stirred up the authorities against me.[17]

2 AUGUST

To the Red Bull Inn to eat & drink with Ned Alleyn. Afterwards we walked to the Fortune, which lies between Golden Lane & Whitecross Street. Ned was brimful with pride as he showed me his theatre, which Peter Street & his men have completed but a week or two since. Ned showed me some fine decoration & painting, for which he have laid out some £80, together with twenty-five shillings for a flagstaff. At the entrance Ned hath placed a figure of Dame Fortune. I told him, and I lied not, that I rejoiced for him & Henslowe, and that it is good they be north of the river [Thames] and we be south. So we may brook our competitors and remain fast friends.

5 AUGUST

Yesterday our James Roberts went to the Stationers' Hall to register some of my plays for fear they be printed by others.[18] I trust this action will succeed. The Lord Mayor is to impress over 300 men for the wars in Ireland. Men have deserted on every side, & some have been executed to serve as an example. From what I hear tell, death immediate may be better than death prolonged.

15 AUGUST

[James] Roberts hath brought me pelting scurvy news: a wretch named Pavier hath registered a play called *Henry Fifth*, which appeareth to be mine own.[19] This is as I feared, and I curse that any man may lay hands on my work. Roberts thinks one of our hired men [in *Henry V*] hath writ out all he could remember to make this book. Would that the traitor could recall nothing, or I might erase all words from his fond memory.

17 AUGUST

Yester afternoon—everywhere was abuzz that James King of Scotland was murdered. Yet it was but rumour. There was a plot against his life, but it hath been thwarted.[20] Herein, peradventure, may lie the germens of a play? I have set down as much of *Hamlet* as I am able, though much must be amended, so burdened is it with excess of words. I shall show it to Dick [Burbage] by and by.

26 AUGUST

Lord Essex is released, and they say he goes to live quietly in Oxfordshire, for the queen hath forbidden him the Court. I trust Harry

[Southampton] will be not hot-headed like Essex, tho' I fear their friendship together. Harry is led too easily, too tenderly, like asses by the nose, when he is hard by Essex; yet he is a brave, rare spirit whom I would have by me—but may not.

>Against my love shall be as I am now,
>With Time's injurious hand crushed and o'erworn;
>When hours have drained his blood and filled his brow
>With lines and wrinkles, when his youthful morn
>Hath travelled on to age's steepy night,
>And all those beauties whereof now he's king
>Are vanishing or vanished out of sight,
>Stealing away the treasure of his spring;
>For such a time do I now fortify
>Against confounding Age's cruel knife,
>That he shall never cut from memory
>My sweet love's beauty, though my lover's life.
>>His beauty shall in these black lines be seen,
>>And they shall live, and he in them still green.
>>[Sonnet 63]

1 SEPTEMBER

This evening Jonson told me this strange tale. There was a man and his wife who came but lately from the Low Countries. The wife, being great with child, did long for the gullet of a pig, and they went to Batholomew Fair to get the same. But the wife could not get a gullet, and straightway gave birth to a still-born baby girl, which was buried then and there. Ben seemed much taken by this tale, and he takes much delight in the round bellies of women. I warrant there is no whit of rhyme nor reason to the bacon-fed knave when he is in this mood.

3 SEPTEMBER

I have given Dick Burbage *Hamlet*, tho' it hath need of great amendment. I was afeard almost to let him see it. Yet, as he needs must be Hamlet, I seek his advice and guidance, for I fear my way is lost in writing. All I have writ could ne'er be played in one afternoon, nor would the multitudes stand in the yard listening to it so long. There is an excess of grain in this hour-glass. Dick's mind was preoccupied with other matters because he hath leased his playhouse in the Blackfriars to Master Nathaniel Giles and one Henry Evans.[21] Dick says he will be glad of the rent, some £40 a year, because the place hath been of no use to him ere this. I trust he will put his mind to *Hamlet* forthwith for, until it be finished, I cannot put my mind to other work.

8 SEPTEMBER

Joan sends news that her boy is christened; would I had been there to share in all her joy. I must make her amends some day.[22]

20 SEPTEMBER

Deep chat with Dick Burbage on *Hamlet*, and 'tis palpable he sees mine intent, most particularly with Hamlet himself. He sees how the play turns on Hamlet's speeches solus, which Dick acknowledged give him fine opportunities and which, it follows, must not be lopped off. We talked as well on how 'tis much to do with family, with fathers and sons, and such like. Ever to the matter, Dick asked me if I am to play the Ghost, a father returned from the dead to visit his living son, this the reverse of Hamnet and myself. Dick knows me all too well, I fear. Justly he said the length will not do; it must be chopped, but he would not lose that part at the centre where Claudius' guilt is exposed by a play. Dick believes that is a wondrous, fine theatrical conceit, particularly when much in *Hamlet* turns on seeming and illusion, the very stuff of our profession. He said much else, and there was barely one word I could dispute. So I am to set about some amendment, though I doubt not more will follow when once all the fellows have seen the play. Well, I must be bloody, bold, & resolute.

24 SEPTEMBER

Today a wonder beyond all expectation. Harry [Southampton] came to the playhouse to see what we were about. He said little save that he hath been away in the Low Countries. While there, he fought a duel with Lord Grey, his adversary of old.[23] Harry looked pale and sick, but naught I might have said would comfort him. Like two barques cast on the seas, we drift apart. Thus am I taught that Time hath come and ta'en my love away—the thought is death, and I cannot choose but to weep at the loss. Courage and comfort—all may yet go well.

8 OCTOBER

Midsummer Night's Dream, much as I wrote it, is to be a book. Tom Fisher registered it today.[24] Dick and Cuthbert Burbage are in a fine fury, for the boys at Blackfriars draw the multitudes *and* Jonson now writes his plays for them in his war (so 'tis called) with Marston and Dekker. This all comes to pass e'en tho' Dick leased Blackfriars to them and coins money thereby. So he asks me to add gibes against the boys in *Hamlet*, which I am loath to do, for the play be overlong already.[25] Still, such augmentation may be cut out once the fashion is passed; the boys are but lapwings that run away with a shell on their heads.

18 OCTOBER

Today Cuthbert Burbage was all smiles, for the suit Giles Allen brought against him for plucking down the Theatre to make our Globe is dismissed. I know not the whys & the wherefores, but I rejoice that Allen must desist; let him pursue his avarice & Puritan ways some other where. Heminges is to play Polonius so the jest I gave him may be made perfect.[26] John worries a boy cannot enact Ophelia, which puzzles my mind, for, as I told him, the role will play itself & with Ophelia's songs cannot fail surely to affect even the hardest of hearts.

10 NOVEMBER

Richard Hooker has died, and thereby is humanity diminished.[27] They say he was a modest, temperate man who ne'er raised his voice. I know that if his precepts were followed no heretics of any stripe would burn, and life would be the more harmonious. There's a great soul gone, yet the blessing is his words remain—a fine epitaph. *Fortune's Tennis* is to be the Admiral's play at the new Fortune two days hence.[28] There is great felicity in the title (tho' what the play be about I know not): we are all like a ball in tennis, knocked about by the whims of fortune. Yea, Romeo's "O, I am fortune's fool!"[29] But Hamlet is like the Stoics—"Since no man of aught he leaves knows, what is't to leave betimes?"[30] which is as must be. There's talk we might play *Hamlet* this Christmastide before the Court, but I think 'twould be impolitic. The play's too long, lacks comedy in the main, and murders at court are not the thing in these days when plots against the queen are sniffed in Essex's doings. I fear he will be not long in this world because he is as proud as any man could be—his pranks have been too broad to bear.[31]

1 DECEMBER

A boy has been born to King James of Scotland.[32] The Lord Essex's ire, rage, and rebellion o'erflow the measure; 'tis open for all to see, and I doubt not his popularity waneth. Not so the boys at Blackfriars, who prove ever popular, and have performed one of Jonson's plays—*Cynthia's Revels*—which by all account I should not care for. 'Tis said to be full of gibes at Marston, Essex, and others. I hear tell one of the boys called Field is, take him all in all, a fine player & acquits himself creditably. Would he were one of our company.[33] The rumour is they play it again for the queen at Christmas, whereby our company will be the loser, for we have no novelty lest we act *Hamlet*.[34]

14 DECEMBER

I met Dick Field in the street; I have not seen him in many a month. Dick is mightily concerned that the boys at Blackfriars have become popular, for the multitude of folk disturb his peace and rest.[35] He told me that yesterday Henry Evans and his man, one James Robinson, had seized & impressed some boy named [Thomas] Clifton to be one of the boys of the chapel. After they had dragged the boy to their playhouse, the child's father [Henry Clifton], a man of some importance, came after them. Many wrathful words and ire passed between the parties, but Evans had to let the boy go free. I muse again on fathers and sons—all in *Hamlet* will keep ever abuzzing in my mind. 'Tis definite we play for the queen at Whitehall on St. Stephen's Day [26 December], & now we are of one mind that old comedies shall suffice for the nonce.

26 DECEMBER

This day were we at Court. As formerly, we acted well, or well enough. Her Majesty seemed cheerful, though that might have been naught but outward show, for Essex is again in London, out of favour, and, they say, speaks loudly & angrily against those courtiers the queen prefers. Sometime I am fearful because I was sometime close with Harry [Southampton], and he and others now cleave strongly to Essex. Yet should I fear even more for Harry, for he knows no bounds, no restraint when he is with Essex. There are several others that urge Essex on to foolhardy deeds, leastways thoughts, I hear tell. Mayhap I should fear the Blackfriars boys more; they play for the Court come January, & may surpass us, tho' we should be the greater, they the lesser. What a fine reversal of fortune would lie therein.

1601

As Shakespeare feared, Southampton's loyalty to Essex draws him into Essex's rebellion against Queen Elizabeth; Southampton enlists Shakespeare's aid in inducing his fellow actors to stage Richard II *in hopes of fomenting unrest in the general population of London. The Essex rebellion fails, and luckily Shakespeare and his fellow actors are exonerated. However, Essex is executed (curiously, Shakespeare's company performs for the queen on the evening before), and Southampton imprisoned. The so-called "war of the theatres" that pits Jonson against other dramatists proceeds apace, although Shakespeare stays largely above the fray. The remainder of the year proves mercifully quieter for Shakespeare; he concentrates on work, but is saddened by the death of his father in September. Kempe returns to London looking for employment, but there is no place for him in Shakespeare's company. Shakespeare writes* Twelfth Night, *a darker comedy with gibes at the ever malcontent Jonson. Edmund Shakespeare plays Viola, and his love scenes with fellow actor Sam Gilburne as Olivia are given new meaning in a private encounter that Shakespeare stumbles upon. In public, before her majesty, Edmund and Sam are very successful.*

6 JANUARY

Much bustle at Whitehall this day. Those wretches, the Children of the Chapel, performed for the queen, as did we. It seemed we were received with equal indifference—polite, not hearty applause. Rather, all eyes were on the ambassador from Russia with whom the court parties would have greater amity. He was a tall, fat man with ponderous face & beard, tho' he carried himself majestically. An Italian duke was present also—Don Virginio Orsino—a handsome young nobleman who comported himself well. Yet did he seem somewhat sad, as though lovelorn.[1]

10 JANUARY

I hear Harry [Southampton] was attacked in the street yesterday by Lord Grey—this the second time or more. Harry's only company was his horse boy, whereas Grey was accompanied by a whole band of followers. It is some relief that Grey hath been committed to the Fleet, tho' I fear for Harry still. I read o'er *Hamlet*, & perceive now much therein be on plays, players, and playing—that huge stage that presenteth naught but shows. Then, for what reason, I know not, I could think only on the word personate and naught else. Yet as soon as I remembered that I had heard the word in Marston, it vanished from my mind.[2] Curious strange. The time has come to turn aside from *Hamlet* and think on some other play, wherein I have a mind to employ more music. That would suit [Robert] Armin well, and furnish him with some fine opportunity.[3]

25 JANUARY

Now I have more reason to pen a comedy, for the rumour is [John] Hayward hath been examined again [on 22 January] about his book on Henry IV. He is like to lie in the Tower until death, so incensed is Her Majesty against him. He must pray nightly the queen will die afore he do, & I would not have it so with me—I am not strong enough to laugh at such misery as the Tower.

1 FEBRUARY

A furious, tempestuous storm raged today which plucked down a windmill near Tyburn. Some folk declare this be a portent, yet 'tis but a tempest.

2 FEBRUARY

Yesterday's tempest now appeareth an omen after all, methinks, for this evening, somewhat after seven o' the clock had struck, Harry [Southampton], all muffled so close that I scarce could recognise him, stepped into my room. Ere I uttered one word, he clapped his hand over my mouth, saying, "I must commend a secret to your ear much weightier than aught else in this realm." Then he swore me to secrecy, and made me subscribe several deep oaths. Because he had surprised me and my joy thereat, I assented right readily. First, he told me of events earlier today. Harry's only scourge, terror, and black nemesis, Lord Grey, was released from the Fleet. Harry & the Lord Essex conferred together, both full of vexation & ire. They believe there is now no law will protect them from their foes, that the queen and all her counsellors are ranged against them, & seek only their destruction. "In brief," said Harry, "we are mightily discontented, and I think we shall, with our good friends, rebel." At this news I was afeard and knew not what to say, for I am sensible of the powers of the authorities, and am coward-like. I would but pen plays and have no need for aught else—save my daily comforts. Harry apprehended my dread, and bade me drink some wine. Then he said, "Sweet Will, I know thou art fearful of what I tell ye, and I would not bring ye any harm. For I remember well my youthful days with ye, and if 'twere possible I'd lie in thy bosom once more. That may not be, for ye wot well I am married to a matchless beauty who is all beauty extant. But I ask one boon, it is a small request." Then he told me how he, Essex, and their close followers would stir up the people so that they would join their band. For that purpose, they would have a play performed to incite the people. Thus Harry asked me if I would speak with some of my fellow players, and so determine if they would meet with Essex's men. If my fellows prove not willing, said Harry, the matter will cease to be, and no one (meaning those in authority) shall be any the wiser. He sought to assure me that the matter of incitement of the people with a play would be known only to Essex's men and himself, and I need not, nay should not, mention aught of that to my fellows. He gave me his word of honour that he only would know what had passed between us this night, and he would go to the block ere he would utter my name, even if racked. I likewise swore to him that I would keep his words close within my bosom, and would but tell my fellows that some of Essex's men desired to meet with them to bespeak a play. This I swore in all honesty, though inwardly I trembled and felt no valour. So, as quickly as he came, Harry left me, but in parting kissed me as of old. I had barely taken breath and drank wine before Harry was again before me. "Sweet Will," said he, "in my haste I forgot to tell ye that I shall send a boy to ye Wednesday night at this hour. That ye know he is my boy, he will give ye this ring, which ye may keep in remembrance. If we are to meet your fellows, tell the boy when and where." And he departed the second time.

3 FEBRUARY

I spoke with Gus Phillips & others upon the matter of last evening, and the men agreed we shall meet with Essex's men this Thursday [5 February]. Coward-like I told them naught of the true reason, of Harry's treason (for such it is), only that Essex would bespeak a play. This was no sooner settled than I received word from Dick Quiney that he is immured in the Marshalsea, & with him Henry Wilson, Henry Walker, John Sadler, & some others from Stratford.[4] I hurried to the Marshalsea as swiftly as I e'er could to render them succour. Dick told me their woe lay all in the hands of Sir Edward Greville, who had enclosed the Bankcroft [in Stratford], that pasture that belongs to all the townsfolk, which sure he may not do.[5] So Dick & all the rest cut down his hedges, and did some other damage & enormities, for so Greville called them, that they were arrested for rioting, & brought thither to the Marshalsea. Dick said, "We sent word to Tom Greene, and he is to obtain our release on bail, though we know not when that might be."[6] I asked them what I might do for them, but all they wanted was some hearty food & drink, which I gladly sent them upon my return home. I pray no harm come to them & their release come soon—tho' in these parlous times naught is certain.

4 FEBRUARY

Harry's boy appeared but minutes ago as was promised, at the appointed hour. I took Harry's ring from him and gave the boy the news. Now I sit, holding Harry's ring, staring fondly at it, almost in mad despair. I fear, as I have feared so oft of late, that fate will o'ertake Harry, and Essex will lead him to a mortal doom. This ring is all I have now in remembrance. Tomorrow I must to the Marshalsea again to see how Dick Quiney and the others fare.

5 FEBRUARY

Today being Thursday, at something past seven o'clock, we met with Essex's men as Harry [Southampton] had spoken. On our side, besides myself, there were Augustine Phillips, the two Burbages, Heminges, and Bob Armin. They of the other part were the Lord Monteagle, Sir Charles Percy, Sir Gelly Meyrick, Sir Joscelyn Percy, and some two or three others whose names I recall not.[7] Sir Charles Percy, whom I have seen with Harry before, spoke for them, and said they desired to have a play this Saturday next [7 February], whereat Gus Phillips said that we had a new play called *Hamlet* that might well content their company, and told them somewhat of the action of my play. But Sir Charles would not hear of that, and then said he knew that some time since we had given a play upon the deposition and murder of King Richard the second. That was the play he desired us to perform, and that as it was also by Master Shakespeare so much the better. He said he favoured it in particular for love of his forebear [Hotspur]. Dick [Burbage] said that indeed it was some time since, and that the play was old and so long out of use that we should have but small company for it. Then Sir Gelly Meyrick spoke loud and forceful, & said we should not trouble ourselves upon that score, for he would promise to pay forty shillings more than we would gather at the doors. He added, "I have an earnest desire to satisfy mine eyes with that tragedy, & naught else will do."

Well, we held a brief conference amongst ourselves and we were filled with trepidation that the authorities might misconster what we did.

Cuthbert thought these men might be confederates in some plot and misliked enacting a play in which a king is deposed and murdered. "For," he said, "these are parlous times when a man must walk softly and be wary." Yet the promise of forty shillings tempted us. Better forty shillings than thirty, for then might we have thought on who sins most, the tempter or the tempted. Thus we made a compact with Sir Charles & the others that we would give the play this Saturday next. When all was done and agreed, I came back here much troubled for, though my fellows knew these were Essex's men, his lordship's name was not uttered once, whether by design or through neglect. Yet sure we must have been mindful of him, because they would have *Richard II* performed. 'Tis true I swore to Harry not to reveal what he had said to me, yet Gus and Dick and the rest are my fellows with whom I must live and work for many a long year. Well, it is done and settled; we shall see what happens come Saturday.

6 FEBRUARY

I apprehend some fear. We have made ready *Richard second* for the morrow. Harry's [Southampton] words to me remain mine alone, though I dread my treachery in this complot. Mayhap naught will happen. I wonder at Lord Monteagle's silence yesterday, though it scarce signifies. Dick Quiney and t'others have been set free and, with Tom Greene, now desire to consult with Sir Edward Coke, the attorney general, over their grievances. I wish 'em joy o' that worm.

7 FEBRUARY

This afternoon we played Richard [*Richard II*] at the Globe as had been arranged. There were many men there who support Lord Essex—Sir Charles Percy, Lord Monteagle, Sir Joscelyn Percy, Sir Christopher Blount,[8] and many more knights, gentlemen and other persons, though there were few ordinary folk. Before we played, Sir Gelly Meyrick, with a Captain Thomas Lee,[9] came and gave us the forty shillings promised last Thursday. Tho' we acted but ill, little knowing a play that hath lain idle so long, Essex's men cheered the usurper Bolingbroke, & roared most when Richard was deposed and then murdered. Tonight all is quiet, as 'tis before a storm breaks ope.

8 FEBRUARY

I kept indoors & know but little of today's events, though I am afeard for the part we took in playing *Richard*. Some time after ten o'clock this morning, the Lord Essex, Harry [Southampton], some other lords, earls, and some two or three hundred men flocked through the streets of the city to rouse up the multitudes. They shouted that a plot was laid against Essex's life. But the citizens that came forth did but gaze upon them while others stayed in their houses, and so there was no uprising, no rebellion. At the lack thereof, the band of soldiers with Lord Essex returned whence they came [Essex House]. Then the Lord Admiral [Charles Howard] laid siege to the house, and after some time Essex, most desperate, yielded, & he & Harry were taken away. Now the queen's men are posted all about the city, and it is best to stay at home. Alas, my fears for Harry have come all too true. Should I burn all this that I have written?

9 FEBRUARY

Today I remained within doors. There hath been a proclamation concerning the events of yesterday which confirmeth much of what I had written before. Essex, Southampton, and all the others are declared traitors to Her Majesty, that they would spread sedition, and kill her subjects—with much more to the same effect. The rest of us are told to preserve the peace and so forth. I muse how many days will pass before our own part in these events is discovered. I fear lest Harry prove not honourable towards me, for the rack is a fearful instrument, & he is yet young—I pray he be as brave as his word. O could we but call back yesterday and bid time return. Later Dick Quiney came to see me, & told me Sir Edward Coke had not seen him & the others by reason of the recent troubles. So they make their way home on the morrow, but will return, Dick said, when the times are more peaceable & propitious. I wished him godspeed.

13 FEBRUARY

Today I heard a rumour of a plot by Captain Lee (who came to see *Richard*). He was arrested in a palace kitchen where he was on his way to the Queen's chamber where she ate with her ladies-in-waiting. Lee desired to force Her Majesty to issue a warrant for the Lord Essex's release. So even a child may count the hours before Lee's death.[10]

14 FEBRUARY

Another proclamation, viz—base, low folk spread rumours and the like, & cause turmoil and disorder. Anyone not living within the city is to return to his own abode upon pain of death. This Sunday [15 February] we are all to attend church, for the preachers shall reveal unto us the treasons of Essex to us. If we go not, we are to be fined severely. I would that this all might pass that we may play again, & I write plays. I feel more secure, for surely Harry [Southampton] hath kept his word & not revealed what part I had in his affairs, his treasons.

15 FEBRUARY

I went to Paul's Cross, for we must, to hear a Mr Hayward preach. Nearby were hundreds of soldiers that there might be no disorder; in sooth, many more hundreds of soldiers were placed about the city. Hayward spake long on Essex's treachery and his passage was "Then the men of David sware unto him, saying, Thou shalt go no more out with us to battle, that thou quench not the light of Israel" [2 Samuel 22.17]. After he delivered his sermon (to which, I confess, I attended not), there was great applause for the queen's deliverance. Well, 'tis easy enough to pray for that.

18 FEBRUARY

Gus Phillips was examined today by the Privy Council on our part in the late rebellion by Lord Essex. He told the Council much as I recorded before, how Essex's men were desirous to see *Richard II*, though we told them it was but an old play, & how they offered us 40 shillings for playing. Gus told me that his testimony appeared to satisfy the Council which, he thought, had much predetermined who was guilty of treason and who not. So our part is deemed an innocent one. Essex and Harry [Southampton] are to be tried on the morrow in Westminster Hall; there can be no doubt of the verdict for, the rumour is, Francis Bacon, that accounted himself Essex's friend, is to speak against him. What man would not, save for sweet Harry.

19 FEBRUARY

Essex & Southampton were tried and condemned today. Some time after six o'clock this evening I heard much commotion in the street outside my window. Crowds of folk rushed about, & I called to a man to enquire of the disturbance. He said all were going where they might see the Earl of Essex led back to the Tower. Though the thought of a glimpse of Harry nearly o'erpowered me, I stayed in my room and prayed instead. My heart is with him, yet he hath allowed himself to be led quite astray. If he is to die, I hope Harry finds peace & rest eternal. God grant him that, the sweet gallant soul. Mine own soul is full of discord and dismay.

20 FEBRUARY

Our company is commanded to play before Her Majesty on Tuesday next [24 February]. She has yet to bespeak the play she desires to see, which we wonder at. But we are comforted that she would see us perform sith we did perform for Essex on the eve of his rebellion. I do suspect there is much method in H.M.'s commands.

21 FEBRUARY

I suspect we are made part of some cruel irony which Her Majesty hath in mind. Today I heard a rumour that Essex is to die the morning after we perform before the queen, but no one is confirmed in this belief. But I think the queen might do such a thing, for she is disappointed that Essex failed her as her favourite, & is full of vengeance because he would lord it over her. She hath not the rarer virtue, forgiveness.

22 FEBRUARY

The queen bespeaks the *Merry Wives* because she would see Falstaff again. Tom Pope is to play Falstaff, for Kempe is in Germany or Italy or some such country, I know not where. We trust Her Majesty does not want to see Kempe, for we would not have her fury fly in our faces.

24 FEBRUARY

We played *Merry Wives* for the queen today, though our playing lacked heart, for I believe we all thought on the affairs of recent days. We were in some fear because we had played for Essex's men before the rebellion. Yet Her Majesty's joy & delight in the play was palpable, though mayhap not unfeigned. After we had concluded, she called our company forth and addressed us thus: "Well, goodmen players. As you did play for the Earl of Essex on the eve of his rebellion, it is but meet, right, and proper that you play for *your prince* on the eve of his execution. Yes, indeed, he goes to the block tomorrow morn, & so perish all such traitors. He can scarce savour his last few hours as we have done." She turned to leave, but then turned back, and said, "We had hoped to see Master Kempe play Falstaff, but it is no great matter. What we saw played did suffice." She left, & we hastened away, glad the thing was finished.

ASH WEDNESDAY [25 FEBRUARY]

Essex was executed this morning, & the tales of his execution abound. 'Tis said that his lordship was dressed all in scarlet (that the blood might not show), and frankly confessed his treasons, implored the queen's pardon, and set forth a deep repentance. Nothing in his life became him like the leaving of it. The executioner struck three blows before the head came off, and then he held it aloft for all the see. Later a crowd gathered to beat Derrick, the executioner, as he left the Tower, but the Sheriff of London rescued him & carried him safely off. I have heard naught of what hath befallen Harry [Southampton], & I may not contemplate what doom doth await him.

27 FEBRUARY

This ballad on Essex is writ already, tho' woe betide the author if the authorities lay hands upon him:
    Sweet England's pride is gone,
        Welladay, welladay!
    Brave honour graced him still,
        Gallantly, gallantly.
    He ne'er did deed of ill,
        Well it is known.
    But envy, that foul fiend,
        Whose malice ne'er did end,
    Hath brought true virtue's friend
        Unto this thrall.

Also today three Catholics were executed at Tyburn, and they were, folk say, joyful at their execution.

1 MARCH

This morning I walked to St. Paul's Cross where Dr. Barlow gave a sermon on rendering unto Caesar [Matthew 22.22], & on the Earl of

Essex. The goodly doctor had been with the Earl at his execution, & had heard his confessions. As by rote, the doctor commended the execution & rejoiced in Her Majesty's safety, at which there were many loud "amens" and "God save Her Majesty," and many another.

6 MARCH

Yesterday several conspirators with Essex were arraigned and condemned.[11] How swiftly they all go to it, for ever the caterpillars o' the state must be rooted out, branch & stem.

11 MARCH

Today an order was issued that during Lent plays shall be suppressed. Thus am I reminded I have penned but little since *Hamlet*, & even in these parlous times I must write or we shall all be paupers. The next [play] must needs be a comedy, for life & events hath been all too dark, and we have seen our own tragedies enacted as flesh. So I shall pen what I will, *quodlibet*.[12]

13 MARCH

I know not why, and there being no Kit Marlowe by to goad me to it, but today I walked to Tyburn to see the executions. First they brought out Essex's secretary [Henry Cuffe] who, before his slaughter, did say some words in his own excuse. After him they brought out Sir Gelly Meyrick, who desired to be despatched upon the gad [quickly], for he was weary o' the world. In sooth his wish was fulfilled, the means of his death as bloody as they ever are.

18 MARCH

Today there were more executions. At Tower Hill, Sir Christopher Blount & Sir Charles Danvers were beheaded before the multitudes.

Having no further stomach for blood, I stayed in my room and assayed some few words, though my mind & heart were not in what I penned. I must be more resolute, bold, but not bloody. I come to think this new comedy shall be naught but a riotous gallimaufry of comedies gone before, for 'tis easy to raise laughter at the familiar, that what we desire to see happen doth indeed befall. Expectation fulfilled. And everyone shall be in search of love, that passion as constant as the lodestar. *Quodlibet.*

5 APRIL

How swiftly might I come by £100, and from his worship the mayor to boot—all for yielding up a name. Alas, I know not the author or authors of the slanders that have stuffed the ears of men, 'tis said, with false reports.[13] And, blast her, Anne wants forty shillings I have not in hand, and all to pay a debt to her father's shepherd.[14]

19 APRIL

The other day [16 April] the two Percys that did talk with us [on 5 February] were released unto the charge of their brother, the Earl.[15] So not all those of Essex's party & rebellion go to the block. Cut off but the head, the snake is scotched and dies.

25 APRIL

In the street today Marston accosted me; we chatted awhiles, & then went, about six o'clock, to the Bunch of Grapes for ale, bread & cheese. We talked of affairs which have passed this year, & Marston hath been as much affrighted as myself. He told me that Francis Bacon's book of Essex's trial hath been published,[16] but Marston thinks it will not win the public's love. He said, "Essex hath been generous to Bacon in years past, & now for Bacon to serve him thus, e'en in death—why folk will not stomach it." I agreed, & then told him of my *quodlibet* that I think to call *What You Will.* He laughed: "Why, how marvellous strange, that is the self-same title of my play for the Children of Paul's, my next hit at Jonson, whenever they may perform it now that Lent is done."[17] Tho' he protested he cared not, I told him I will bethink me some other title for my play, for I care not to be a part of their "war," as folk people might think. Then we talked on many another matter for some three hours together.

20 MAY

Supped with Tom Dekker & John Marston at the Mermaid, where we three had not been in several weeks or more. 'Twas an excellent repast with fine wine aplenty. They talked much of their "battles" with Ben Jonson, & marked how he would engage them further. They marvelled at the fervency of Ben's bitterness and bile, &, for their part, they bethink themselves generous and forgiving, Tom much so. Tom said he thought Jonson purposed another play already,[18] & he believed word of their "war" brought in the multitudes—at least, some folk who would not bestir themselves otherwise. Tom also said there was talk that the brother of Francis Bacon had died,[19] but there was no public notice. It would seem Anthony, this brother, was grieved by the execution of the Earl of Essex, his great friend and master. I marvel at the reach of one man's death, and at the loyalty such a fiery man inspired in friends & followers alike, & how many he led to their appointed end. Yet I rejoice Harry [Southampton] was spared, e'en though he lies in the Tower.

11 JUNE

At the Bell Inn in Carter Lane to sup with Dick Quiney, who had with him a petition of their grievances against Sir Edward Greville, against enclosures and what not.[20] Dick was full of hope that the authorities would attend to the petition, for it comes from the Corporation & those well-versed in ancient practice in Stratford, father amongst them. I wished him well; I was right glad to see him & have his company.

7 JULY

A levy of 1,000 men is ordered to be taken from the City; they are to go into the low countries. Some say the Spanish are in Ireland, though I know not if this be but idle rumour, like most such rumours prove to be.

23 JULY

More levies are to be made; they say over 5,000 men are wanted because the Spanish aid the Irish rebels. Will there ever be tranquillity, save in death? Such a year as this hath been, methinks this land will be for ever racked with domestic fury, fierce civil strife, & suffering.

1 AUGUST

These several weeks past I have read o'er a number of my plays, seeking out some inspiration for this quodlibet play which haunts my mind. These are to the purpose—*Comedy of Errors, Merchant of Venice* (that was called the Jew of Venice), *Two Gentlemen, Merry Wives*, perchance *As You Like It,* and I forget not Plautus. Parts of *Hamlet* (eavesdropping, love letters) from which I might take some cue. No role shall be larger than another, for this practice suits our company well; none may envy, all harmonious. I must talk with Bob Armin, and with neighbour [Thomas] Morley for some music I would have him compose. Love and music—there lies my path. Both delight us, but they vanish as swiftly as a morning's dew; yet we pursue love with might & main. One moment no love, next, all love.

2 AUGUST

They say there is a fleet of Spanish ships off the western coasts. Moe men are impressed. Jonson has told me somewhat of his next play, which he calls *The Poetaster*, though I care not either way. In his eye there is, as so oft, an evil glint; he desires to do ill, so mayhap I may shoot some gibe or jest in his direction. An evil-wisher, Malvolio, shall be a character in my madcap comedy, & thereby might I recall Benvolio in *Romeo*![21] I have settled on twins and disguises, that the boys might act women the easier. Ned [Shakespeare] hath some difficulty with his voice, & he is more a man than a boy/woman these days. Yet he thinks he can still play for us, and I would have him do so if 'tis possible.

15 AUGUST

My brain is idle. I would write. I know what I would write, yet I cannot. Then today came word that father ails sorely; so tomorrow Ned [Shakespeare] & I return to Stratford. It hath been an age and more since Anne & I saw each other. The madcap, quodlibet play shall be called *Twelfth Night*—that, at the least, is something. Peradventure few thoughts may come in Stratford, for the circumstance be not propitious.

25 AUGUST

Home. Mother much troubled about father. Ned & I do what we can, but father, I believe, hath not the will to live. Anne & I are tolerable well together.

7 SEPTEMBER

Tomorrow father will be laid in the churchyard [of Holy Trinity], and he ends as all must. Mother is grievous grief-struck, but Anne is a great comforter to her, and sister Joan ever a blessing. I must attend to father's affairs before I may return to the city—Ned says he will return once the funeral is done.

8 SEPTEMBER

'Tis done; father is buried. A multitude of folk, all of Stratford it did seem, saw him laid to rest, even some people that liked him not in life.

Welladay, the rude wind will ne'er hurt him more. Leastways matters will be soon settled over father's houses, which are to come to me, & Joan is well pleased with her portion.[22] I stay some days more for mother's sake, & to please Anne.

16 SEPTEMBER

I had returned to the hurly-burly of London but an hour or two when I met with Kempe. Or the rather, he did seek me out, for he wanted my good word & opinion, and he desired to become once more a sharer in our company. He said also he wished I might pen some part for him to personate. I told him that Robert Armin was now one of our players and enacted such roles as he, Kempe, had done heretofore. I did not tell Will that Bob acts the better and sans broad sawing of the air, speeches extempore, and such like that Will would do in his perversity. Kempe looked much downcast, but afore long he told me a long tale of his journey into Germany and Italy whence he had returned but a few days before, but with poor fortune. He told me that in Rome he met Sir Anthony Shirley who recounted to Will his wondrous adventures into Persia, and how he and his brother had served the Sophy [Shah] of Persia.[23] These reports, I had almost called them fables so fantastic were they to hear, did engross my mind, and hath occupied my thoughts since. After some while I began to sorrow for Will and his condition, & so I said that, though the company hath all the sharers needed, yet if he were not too proud he could be one of the hired men, for those we always need. For a moment Kempe frowned, then he laid aside his pride, his face gladdened, and he said, "Those be fair words, sweet Will. I know I always played fast & loose with my part; that was but my way of playing, as you know. I should be right glad of any work you & the fellows might put my way, & I shall thank ye right heartily."

So we parted better friends than we have been in many a long time. I know not what Will might play, for Armin *is* our clown, but forsooth Kempe deserves something from us, for he was ever popular with the multitude & served our turn well.

17 SEPTEMBER

Yesterday Kempe, & this evening came to me Dekker, Marston, & some others, all full of Jonson's last gibe in their "war."[24] They were in high roistering spirits & seemed not angered by Ben's satire on them, of which they told me much. Marston said Ben called him Crispinus in this *Poetaster* & Ben appeareth as Horace. In one scene Horace tells Crispinus that he is a "strong tedious talker, that should vex and almost bring Horace to consumption," & that he is a "long-winded monster" [Act 3]. Later, Horace gives this Crispinus some pills which cause him to vomit up and disgorge words from Marston's plays [Act 5]. As he told me this, Marston laughed heartily, whereat I wondered why he was not angered. Marston said he cared not, for Ben's play was weak, thin gruel—indeed scarce a play at all, and acted but by boys, & so wanted true satire.[25] Dekker laughed also, & said Jonson named him as one Demetrius and called him a "very simple honest fellow, a dresser of plays" [Act 3]. "Well," said Dekker, "beshrew me if that is not true, though I have gained but little from that craft." Yet, for a minute, Dekker's visage took on a serious aspect, and he said Jonson must think all players are catamites and seek after others.[26] "Well," said Marston, "'tis common enough, & no harm is meant. Remember poor Kit Marlowe. And for all that, what of Ben & the venery he confesseth. 'Tis all one." I said nothing and held my thoughts. Then Dekker told me he thought Jonson did also satirise me as one called Ovid junior. "Why," I said, "all the world knows that I am much enamoured of Ovid & read him oft." "Well," said Dekker, "there is a scene [4.7] where this Ovid, in Ben's play, is much like Romeo in your play, Will. And Ovid's Juliet is called Julia, and she appeareth on high to him from her window. Yet Ben gives them fustian, the merest parody of those beauteous words you had those young lovers speak." Dekker described the scene further, & the more he did so, the more angered I grew, though I knew I should not.

The chat continued some while, & then Marston said that he & Dekker had their revenge on Jonson well in hand, a play they call *Satiromastix*, and told me somewhat of it. They employ the self-same characters as did Ben—Horace whom Demetrius and Crispinus reprove for being quarrelsome & such like. Then I said that if they desired to anger Ben thoroughly they should call him a bricklayer or mortar treader, and say how he escaped hanging by saying his neck-verse—for such be what Ben hath done. Dekker & Marston laughed, agreed, & said they would do so. "And forget not," I said, "he writes his plays but slowly, tediously."[27] Marston said this last would be a good hit, for now he recalled Ben's mock of me and my swift facility. He said, "Ovid junior writes law cases in verse and says he knows not why: 'they run from my pen unwittingly if they be verse.'" Well, there was much more said, and I trust they drag Jonson across the stage as the condemned are dragged on hurdles through the streets to the scaffold. Blast him! But I can be frampold and piss o' th' nettle as well as him!

26 SEPTEMBER

Today I met Dekker in the street, he brimful of mirth, for yesterday Jonson told him that Henslowe had given him £2 for additions to Kyd's *Spanish Tragedy*. Dekker said Ben recalled not how he had called him [Dekker] a dresser of plays, but thought he, Ben, had done well![28] I laughed right heartily, and said humility was something Ben thought not on greatly, nor would he ever possess it, and that pride goeth before the fall, and so forth. Then I told Dekker I had spoke with my fellow sharers, who are annoyed somewhat with Ben, for he left us so that he might pen his mockeries for the little eyases, that eyrie of children. "We are agreed," I said, "that we will play your *Satiromastix* when 'tis complete, if you & Marston wish it." Dekker was much overcome with joy, and said the piece was well nigh complete, and asked me whether we could play it a month hence or thereabouts. I told him I knew not surely, but things done well and with care exempt themselves from fear.[29]

1 OCTOBER

Twelfth Night is now lodged firmly in my mind. When I write the part called Malvolio, I needs but think bitterly of Jonson, & all is then made easy, as is the rest of this love play. 'Tis no great thing, but it will suffice. We might play it well enough this Christmastide when we are called for, as surely we must.

13 OCTOBER

Yesterday Nicholas Brend died. God rest his soul, for he was a good man to us, and I doubt we shall look upon his like again. We are fortunate his affairs were well settled & we have naught to fear.[30]

1 NOVEMBER

Though it needs amendment (but a little) *Twelfth Night* is finished, and we are agreed on our parts. Bob Armin is Feste (& pleased with his quips), Tom Pope is Toby Belch, & with him Dick Cowley as Sir Andrew [Aguecheek]. All three promise fine merriment. Dick [Burbage] is to be Orsino the Duke (after the noble whom I did remember from last Christmastide at Court), though Dick longs more for tragedy and Hamlet. Gus Phillips said he cared little for Jonson, and thus desired to be Malvolio to jest and mock at Ben. Ned [Shakespeare] is to be Viola, & Will Sly the twin Sebastian, for they do look something alike. And, on the sudden, I am struck with remembrance of that dear twin [Hamnet], tho' I must rejoice that t'other is spared yet to me. But to the purpose—Olivia—Sam Gilburne; Maria, the other Sam,[31] most pert. The rest—John Heminges, Fabian; Henry Condell, Antonio; and I am to be the Sea Captain, for I would not have a lion's part! Yet no date is fixed on, which is no great matter provided that it be performed ere long. We shall not need to rehearse much, simple thing that it is, tho' I do confess I am half in easeful love with the music Morley hath composed for the play.

11 NOVEMBER

Today we played *Satiromastix*, and the Children of Paul's also play it privily. Lord, how we enjoyed the jests at Jonson, called Horace, and many was the time we all fain have would fallen down laughing, so fiercely did we bait Horace. The crowd, though not large, was a goodly size, & perceived keenly whom and what we mocked. The multitude roared when Horace was crowned with nettles, at which in the midst of the audience someone called out how did he like the stings now? I might feel sorry for Ben, but he hath brought his troubles upon his own head. Mayhap now this so-called war is dead and gone.[32]

20 NOVEMBER

Twelfth Night—I have done little but blot a line here and a line there. Thus it is complete and I care not greatly for it, though I would see it personated. It is comedy enow, but my mind dwells on darker matter—*Hamlet* hath more savour than twins and love. Oft I have recalled the line "If this were played upon a stage now, I could condemn it as an improbable fiction" [*Twelfth Night*, 3.4.119–20], for much we do is but fiction most improbable. Bob Armin & Tom Pope, most friendly, told me yesterday of some conference they had of cakes, ale, and ginger spices—all which they would have me add if I were so pleased.[33] So I have pleased them.

29 NOVEMBER

A joyous day, for Gus Phillips' son was baptized this day at St. Saviour's [Southwark]. They have named him Augustine after dear Gus himself, which is well enough. We drank and ate heartily. The babe quiet & grave.

1 DECEMBER

We are to play at Court come Christmastide, tho' *Twelfth Night* is not yet called for.[34]

9 DECEMBER

My Lord Hundson hath commanded us to play for him at his house in Blackfriars; Her Majesty is to be his guest of honour. We play *Twelfth Night*, for H.M. demands naught but comedy; it brings her such comfort & joy as she can summon.

10 DECEMBER

Today with Ned [Shakespeare] and Sam Gilburne, for they would rehearse together and seek my opinion. They had chosen the scene in which Viola all disguised as Cesario woos Olivia for Count Orsino [3.1.91–161]. They played right prettily, tho' they would stumble and fall over my words, which they knew not well. 'Twas but flimflam. For awhile I played Viola, then Olivia, not for imitation though, for I am not a glass wherein they may find themselves. After a short while they did well, tho' Ned worries his voice will not hold. He said, "Most days, Will, it cracks not, but I do fear the day is nigh when my voice will drop for ever." After some ale, bread, and cheese, they rehearsed the scene again, and whether it was the ale, I know not, but they spoke with much fervour. I marvel that Ned spake but one line, "I come to whet your gentle thoughts" [3.1.102], and the flame was lit.

12 DECEMBER

How mightily astonished have I been! I walked to Ned's lodging to speak further with him on playing Viola. I could not make him hear when I knocked at his door, which being open, I entered, thinking I might await his return, for the evening was cold, & I would fain not stand out of doors. Once inside I saw him with Sam Gilburne in the height of carnally coupled passion. So lustily did they go to it, they knew not I had entered. Thus did I retreat and came again to mine own lodging. Now I know not if I should say aught to Ned, yet condemn him I cannot, for I know what sweet pleasures they did enjoy. 'Tis better left so, I think, leastways for awhile, for such a notable ardent passion endures but rarely. And our play may yet profit by it. But what & if these two live, & have the agony of love about them?

17 DECEMBER

This night at the Mermaid, Jonson accosted me and sneered, for he had drunk much wine and had not eaten. He said he heard I had written a play in which he appeared as an evil-doer, and he asked what was my purpose. I told him that in my play *Twelfth Night*, that is to be played before the Queen come Christmastide, there is one called Malvolio who is "sick of self-love" [1.5.85]. "Why," said Ben, "you call to mind my *Cynthia's Revels*, and all the world will think it a hit at me."[35] I asked Ben why this should trouble him, for had he not done like things in his plays, and he cared not for those he held up to public view. I told him I may have thought on him while I wrote, but that it was no great matter, for I have thought on many persons, and he should not be so vain. So, Ben snarled, sneered, and fleered for some time. Then he said that he would be avenged, for his *Poetaster* was to be registered ere long for all the world to read.[36] He continued to quaff off the muscadel, & I was afeard he would grow riotous—so I left him, & I know not whether to hate or pity him.

CHRISTMAS EVE [24 DECEMBER]

Today, great thunder, lightning, and quaking of the earth almost upon the stroke of noon. I might believe these are dread portents, yet 'tis but thunder. For all that, I was afeard a little. I shall to church for the Christmas mass.

26 DECEMBER

Today we played at Court, and were feasted right handsomely afterwards. Her Majesty was pleased with our company. I was loath to return to my closet for I had need of merriment & goodly company. I thought to seek out Ned [Shakespeare], but remembered 'twas like I should find him & Sam [Gilburne] hot & lusty together. I would I had the comfort of Anne, the children, & home.

29 DECEMBER

This evening we played *Twelfth Night* for the Lord Hunsdon and Her Majesty at his lordship's house in Blackfriars. The occasion was festive, the house full of garlands and delights. We played passing fair, but better by far were Ned [Shakespeare] and Sam Gilburne as Viola and Olivia. Yet only I, as well as themselves, knew why or how love shone through their eyes. I am glad I said naught of what I had seen betwixt them. Gus Phillips, Malvolio to perfection, caused much mirth, and how the Queen laughed. 'Tis clear as broad day she cares not for Puritans. Master Morley's music did affect me much, and Armin sang the songs to ravish the ear. Most poignant. As of yore, H.M. called for me and told me of her delight in seeing the play. "Think not on tragedy, Master Shakespeare," quoth she, "for you do excellent well in comedy, which doth please us much. We do charge you to write more after this vein for us, & you shall be rewarded handsomely." She wished me joy of the season. I mumbled a "your majesty." Tomorrow Cuthbert's daughter is to be baptized, and I rejoice, and my heart is glad.[37]

※ *Shakespeare is at his height of fame and fortune, and recognized in many ways both far and near; he is again made a character in a play performed at Cambridge University. He changes his lodgings and moves north of the River Thames where he finds himself closer to friends.* Twelfth Night *continues to be popular, and is well received at the Inns of Court. At the urging of others, rather strangely Shakespeare turns to the story of* Troilus and Cressida *for his next play, which fails to be performed. In May, Shakespeare's Stratford friend Dick Quiney is attacked brutally by the local squire's thugs; Quiney dies in June, and Shakespeare's mood darkens once more. Nevertheless his friendship and debates on drama with Jonson resume, and a respite at Stratford after an illness in London results in him reworking a juvenile effort: it is called* All's Well That Ends Well. *It is not one of Shakespeare's favorite plays, and the ever more frail Queen Elizabeth falls asleep during its Christmas performance.* ※

2 JANUARY

Yesterday at Court. We were applauded heartily, & Her Majesty was as light in heart as I have e'er seen for many a long month. Today I saw Kempe, who was jocund. He hath joined Worcester's Men, and tomorrow they play at Court.[1] I told Will I rejoiced in his new-found good fortune, the more so because our company could do naught for him. Will said he bore no ill-will, and fortune had indeed smiled on him, & he was thankful. Then he told me that Tom Heywood desired to chat with me, for he hath been to Cambridge this Christmastide, and saw some play there much like one a year past. "Tom saith we two and Burbage were personated therein, & I fain would learn more," Kempe said. "If thou art curious to know, Will, let us three sup together ere long." I thanked him &, because I bear him no grudge, said we should seek out Heywood and hear his news.[2]

7 JANUARY

Though I never cared for Kempe while he was of our company, my affection for him hath increased since he hath returned from abroad. Mayhap 'tis because no longer must I write for him those parts that, wilful-negligent, he would mangle, as was ever his custom. But let that go. Yesternight I passed in pleasant company with Will and Tom Heywood, as I had promised with Will. Tom I have scarcely seen since I met him first a year past; as before, he was a pleasant, honest, open fellow with whom I desire more acquaintance. While we drank malmsey and ate a passing fair venison stew, Tom told us the tale of his visit to the university at Cambridge at Christmastide. He was saddened that Tom Nashe was not alive to accompany him, for Nashe would have enjoyed the satiric revelry. I felt my colour change and some fear grip my heart, for, on that sudden, I recalled that I had not seen Nashe in many a long month. I said, "So Tom is dead?" "Aye," Heywood said, "that is what I have heard tell, but where and how he died, I know not, and cannot tell ye." Kempe said Nashe was but a stripling, and could scarce be thirty years old. Tom said, "There's many, nay thousands that die before they be thirty, but I believe he was more than thirty." I said Tom was in the right, but I knew Nashe was younger than myself by a good few years.[3]

Then we fell silent for awhile, thinking on poor Nashe—leastways I did so. Then Heywood said, "Well, my tale of Cambridge may make you jocund," and he told how, as the year before, he had seen a play at one of the colleges acted by students and how it was called *Return From Parnassus*.[4] Heywood said two characters were called Burbage and Kempe (here Will laughed loud), and they spoke on actors and writers.

Tom said they called Jonson a "pestilent fellow," while I did surpass all writers, which I called a goodly jest. "Nay, Will," said Tom, "indeed, I do believe you do put down [surpass] all the others, & ye need not be so modest as a maid. Then this Burbage and Kempe (in the play) said ye had given Ben a purge, which I understood not." I said that puzzles the brain, unless, mayhap, Ben knew I had a hand (but a small one) in *Satiromastix*. Will nodded his head, and said it was no doubt the matter. Tom then told of how in the next scene two students come to Burbage and Kempe to see if they be suited for the stage and to rehearse some parts. "The jest here, Will, was Burbage had the student act Richard III, as though there could be any that might surpass Dick!"[5] Again, we laughed heartily, & so on as Tom told us more of this and that. When it came time for me to take my leave, Tom told us a curious thing. After the play, a student had spoke with him and said he would fain see Shakespeare's *Hamlet* acted there—curious, for how did he know of my play? Howsoever, I said that, mayhap, some time when the plague doth drive us forth from the city we might well act *Hamlet* at Cambridge.[6] Yet I muse how the play be known so widely already. Then to bed.

20 JANUARY

I hear that my *Merry Wives* is to be published, e'en though the company nor myself have authorised this. In all such matters I am as helpless as a new-born babe and as pitiable.[7] How occasions do inform against me!

21 JANUARY

What a curious strange conflux of events. This morn came news from Heminges that we are to give *Twelfth Night* this coming Candlemas [2 February] in the hall of the Middle Temple where the lawyers dine and keep their revels. Heminges said, "I hear tell 'twas your kinsman Tom Greene, who be a lawyer there, had something to do with this quest. The occasion promises fair, and in truth we have the play well in hand." I said belike Tom had said something, but I knew not. Then, some while before six o'clock, and after I had been to [St.] Paul's to see what books there might be, I walked up Ludgate Hill and found the Bel Savage Inn marvellous convenient to hand for food and drink. I sat near the fire, for the cold had pierced my body down to the very bones. As I awaited food, two gentlemen took their place close to me, and we fell atalking ere long. One of the gentlemen was called Mr Curle and his friend was Mr Towse, lawyers both.[8] How he knew, I know not, but the man Curle said that I must be that excellent writer of plays Master Shakespeare, and that he would fain be well acquainted with me. Curle said he had heard from his friend, John Manningham, with whom he shared rooms, that one of my plays was to be given at the Middle Temple come Candlemas.[9] I said I had received that self-same news that very morning, & I marvelled they knew it already. Then Curle said he desired to know more of this play, its nature and who might play in it. I told him it is called *Twelfth Night, or What You Will* and that I had looked well about me for inspiration—mine own plays such as the *Comedy of Errors*, as well as Plautus' *Menaechmi* and an Italian play called *Gli' Ingannati*. Then I told them who would personate the characters on Candlemas.

When he heard me name Dick Burbage, Mr Towse asked me to tell him more of that "illustrious actor." I agreed that Dick was indeed illustrious, some call him the finest actor of our age, though others incline to Ned Alleyn. Both men nodded. Then, for a jest, I told them a tale of Burbage and myself, though I did not tell them it was mere jesting. The tale: "Once a lady citizen waxed greatly amorous for Burbage while he played Richard the third. She appointed an hour for him to come to her that night by the name of Richard the third. Overhearing their complot, I went to the lady beforehand, and she entertained me. Then came a message that Richard the third was without at the door. I returned the message to Burbage that William the Conqueror was before Richard the third." The two men laughed right heartily, and Curle said he would relate the tale to his friend Manningham, for he noted down such tales in his tables.[10] We enjoyed much other chat ere we departed.

25 JANUARY

This day I walked over to Wood Street and supped with Dick Field, his wife [Jacqueline] and sons [Richard and Samuel]. They were all in good health and prosperity. We talked of much, and of home. I said I had a mind to seek out new lodging on this [north] side of the river. Jacqueline said she knew of a French Huguenot family called Mountjoy that had lodging in Mugle [Monkwell] Street, which might suit. She did not know if there were rooms now, but, if I wished, she would speak with Mme Mountjoy. "Why, dear Will," Dick said, "ye would be around the corner from us, so to speak, and that would be a blessing." I said I would be right glad to be near them, and that mine own wants are few—a peaceful room to pen my plays is all my desire. Jacqueline doubted not all would be harmonious charmingly there, if there is a room—which now I desire.

27 JANUARY

All hath been agreed swiftly, and today I lodge with the Mountjoys. Our household is thus: Christopher, the husband, who is a maker of tires and ornaments;[11] his wife and daughter, both called Mary; and a fair maid, Joan [Johnson]. My room is at the topmost of the house which lies at the corner of Mugle Street and Silver Street, hard by Cripplegate. Heminges and Condell are convenient close, so all will be well.[12] It was a happy thought which found me here.

3 FEBRUARY

Yester eve for a feast at the Middle Temple, we played *Twelfth Night*, as we did before for the queen. We were placed in the Great Hall of the Temple which was most convenient for our purpose. At one end was a large screen with lofty portals which we covered with hangings for our entrances. Before the screen we laid a platform for our stage. Opposite us, at the far end, was a large dias for the notables—nobles, judges, and such like as had to do with the affairs of the feast. These sat together with a large boisterous-noisy crowd of young gentlemen who would be lawyers and the like, though Tom Greene was not amongst them (I know not why). Our play fared well, and Malvolio much jeered. Ned [Shakespeare] pleased them well, but I fear his voice is not now suited for young women, & he must look to other parts. After we had played, a young gentleman sought me out and said he was John Manningham. He begged me to join him and his two friends I had met already [Curle and Towse], for all three desired to drink my good health. I thanked him for his kindness but told him I had already pledged myself to others. We parted good friends, Manningham declaring he would seek me out some other time.[13] As I was leaving, he asked me did I know that John Donne hath been married secretly these past three weeks to Anne, daughter of Sir George More, but now all is revealed. I knew not what to say; I scarce know Donne.[14]

11 FEBRUARY

These past four or five days my bones have ached severely, my head hath been pained, and I have had a burning fever. I have lain in bed all the while—Joan [Johnson] the maid hath tended me, & saith many folk are in like condition, but few have died.

14 FEBRUARY

Though hardly well, my sickness leaving me weak, I joined my fellows today at Court. We played *Twelfth Night*, for the queen did request it once more. I rejoiced my part—sea captain—was but small. I took to my bed as soon as all was done, Joan Johnson again tender in her ministrations unto me.

12 MARCH

Today at the Bel Savage Inn, I made a goodly repast. As I was supping ale and musing on what next I should write, Mr [John] Manningham entered and came to me. He asked me if I remembered him, & if I would oblige him by drinking with him, as he had to forgo that pleasure some weeks past. I said the honour would be mine, & so he sat with me, and we fell to drinking and chat. Manningham questioned me on plays, actors, and theatres, which I was pleased to make answer. I began to tell him the tale about myself and Dick Burbage which I had told to his two friends,[15] but I had hardly begun when he said he had, forsooth, heard it from his friends, & it delighted him greatly. I refrained from admitting 'twas a fiction, like so much else. Then Manningham asked me what new plays I had in mind, and he trusted we should play before one of the Inns [of Court] ere long. I told him that my purpose that very evening had been indeed a horse of that colour—to think on some subject for a play, though I knew not, of course, whether whatever it might be would suit the Inns. He said, "Mine own advice would be to take some tale from antiquity and write it anew. I knew your *Twelfth Night* was much like Plautus in some regard, yet you placed it not *in* antiquity. And, if you would permit me to remark, for I intend no offence, the tales of love were too honey-sweet. I speak now not of your Malvolio and his passion for, what was her name, Olivia. Yet in that Malvolio I did descry some bitterness, some satire, yes, and perchance that might be the fashion to follow. The fellows in the Inns like to think themselves above mere passion, mere love; they think themselves worldly and knowing." I commended him for his observation, and said there was no offence in't, for he had surmised my method. I told him that, indeed, the plots of near all my plays belonged to others and thus were ready made. Yet I hoped that what I wrote breathed life anew into the old tales.

So we chatted more on this purpose awhile, & the more Manningham spoke, the more I found I cleaved to the man and his thoughts. After some time who should enter but Tom Dekker whom I had ne'er encountered at the Bel Savage. Tom sat down with us and commanded more ale, cheese, and bread. I told Tom of our conversation and begged him for his thoughts on the matter. Tom said that there was indeed much matter in antiquity, as perpend, Virgil's *Aeneid*, or Homer's *Iliad*, and that I might look to them for inspiration. I said that but some time past I had made use of the *Aeneid* in *Hamlet*,[16] so I would have none of that. "Well," said Tom, "awhile ago Chettle and myself wrote a play on

Troilus and Cressida for Henslowe. In truth it was much on Cressida after she gave herself up to be the strumpet of the Greeks. 'Twas much after Henryson."[17] "There," said Manningham, "is such a subject as I describe—Troilus and Cressida. If Master Dekker followed Henryson, perchance you might improve upon Chaucer." So we talked more on the matter, and verily I believe I have hit upon my theme, and mayhap we might perform such a play for the Inns.

25 MARCH

Tom Dekker to my room, he most pleasant. He had with him Chapman's *Iliad* for me to read.[18] I thanked him thoroughly, & told him I had these past few days read Chaucer's *Troilus and Criseyde* which I had by me. Dekker said he could not find his play on Cressida, & knew not what fate had befallen it. Yet he thought it no great loss, for he did not think much of it. "'Twas poor matter, Will, leastways in compare to your fine plays." I told him he was too modest by half. Tom said he had work aplenty in hand, yet he hoped he might find employment with Worcester's Men if they do but get their licence.[19] I told him I had in mind some small hit at Jonson, but I had not devised the business. Dekker laughed, & said mayhap we should let poor Ben rest in peace.

1 APRIL

Dinner with William Combe. He came late, for he was detained by his affairs at the Middle Temple for which he came also to the city. After a pleasing repast, we agreed on his land in Old Stratford to be sold to me within the month or thereabouts—Gilbert [Shakespeare] to be my agent. Combe exacted a heavy price, though for all that, it is fair enough, & I am contented. I may not write plays for ever, & we come to depend upon land.[20]

4 APRIL

Troilus play [*Troilus and Cressida*]. Perchance 'tis because I think on that land in Stratford, but my thoughts are as frozen as the Thames in deepest winter. I think in jest of Jonson when I think of Ajax and his o'erweening pride o'er naught; but that is but to suckle a fool & chronicle small beer. Jest—Ajax—a jakes. I can go no further; I must to bed.

5 APRIL

I espy an irony. If this play, this *Troilus and Cressida*, be writ for the Inns [of Court] then 'tis much like the plays Jonson writes for the Children of the Chapel. Thus should I fashion it more after his work? Mayhap. There needs be little fighting in it, for methinks the lawyers desire debate, not action (and thereby shall we require fewer hired men to boot). The characters shall exchange speeches merely, not swords. One scene might recall Romeo's passion with Juliet, but there shall be more bitterness in *Troilus*.[21] 'Tis best I write what I may, and amend thereafter, thinking how we might play it at the Inn where we gave *Twelfth Night*—yet it must provide variable service, there & in our own playhouse.

12 APRIL

Gilbert [Shakespeare] arrived at my lodging today, tired from his journey. He marvels anew at what he hath seen and heard in London, though, he said, he had not forgot the noisome stench.[22] "But I'd rather be by the hearth at home, when the moon is down, & the crickets chirp, Will." I had forgot the sweet air of Stratford; Gilbert's presence recalls the joys of home, e'en when the screech owl calls in the dawn. Yet my work is here, and surely I would find Stratford a prison in mind and spirit if I returned there for ever—though I fear I must one day. We have eaten and drunk together heartily, and talked of the folk at home. Gilbert hath not found him a wife, and he believes he hath grown too old to take one. "I' faith, Will," he said, "I know not if I care for a wife.

There may be pleasure and comfort with a wife, but there's many of 'em be shrewish, and that I could not abide. Why, look, you yourself have managed well enough with a wife a hundred miles away, which is as good as to say you have no wife." I thought to expostulate with him, but then thought better of it. Gilbert returns home two days hence with money for [William] Combe's land, and I fear lest he be robbed on the highway. He thinks naught of the danger.

1 MAY

Troilus [and Cressida] is complete, yet I think it hath gone awry. Mayhap my heart was not in it. Perchance I have tried to serve two masters, the Inns [of Court] and our own playhouse, when I should have penned the piece for the Globe, and we could make do if we played it at an Inn. I know not, & I care not greatly for the work. I have shown some of it to some of the fellows, and they are of one mind that we should play it for the lawyers when they command it. There is no certainty we shall play it at the Globe.[23]

10 MAY

Word from Gilbert [Shakespeare] that the land in Old Stratford hath been conveyed, and all is as it should be. Gilbert's other news is troublous. Some drunken men have brawled with Dick Quiney, striking him about the head and wounding him grievously. I pray he do recover, but the news is heavy ominous.[24]

12 MAY

Today, while we played, our playhouse was beset by numerous men who impressed as many in the audience as they could lay hands on. Such was the hurly-burly, we ceased our playing. Many of those taken were not lawfully impressed, but we had no remedy. I heard tell that the bowling alleys and bawdy houses alike were set upon. I could by no means discern the reason for this violent impressing of men.

22 MAY

To me this morn, Anthony Munday; I had not seen him in some weeks. We chatted, & he said he had scarce escaped being impressed two weeks past. I told him of the hurly-burly at the Globe. Then Munday told me that he and some several others were to write a play on Julius Caesar for Henslowe (he had Henslowe's £5 in hand today). "Yet," he said, "we lack all inspiration."[25] I asked him if he had seen my *Julius Caesar* when we played it, which he had, & he said how the multitude had given its ready approbation. He asked me if the play had been published, and I told him it had not for, indeed, it is popular.[26] I told him that, but for it being popular, I would let him have my copy, but I might not do that, for in truth it belongs to our whole company. Munday understood this well enough, and said that he and his fellows might surely knock their heads together & pen something. To show I bore him no ill will, we went to drink ale together. Yet how I am reminded of those early days when I had to do the like; 'tis no way to write a play, for it must be of a piece, it must be mine own. But needs must, and beggars may not chose.

10 JUNE

From Gilbert [Shakespeare] dread news that poor dear Dick Quiney hath died of the blows Sir Edward Greville's men gave him. And what of Dick's nine children, his wife? The man was but keeping the peace, trying to restore order, & for this he dies at the hands of men who should know better. How can there be peace in the realm with the likes of Sir Edward who does as he pleases and choses, & to non-regardance casts the law. Who may be safe? And but last year Essex rebelled. Such hath oft been my deadly theme in chronicles, yea, e'en *Troilus* where men die for a woman stole by another—where is degree and order when Dick can be murdered? And what will come to pass when our queen die, as she will ere long? Shall there be fighting then? I know not. Fear whirls me round; how can I write? Yet I must, but I am afeard I cannot write a tragedy, for my thoughts lie in too dark an abyss. Comedy? Yet I cannot shake off despair, and inspiration have I none to please these curious days.

15 JUNE

I have been downcast and in ill humour several days; the fit will not pass. The death of poor Dick Quiney, his murder, preys upon me still; something deep within ails me. Nonetheless I betook myself to the Mermaid, for I had promised Jonson I would drink and eat with him there. He hath more friendship in him of late, and, when he is not in an ill temper, he is welcome company. Besides, not one of us may be long in this world—we may follow Dick soon enough. Ben had arrived at the Mermaid before me by an hour or more I thought, for 'twas plain he had drunk a sufficient quantity of wine, and he was in high spirits. So we did chat and drink as several hours stole on. Ben was remorseful for his past ill humours, and wished we would be better companions. I told him that he had truly slighted me and others, that he took things ill which were not so, or being so, concerned him not. "But Ben," I said, "none of us hold grudges long, and we shall be better friends from this day forward."

After some while we fell to talk of our plays and, like myself, Ben wants inspiration. He cares not for our audiences; he said, "The multitude, that beast, loves nothing that is right and proper. The farther it runs from reason and possibility, the better it is with them." But he hath, he said, penned some amendments and scenes for *The Spanish Tragedy* which Henslowe did ask him for, though Ben said these be not complete. Then I told him of my conversation with Munday some weeks since [22 May], and for an instant, at mention of his name, Ben scowled but then smiled again. Ben said, "Well, that's mighty strange, that Munday would cast his eye on Julius Caesar, though in truth 'tis a well-worn tale that any one might retell. Yet I had thought you held the field there, Will." I said that I was well pleased my play was popular with the multitudes, but that I cared naught if Munday & the others wrote on Caesar too. "For," I said, "the story can scarce be called mine own. And I see no fault in that. The worth of a thing lies in the writing, for, as you know well, my plots are not mine own." Then Ben said that put him in mind of something he had pondered a year or two ago, a play on Richard Crookback, but when he had thought further on't he recalled my play. So I said it was some ten years since my *Richard III*, & out of doubt the time was ripe for another play upon him. "And besides, Ben, you know your play could not be like mine, for our styles do differ as much as night from day." Ben said he would think more on't.[27] We drank, and ate some more, and parted good friends again.

30 JUNE

In great pain, I have been lying abed these several days. I would send for a physician, though I fear there be no remedy for whatever aileth me. I' faith, remedies and physicians keep little company. There is so much thunder and lightning today that might be an omen of worse to come, if I did but believe in such childlike folly. *Later.* Joan [Johnson] hath been with me and asked me how I fare. I told her all my condition, & she asked me if she might look at my body. Since the pain was great, I did allow her. So she looked at my body carefully & closely, & after some while she said there was a fistula and she could furnish a remedy. She prepared and did apply a poultice or cataplasm, which presently brought me much ease. I am to drink a potion of herbs and I know not what else. I am in hope that all will end well. So much the less is my pain now that I have read somewhat in *The Palace of Pleasure* for mine enjoyment.[28]

4 JULY

There is now little pain, and greater ease, for which I have given Joan [Johnson] much thanks. She hath tended me with gentle care, I had almost writ loving care. She hath been all the comfort a man might desire. During these long days I have read *The Palace of Pleasure* which hath in the past been like an old friend, and wherein I have found goodly tales & stories for my use. I recall, too, that many years ago I wrote the shadow of a play wherein I did employ, for the plot, a story from the *Decameron*. In it a fistula was healed, or some such thing—not unlike mine own anguish and calamity which would have carried me off. I have not found it in this room, & so I think it must be with Anne in Stratford. Now I have more strength I shall return home, as indeed 'tis time, & search for it, for I think I can amend it, since I lack all inspiration else. It would be right & proper to enquire how Dick Quiney's family shog in their parlous days. I shall leave tomorrow.

11 JULY

A long, hard ride home to Stratford. Weather fair. Anne hath received me kindly, & we agree well together. I have seen Elizabeth [Quiney], and she grieves quietly for her dear Richard; life goes hard for her for the time being. She says she keeps herself busy, for otherwise she would dwell too long in her thoughts & might despair. I believe it is the manner of Dick's death, his murder, that afflicts her most, as well it might.

12 JULY

I have found what once I was pleased to call a play, but would be loathed to do so now, for it is a paltry thing. It is stuffed full with rhymes and sonnets that I would scorn to employ these days, though the thing could suffice if I might amend it.[29] There is no part for Bob Armin, which would not please him nor the crowd, so one must be fashioned for him.[30] Yet the betrayed wife [Helena] is such that the heart might be stirred. So, I shall set to it here whiles I regain my strength & health. London may wait, for home proffers savours sweet and fresh air—& I must tend to my land & affairs.

29 JULY

I rejoice in my safe return to the city; riding yesterday harrowed me with wonder & fear. There was great rain, lightning, tempestuous winds, hurricanes, and, at the last, hail of such bigness I have ne'er seen before. I was returned but two hours when Ben Jonson called upon me, and he was much saddened. He told me Salomon Pavy, no more than a boy, had died some days since.[31] "Will, that boy was a jewel, and full of grace. 'Tis indeed a harsh Fate that can turn so cruel and take him from us. I' faith, I believe he could have been the rival of Ned [Alleyn] or Dick [Burbage] in years to come." I told Ben that I was of his mind, tho' verily Dick and Ned are above compare. We sat in such chat some while, after which we ate and drank at the Bunch of Grapes. Ben remained morose and sour-tempered. He asked me if I knew that James Roberts had registered my *Hamlet* book; this I did not know,[32] but said that no doubt it was to stop others printing it. I have not prepared the book; indeed, I have it not about me, for Gus Phillips was fashioning a brief version of it some months ago. Ben also told me that he had heard the Duke of Biron was beheaded in the Bastille, for treason against Henry.[33] Much else I remember not, for I grew weary & tired. Home & rest after midnight, tho' no cricket chirped me asleep.

1 AUGUST

I read *All's Well That Ends Well*, for such is now the title of my new play, to the company. No one disliked the book, though Bob Armin said he did not see much opportunity in his part [Lavatch]. No one praised the play, yet one or two did opine Helena was a sweet, virtuous wench the crowd might take to its heart. Well, I have lost little enough, for all I did was write o'er a youthful piece I had long forgot. If we want for something, we might play it, but I hold little hope or much desire that 'twill be so. I must think on new work, though curious strangely the tale within the play doth haunt my mind. Mayhap I might use it [the tale] again. I know not.

13 SEPTEMBER

Today we gave a play, though why we have done it, I know not, for the plot I could scarce follow. 'Twas the silliest stuff I ever played; naught but little business of a silly fraud. But the multitude liked it well enow. So why make moan? In this play Turks did capture Stuhlweissenburg, for all the good it did them.[34] Yet the horror (with delight) of the crowd at the Turks & their slaughter might serve my turn some day. Turks are all we are not, leastways what we say we are not. There may be some sport & profit in't after all.

1 OCTOBER

In the street I saw Jonson with George Chapman, they in deep conversation until I assailed them. When they saw me, both smiled, and Chapman said, "I see, dear William Shakespeare, ye have given us another play." So saying he held up a book for me to see. I told him I knew naught of what he said. "Why, see here," Chapman said, "here are your very initials, W.S., where the book says the play was lately acted by the Lord Chamberlain his servants. Wherefore, Will, I do believe 'tis thine." So I took the book from him, and saw it was a play called *Thomas Lord Cromwell,* and thus all was clear as broad daylight. I told him I doubted not that "W.S." was Will Sly, who had tried his hand at a play, though I had thought to give him some little-seeming assistance here and there, which he had entreated from me. Ben said, "So, Will, it be not for your work that I have laid out what little good money I have. I am the sorrier for that." "Indeed, no, 'tis not mine," I said, "and I be sorry you are deceived, Ben. There's not the smallest doubt it is some jest of Sly's—sly by name and sly by nature." Because I would not have Ben harbour a grudge against Sly which would fester rancorously, I asked him & Chapman to go with me to an inn hard by and drink.[35] So all passed off amicably enough.

8 OCTOBER

A happy day. News from Gilbert [Shakespeare] that the cottage and garden are mine, and Anne is mightily pleased she is to have a gardener as well.[36] Later. Now sadness, for I hear that Thomas Morley is grievous sick and like as not will die ere long. So shall no more sweet music, honeyed airs that give easeful delight, flow from his hand.³⁷

16 OCTOBER

To the Rose [Theatre] where was given a new play of the life & execution of the Duke of Biron, who was beheaded this July past. I had thought it might be from Jonson's hand, but it was too hasty written and, taken all-in-all, too careless by far. Yet the subject bewitched the popularity, and we are born but to please our many-headed hydra; we must please one and please all.

25 OCTOBER

We are to perform again for the Queen this Christmastide, though many folk say her health is doubtful. As is my fate, alas, my fellows desire me to dress up and trim *All's Well,* for we otherwise shall lack all novelty. They say the love tale will suffice, and I need but give Armin more jests and the like. I had thought no more on the play, for it is a truant unruly, a wayward child I can no more shape and control. I can bring no rod to it. I' faith I do not much like it, and wish I had let it lie amouldering where it lay in Stratford. Well, needs must, tho' it be a paltry thing.

7 NOVEMBER

I passed a pleasant evening in the hearty good company of [Michael] Drayton. We talked on much, tho' most on Drayton's work—he is a marvellous prodigious writer whose pen ne'er stands still. He admired my *Julius Caesar,* and did enquire whether I would write more plays on the Roman empire in like vein. I told him I knew not, tho' there are histories aplenty for the telling. After some while he told me a merry tale of affairs at the Swan [Theatre] to which he had betaken himself yesterday. It seems there was a gentleman of Lincoln's Inn, one Richard Vennar, who put about some bills for a play called *England's Joy*. This play, so said the bills, was to be enacted by men and women of note and quality, and for which this Vennar took eighteen pence or two shillings [admission]. When he had gathered in most of the money, Vennar fled, but he could not mount his horse, for the audience plucked him therefrom. Then the crowd took him to Sir John Popham, the Lord Justice, who declared it was but a jest, tho' he bound over Vennar. At this the people grew riotous, and went & pulled down the hangings and curtains at the Swan, & revenged themselves mightily upon all they could seize. I asked Drayton how it came that he went to the Swan at the first, & he said the bills had proclaimed *England's Joy* was a play and satire of history, in which he, Drayton, takes much delight. Tho' we laughed at the tale, I marvelled also at the harm it could bring upon our work, for folk care not to be deluded & deceived, and truly they are our masters.

26 DECEMBER

Today at Whitehall, for the Queen, we played *All's Well* all unhappily. Dick Burbage cared not for Bertram, nor Armin for Lavatch. We could not discern whether the Queen was displeased or not, for she would fall into a sleep from time to time. At the end there was small applause, and H.M. was carried out of the hall. She seemeth thoroughly sick and ill at ease. I wonder if the Admiral's Men will fare any the better on the morrow.[38] We were entertained afterwards with food & drink, but there was none of our accustomed mirth.

※ As Queen Elizabeth lies ailing, a play by Thomas Heywood causes Shakespeare to reflect on his life and marriage. He ponders notions of fidelity and jealousy that provide the germs for Othello. The early months of the year are marred by the plague (always a present threat) and then by the death of the queen. However, there is no disorder, nor a Catholic insurrection, but rather an orderly transfer of the crown to James VI of Scotland. Jonson outlines his plans for a tragedy, which Shakespeare dislikes; its performance is unsuccessful. Shakespeare witnesses both Queen Elizabeth's funeral and King James's progress towards London, though the plague causes James to avoid the city of London itself. Shakespeare's company is now named the King's Men. A pirated edition of Hamlet angers Shakespeare, while for his part, Jonson begins on a path of ingratiating himself with the Court, and later writes numerous masques for the king and queen—something of a sellout in Shakespeare's eyes. In August the plague is at its height. While Southampton has been set free and restored to royal favor, Sir Walter Ralegh is imprisoned and tried for conspiring against James. Always curious, Shakespeare journeys to Winchester to see Ralegh's trial, and to perform As You Like It for King James at nearby Wilton House. ※

2 JANUARY

A blessed, happy day for Dick [Burbage]—his daughter, whom they have named Juliet, was christened. Dick jested he did it because of my play. I said I trust she do not fall in love with a fellow named Romeo. A goodly repast after.[1] I pray I suffer not on the morrow.

1 FEBRUARY

Today is bitter cold, and like to be again tomorrow when we are commanded to play for the queen once more. It is a deal of trouble for little recompense, & yet we must, for we are but servants obsequious.

3 FEBRUARY

Yesterday we trudged to Richmond in weather so cold and bitter I marvel we were not frozen to death. I have ached since, and am as bone-cold as a hoar-frost. We played as well as we could for the queen, but our hearts were not equal to the task, or rather barely. We were cold, the queen grievous sick at heart and in body, the courtiers as gloomy as the night. I could not discern if the queen understood our play, for she scarce moved. When we had concluded, there were but feeble plaudits. The queen, assisted by several of her ladies, left the chamber as soon as we were done. But we cheered our stomachs with a hearty repast before we repaired to the city.

8 FEBRUARY

There was a curious accident, leastways I believe 'twas so, yesterday at the Swan [Theatre]. Two master fencers, John Dun and John Turner, who have been famed here and their skills bruited far & wide, duelled each other, during which Turner hit Dun so far in the eye with his sword that he pierced Dun's brain, and Dun dropped down dead on the instant.[2] This struck dumb with fear & amazement all those present, or so the report goes. I have oft thought what danger we incur when we fight on stage, though we rehearse o'er & o'er lest we might injure one another by accident. But we would have our auditors believe those deaths they see upon our platform are real, what with pigs' bladders full of blood and the like. So yesterday, at the Swan, was death portrayed in his awesome reality, tho' 'twas but an accident—a greater power did thwart their intents.

14 FEBRUARY

Today I have reaped the rewards of feasting and drinking Rhenish to excess yesterday. Yet it was a joyous day brimful of happiness and delight for all our company. We wished Bob Gough and his bride long life, health, & happiness and, i' fecks, we are but as a family.[3]

25 FEBRUARY

Tom Heywood's *A Woman Killed with Kindness* hath caused me to pause & ponder.[4] It is unlike mine own plays, tho' 'tis evident Heywood hath pillaged *The Palace of Pleasure* for some portion of his plot—not that I blame him for that, because I have done the like myself.[5] No, tho' Tom's play be a tragedy, it is a domestic tale. He, as doth Dekker, writes of commoner, humbler folk than I place in my tragedies—I mean the chiefest characters. And those folk, those characters are but simple, as, in truth, is his language. Most odd, he metes out two plots which, until the final scene, are as separate as Anne and me. One speech did affect me quite—"call back yesterday."[6] Now I have it—poor Kit Marlowe wrote the like, yet all the better: "Stand still, you ever-moving spheres of heaven that time may cease and midnight never come."[7] What is owed to that dear, rash, impetuous fool; what might have been! What a loss was there. *Later.* I do now perceive that Heywood's play hath provoked me to guilt, for I am like Frankford.[8] I have banished mine own Anne, with kindness. True it is I visit her, and true it is she is no adulteress—least, I have no knowledge she is; indeed, I am tongue-tied in guiltiness in regard of that. I might not blame her if she did stray. Yet my work lies all here in London, and we are reconciled once in awhile; but, haply, I feel I am Frankford. Perchance things past remedy should be without regard? *Later yet.* I muse still on what a man might do with an adulterous wife, or one that he supposed so. What Heywood hath writ is of note because his Frankford lies beyond our imagination. Surely, a betrayed husband would be like a savage beast that wants all sense or reason, and racked all o'er with jealousy. Here lies the stuff of some play or other I might write. Husbands, wives, men, women, fidelity, betrayal, sex, death. What doth provoke a husband to jealousy?

3 MARCH

There is a case of plague in Southwark, & I doubt not this will bode ill for us if the playhouses are closed.

FRIDAY [7 MARCH]

At the Mermaid where, as is our custom, there was a goodly company of what we are pleased to call our fraternity—Jonson, Inigo Jones, John Donne, Michael Drayton, Thomas Campion, two young men named Beaumont & Fletcher.[9] 'Tis Ben's idea we should meet once a month to joust in wit-combat, as he calls it. Some of the men I know scarce at all, but there was merry sport, and the evening was pleasant enow. Perchance I shall venture again.

10 MARCH

Many rumours are spread abroad of our queen's health, or rather sickness. I remember how ill she looked when we played at Richmond last month. I have heard many folk talk on who will succeed her, though I should be mightily astonished if it be not the Scottish King James. A fine thought—James to succeed where his mother [Mary Queen of Scots] failed, though she persevered and he has but awaited his time.

19 MARCH

As I had feared, we are restrained from playing, tho' the cause be the queen's sickness. Yet the plague doth increase also.[10]

21 MARCH

As I had a mind to sup at the Mermaid, I went by Fleet Street to seek out Drayton at his lodging there & ask him to join me. Michael was joyed to see me, but, before he would leave his room, he would have me o'erlook a poem he had writ. I was amazed mightily because this poem was a poem gratulatory to King James of Scotland, lauding him as king of England—this, and our own queen not yet dead. Drayton's true purpose in the poem is to seek the grace & favour of King James. "When our queen is dead," quoth he, "I purpose to ride north to Scotland and present my poem to the king himself."[11] I knew not what to reply, but to tell him I wished him well. I did not say I thought his poem too forward, & that he ought to bide until her majesty *be* dead. At the Mermaid, many of my fellows were assembled (as is now the custom), & there was much disquiet upon the queen's illness. Drayton with prudence said nothing of his poem. There was talk on what Catholics might chance to do when the queen dies, as die she must. Some are for taking up arms, tho' for mine own part I could not do it. 'Tis not fighting we shall need, but peace & harmony. I did not stay long, but came away to keep my own counsel.

22 MARCH

Doubt, fear, and uncertainty continue unabated as Elizabeth lies adying. Yester night at the Bel Savage Inn I overheard a consort of Catholics talking loudly that they would oppose King James as our monarch. They were so flushed and brazen, in open defiance, that I did fear for their safety. Yet none said aught against them, for these days make some mouths bold. But I think order and reason shall prevail.

Many, nay most folk will accept King James, Protestant or no, because there is none other with so near a claim to the throne. Howsoever, I doubt not some folk care not for legitimacy, & may seize the throne when the time comes. I fear my cowish spirit shall make me irresolute, not bloody brave.

24 MARCH

The queen is dead.[12] I went to Cheapside where Sir Robert Cecil read the proclamation declaring James the King upon whom now the safety and health of this whole realm depends. There was assembled a great multitude of folk, nobles & commons alike, yet in silence did all hear Sir Robert read the proclamation. Every minute was expectancy, & sure some folk were filled with joy, for we have a new monarch. There was no tumult, shouting, disorder, fighting or the like, as some (Catholics) had foretold. As I returned to my lodging, the day appeared much as any other day—men and women going about their ordinary business, tending to their affairs. I do believe now we are happy because we have a new king, whereas erst we knew not what might come to pass when Elizabeth died without issue. We may rejoice, for we are as certain of our future as any people in this world may be. Tonight there were bonfires, bells ringing, all manner of folk making merry.

> Not mine own fears nor the prophetic soul
> Of the wide world dreaming on things to come
> Can yet the lease of my true love control,
> Supposed as forfeit to a confined doom.
> The mortal moon hath her eclipse endured,
> And the sad augurs mock their own presage,
> Incertainties now crown themselves assured,
> And peace proclaims olives of endless age.
> Now with the drops of this most balmy time
> My love looks fresh, and Death to me subscribes,
> Since, spite of him, I'll live in this poor rhyme,
> While he insults o'er dull and speechless tribes.

And thou in this shalt find thy monument,
When tyrants' crests and tombs of brass are spent.
[Sonnet 107]

28 MARCH

To supper with Jonson at the Mermaid. We talked o'er our doings. Ben said that, tho' of late he lacked all favour else, now had good fortune smiled on him and procured him a patron. Ben said, "A poor man must gain riches, Will, rather than seek philosophy," which seemed true enough. Ben's patron is Sir Robert Townshend, of whom I know & have heard nothing.[13] Ben said Sir Robert hath been kind, generous, & courteous to him. I asked Ben what he had been writing, and he said he had thought on my *Julius Caesar* and how it had won the hearts & minds of the stinkards. Thus, taking but some little hint & inspiration from it, he had set his mind to write a Roman tragedy which he calls *Sejanus, His Fall.* I told Ben I rejoiced my work had pricked him on, all the more because this *Sejanus* must be much unlike his other plays. "Indeed, Will, you are in the right; I have ne'er assayed tragedy before, & was't not Spenser who said 'Never aught was excellent tried which was not hard to achieve and bring to an end.' Yet I beg to say that my Roman play is unlike your own, for I have studied the ancient authorities carefully— Tacitus, Suetonius, Seneca, and many others. I think you used, what shall I say, a hand more liberal when you wrote your histories." I smiled, for here was the Ben of yore, setting the world to rights, telling me frankly how plays should be penned. Yet I forbore to be disputatious with him because I knew I would not change his mind. Moreover, he was in general good humour, and to dispute his view would but anger him. So I smiled, and said I hoped he would allow me to read o'er his play, and mayhap the other fellows might care for it too & enact it at the Globe. Ben said he was pleased to hear that and he would send me the play ere long. "I have asked [George] Chapman for his opinion on some matters in the play, but as soon as he hath done, which shall be but a day or two, I shall send it, or bring it myself."[14]

So there we let the matter rest and talked on other affairs, though in the main on the late queen and our new monarch. Ben said he had heard Elizabeth had refused to lie down for nigh on a week, for she had a terror that she would ne'er rise to her feet again. I jested that she will lie forever now.[15] Ben laughed heartily, and commanded more malmsey and some pickled herrings. We drank long.

1 APRIL

I passed by Whitehall today where lies the queen. They say that there is to be no funeral until the new king doth command it, & when that may be none can tell. Some say 'tis like she will lie there a long time. Yet the new king will not present himself to the kingdom until the queen's funeral is done.

2 APRIL

Today, from Jonson, *Sejanus, His Fall*. Ben is surely right—it is as unlike what I have written as cheese is from a pippin, and I doubt it will please the multitudes, the beast as he calls them. And I do cleave to pippins of mine own grafting. Yet I did promise him I would show the play to my fellows, & that I shall do tomorrow. Ben is to attend the gathering. More pestilence in Southwark.

4 APRIL

Jonson & all the rest gathered together yester afternoon, and we looked o'er his *Sejanus*. I said naught touching my disfavour because I have lately writ nothing myself—leastways anything I would show unto others, for I lack invention—and I desired not to anger Ben. All the fellows were courteous, Ben above all. The upshot is we will play this tragedy; we lack novelty else, tho' Ben does not know this. He went away happy enow.

11 APRIL

Yesterday I heard one tell that Harry [Southampton] is released from the Tower by order of King James. I rejoice heartily for Harry's safety, his freedom, tho' it is doubtful he will seek me out, for his family & noble friends will come before a lowly maker of plays—but 'tis no matter. I perceive King James hath shown wisdom, for in this action he gives many folk joy & hope, e'en tho' there's many who think back on Essex as well. Yet it was the queen that lies in state that did execute Essex, not James. I heard also of a cutpurse who had followed the King all the way from Berwick, cutting purses and robbing folk. When the thief was apprehended, the King had the man hanged straightway, without a trial. Such swift merciless justice unsettles some folk, but mayhap this will be a time when the unjust man shall not thrive. All is not certain, as it may never be in this world.

14 APRIL

We are in some measure of doubt & uncertainty since our patron, the Lord Hunsdon, is relieved of his position, though, i' faith, his lordship hath been sickly long sithence. So our company wants protection and a new patron. Rumour hath it that the King himself would make us his own players. Gus Phillips & Dick Burbage swear that this will come to pass; I think they do but dream. I am set down to play Tiberius [in *Sejanus*]. I wonder if I should act at all—I had rather pen plays & poesy. Yet my fellows have need of me, & 'tis no great hardship. Today Condell's daughter [Elizabeth] was baptized, but I fear she will not live long. She is a weak, sickly, puling child. Condell was brave in smiling, his wife as well. They know the child will die ere long, & would not for the world that it will be so.

18 APRIL

So help us mercy, plague.

22 APRIL

Today I accompanied Henry Condell as he buried his child. As I feared, her life was but a brief candle, now out.[16] It is ever true that all that lives must die, passing through nature to eternity. 'Tis said the queen's funeral, long delayed, will be next week. So high and low may fear no more the heat of the sun nor winter's rages; our task, being done, we all come to dust.

25 APRIL

I would write a play, on husbands, wives, and jealousy. My brain seethes on such matters, but the words come not forth. Perchance some book might give shape & form to my dim conceits, prick up my sickly thoughts.

28 APRIL

Today, so many a week after her death, the old queen's body was taken to Westminster Abbey. I stood in the street with crowds of folk to watch & pay our silent homage. Four horses draped all in black velvet drew an open chariot with the coffin on it. Atop the coffin was a wax figure of the queen, and over all was a canopy carried by six noble earls. Next came the queen's palfrey, bearing no rider this day. Then came the ladies-in-waiting who looked for all the world like nuns, clad all in black, and behind them, all jet black, a thousand or more other lords, councillors, gentlemen, courtiers, heralds, servants, and in their train two or three hundred poor women. In the rear marched Ralegh and the Gentlemen Pensioners with their halberds down-pointed. I could scarce count the hundreds, nay thousands of people along the path of the funeral. As the coffin passed by, there was great sighing and weeping from folk of every degree who stood in the street, in their houses, hung in windows, and e'en from the roof-top gutters that they might see. 'Twas such a pageant—I was mightily moved withal, & I recalled memories of those better hours when we had played before Her Majesty, & afforded her such pleasures as our humble labours might give. Haply our new king will provide for us, whene'er he is pleased to grace us.

7 MAY

Today I made a brief repast at the Mermaid, after which I joined the vast throngs & multitudes of people jostling along Bishopsgate Street. Though there be plague about, folk were concerned not a whit, though the noise & stench were mighty. We made our way through Shoreditch, on to Stoke Newington, thence to Stamford Hill, for it was here 'twas said the Lord Mayor would present King James with the Keys & Sword to the City. At Stamford Hill the enormous crowd gathered there beggared belief & description, & in the unruly hurly-burly many folk must have been hurt & injured, for with utmost difficulty did I keep to my feet. People hung high aloft in trees, and everywhere they filled the meadows, fields, highways; verily, naught was to be seen but people, so my head swam & I felt faint. I had bethought me to carry a flask of wine and some bread, & with these I revived my spirits a little, though the great press of folk & their foul breath were noisome, the air stifling. A space had been cleared for the Lord Mayor, the attendant knights, aldermen, officers of the city and a considerable number of notable citizens, all decked up in their finery, golden chains, velvet coats, scarlet gowns, & I know not what else. After we had waited a long while, the crowd growing all the more restless & unruly, the King appeared. Alas, I could see little of what passed, & heard naught. Indeed, I marvel now what my expectation had been & which was mocked this day. But like so many folk, I had longed to see what this new King might be; my seething brain had shaped a fantasy, and I would have it turned into more than a name. So, frustrate, I came home, ate, drank, & went to bed early to rest.

11 MAY

Today I counted the sound of 130 cannon—this a salute to King James at the Tower. He did not pass through the City, for fear of the pestilence, they say. Others say he is modest & desires not to show himself to the people. Mayhap, but he be monarch, & 'twould be wise and circumspect to humour folk, to satisfy their desire if but a little.

20 MAY

We have received our Royal Patent; henceforth we are the King's Men.[17] Such is our good fortune; my heart is light, & I rejoice. Perchance our way will now lie clear before us, though the plague is a present & constant danger. Our licence be curious for included in our number is a fellow called Lawrence Fletcher.[18] I asked Gus Phillips & Dick Burbage about him, & they know little save the man hath been one of the King's favourites in Scotland, and waits upon the king. T'other curiosity is my name placed before the names of all my fellows. I asked Dick what he thought, but he laughed & said mine had the greater fame. "And, truth to tell, Will," he said, "thou art no less than fame hath bruited." I replied, "What fame I have is little enough and unsought, & you are more than equal for acting." Dick laughed once more, & said, "Well, someone's name must be first, & it might as well be yours, Will, as any other. Besides, if we fall afoul of the authorities they may haul you off first before the rest of us and hang ye."

24 MAY

The plague abates a little, & tomorrow we play Ben's *Sejanus*. Though we have rehearsed & such, I fear the play will not fare well. I said as much to my fellows, but they did o'errule my voice.

25 MAY

As I had feared, the crowd took not kindly to it [*Sejanus*].[19] We were booed, hissed, & hooted off the stage—the crowd grew unruly from the moment we began, & nothing we could do would quiet them, as if the tragedy were played in jest by counterfeiting actors. Dick Burbage acted most gallantly, but nothing assuaged the multitude's anger. I take comfort that it will not be played again. I have not seen Jonson since, but I expect a black humour sits heavily upon him.

26 MAY

Plague deaths increase from one week to the next. We may not play again, which may be as well after what befell yester afternoon.

27 MAY

A plague upon whoever hath done this—it irks my very soul. Today as I passed through Barbican, I happened upon Trundell's shop, & there I saw a book of *Hamlet*.[20] What a mangled gallimaufry of what I wrote down, & we did enact. Some one of our company must have set down what he recalled & with no regard for my play. Where be honesty? I expostulated with Trundell, who did but shrug his shoulders, & hummed & hemmed, & would do nothing. After some time, mine anger increasing, in came Michael Drayton who asked me what might be amiss. After I had told him, Michael said, "Will, there may yet be some remedy. Come with me to Nick Ling's shop in St. Dunstan's churchyard, hard by my lodging, & talk to Nick. He did publish my *England's Helicon* [1600], as ye know well. He will make all right." Thus we went & saw Ling who promised swiftly to set all aright, if I will but give him a fair copy that they may publish. This I have determined upon, vexatious though the task may be.

30 MAY

Yesterday was issued an order for folk to leave the city because of the pestilence, & there will be no coronation of the king anytime soon. Perhaps I should retire to Stratford awhile, e'en tho' there be little delight enow these days in Anne—though the fault there be all mine, I do confess. Yet I could write in peace, and fear no plague.²¹ There would be comfort in the girls, but alas no Hamnet—all blessings come with sorrows.

7 JUNE

The Lord Mountjoy hath returned from Ireland victorious. With him is the Irish rebel Tyrone who, they say, hath submitted to King James &, howsoever it is strangely achieved, is to be pardoned. I marvel how many men have lost their lives for that little patch of ground, that veritable eggshell. Forsooth, 'tis said many moe thousands of men remain yet in Ireland; what of them? & can there ever be true & lasting peace? Yet all wars must end at some time, surely. Also yesterday, there was executed some poor soul [Valentine Thomas] at the same place "Marprelate" Penry died.²² The wretched man had languished in assured bondage in the Tower a sore long time for plotting against the life of the late queen. So is one man who caused the deaths of thousands forgiven, whiles the man who failed to kill even one man dies. We are but flies in the hands of fate and death may come on the instant.

8 JUNE

Tyrone hath been pardoned &, so says the proclamation, he is to be respected and esteemed. For this, so many men have died; 'tis cause enow to drink deep & long, & cast my mind to oblivion.

9 JUNE

Some of our company go into the country to play three or four of our works. For now, I shall remain here in the city, for want of better entertainment, though mayhap I shall join them if the plague abates not.²³

10 JUNE

With Jonson today, we ate & drank. Ben is marvellous happy, for he goes to Althorp to present some brief masque he hath written for the Queen [Anne] who makes her progress there from Scotland.[24] Ben said his piece is but the merest trifle, yet he believes more will come of it. "Will, Althorp is home to Sir Robert Spencer, who is reputed to have by him the most money in the kingdom, so who may know what will come of this adventure. I find little enough favour with the popular multitude; it did not applaud *Sejanus*. In truth, I care not for its opinion. And, by my faith, I must live & provide for the family & so forth, & if this masque is well received there may be more favour to be found at Court." I wished Ben well, & said I thought he had already found some favour & a patron. "'Tis true," he said somewhat haughty, "I reside betimes with Lord Aubigny, & I think I shall dedicate *Sejanus* to his lordship."[25] More chat, & then to bed.

11 JUNE

Today to Stratford. My affairs do even drag me homeward.

19 JULY

Perchance I should have remained at home with Anne, for London appeareth all awhirl. Since last I was here, Harry [Southampton] hath been made a Knight of the Garter, & is to be restored to his earldom ere long.[26] Harry is now as much in favour with the King as he was out of favour with Queen Elizabeth. But the wheel hath turned for Ralegh; he and some other lords and conspirators, so named, have been arrested and sent to the Tower. 'Tis said Ralegh would depose the King, and place the Lady Arabella upon the throne.[27] Though 'twould be treason to say so, I think we have more need to worry o'er the plague which increaseth everywhere and every day. All the pomp & ceremony of the King's coronation is postponed until the pestilence be abated, & we may all be dead afore we see a proper ceremony. Yet I would not be Ralegh, nor of his company, for 'tis like they all will lose their heads. Greatness is best discovered in others, & 'tis better not to exalt oneself above other men.

22 JULY

The rumour is that two days past Sir Walter Ralegh attempted to stab himself, & thereby end his misery. Yet his knife struck one of his ribs, & he was prevented. Methinks such a soldier, had he wished to accomplish the act, would know full well how to finish the deed. I doubt not that my Lord of Essex would have played the noble Roman had he been of Ralegh's mind. For all his hot rashness, Essex cleaved to his beliefs.

26 JULY

Yesterday King James was crowned at Westminster, but few did see it, for all were commanded to stay away because of the plague. We are promised a celebration when the pestilence is abated, so all may be well then. Mayhap 'tis for the best; yesterday the rain fell so heavy and thick I doubt many folk would have been abroad. They say 300 or more were made knights by the king. Every jackanapes becomes a gentleman, and there's many a person made a Jack.

1 AUGUST

Plague rages, & I venture abroad but little & of necessity only.[28] It is all around me, & I cannot close my eyes to it. Throughout the streets the body bearers push their carts crying "bring forth your dead," & ringing their bells, tolling for the dead. They stand in particular in front of those doors marked with a red cross. On some are written "Lord Have Mercy Upon Us." They say the dead are beyond count & number so many that the graveyards be full, & graves cannot be dug quick enough, & rich & poor alike are thrown in together. Tom Dekker told me he hath seen bodies piled in heaps of ten, twenty, or more. Some folk have tried to fly the city, only to fall down dead as they flee. There is no remedy. Those with the disease are a fearsome sight, with swelling buboes, spitting blood, coughing, & I know not what else. Some poor souls are sent to the pesthouses where naught can avail them, & the women-keepers there bring on their deaths as swift as may be, which I doubt not is a merciful kindness. I have heard of the afflicted in such pain that they run & cast themselves into the river to die. I wonder why I am yet spared while this passeth all around me; 'tis but the merest chance.

10 AUGUST

Today an order that this and every Wednesday is to be a fast day, & we are to pray for relief of the plague. 'Tis well enough. There is a special providence in the fall of a sparrow. If it be now, 'tis not to come; if it be not to come, it will be now; if it be not now, yet it will come. The readiness is all. Since no man of aught he leaves knows, what is't to leave betimes? Let be.

26 AUGUST

Today I might believe there was some conjunction of the stars, if I did but believe such stuff. Howbeit, 'twas a curious coincidence. I decided to venture forth for a brief while, because despite my fear of the plague, I could not abide my room and desired to walk about in the air. I had walked but a little distance, no further than Silver Street from whence I turned into Philip Lane, when I encountered William Leveson just as we were both before the house of the late Thomas Digges.[29] Leveson hailed me in his hearty good fashion, & said we were well-met on that very spot today. He asked me if I knew the latest news and, goodly gossip that he be, Leveson began to recount his news. "We are well-met, Master Shakespeare, & you see the house before which we stand." I told him I knew well it was the house of Thomas Digges, & that forsooth I had been therein upon several occasions. "Do you know," I asked him, "that I owe some small inspiration to a portrait within these walls? Upon one of them there is a portrait of that famed astronomer, Tycho Brahe who died but two years since.[30] Well, surrounding this portrait of Brahe are the coats-of-arms of his ancestors, & from those I chose the names of Rosencrantz and Guildenstern for my play *Hamlet*." Leveson said that was remarkable & noteworthy, & he would remember it that he might recount it to others upon occasion. Then he continued his news. "Today Mistress Digges is to be married to Thomas Russell, whom I believe ye know well."[31] "Verily," I replied, "I know they have long desired to do so, but Mistress Anne was bound by certain conditions of her husband's will that prevented her." Leveson said, "Y'are in the right, tho' that will hath not prevented them from living quietly together. I do believe she hath been living with Master Russell at Alderminster, not far from your own Stratford, and her two sons as well."[32] I told him I had heard as much, and had hoped one day they might marry & set all to right. Leveson said, "It appeareth that the main impediment lay with the son, Dudley, for he was to remain his mother's ward until he was twenty-four, and Mistress Anne hath been sorely tried by a bond, they say worth £5,000, which prevented her marrying again. Somehow, it hath all been settled: the boy is to get his patrimony, & Anne is released from the bond. Why, I am certain affairs are much more muddled and tangled than what I have heard & tell ye, but there is no doubt that all is now resolved and they will be fast married this very day."

So I thanked Leveson, & I rejoiced inwardly that the two dear souls have found the happiness they had long desired. Leveson then pressed me to eat and drink with him; I thanked him & told him that I had other affairs to attend. However, just as we were taking leave, I recalled another coincidence which I recounted to him. "You will know," I said, "that Thomas Digges published an arithmetical military treatise, called, I believe, *Stratioticos*." "You are correct," Leveson said, "for I recall several occasions when he spoke to me about it. You know he had a pew in St. Mary's, where I am churchwarden." "Ah, yes," I said. "Well, did you know that in 1590, my good friend & neighbour from Stratford, Richard Field, printed an edition of that self-same book? I do think that shows how, in some strange fashion, all things be conjoined." After that more chat, and then we went on our ways.

30 AUGUST

I hear William Wayte and his wife have both died of plague.[33] After all these years I bear him no grudge, no ill will, & I wish no one a plague death. I' faith, I marvel I am alive and not tortured like so many poor souls. Gus Phillips is possessed of more sense than many: he hath taken a house at Mortlake, in the country, far enough from the city's pestilence. Mayhap I may go & stay with him.

31 AUGUST

Left & right dogs are killed by the hundreds, for 'tis said they spread the plague. I would rats were killed along with them, for they are filthy creatures which crawl incestuously about. The Mountjoys keep a good house; e'en so, I found a rat beneath my bed the other morning. It scudded away ere I might catch it.

10 SEPTEMBER

Heminges told me our patron that was, Lord Hunsdon, died yesterday. He had been sickly for many a month. I doubt not he died of plague; John knew not but that his lordship was dead.

15 SEPTEMBER

Today came a letter from Jonson. He hath been, with Master Camden, at a house in Huntingdonshire.[34] His news hath rent my heart—his eldest son, but a boy of seven, is dead of plague—such grief is hard to bear—and in the instant I remembered my poor Hamnet, dead these seven years—how may seven be a sacred number? Ben writes that, beforehand, he had a vision in which he saw his son all fully grown and with a bloody cross cut into his forehead. I marvel how that might be. I must drink myself into deepest oblivion tonight lest I recall aught of this, which I most thoroughly would not do.

16 SEPTEMBER

From the Lord Mayor comes a proclamation to pluck down the houses and rooms in the suburbs that, thereby, the plague be not spread by dissolute and idle persons. Thus all the brothels, gaming houses, and the like are to be pulled down. I doubt this will prevent a man from scratching where'er he doth itch.

10 OCTOBER

Dissolute & idle persons abound and spread the plague, for it abateth not one whit. All around, people die by the hundreds.[35] The authorities must need send forth succour to aid folk in their distress.

15 OCTOBER

Ned Alleyn buried his servant today.[36] Ned thinks to leave the city until the plague be passed. All our company is to gather at Gus Phillips' house at Mortlake where the air is clear, clean, and fresh, and where we may be spared, God willing, from the pestilence. There we may also think on what we shall attempt when we are permitted to play again at the Globe. I long for converse, and peradventure come by some inspiration from the fellows. Tomorrow I gather my necessities and ride to Mortlake.

17 OCTOBER

Gus Phillips' house is splendid—commodious & appurtenanced with every necessary for our comfort—& 'tis a joy to be far from London's fetid air. We are a goodly, amicable company, with fine food and cheer. We chat—what plays we might perform or rehearse, what I might write. There is much talk of Ralegh's imprisonment and what the authorities intend with him. All the fellows think the haughty man will to the scaffold ere long, & so too the priests arrested thereabouts. King James, they say, is in Wiltshire to avoid the plague, & Ralegh will be arraigned at Winchester, nearby. I have a mind to journey to Winchester, for the affair may prove to be of use in some play or other.

22 OCTOBER

More chat on plays with Dick Burbage and others, & how I might write on recent events—the plucking down of the stews and such, but to place my plot in France, Italy or elsewhere so it offends not. John Heminges gave me an old play to read, *Promos*.[37]

1 NOVEMBER

Today we received a royal summons to perform for the King at Wilton House in Wiltshire, where he hath been some time because of the plague in the city. We are to play on 2nd December. What play we shall perform is not decided. The company inclineth to *As You Like It*, for we know it well, there would be small difficulty in playing it in the country, and 'tis like to please. We are fortunate this new King hath not seen what plays we have presented before; thus we may play them again. Since we go to Wilton, I am the more determined to ride on ahead to Winchester for the trial of Ralegh.

4 NOVEMBER

We heard a rumour today that Will Kempe was buried at St. Saviour's on Bankside the second day of this month.[38] I know not if this be true, and none of the fellows hath seen nor hide nor hair of Kempe in many a month. I shall ride to Winchester in a few days.

12 NOVEMBER

Winchester. My journey here was as comfortable as I could expect at this time of the year—some rain, mists, and cold marred my ride, though I had wrapped myself well against the chill wind. My way o'er the Downs might be pleasant enough in summer, & some valleys with their ample trees provided shelter most welcome. What little sun there was shone pale and watery; but, for the greater part, 'twas all grey and dark clouds, & I was thankful for an inn and a night's warm rest. Tomorrow I shall look about the city. Ralegh's trial hath been set down for the fifteenth of the month. All the folk in this inn buzz in great expectation of the trial & Ralegh's downfall.

13 NOVEMBER

The chiefest features of the city [Winchester] are its cathedral and the castle. I climbed the tower of the cathedral, and looked o'er many miles of what once was that ancient kingdom of Wessex & our Anglo-Saxon forebears. Some folk believe this city was King Arthur's Camelot, in which I might lay some credence. It was a sight to rejoice the heart, e'en tho' my mind was ever on the trial to come. I did marvel how a place of such beauty might be sacked and pillaged in Henry's [VIII] time; what men will do in the name of religion and such. After awhile, I walked about the town and then partook of a good repast.

15 NOVEMBER

The priests [Watson and Clarke], Lord Cobham's brother [George Brooke], and some others have been sentenced to death for their plot to kidnap the King last summer. The trial, the guilt of Sir Walter Ralegh, I doubt not, will be construed after the same fashion.

18 NOVEMBER

What I have gleaned and winnowed of the trial of Raleigh is this. Ralegh was accused, with Henry Brooke Lord Cobham, of plotting to depose the King and to make the King's cousin, Lady Arabella Stuart, queen.³⁹ This Lord Cobham is that self-same Cobham whose family did protest against Oldcastle, and obliged me to change the name to Falstaff.⁴⁰ Thus is this world a small space! They said that Ralegh was discontented, that discontented men do plot treason, and thus Ralegh is a traitor. Yet the King had taken away Ralegh's house [Durham House] and given it to the Bishop of Durham, & who would not be discontented? Be that as it may. The Lord Cobham testified against Ralegh, and said he possessed books against the King's title, and had said the king should be deposed. Yet Ralegh did protest he had such books as might be possessed freely by any other citizen. Against the which the Attorney General [Sir Edward Coke] said that Ralegh was not of the government and should not be in possession of such seditious matter. The Attorney remarked as well that Ralegh was a Spanish spy, a monster with an English face and a Spanish heart, and did call him base trash, & many like insults. Ralegh was condemned. Yet it doth seem that, though before this trial many folk would have journeyed from miles around to see Ralegh hanged, at the end many were persuaded of his innocence and would now save his life. I do confess that before, because of the love I bore for Harry [Southampton] who with Lord Essex did hold Ralegh in enmity, I desired to see Ralegh hanged. Now, haughty though he be, I believe that the authorities abuse their powers beyond the mark of thought, and exercise hatred, not justice. Mayhap I should not hold that thought nor write it down, yet I must. What will come now, I know not.

25 NOVEMBER

Today all our company and the cart with our necessities arrived safe & sound. We set out from Winchester for Salisbury in the morn; our way there lies some twenty miles or more to the west, and we needs must arrive in good time. I recounted what I knew of Ralegh's arraignment as we sat & ate at the inn this evening. We were agreed it is a lamentable business, but we are the King's Men & must give no words but mum.

27 NOVEMBER

Today we rest at Michelmersh, our journey from Winchester being slow & tedious hard on account of the weather. There hath been much rain. This hamlet is hard by Mottisfont Abbey, which was a priory, but now is a mansion with fine grounds that abound in oak, cedar, beech, and plane trees. A peaceful stillness lies across the land &, blessedly, we are far from the turmoils of London & Winchester.

30 NOVEMBER

Salisbury. The slender soaring spire of Old Sarum's cathedral could be seen many leagues before we reached the city. Folk say it reaches more than four hundred feet into the heavens, & I doubt it not. We rest at a fine inn. Tomorrow we journey the four or five miles to Wilton House; we play come the second of the month.

1 DECEMBER

Wilton House is magnificent, but chiefly the tower. We are well provided for, & we have prepared our platform where we play *As You Like It* tomorrow. I have heard Harry [Southampton] attends upon the King, but I have not seen him nor made myself known unto him. All the talk amongst the servants is of the execution of the two priests Watson & Clarke at Winchester two days past [29 November]. It is said that the executioner cut them down alive, & handled them very bloodily. The priest Clarke did also speak after he was cut down. Their quarters are set on Winchester gates and their heads on a tower of the castle there. I am right glad I did not see this inhumanity, & marvel it is done in the name of justice & the King. Yet must I think on our play tomorrow, but with a sad heart.

2 DECEMBER

We gave the play [*As You Like It*] tolerable well, the King & Court, above all the Queen, were pleased, and applauded lustily. The King is of middling stature, with large eyes which wandered after persons about the room, & 'tis said his legs be weak, for he ever leans upon somebody when he walks. I saw Harry [Southampton] close by the King, by whom sat one of the King's favourites with whom his majesty dallied from time to time. Harry gave me a friendly nod. After we had concluded Heminges said we are to receive £30 for our present pains, travails, & expenses, & I warrant it is a handsome sum. Then, as we were to go eat, Harry accosted me, and said he was instructed to show me to the countess who wished to speak to me.[41] I assented, though I wondered inwardly what this might portend. The Countess was pleasant and received me courteously, lauding my plays, and spoke many another deep premeditated line. Then she asked me to read a play on Mark Antony which she hath translated from the French, for, she said, she would have it weighed by my valued opinion rather than her own.[42] I have looked o'er the piece, and 'tis horribly stuffed with rhetoric, epithets, and I know not what else. I confess I am in a quandary what to tell her ladyship, though I doubt not she desires but pleasing words and glass-faced flattery. 'Tis best I give her what she most desires. I have not seen Harry since. Tomorrow we play for the burgesses of Wilton & for the King again o'er Christmastide, tho' we know not what.

5 DECEMBER

From the good burgesses of Wilton six pounds and five shillings. So says Heminges, and we are in good spirits. The rumour is Harry's [Southampton's] adverse pernicious enemy, Lord Grey, is to be tried for the Catholic plot against the King, & Harry is to be one of those that judge him.[43] I would not be Lord Grey for all the world. I ride for home, there to abide until I must return for our plays at Court.

15 DECEMBER

I have been at home with Anne these several days. She gave me a fair and loving welcome, & we have jostled well together. Judith and Susanna are grown to be fine young women and in no hurry to wed. Belike they will find themselves steadfast men when the time is ripe. I have sifted this news of what remained of the trials of those that plotted against the King. Lord Cobham's brother, George Brooke, was condemned and beheaded [5 December] in Winchester Castle. They say he asked the executioner what he must do because he had never been beheaded before. No one said "God save the King" afterwards, save for the executioner and the Sheriff. Some days later [10 December] the other condemned were brought to the scaffold in the castle yard. First, Sir Griffin Markham was led in, then taken away to a hall. Likewise Lord Grey, and, last, the Lord Cobham, but him they left at the scaffold. Then the other two were brought forth like unperfect actors on the stage who in their fear are put besides their parts. Then they were told the King had spared them, and they were to go to the Tower. Well, such is their fate, & I trust his majesty stores not up trouble for himself and this realm. We do but desire peace. But a few more days here & I must then ride for London. I know not yet what we shall perform for the Court, but pray my part be but a small one, lest I be unperfect too.

23 DECEMBER

We are in a rare pickle and there is ill humour, for we have yet to choose what we perform for the King, though there be a plentitude of plays we might act. Some of the fellows wish to play Jonson's *Sejanus*, e'en though this was hissed by the multitude when first we acted it. I said there are those folk who think Ben touches on Essex's rebellion and think Sejanus be Essex himself, which being so, then Tiberius would be our late queen. And others aver that Macro, Varro, and Afer do personate Cecil, Howard, and Coke, which being so, our company might well offend them, & we find ourselves in much trouble. Yet the other fellows say the play is no such thing, & we should act it for Queen Anne does favour Ben, and desires him to write masques and the like for her, and that if Ben be favoured then shall we be in like fashion. The upshot is we play *Sejanus* on St. Stephen's night [26 December]. Dick Burbage is to be Sejanus, me Tiberius. I trust we displease no one.⁴⁴ Poor Tom Pope is grievous ill, and I fear he is not too long for this world.⁴⁵

27 DECEMBER

Yesterday at Court we presented *Sejanus* for the King who entertained ambassadors from France, Spain, and Venice. The court was splendid, though I wish I could think the same of our play, which did not, I think, please o'er much. Today Jonson hath received word that Lord Henry Howard hath accused Ben of popery and treason in the play, & Ben is called before the Privy Council to give answer. 'Tis as I feared—naught but trouble, and all for a play that is not worth a beggar's spittle.

29 DECEMBER

Jonson came to me this even, & was all smiles. Yesterday he was called before the Privy Council to answer for *Sejanus*. Ben laughed when he said, "They said it is full of popery and treason. I replied it was no such thing. Well, Will, it appeareth that Lord Henry Howard holds some grudge or other for me, & dislikes me. However, the King himself intervened, & despite my friendship with Sir Walter [Ralegh], said there was no case to answer, for he had seen the play himself. Besides Her Majesty desires me to make more masques for her and her ladies. So you see, Will, I am a made man." I told Ben I rejoiced at this good fortune and wished him well. Leastways, we will not perform *Sejanus* again in many a long year.

1604

※ *Performances at Court have changed somewhat, for King James is now more interested in his male favorites than the plays, despite the presence of the queen. Shakespeare examines love, marriage, and jealousy in* Othello, *yet another reworking of a well-worn tale that he reanimates. (Richard Burbage excels himself when he performs the title role in November.) The King's Men find themselves in another role, as Grooms of the Chamber and a part of the magnificent coronation procession for King James. Alas for Jonson, the king is too tired to listen when it is Jonson's turn to deliver an address. In midyear Shakespeare plays matchmaker for his landlord's daughter, Mary Mountjoy, though he cannot remember much about this event when he is called to testify about it several years later.* The Malcontent, *by a newcomer John Marston, bears singular similarities to Shakespeare's* Othello, *but is still performed for all that. However, Shakespeare's mind is now on a dark, disquieting comedy that's also full of bawdy innuendo and deals with notions of justice and governing*—Measure for Measure. *August is an irritating, idle month when the King's Men have to dance attendance on the Spanish ambassador. Year's end sees the publication of* Hamlet, *in a new edition Shakespeare has corrected.* ※

2 JANUARY

Yester eve, before the King with Prince Henry, we played *Midsummer Night's Dream* tolerable well if I consider how long it is since last we played it. As of yore I played Theseus, which is as much as I care for these days. The King seemed pleased enow, the Prince much delighted. The Prince hath a long, lean face, strong body, and a graceful countenance—more pleasing to the eye than his father. When we had done, the King spoke some words to the company, but I confess that I discerned but a little of what he said, for I could not understand his Scottish tongue, tho' it seemed agreeable enough after its own fashion. The King directed some of his speech to me in particular, & I caught words of fulsome praise. I think the King takes much interest in witchcraft and such.[1]

4 JANUARY

I marvel how, as in a blinding flash of lightning, all may be resolved and the way made clear. I have pondered long and deep on what to write, & my fellows have chid me for my sloth, for we want novelty. Then, yesterday, idly, for I knew not what to do, I took down a book of tales from Italy which I have perused from time to time. The first story I turned to was of a Moor of Venice and of how he came to murder his wife at the behest of his ensign.[2] Here is a tale that may be fashioned anew & the like of which I have thought on since Heywood's *Woman Killed with Kindness*, for the heart of the matter is love, jealousy, & fidelity. I think my Moor must needs be deluded in himself; outwardly he shall be noble, fine, and speak glorious rhetoric that shall seize the imagination. Yet within himself he shall be doubting & a prey to jealousy. His ensign shall in like manner be jealous, for he desires greatly what all others have but which he cannot gain. He shall lust for devilish power over every man, & be a duteous, knee-crooking knave such as hath not been known before. The wife shall be pure, loving, trusting, and loyal—too good for this world in which evil triumphs ever. The Moor shall kill her & himself, but the villain ensign shall remain alive, leastways upon stage, for his evil cannot be killed. And there I have it, & will set upon the play tomorrow.

There was a second tale in Cinthio's book which, when I read it, called to mind Whetstone's *Promos*.[3] This lays clear the way for a second play which shall be on justice & power, love, & lust, & how in all things there must be equal & merciful justice. Folk must not make a scarecrow of the law. The law must needs reach forth its hand with equity, and all shall be judged as they would judge others and be judged by others. "Judge not, that ye be not judged. For with what judgment ye judge, ye shall be judged: and with what measure ye mete, it shall be measured to you again. And why beholdest thou the mote that is in thy brother's eye, but considerest not the beam that is in thine own eye?" [Matthew 7: 1–3]. Thus. And I recall how at Winchester King James spared the lives of some of the conspirators whiles others were hanged and butchered. Well, this second play may bide whiles I pen t'other, for I feel a white heat now upon my brain, & know what 'tis I shall write.

7 JANUARY

Jonson came knocking at my door early, & I yet abed. I asked him, "Why this haste to rise so early?" Ben but scowled; he was in a black humour, a foul contending temper, & he could scarce relate the cause of his distemper. Yester evening at Court there was played a masque written by Sam Daniel entitled *The Vision of the Twelve Goddesses*. In this masque the Queen herself appeared as Pallas decked up in a blue mantle & jewelled buskins. The success of this masque angered Ben, for he had desired to present a masque, but Daniel was preferred instead. Ben said he was so angry that he and Sir John Roe (whom I know not) were ushered from the room by the Lord Chamberlain. Said Ben, "Daniel is a good honest man, but he be no poet," & he railed in this fashion a wearisome long time. At length I told him I must dress, and then we should go eat, & at last the black cloud left him. Poor Daniel—Ben is like to be rude & merciless with him ere long.

10 JANUARY

The play, which I now call *Othello and Desdemona*, doth proceed apace; I am well pleased. Forsooth, I marvel amazedly at the words which flow from my pen with such felicity. I have talked with Burbage about the play and shown him such speeches as will be his, Dick to play Othello. Dick said he thought they were fine and he could bombast forth the rhetorical devices that he hath to speak. We passed an hour or more in discussion on how he would personate Othello, for I told him that, though Othello's speeches be magnificent, yet are they but a disguise, as 'twere; Othello be a hollow man. He is a stranger in a strange city (Venice—and here I recalled the Jew Shylock, tho' the men be not alike). Though the senators honour him, he is uncertain of himself. This defect he cloaks with his speeches. And he may hardly believe his good fortune in winning the pure & divine Desdemona. Forsooth, he is jealous for he's jealous. We talked much on jealousy. Dick said, "I see now, Will, that this Othello's black face is some species of mask." I replied that there was a chasm between Othello on his outside and his reality within. "You will recall, Dick," I said, "how Hamlet repeated 'seems,' and that is how this Othello is—he seemeth on the outside, as his rhetoric revealeth, yet there is little or naught within. It is for this reason the villain Iago can so work his treachery upon him." Dick nodded, and doubtless he will become this man. How blessed am I, and the whole company, that Dick is an actor sans pareil—yet are the other fellows fine actors too.

16 JANUARY

While I supped at the Bel Savage Inn this eve, I heard one tell this lewd rhyme about the Lord Cecil:
> Backed like a lute-case
> Bellied like a drum,
> Like Jackanapes on horseback,
> Sits little Robin Thumb

There was much laughter at this; I do believe 'tis dangerous to utter such things, though some folk care not one whit. Another man I spoke with over some ale told me that there had been some conference or other about the Book of Common Prayer, which all must use in church, & that the Puritans be greatly vexed.

3 FEBRUARY

The company performed for the King yesterday. I was sick abed & my role, being but small, was given by one of the hired men.[4] But that 'twould tempt fate to deal severely with my life, I fain could be sick more often. Alas, I must con my part in *The Fair Maid*.[5]

5 FEBRUARY

Today I walked along Wood Street, through Cripplegate, on to Whitecross St. There I turned into Old Street, and by good fortune did encounter Sam Daniel. He accosted me in hearty good fashion. "Why, Master Shakespeare, I am well pleased to meet you," said he, "and I have just received good news that I would share with you, though I daresay your friend Jonson is today not in the good humour I am." I asked Daniel his news. "Well, 'tis thus," he said. "Yesterday a patent was issued that declares that henceforth the Children of the Chapel shall be known as the Children of the Queen's Revels, for, as you will know, Her Majesty takes great delight in such entertainment.[6] I am appointed to have oversight of the plays the Children shall perform for Her Majesty, as well as publicly. I do think Master Jonson had some thought he would be so appointed, but I believe Her Majesty was much delighted with the masque I wrote for her,[7] and so the position be mine." I congratulated Daniel on his good fortune, and we had chat on this & that. Before I took my leave, Daniel said he would be pleased to see me and talk any time I had a mind to pass by that way. I thanked him kindly, and I hope I shall not encounter Ben for some time; I fear he will be in a black humour once again.

9 FEBRUARY

Welcome news from Dick Burbage. He hath received £30 from the King for our maintenance & relief because the theatres be closed because of plague. 'Tis a fair sum, though we are in need of more. Dick thinks he will proffer some speech of thanks when we perform next at Court, ten days hence.

19 FEBRUARY

This day at Court we played *The Fair Maid of Bristow* indifferent well. My part was but small, and I cared not for it, nor, it seems, did the King, for he paid but little heed and departed as soon as we concluded. Thus Dick Burbage rendered not his speech of thanks to the King.

23 FEBRUARY

Othello goes well & is nigh completion. I have laboured hard on a scene in which Iago (such is the villain called) provoketh Othello to great jealousy by means of questions [3.3]. A good device—Iago kneels with Othello so that they seem as one, as bride & groom at their nuptials. Tomorrow the scene of Desdemona's death, on her wedding linen.

29 FEBRUARY

I have heard that the Archbishop of Canterbury died earlier today, in which Catholics & Puritans alike will rejoice, leastways inwardly.[8]

14 MARCH

Tomorrow is the coronation procession of the King, long delayed. For the occasion each man in our company hath received four and one half yards of red cloth that hath been made into liveries—we are Grooms of the Chamber! Though I am I think modest in such matters, I confess the livery be splendid. I doubt not there will be magnificent sights, marvels, & wonders when we pass through the city on the morrow, tho' I think much o' the day will be tedious. Jonson is horribly stuffed with pride; he hath writ some speeches to be delivered as the King passes by the gates of the city. Well, we shall see what we shall see.

16 MARCH

Yesterday was the King's procession. We were nine King's Men, "Grooms of the Chamber," and marched from the Tower to Westminster, amidst lusty cheering and huzzas. Every now and then we passed under fantastical triumphal arches.[9] Prince Henry was on horseback, some ten paces ahead of the King, who rode under a canopy borne by four-and-twenty gentlemen, all dressed in splendid finery—all gold and pearls. Then the Queen followed some twenty paces behind; she was seated on a royal throne drawn by two white mules. Behind Her Majesty came the Lady Arabella [Stuart] in a finely furnished carriage, and then followed many maids of honour. The first gate was Fenchurch and represented buildings in London. On the arch were twelve or more actors and musicians who rested like statues until the King arrived. Ned Alleyn, dressed all in purple, was the Genius of the City, with a boy actor (whom I hath seen at Blackfriars, but know not) reclining beneath him. This boy wore a crown of sedge and reed upon his head, his arm lay on a pot from which water issued and live fishes swam about him. Ned spoke his speeches excellent well, his voice as fine as ever I have known it. The second gate was at Gracechurch Street and crafted in wonderful Italian workmanship. At Cornhill, the third gate represented the seventeen provinces of the Dutch nation, this to honour Her Majesty. Some of Her Majesty's native music was played upon a scaffold at St. Mildred's Church, Poultry. The fourth gate was at East Cheap. An arbour of music was the fifth gate at Paul's Gate. At Fleet Street the sixth gate was most elaborate—a globe of the world, with presentations of Justice, Virtue and Fortune, and of the four elements. The seventh and last was at Temple Bar, and here was built a temple dedicated to Janus. Alas, for poor Ben Jonson, his majesty was by this hour wearied, as I confess were we everyone. Thus the King would not stay for the speech Ben had written to be delivered. The crowd was clamorous and noisome. And so, after this long procession and day, we, the "Grooms" betook us to the Mermaid, where we ate and drank long into the night, the hours stealing on. Abed all morning.

18 MARCH

Tomorrow Parliament is to assemble & the city is abuzz with what will be done.

25 MARCH

A year ago yesterday did King James ascend the throne. It is for the better, I think, that affairs are much as they were before, though Puritans and Catholics alike might disagree. I heard there was a solemn tilting at Whitehall where Harry [Southampton] did acquit himself very commendably. I am sure Harry is well pleased James sits upon the throne and not Elizabeth—tho' there be folk who would agree not with him. The wheel lifts some, while other folk do fall.

1 APRIL

Mr [Christopher] Mountjoy came to me today, and asked me to aid him in some affair he has in mind. I said that if I could be of service he might command me. Mountjoy said it would please him and his wife if his daughter, Mary, would marry his former prentice, Stephen.[10] I said I did recall Stephen was a good man & prentice, & like to be a worthy husband for Mary. I asked Mountjoy to give me a living reason why Stephen must needs be persuaded. He said that there might be some delicacy for the very reason that Belott (Stephen) had been his apprentice, & mayhap Belott might talk more freely to me about the dowry & like matters. After some little while, Mrs Mountjoy came in, and in like manner did entreat me past all saying nay to persuade Stephen to the marriage. So I agreed, and Pandarus-like I am to go forth on my errand.

2 APRIL

As I was to set out to see Belott, Daniel Nicholas, friend to Belott & his family, called by my door. At the first, he was like some old love-monger, and spoke skilfully some enigma, some riddle or other. But, in truth, he was anxious to know what Mr Mountjoy might offer Stephen as a dowry and so forth. I told him what had passed yesterday between Mountjoy and myself, and that it seemeth the marriage would be pleasing to Mountjoy, but what the dowry might be, as yet I knew not. We talked a little further on the affair, after which I departed to see Belott. He was amiable, & said Mary Mountjoy would please him as a wife. He said too that for some time he had been desirous to rejoin his former master in his business. After some time, we talked about the dowry, & he said he would accept whatever Mountjoy thought handsome & proper, & then added, "Mayhap Mr Mountjoy might also promise to leave me something in his will." This all being settled, I took my leave and returned to my room. No sooner had I taken my ease & sipped some wine than Mountjoy knocked at my door & came in. I told him what had passed between myself & Belott, & he seemed well pleased. He said that he could promise a handsome dowry, & leave Belott a goodly portion in his will. Thus am I to tell Belott this, and that a wedding may be arranged in six or eight months.[11] Thus is the tangled business of marriage conducted, but how unlike how Anne & I were wedded.

8 APRIL

Our company is well pleased, for tomorrow we may play at the Globe again, though we are warned that if plague deaths do top thirty in a week the theatre will be closed again. Now have I reason enough to write. *Othello* is near complete, & I think to turn to t'other play I have in mind [*Measure for Measure*].

20 APRIL

They say that these past four days Parliament hath debated long on the union of the kingdoms, which our King desires greatly. Some would have the new kingdom called "Great Britain," which hath a fine sound to it in my opinion, though many are opposed. What's in a name if the union provide us lasting universal peace, which all do desire?

30 APRIL

Jonson be all cock-a-hoop, for tomorrow his new masque for the King & Queen is performed.[12] Well, I wish him joy o' the worm, though I do think there be little worth in these masques which are mere show. The play's the thing to catch a queen & king.

[MAY]

Now here is a strange affair. Our company hath come by one of Marston's plays which hath been acted by the boys earlier this year. It is called *The Malcontent* and is well named.[13] To my mind it is a tedious play, & I confess I can scarcely comprehend the plot at times. Nevertheless, the work hath some admirable qualities. What is curious is how alike to my *Othello* it is— there is a character named Mendoza who might be my Iago.[14] Then there is a Duke [Malevole] who hath been deposed and goes about in disguise to see how people conduct themselves that is akin to mine own Duke, leastways as I have conceived the play [*Measure for Measure*] thus far. Yet Marston is most bitter & satiric, like Jonson—indeed they might be one and the same for bitterness. Well, we are to play this piece ere long, for Dick Burbage hath taken some fancy to enact Malevole, and in truth if there be any actor that can personate Malevole Dick is the one (save Alleyn).

[MID-MAY]

Today we presented Marston's *Malcontent*, which played well enough. The crowd delighted in Burbage as he spewed Malvole's invective—lord, how Dick did rant & rail. For my part, the best scene was the Induction, which young John Webster had penned especially for the occasion. Therein did he bring on stage some members of our company as themselves—Will Sly, John Sinklo, Dick Burbage, Henry Condell, John Lowin, & e'en our tire-man. What is reality then? There were some good jests against the boys of the revels and such stuff. A line worth the remembering—"Did your signiorship ne'er see a pigeon-house that was smooth, round, and white without, and full of holes and stink within?" [1.1.290–92].

15 JUNE

Marston again hath been most satirical, & I wonder he be not clapped in prison. Yesterday the Children of the [Queen's] Revels played his *Parasitaster* [*or The Fawn*] in which one character, King Gonzago, is said to assail King James himself. This Gonzago is given much to rhetoric, & holds his own opinion in high esteem. They say the Queen is delighted that her husband is held up thus to ridicule (why I know not), and enjoyed the laughter against her husband. Thus is Marston safe for the while. Curious Marston should call the King "Gonzago," for I used that name in *Hamlet* [3.2.23–31]. Of late it seems our two minds are as one. I must speak with John on this when next we meet.

27 JUNE

I have heard that some three days past that Harry [Southampton], Lord Danvers, & some others with him were arrested, taken to the Tower to be questioned, & were released the next day. This puzzles me, for Harry hath been in favour with the King from the moment of the late queen's death. The rumour is that Harry may know something of the late Earl of Oxford, who hath died of plague.[15] When I was at the Bunch of Grapes yester eve I overheard a tale about this earl, which went thus and caused great merriment: One time, upon making his congée to Queen Elizabeth, the Earl, with great misfortune, did break wind. So afflicted with shame was he that he travelled abroad, and did not return to

Court for seven years. Then the Queen welcomed his return and said, "My Lord, I had forgot the fart." This tale was told o'er several times as the evening wore on, and each time there was loud laughter and such.

28 JUNE

It is indeed true Harry [Southampton] was arrested and released, & the cause therefor is unknown. Even the favoured nobility are not safe in their beds, let alone the common folk.

1 JULY

Today we buried Gus Phillips' son, who was named after Gus himself.[16] We were all downcast, solemn, & grave, & Gus weighed down so mightily with grief that I do believe he would have lain in the child's grave with him. I fear Gus is not long for this world, nor cares he greatly for it.

3 JULY

My *Measure for Measure*, as now 'tis called, proceeds apace. I am more enamoured with the low, bawdy comedy in which plain truth issues forth. I have fixed upon one scene in which a condemned man [Barnadine] drinketh all night and says he is not fitted to put his head to the block [4.3]. Thus are the plans of the Duke in disguise frustrate. I ride to Stratford tomorrow to see my family, find some easeful rest, & mayhap write *finis* on this *Measure*.

20 JULY

Stratford. Today a letter from John Heminges in which he says I am to return to London by month's end, for we are commanded by the

King to wait in attendance at Court, as Grooms of the Chamber. I muse what this may mean, for more he did not write.

1 AUGUST

London once more. The Mountjoys and Stephen Belott have settled and agreed together upon all matters. Belott and Mary are to wed sometime soon, this news from Mme Mountjoy, though the day be not certain. I shall wish them all joy & happiness.

3 AUGUST

This morning there was mighty thunder, rain, and hail for upwards of an hour or more. Afterward folk spoke of what this might portend, though they were best to dry out their cellars methinks.

8 AUGUST

On the morrow we attend upon the ambassador from Spain, & Heminges believes we shall lie at Somerset House for two or three weeks, mayhap more. So my newest plays are put off & set aside until September, mayhap October. No one can tell what we shall do as Grooms of the Chamber, save we are to dance attendance on their lordships' pleasures, and play the spaniel. We are to have rooms & food & such, and, says Heminges, we shall receive some small payment. All twelve of us. Well, I have no great stomach for it, but we are commanded royally & must perforce obey.

9 AUGUST

Today I lie at Somerset House which the Queen hath been pleased to give o'er to the Spanish ambassador. He is called Juan Fernandez de Velasco, Duke of Frias and Constable of Castile, and Ambassador

Extraordinary. I marvel I am plain Will Shakespeare. The other men of our company and myself do little or nothing; we do but swell a progress. There's much else I might put my mind to than stand in attendance.

11 AUGUST

The Spanish Ambassador entertains & is entertained right lavishly. People without number have flocked to Somerset House. He is fond of buying jewels, rings, & such, & is beset upon all sides with those offering their wares. I believe he wants sense & discernment, & hath an inordinate love of flattery.

13 AUGUST

I had not thought hours spent amid such splendour could be so tedious—we might well be dunghill grooms. More like days of enforced idleness are yet to be endured.

19 AUGUST

Today, amidst much ceremony, King James and the Spanish Ambassador swore peace. The King declared that peace with Spain was what he desired most in this world for this kingdom & for his people. Afterwards there was great feasting at Whitehall, after which came bull and bear-baiting. I had bethought we would be commanded to perform a play for the King & the Ambassador. Howsoever, the Ambassador does not speak English, and our pains would have been for naught.

20 AUGUST

The ambassador is taken with the gout & lies abed. Thus he departs not for Spain, nor we to our homes.

28 AUGUST

We departed Somerset House yesterday & good riddance to it all—pomp, splendour, idleness. Heminges tells me that the twelve of us are to receive £21 12s for our pains—this the sum for us all! I have no great desire to be a Groom of the Chamber again.

1 SEPTEMBER

Today we looked o'er *Measure for Measure*, & all the fellows were contented with their parts, viz:—Condell, the Duke; Dick Burbage, Angelo; Heminges, Escalus; Will Sly, Claudio; Bob Armin, Pompey. Gus Phillips' prentice, James Sands, is like to be Marianna, for he seems ill-suited for Isabella. In truth, who can personate Isabella aright I know not, tho' Dick says I need not fret, for we can find someone to strut his hour upon the stage. Armin is perfection as Pompey, and I marvel Dick can ne'er do wrong.

16 SEPTEMBER

Today I walked to Shoreditch for to see Dick's daughter baptized.[17] There was little joy; I believe we all know the poor dear child cannot endure more than this week or next.

19 SEPTEMBER

As I foretold all too readily, poor Dick Burbage's Frances is dead, & was buried today. Next week we shall play *Measure*—I have but a small part. I now dislike what I have set down for the last act, yet it must suffice, for a play must end in some fashion or other.

3 OCTOBER

Our Bishop of London is to be made Archbishop of Canterbury,[18] so it will go hard on Puritans & Catholics alike. This same Bishop banned Tom Nashe's books, and was chief in the arrest of the Marprelate folk—John Penry and the rest.[19] They say the bishop is severe & cannot abide dissenters nor any who would stray from the doctrines of the church. Yet I hear tell he flatters the King most servilely. Is this the measure of the man?

11 OCTOBER

There is a rumour that the King's sickly son hath travelled from Scotland and now lies at Windsor. He cannot walk nor speak; such is the blood royal.[20] Be that as it may be. We have determined to play my *Othello* for the King on the first of the month coming. Dick Burbage hath studied Othello closely, & I believe he will surpass all he hath done before, for he sees how the inner man is but hollow, the outer man but words & show. Whether John [Lowin] be equal to Iago I know not, but he works with accustomed diligence at his part, and is a fine fellow. Brabantio—Heminges, Cassio—Condell, but we have not yet our Desdemona.

24 OCTOBER

All is in readiness for *Othello*. The boy [unknown] is a sweet enough Desdemona, & verily need do little else. It is said King James hath proclaimed himself King of Great Britain, which he hath long desired, tho' I know not whether Parliament have agreed. 'Tis no great matter in my mind, but kings savour titles. Some folk now think upon our late queen with more favour than when she lived.

2 NOVEMBER

Yesterday at Whitehall we played *Othello* before the King and all his court. Burbage towered over all like a falcon in the skies, as becomes him, & I marvel ever when I hear my words issue from his mouth. He understands all &, i' faith, renders them better than I could conceive.

Lowin did surpass himself in the scene with Othello, & I believe few could resist his base insinuating flattery & temptations [3.3]. Most dramatic was when together they kneeled down. The murder of Desdemona was piteous, and I heard some of those ladies who looked on weep. After we had done, the queen herself called me forth, and spoke several kind words, & I did mark two tears upon her cheek. Today I saw Jonson who rejoices that his *Sejanus* is to be printed.[21] Sunday [4 November] we perform *Merry Wives* for the King.

4 NOVEMBER

This eve our company played for the King at Whitehall *The Merry Wives*. John Lowin did enact Falstaff to mighty applause and approbation, & I did observe Her Majesty was much pleased. Afterward she said, when I had been called forth, that she was pleased both to weep and laugh at my plays, but she preferred laughter the more. I bowed low and murmured my thanks, & said I hoped I might please her further. Our company was feasted right well.

16 NOVEMBER

Today, at St. Leonard's Church, Christopher Beeston's son was baptized & named for Gus Phillips. I walked over to Shoreditch with Tom Heywood, a good friend of Beeston. The latter I have seen the less of since he left our company for Queen Anne's, Worcester's Men that was.[22] Yet Beeston is a good man, & I rejoiced in his happiness, & wish his family all joy & prosperity.

20 NOVEMBER

Though I did entertain many a doubt whether it would come to pass, yesterday Mary Mountjoy married Stephen Belott hard by here, in St. Olave's.[23] They were a happy enough couple I think, & afterwards we had a fair feast—leastways there was plenty to drink, & I have not been well in the head today. There was some talk of the promised dowry, but I know not what hath come to pass upon that score. George Wilkins[24] was amongst the assembled throng &, as ever, scowled and uttered gibes. I told him I marvelled to see him at the wedding, knowing of his hatred for women & how they vexed him. George said there was small cause for amazement, for he knows Belott well, & the couple are to live in one of his chambers. I said I had not heard this news, & Wilkins said it was to do with the dowry that Mountjoy had promised but was not like to pay. Much more chat of same, & then George said he was going to a whore. Some of what he said I think to add to *Measure* when we perform it next, for the King.

30 NOVEMBER

To hand from Nick Ling the new copy of *Hamlet*, which I had corrected, though I did omit some lines so as not to offend the Queen.[25] So Nick hath been as good as his word, and I am well pleased.

1 DECEMBER

Today news from Tetherton that Rogers will pay his debt.[26]

16 DECEMBER

There is no small displeasure with the Gowry play we have played twice; an exceeding concourse of all manner of people have seen it. From what I hear tell, though the play was complimental to the King, no Prince should be enacted upon the stage during his lifetime.[27] Nonetheless, we are commanded to play before the King this Christmastide, but not Gowry!

17 DECEMBER

We are not alone in our troubles with authority. I hear now that Sam Daniel hath provoked the authorities with his *Philotas*, because they say it hath a sympathy for the late Lord Essex. So it shall be played no more; Sam says he's much troubled and fears for his place at Court.

27 DECEMBER

Yester night we played *Measure for Measure* at Court for King James. His Majesty took some interest in the Duke, I think, for he seemed to nod approval here & there when the Duke spoke. Her Majesty laughed heartily at the bawdy; indeed, I believe she had drunk a goodly quantity of wine. We play again for their majesties on the morrow—we are to give the *Comedy of Errors*. I can scarce believe it is now ten years since we did first perform it at Gray's Inn.

1605

❧ Performances at Court are disappointing—stupid masques by Jonson, and his dismal Every Man Out of his Humour; *and yet the man remains in favour. Still, Shakespeare's* Henry V *and* The Merchant of Venice *are well received, and Shakespeare is gladdened by a now infrequent meeting with Southampton. There will be no more meetings with old friend and colleague, Gus Phillips, who dies in the spring after telling one of his famous theatrical anecdotes. At the last, Gus commended the story of King Lear to Shakespeare as worthy of his attention. In September, Jonson again finds himself briefly in prison over the play* Eastward Ho!, *in which he had a hand. Shakespeare and his fellow actors travel to Devon and then to Oxford where Shakespeare is pleased to see his old friends the Davenants once more. However, all events this year pale into insignificance in comparison to the November Gunpowder Plot to blow up the Houses of Parliament. Jonson is peripherally involved in the affair (as a spy for the government) while some of the conspirators from his native Warwickshire might be known personally to Shakespeare. Shakespeare can only marvel at the turbulent days he finds himself in. ❦*

5 JANUARY

Thus far this month we have given but *Love's Labour's Lost*. I hold it one of my lesser plays, & indeed now I could not write it, leastways not as 'tis; I have done better. The whole no longer pleases, though there are parts I yet admire—some characters delight, and some of the wit. I believe I unmasked the excellent foppery of the world. George Chapman is much delighted that his *All Fools* hath been played.[1] I am pleased for his sake, e'en though his theme—the smooth course of true love—is a path much trod by many, as I know forsooth.

7 JANUARY

Shortly before noon Jonson came to my room stuffed with news of his masque which was played last night at Whitehall, though that might well be "by" Whitehall![2] This is all his story, as much as I can recall. Inigo Jones had drawn up and painted the scene, which was concealed by a curtain until the moment the masque began, so that a great effect might be achieved. There were pictures of sea horses, other fish, and a scallop shell, wherein sat Her Majesty (who is big with child) with several ladies of the court.[3] Their apparel was rich and gorgeous, though Ben did allow some folk might mistake them for courtesans! They did not wear masks; instead their faces and arms all up to their elbows were painted black, so that they looked like blackamoors. Ben said those in attendance were greatly amazed at this sight. The King was there present, and sat next to the ambassadors from Spain and Venice. Afterwards there was a banquet where tables and trestles were turned over in violent array before anyone had eaten. Ben seemed pleased by this affair, for what he desires most is to be at Court. Today our company plays *Henry the Fifth* for the King, which shall be like chalk to the cheese of yester evening. Yet I would choose my chalk o'er Ben's cheese, e'en tho' the Queen performs in Ben's stuff.

9 JANUARY

Yesterday we played *Every Man Out of his Humour* for his majesty, though I cannot think why we did so, save that Jonson be much in favour at Court. Upon the last occasion we played it at Court, the piece was ill-received,[4] and fared little better yesterday. The King seemed much distracted by those courtiers around him, those he favours most,

& gave us little heed, tho' we were provided well with food & ale afterwards. I was well pleased to conclude & return home to rest.

[C. 13 JANUARY]

Dick Burbage said he had been to see Sir Walter Cope,[5] & told him we have no play Her Majesty hath not seen already. Dick told Sir W. we had revived *Love's Labours,* and he thought this might suit, for it is witty enow. So we play it tomorrow night at Harry's [Southampton's] house. I think I am now like a maid new in love, for I have not seen Harry in many a month and long to do so.

[C. 14 JANUARY]

This night at Harry's [Southampton's] house we played *Love's Labours* for the Queen & the Duke of Holst. Our audience was but small, for the performance was a private one. Her Majesty was full of mirth & was pleased exceedingly, for she gave all our company many gracious thanks when we had done. Harry was one of our audience, & he sought me out quietly afterward whiles the fellows were given food and drink before we took our leave. Harry did lament we had not seen each other in many a long month or year, & recalled those times we had spent together. He rejoiced in the renown my plays have found, and asked me if I had any sonnets or other poesy that I might send to him to read, & I said I would do so. Harry was also happy because his wife, like the queen, is great with child, & he wishes that with the next child he might be blessed with a boy, for his loins have yielded girl children only.[6] Alas, there was little other chat before Harry returned to the Queen & her guests. I must place in order some several sonnets for Harry to read.

Be as thy presence is, gracious and kind,
Or to thyself at least kind-hearted prove.
    Make thee another self for love of me,
    That beauty still may live in thine or thee.
    [Sonnet 10, 11–14]

1 FEBRUARY

On the morrow we perform Jonson's *Every Man in his Humour* for King James. Ben hath revised the play for this occasion, & hath now placed the play in England. I am to play Knowell who was Lorenzo Senior before. How this came to be is of passing interest. When we played my *Othello* in November last, the King was much pleased. Thus, said some of my fellows, after a tragedy on jealousy we might please the king with a comedy of jealousy. Ben, on hearing this, said he would make this English *Every Man* for the occasion. I care not, but I think Ben would make us rivals at every turn.

SHROVE SUNDAY [10 FEBRUARY]

Today we presented *Merchant of Venice* at court for the King, who was so mightily pleased with the play (& all our company) that he hath commanded another performance for Tuesday [12 February]. Dick Burbage was Shylock, & no praise be superfluous for his personation. The King did congratulate him heartily, and spoke kindly words to me

11 FEBRUARY

Today early, though why I know not, George Wilkins came to my room and asked me if I would attend the christening of his boy, Thomas.[7] I told him this request was all unexpected, and I did flatter him, saying I was most honoured, though I care not for the man one whit. Yet, I said, I could not go with him, for we are to play at Court today for the King, and have many preparations in hand.[8] At this Wilkins looked somewhat surly, or mayhap downcast, and then said he was right sorry I might not attend. I do believe he had hoped some person of import might be present at this baptism, though I flatter not myself that way.

3 MARCH

I have heard Harry [Southampton] hath been blessed with the boy child he desired so earnestly. I have not sent Harry the sonnets I did promise him two months past, though I expect this present joy hath cast my paltry offering far from his mind.

26 MARCH

Tomorrow Harry's [Southampton's] son is to be christened before King James at Court. What boundless happiness and joy Harry must feel in his very senses, & I rejoice for him.

30 MARCH

I journeyed to Mortlake to visit Gus Phillips who is grievous sick, and, I fear, will dwell not long in this world, though I could wish many another an earlier grave afore good & kindly Gus. He is the most loyal of fellows. I found him resting peacefully enough, and what 'tis that ails him I know not. We talked for some while and sipped wine, which seemed to restore Gus a little. I told him I knew not what to write, though nowadays I care only for tragedy, not comedy. Gus said audiences ever desire to hear about families, fathers, daughters, sons, & the like, and mayhap that should be my theme once more. He recalled the old play *King Leir* played so many years ago at the Rose.[9] "You will remember it, Will," he said, "for as I recall you enacted some part or another in it; what was that?" "Perillus," I said, "and I marvel that you can recall it so. Yet I liked not the play greatly for, rightly, it should have been a tragedy, but all ended happily." "Ay, true enough, but that need not prevent *you* penning a tragedy from the same stuff," Gus said.

So we chatted more on that for some time, & after awhile Gus's wife brought in food to eat.[10] Then our talk turned to other affairs, & I told Gus that I had heard the notorious robber, Gamaliel Ratsey, was hanged some days past.[11] "Well, I never," declared Gus. "Many years ago, when I was travelling the highway with Ned Alleyn & some other fellows, we encountered Ratsey at an inn, though we knew not then who he was, for he was disguised like some lord. Howsoever, he asked if we would entertain him, & so he heard our play, & thereupon gave us some forty shillings. We were full of joy at such generosity, for forty shillings far exceeded what our audiences had given us thereto. And so we went to bed right happy & satisfied. Well, the next morn, we had scarce travelled upon the highway two miles or so when this Ratsey came upon us, cried 'stand and deliver,' and robbed us of the forty shillings he had bestowed upon us the night before. As he did so, he reproved us for our idle profession and the like." Gus laughed at his tale, though I saw he was much tired in the telling. We sat awhile longer quietly together, and then I took my leave, promising him & Anne I would return to see them again ere long.

8 APRIL

Today was buried Master John Stow.[12] I ne'er knew the man, but people do say he was most cheerful, sober, & courteous. I did, nay do, admire his *Chronicles* by Holinshed; indeed, many a time & oft have I had cause to consult those books. I hear tell that Stow would spend two or more hundred pounds a year to buy books and the like. Well, may he rest in peace, for he lived a long & goodly life—would that all men might do so.

9 APRIL

The sound of church bells awoke me, though I would fain have lain abed, for I felt unwell. Bad wine or rotten food doubtless was the cause. In the street I enquired of one passerby the reason for the bells, & he told me that yester night, a little before midnight or thereabouts, Queen Anne was delivered of a girl child [Mary], for which all rejoice.[13] I too might rejoice, but for my sore head and stomach. Mine intent today was to journey to Mortlake to visit Gus Phillips, but that must wait a day or two more. I pray Gus be not too sick.

15 APRIL

"Will, sweet Will, pray you bide awhile"—this from Marston this morning in the street. He ran from behind me to greet me, & then said "I pray you be not greatly vexed, for it is no fault of mine, I do assure thee." I told him I could not be vexed, for I knew naught of what he spoke. "Ah, then it must needs be ye have not seen it. In brief, Nat Butter have published a play called *The London Prodigal*, & says the play is yours.[14] But in truth it is, in part, some of mine own work (& some others), though I took some hints of the plot from something we had talked on many months ago. I believe Butter hath affixed your name to the wretched piece that more copies might be sold thereby." When Marston had finished, I told him I doubted not that such was the case, & I blamed him not for Butter's actions. I said some two years ago people said *The Merry Devil of Edmonton* was mine, & tho' it be a fine play & tho' we did act it, it was not mine verily. We talked some while on such affairs, & then Marston went on his way. I know not what I might do about such stuff, though another way this flatters me, for my name is, 'twould appear, held in high regard. Yet I would not have paltry work foisted off as mine own.

4 MAY

Almost too late, I went this morning to see poor Gus Phillips who now lies adying, though he is peaceable enough. We spoke of many a thing & of the pleasures we have shared in times past, & of good Sam Crosse so lately died.[15] Gus asked me to stay with him whiles he made his will & testament, which I did. He remembered all the fellows, leaving each some portion of gold.[16] After he had concluded, he grew very tired, & said he would rest but desired to see me again. I told him I would return soon, though I fear I may never see him alive again. I think Gus knew that in his own mind.

11 MAY

As I was afeard, I ne'er saw Gus Phillips alive again. He's dead & gone, but shall not be forgotten, leastways not by myself. I shall cleave ever to sweet memories of him & of our days, nay years, together.

1 JUNE

Strange are the ways by which we remember the dead. Today I bought a copy of the old *King Leir* play,[17] the self same that Gus Phillips commended to me as something I might amend & improve. Indeed, after I had read the old play again, I saw straightway what course I might take. Alas, there will be no part now for poor Gus.

27 JUNE

Marston today was most content, for his play was registered for printing yesterday, & he takes much pride in that.[18] I know it not, for it was but acted by the boys at Blackfriars, & so I asked Marston what was the purport of his work. He said, "The difference betwixt the love of a courtesan and a wife's the full scope of the play, which, intermixed with the deceits of a witty city jester, fills up the comedy." I commended him on such brevity, & no doubt his *Dutch Courtesan* is stuffed with matter satirical. Also today a man called Thomas Douglas was hanged & quartered [at Smithfield]. He tried to forge the King's signature so that he might procure the Great Seal [of England]. I marvel at his foolishness and simplicity.

1 JULY

Bob Armin hath lent me a pamphlet called *Ratsey's Ghost* which tells of the adventures of that Ratsey who was hanged last March. And, wonder of wonders, in it is the tale Gus Phillips told me.[19] I was pleased withal by another tale of a Parson's daughter: a Parson's daughter dwelling near Stamford, being sent by her father upon a market day to buy stuff to make her a new gown, was given forty shillings to do her markets. Travelling forward, Ratsey met her, who bade her stand and deliver her purse. The maid fell down on her knees, and besought Ratsey to be good unto her, and to use her well for, she said, "I am a very poor maid and have not that you look for." "Come, come, you are a dissembler," replied Ratsey, "and therefore dispatch, and yield me your purse." "Indeed, sir, I will tell you the truth," said she. "I have here forty shillings which my father hath given me to buy me a gown, and if you take that away from me I am utterly undone, for God knows I shall not get another of him these seven years." "Let me see your money," said Ratsey, and she delivered it to him. Ratsey, seeing there was just so much, put his hand into his pocket, and gave her three angels more, which he gave unto her with her own money, and bade her buy a new petticoat also. "And do not forget to speak well of Ratsey wheresoever you go." The maid thanked him most joyfully, but if there passed any other kindness between the parson's daughter and Ratsey is more than can be told.

24 JULY

Stratford. This day hath inspired new comfort, for Joan's son was christened, and I was present.[20] The little tyke bawled so lustily we scarce heard the parson. Also the tithes are settled and should provide fair enough for us.[21] I would remain here longer, but I must return post-haste to London.

15 SEPTEMBER

Jonson be in prison once more—on this occasion with Chapman. Ben, Chapman, & Marston (who hath fled to the continent) have written a play which hath given offence at Court; Sir James Murray, who I know not, believes that he hath been insulted. The good Lord alone knows how that affair will be settled.[22] For mine own part, methinks Ben aimed another hit at me, for, as I hear tell, in the play a footman is called Hamlet and is mad, and some other character is called Gertrude. But I have not seen the play, and care not a fig for it or Ben's gibes. As for our company, we leave for the West Country, for the plague, though not great, doth increase. Our playing in London is not yet restrained; we leave as much for our recreation as for our health.

1 OCTOBER

Our journey to Barnstaple hath been a long tedious business, though I confess there was much to pleasure the eye as we journeyed through verdant fields. I passed much of the time in contemplation of this Lear play which takes shape in my mind's eye. An eclipse [27 September] gave me a hint on fortune, the stars, and superstitions. Along the way, our company was joined by a fair youth named William Peter.[23] He said he was a scholar at Oxford University, though his heart was not in his studies. He was overjoyed to make mine acquaintance, and spoke much on my plays (which he had seen). He rode with us until his way took him to Exeter (where lives his family) and ours to Barnstaple. As he departed, he said he hoped we would meet again. He was a kindly young man, and he reminded me of my unsullied gloss of youth and of the days I shared with Harry [Southampton]. How relentless is time and life. Yet do thy worst, old Time; despite thy wrong my verse shall ever live young. When we rested at inns along the way, I observed closely the speech of Devon folk and the like, & think to employ it in some fashion in *Lear*.

2 OCTOBER

Today there was another eclipse, which again strikes fear into the hearts, minds, & souls of the timorous, and portends unto them momentous events. I smile inwardly.

5 OCTOBER

We returned to London to discover that playing is now restrained; the pestilence hath increased.[24] Dick Burbage says we leave on the instant for Oxford where we might play for the Mayor & Corporation.

9 OCTOBER

Oxford, where I take my ease with my good friends John and Jane.[25] John is grave and saturnine, but no heavy-headed blunderer, and he loves plays. He told me of a curious interlude he had witnessed when the King had visited Oxford this past August. Before the gate of St. John's College, three youths dressed like sybils had appeared before the King, and prophesied King James and his heirs would rule the kingdom for ever.[26] I said I doubted not that his majesty was most pleased at this vision, and John told me somewhat more of the interlude. Jane is as beautiful as ever she was, full of wit and agreeable conversation. We talked much of London, & John oft regretted they had left the city, though that were for the good of their health. I gave them an account of our playing before the Mayor today, which was well received, though with much formality beforehand. John said he wished he might have seen us, in particular our famous Burbage. I told him I would bring Dick to see them before our company goes upon its way.

20 OCTOBER

This night to my room came Jonson in apprehensive mood, & asked if he might sit & talk awhile. Much of his chat was pure mystery, & I could scarce divine his meaning, though he had drunk but little wine. As best as I can surmise, nigh on two weeks ago [9 October], Ben went to supper provided by one Robert Catesby—this at an inn, the Irish Boy, in the Strand. This Catesby is a well-known Catholic & fanatic, and I believe I have heard his name before. Several other men were there present.[27] Ben did remind me, though I needed it not, that while in prison some six years ago [1598] he had converted to the Catholic faith. Ben said all present were seized with deep & dangerous discontent of the King, who had promised them toleration of their religion (indeed, the Queen herself be a Catholic). But the King had not kept faith with them, and they are as persecuted as ever they were. I told Ben talk of such matters was like to be treason, and he should have naught to do with those men. Ben was surly & sad, like a young child robbed of all expectation. We talked on thus for nigh on two hours, after which he left. I mused on Ben's news, & then on Lear, which in like manner will be a play touching upon dissension in the kingdom, a kingdom divided, & in families where sons and daughters are pitched against each other, all for the love of the fathers.

22 OCTOBER

No further word from Jonson, & I am disquieted. I sense something in the whirligig of time is out of joint; e'en in the street some folk avert their eyes, no cheery smiles or a God give you a good day. Heminges says we play at Court again this coming Christmastide and must prepare some ten or dozen plays for the King. *Mucedorus*, for it be popular, is to be one of them.[28] John said Ben hath finished a new play which he calls *The Fox*, & 'tis like we shall give that as well.[29]

28 OCTOBER

The Lord Mayor's pageant be tomorrow, but as I care not for him nor the multitudes that will crowd every street, I shall bide in my room. Besides, I have work aplenty to accomplish. Passing by Bedlam t'other day hath put me in mind of what might be done in *Lear*.[30]

5 NOVEMBER

Out of doubt, this day will be remembered far above all others, and I marvel that such a deed hath come to pass in mine own lifetime. It seemeth that early this morning the authorities discovered a conspiracy against King James. The conspirators had plotted to kill the King by destroying Parliament House by use of gunpowder, whiles the King, all the lords, & Parliament were therein. I know not yet the names of those apprehended, but my mind misgives they will live to see many more days. Tonight about the streets there are more bonfires than I can count, and people on all sides offer praises and thanks to God for his mercy in exposing this treachery. Folk swear they will not forget this day. I now believe that the supper Jonson told me of [20 October] had somewhat to do with this treason. I pray God Ben be not one of these foul conspirators, though I tremble at that thought, for he is a Catholic and he can be wild, furious, and passionate. What else will come to pass, who can tell, & I know not.

8 NOVEMBER

More news of the Powder Treason. The principal conspirator is now said to be that Robert Catesby that gave supper to Ben Jonson this past month. Others were also there—Francis Tresham and a Thomas Winter (or some such name), though the man apprehended with the gunpowder in the cellars below Parliament is one [Guy] Faux or Fakes. The plot was uncovered because Tresham sent a letter to his brother-in-law, Lord Monteagle, with a warning to stay away from Parliament. This is that same Lord Monteagle that was party to Lord Essex's rebellion, and asked our company to play my *Richard II*.[31] (I tremble to think on that business, & pray the authorities think not on us in this matter.)

About an hour past, this evening, I spoke with Ben as we ate and drank at the Mermaid. Ben said we should sit apart from other folk for he had news to relate that others might not be privy thereto. Then he swore me, by sacred oath, to deepest secrecy. At the first, I said such an oath must portend matters of high concern which, for safety's sake, I would not hear. Yet Ben urged me to reconsider for, he said, he had to tell some close, dear friend so that thereby his own burden might be the less. So I swore the oath. After I had sworn, Ben spoke closely to me. "Yesterday the Privy Council summoned me to them and demanded of me that I might find some Catholic priest that they thought knew something of this powder complot. I agreed to find the man for, as you know, I have been in difficulties with the authorities with that play, *Eastward Ho*. Thus I thought I might restore me to their grace and favour." Ben recounted much of what he did to find this priest, but all his efforts availed him not one whit. Leastways, I believe that 'twas such, for in one moment Ben seemed to say the priest did not trust him nor the promised safe conduct. Either way, the affair came to naught. Yet Ben hopes he hath found favour again at Court. When I returned to my chamber here, I did heartily wish Ben had not revealed all his story to me, for these are dangerous times when 'tis best to know nothing—for knowing nothing, nothing can I lose. Leastways, Ben did attempt his task for the authorities—a small comfort.

9 NOVEMBER

The King, in Parliament, hath given thanks for his safe delivery & the discovery of the Powder Treason. I heard that he said much on the nature of his kingdom, such as "The Head is the King, the Body are the members of Parliament. This Body again is subdivided into two parts: the Upper and Lower Houses." I have said as much in several of my plays; it is a fine & goodly conceit to make compare the kingdom and the body.[32]

10 NOVEMBER

Today news of the powder conspirator [Robert] Catesby who has been killed by the Sheriff of Worcester & his men at Stourbridge.[33] When I heard this news, I trembled a little because Stourbridge is but small distance from Stratford, and I wonder if any one there might be part of this tangled web of conspiracy. I pray it be not so.

27 NOVEMBER

The Earl of Northumberland and some other lords have been sent to the Tower. He was not in Parliament the day the Powder Treason was discovered, and he is said to be a friend to some of the conspirators. So he is suspected, & I pray Jonson hath fallen on the right side of favour.

CHRISTMAS DAY

In this deep midwinter, I marvel at the turbulent days in which we have lived, and continue so to do. This Powder Treason hath been a wondrous, fearful affair, for what might have ensued if the King, the Lords, & all of Parliament had been blown unto the heavens? How dearly do most humble folk desire & yearn for peace. The conspirators will suffer the severe retribution & punishment which they have called down upon their own heads. I hear that one [Francis Tresham] hath died already in the Tower, though he was not executed. They say his head is cut off, and will be placed on London Bridge alongside those of the other traitors when they be executed. All this in the name and cause of religion. Does our God wish such business? Yet they were traitors, & they would murder. I scarce know what to think or believe, yet surely Jesus preached humility and mercy, & I know not what. I must leave off for my mind's awhirl.

1606

❧ *The effects of the Gunpowder Plot linger on, with trials and bloody executions that Shakespeare witnesses with fascinated revulsion; he sees the heads of the plotters set on London Bridge and Parliament House. In March, Shakespeare makes a special effort to attend the christening of William Davenant in Oxford, and, as the year progresses, he finds satisfaction in encouraging the work of younger dramatists such as Tom Dekker and John Marston, while his own work proceeds apace. He writes* Macbeth *with King James specifically in mind, and incorporates gunpowder plot references into the play, while the April performance of his* King Lear *moves him as he has never been moved before. Back home in Stratford, Shakespeare's daughter Susanna wants to marry the local physician, John Hall, and a summer visit home persuades Shakespeare that Hall will care deeply for Susanna. He gives the couple his blessing, despite some reservations about physician Hall's Puritan outlook. Shortly after, the first performance of* Macbeth *for King James is marred by the death of the boy actor playing Lady Macbeth; it begins the curse that has dogged the play's history ever since. Shakespeare finds acting less and less to his liking, and Stratford more appealing, and there he continues his work on* Coriolanus, Antony and Cleopatra, *and* Timon of Athens *(begun in collaboration with another young dramatist, Tom Middleton). In October his landlord's daughter dies, while in December brother Edmund surprises Shakespeare by fathering a bastard child. The year ends with a Christmas performance of* King Lear *for King James.* ❧

5 JANUARY

Jonson is all smiles and like one who basks in the sun, for he hath found royal favour once more. Tonight, & again tomorrow, another of his masques is to be performed at the Banqueting Hall, Whitehall. It is called *Hymenaei*. He is most pleased with the music which his right good friend, for so he calls him, Alfonso Ferrabosco hath composed.[1] Ben said also that the dresses are sumptuously bejewelled. I marvel he cares so much for such matters. Nonetheless, the gossip of note is that the masque is written in honour of the marriage between Lady Frances Howard and the Earl of Essex. She is but thirteen, and he but 14. It hath all been arranged to patch some political feud or other.[2] Such are the ways of the mighty.

11 JANUARY

This Powder Treason must be a fearsome thing, for yet two more conspirators [Robert Winter and Stephen Littleton] have been captured and lie now in the Tower. 'Tis said they have lain in hiding somewhere these last two months or more. I suppose they have been betrayed by someone for some reward or out of fear. Yester eve I was supping ale with Will Sly at the Bunch of Grapes, & he did think this powder plot might have in it the stuff for a play. When he said this, his grim face smiled as much as I have ever seen. I told him perchance it might, but such a play must needs be as a buttress to our monarch, & condemn soundly those men that would disrupt our order. Then I thought some more, & told Will that such a play could be penned, but it must be set backward in time, and but glance at what hath passed these several months. After we departed I thought more on this and believe I would do well to write a play [*Macbeth*] that, in whatever fashion, praised our king & his forebears.

27 JANUARY

Today the arraignment of the powder plotters.[3] There required no prophet to declare them guilty. 'Tis said the King, the Queen, & Prince Henry were in Westminster Hall to see the trial, but all were disguised.

30 JANUARY

Though I fain would have stayed home, Marston dragged me to St. Paul's Churchyard to witness the execution of some of the powder conspirators.[4] There was set up, in that western part where old Queen Elizabeth had given thanks to God for our deliverance from the Spanish Armada, a scaffold which was built for the purpose of this execution. Marston was intent & fixed upon what passed, tho' I did avert my eyes as much as I could. What passed was much like those executions I had witnessed before with Kit Marlowe, who took blood-thirsty delight in these affairs. Sir Everard Digby was first upon the scaffold, and confessed his guilt, and begged forgiveness. He was cut down almost as quick as he was hanged, and some said it did appear he spoke when his heart was cut out, though I heard it not. Then followed Robert Wintour, who did naught but pray before he died. Then the other condemned confessed their guilt and such to the gathered multitude—such a monstrous press of folk can scarce be imagined. All died bravely enough, bloodily enough—all done as the law requires, for thus only may the body politic be satisfied.

1 FEBRUARY

Today all the world would gawk at the heads of the powder plotters, for some have been set upon London Bridge & those of two others at the very top of Parliament House. Yesterday were executed four more in the Old Palace Yard [Westminster].[5] One of them [Ambrose Rookwood] asked for forgiveness, and then prayed to God to make our King a Catholic. I marvel the man was not hanged twice for such an impertinence. The last to hang was the man called Guy Fawkes, who was found in the cellars below Parliament setting out the barrels of gunpowder. 'Tis said his father was a notary and found employment with the Archbishop of York, but his son turned from Protestant ways and converted to the Catholic faith and hath fought with the Spaniards against us. Then he turned conspirator against our king. I believe he had been tortured, for he was weak, stumbled, and could scarce climb the scaffold—tho' in his day he must have been a strong man, and I recall still his red hair and beard. Well, all their worldly woes are ended for ever. When all is said & done, this life is but a dream as tedious as a twice-told tale, or a strangling nightmare.

10 FEBRUARY

This evening I supped at the Boar's Head with Dekker & Marston. I had not kept company with the two of them together in some while. Tom told me his friend John Day hath caused trouble with his play called *The Isle of Gulls* which hath been played by the Revels Children at Blackfriars. This is the same John Day that killed Henry Porter some years ago [1599]. The play is a satire which, said Tom, "Complaineth greatly of this nice and difficult age." For a long time we talked on what we might or might not write in these heated, dangerous days. Mayhap 'tis best to write naught. Late to bed.

11 FEBRUARY

Today I thought on what Will Sly had said a week or two past on some play or other to please our King. I took down Holinshed's *Chronicles of Scotland*, and read somewhat therein, and think, forsooth, there be matter enough for a play on King James's forebears.

12 FEBRUARY

The gossip this today is that the Jesuit priest who was party to the Powder Treason hath been brought from Worcestershire, where he was in hiding.⁶ Not many days will pass before he faces his day of judgment, in this world & the next. Also today, news from John Davenant that Jane is near her time. He says he would be honoured if I would stand as godfather to the child when it is born. And I believe I shall manage affairs to do so.⁷

20 FEBRUARY

I am racked with agues and lie abed. I wish for better health that I may ride to Oxford and Davenant's christening.

3 MARCH

Oxford. Despite some pains, I was right glad to stand as godfather to Davenant's son, William—named for me, they said—christened today. He is a bonny, lusty boy. The church was bone cold and, as we stood at the font, the boy cried heartily. But we passed a joyous day; i' fecks, I have ne'er seen John [Davenant] as happy. Mostly he is as solemn and grave a man as may be found, for he ne'er smiles; but today he might have been another man. Jane, as ever, was brimful with wit and conversation. I declare I could marry her myself if matters were otherwise. Robert, their eldest son, was pleased to see me, and hung much about me as we feasted upon the banquet of savoury dishes, & drank the fine wines John set before all our company.

10 MARCH

I give more thought to this Scottish play [*Macbeth*], which shall consider usurpation by murder. The chief character is possessed by ambition; superstition & fate drive him like devils, and so shall his wife, who would have all. Our king is reputed to be rapt by the supernatural to which he dedicates close study, & that shall have some part. John Davenant reminded me of those sybils that entertained the King some time past, & perchance I might do likewise.⁸ Of powder plotters 'tis said Father Garnet's servant [Nicholas Owen] did commit suicide by cutting open his own belly. This in the Tower [on 2 March]. Yet I have heard other folk say that the man was so much tortured he had ne'er the strength to do it; besides, suicide is a mortal sin. I doubt not he was desperate, and pray his soul may find repose at the last.

[C. 20 MARCH]

This afternoon our company played Jonson's *Volpone*, Dick Burbage being the Fox himself. I did not perform. I think this play is the best that ever Ben hath penned. True it is that all his characters are still possessed by "humours," as he so calls them. Yet, his plot holds the mind, and his satire hath wit and gives delight. Never a modest man, Ben said to me, as we walked to the Mermaid afterwards, "That play I am positive will last to posterity and be acted with applause." Well, that may be so. Then we sat & drank for a goodly part of the evening, & I told Ben somewhat of my Scottish tragedy. Ben forbore to tell me that I should write after his own style, for we shall always differ on that matter, and I have but to remind him of *Sejanus* to quiet him. We chatted on the Powder Treason, the king, and much like. Ben admitted that, tho' he be popular at Court with his masques & such, he is fearful because of his Catholic religion. I said that, if he had converted once before, haply he might convert again. I intended no offence, but Ben was offended, & it was some while afore we were friendly again. Late to bed.

SUNDAY [23 MARCH]

Yesterday throughout the city ran a wild rumour that King James had been stabbed with a poisoned dagger. Some folk took up arms, shops were shut tight, & there was general uproar. However, sometime late in the afternoon and to the ringing of bells, the King returned safely to London from Woking, where he had been. In the evening I supped at the Bunch of Grapes where one gossip opined that the authorities themselves had spread the rumour of the king's death. I asked her why she said so. She replied that the reason was as clear as day—to make folk more favourable to the King that he might obtain the subsidy he needs from Parliament.[9] I told the dame I had not thought of that, and I was astonished that such a crone would think on high affairs of state. She said, "You just wait & see if I'm not in the right." At that she cackled loudly, & her visage did remind me of a witch or hobgoblin. I recalled the sybils at Oxford, & I think some three witches to prophesy to Macbeth his fate would make a quaint device. Yet they shall say one thing and mean another, whereby Macbeth shall be misled, because of his desire, his ambition.

26 MARCH

Dame Trot at the Bunch of Grapes was right indeed—Parliament hath granted the king his subsidy.

29 MARCH

Towards early evening yesterday concluded the trial of Father Henry Garnet who, 'twas said, was party to the Powder Treason, along with Fawkes and all the rest of them. He is to be executed, which astonishes us not a whit. At the Mermaid, all the talk was of Garnet & the other conspirators, for some of the plotters had used the tavern off and on over the months; Goodman Johnson is afeared 'twill bring the tavern into ill repute. Yet, thus far, the authorities have not been nigh the place. Someone said Attorney General Coke had called Garnet a doctor of the five Ds—dissimulation, deposing, disposing, deterring, and destruction—fine rhetoric forsooth. Yet it would seem that Garnet was not deterred, e'en though he was weak from long confinement in the Tower, and, when he was posed such & such a question, he would equivocate, saying one thing and meaning another. He did defend this equivocation, protesting he was not bound to accuse himself, seeing that they had no proof. There was much argument after this kind, but it availed Garnet (also called Farmer) not a whit, & he is to hang come May Day.[10] I fear the Catholics will see hot days, and suspicion's ready tongue will name any folk who keep not closely the Protestant faith. I do but write plays, eat, drink, and sometime take my pleasure—'tis the safe path so to do.

30 MARCH

More violent winds today, as yesterday. Much talk that this bodes ill, one way or another. I had thought to write that God hath vented his anger at Protestant and Catholic alike, yet that might be blasphemy.

[APRIL]

My *Lear* hath been acted by our Company, and I know not what to write of it, for I find it hath so affected mine own senses, more than any other play I have penned thus far. Dick Burbage enacted King Lear so thoroughly, to the topmost of perfection, that I was moved to tears withal. When he had carried the dead Cordelia upon the stage, I could not endure the howls which came forth from his mouth. Many folk in our audience wept openly, and held one another lest they fell down in a faint. At the very end there was no applause for above a minute or more, so moved were the audience. Then the applause thundered loud and long, most for Dick. Yet Bob Armin, our Fool, drew forth plaudits, and rightly so, for he personated the antic as well as any actor in London could. He hath humour and pathos in perfect degree. I played Kent. I had wished Edmund [Shakespeare] might play my Edmund, for I had him much in mind when I wrote that part, but he hath occupation with the Queen's company. Afterwards, to my surprise and delight, Harry [Southampton] came into the tiring house, though I scarce recognised him. He was much disguised, for he wished to be incognito, though he gave no reason for that. Harry congratulated me and all the fellows, & I could see he had shed more than a tear. Whiles we talked afterwards, he asked me if I had heard of Cordell Annesley and her father when I wrote *Lear*. I told him I had, and that the sad tale had given me a hint and more for mine own Cordelia.[11] Harry said, "I had thought as much. The curious thing is my step-father is much acquainted with this Cordell." I thought Harry would say more, but he did not, and he looked somewhat vexed. Then I recalled he had objected violently when his mother married Sir William [Harvey]. After that Harry departed. I marvel now how small this world can be in such matters, how little the degree that separates one from another.

27 APRIL

When I met Jonson this morn, he was most grim. Yesterday he and his wife were summoned to the Consistory Court & charged with recusancy. Ben said they had been attending church at St. Anne's, Blackfriars, this past six months, but they had not received the communion host on account of scruples he holds. My mind misgives whether Ben hath told the whole truth in this matter, but I cannot believe he is foolish enough to seduce any folk to popish ways, which he said the authorities said he had done. He fears they would make him a conspirator in the Powder Treason, yet from what I know, Ben hath done naught that way. He desires his favour at Court too greatly. Before he departed, Ben said he & his wife must appear before the Consistory Court again, & take instruction in the true religion. I know what the authorities mean thereby, but I ponder what the true religion might be, or if there be such—a certain heresy.

1 MAY

Garnet did not hang today because the authorities feared the prentices & like bloody-minded folk would be unruly. I thought more upon *Macbeth*, and think Macbeth's wife needs must be some spur or prick to his ambition. Macbeth would falter without her and her bloody thoughts. Later I read Marston's *Sophonisba*, this play he gave me some week past.[12] The Children at Blackfriars acted it, but I saw it not. It hath some fine lines, and I needs must compliment John heartily when next we meet.

3 MAY

The jest all this day hath been that Garnet hath been hanged without equivocation. He was taken from the Tower, and dragged on a hurdle by three horses to St. Paul's Churchyard where the scaffold lay (as before for his fellows in conspiracy). It was not mine intent to be a witness, but as to a mystery, I was thither drawn. On the scaffold, Garnet disputed his guilt for some time, e'en though two clerics exhorted him to confess. At the last he turned to us & said he was, peradventure, guilty, & sithence the pardon (which he had expected) arrived not, he made himself ready to die. Before he began to pray, he said "Now is no time to equivocate," & then he prayed in Latin. He was hanged while he prayed. I did not stay to see him quartered, for that I could not endure. I heard afterward that the multitude stayed the hangman from cutting him down, and thus did Garnet die while he hanged, and was spared the pains of quartering. May this be the end of the Powder Treason, conspiracies, recusancy, and all else.

8 MAY

"I have bought the Manor of Dulwich for some thousands of pounds"—these Ned Alleyn's words today as we drank a fine canary wine. I had not thought Ned had so much money about him, but I doubt not his affairs have prospered mightily. He told me what he intends to do at Dulwich, though he will continue to live on Bankside for some time to come. Well, may all joy & prosperity be his.

10 MAY

I have received word from my dear Susanna that she hath a fancy for the physician, John Hall. She seeks my approval &, i' fecks, she might do much worse in this world. I am troubled that her name was placed on a list of recusants, tho' Susanna says there is no cause to worry. Mayhap I should write to the parson, or perchance John Hall might attend to the affair.[13] These be parlous days when all men and women are doubted of their religion. *Later.* As I was passing by Marylebone Church, a bride and her groom appeared at the west door. The bridegroom was Sir Francis Bacon all bedecked in purple garments! I think he did intend all eyes to be upon him and not upon his bride, who was but the merest child.[14]

13 MAY

John Heminges called together all our company, and told us we have been commanded to perform for King James when the King of Denmark visits the court this coming summer. John said this will be in July & August, and 'tis expected we shall be commanded to play thrice, mayhap more. We talked about what might be our plays. I said my *Macbeth* is well nigh concluded, and I thought it would please King James, for it touches upon his ancestor, Banquo, together with witchcraft & the like. "'Tis well known the King delights in just such matters," I said. Then there was much chat on other plays, with mention of playing *Hamlet* again. I agreed it might please, if pared & trimmed—and there may be no mention of Danes & surfeit of drinking. "E'en tho' it be true," said Will Sly, laughing violently. Condell counselled we must give no offence. There was some discussion of this matter, but I paid little heed, for I have my task set firmly before me & needs must accomplish it swiftly.

28 MAY

Yesterday was issued a new law against blasphemy upon the stage whereby there may be no jesting nor profane use of God's name, nor of Jesus' name, & so forth. I must amend my work but a little.

5 JUNE

Several fellows & myself gathered at the Mermaid in goodly fellowship to quaff quantities of ale—John Marston, Jonson, Tom Dekker, young

John Webster, Tom Middleton, Francis Beaumont, & some others. I drank too much & can scarce recall our conversation. I remember someone told me he had read a play called *The Fleir* and that parts of it were like my Lear play.[15] I am angered no more by such things, for imitation doth flatter, & I must be of much repute if my fellow dramatists do so. I recall I spoke much of my *Macbeth* to which Tom Middleton gave close ear.[16] Strange that bricklayers give birth to dramatists.[17]

6 JUNE

This eve Tom Middleton came to my room, and seemed meek & modest, uncertain his visage. I gave him some wine, & we soon fell atalking, & he was more at ease. He desired to talk with me about writing plays, what I did, how I write. He was attentive to what I said about *Macbeth*, which is most immediate in my mind. After some time he became shy & coy again, & asked me if I would read a play which he hath penned and calls *The Revenger's Tragedy*.[18] Though I hesitated for a moment, for I have much work in hand, I said I would, & thereupon he produced it from his gaberdine. "If I may be so bold & brazen," Tom said, "may I ask you whether the King's Men would perform such a thing, only if you took a liking to it, of course." "Indeed it is true we always have a need for novelty, to please the multitudes," I said. "And I will be honest and fair with you, Tom. I will read your tragedy carefully, & if it hath merit & is like to suit our company—the two be not the same, you understand—I will indeed commend it to my fellows. More than that, I cannot avouch." Tom smiled and thanked me several times o'er, and said that now the Children of Paul's played no longer—he had written things for them before—it would be a mighty blessing if the King's men played one of his works. Then more chat & wine.

7 JUNE

Middleton's *Revenger's Tragedy* is laudable, & I shall commend it to my fellows. I have told Tom whether we perform it or no is a matter for the fellows. He was greatly joyed.

15 JUNE

"Nay, Sweet Will, there be murder, incest, poisoning, mayhem, & I know not what. And, tho' 'tis in Italy, these dukes & duchesses might be taken for our own. Nay, 'tis not fit for our royal presentation." Thus spoke John Heminges, and the others nodded their assent. I had proposed Tom Middleton's *Revenger's Tragedy* as fitting for us to play in August for the King, but to no avail. I said, "John, there's no more in Tom's play than in my own *Hamlet*, or e'en *Macbeth*, and those we are to perform." Dick Burbage said it was a matter of degree, and besides my plays were without rivality, "the top of admiration." "What's wanted, Will," Dick said, "is a comedy that there may be some variety in our presentation, like variable dishes at a feast that stale not. Tom's play would be a fine enough work for the Globe; you remember how well Kyd's *Jeronimo* [*The Spanish Tragedy*] pleased the multitudes. I think this *Revenger's Tragedy* might do the same." There was more chat by the other fellows to the same purpose. So it was settled, and leastways Tom will have his day with us, & for that am I pleased.

23 JUNE

The common fate & dole of all parents hath visited our queen. Her daughter, born but yesterday, hath died today. Neither rank nor degree may stay the hand of death, & thus is my mind smitten by fond remembrances of my own dear Hamnet. Ever I think on what the dear child might have accomplished.

28 JUNE

Yesterday the Earl of Northumberland was tried by the Star Chamber, & sent to the Tower for the remainder of his life. He is no Catholic, but he hath great sympathy for Catholics—such is the rumour. He hath been suspected in the Powder Treason. The authorities have laid also a grievous heavy fine upon him.[19] 'Tis best I am content with mine own station which is sufficient in this world wherein I find joys & pleasures enow.

7 JULY

Home with Anne and restful days, tho' I must join my fellows in Oxford before month's end. I shall do naught but tend my garden, walk by the river, & breath deep the fresh clear air. Susanna talks of little but the physician [John Hall]. I have told her that it is a fair match, but prudence now brings lasting joys. I remember the haste with which Anne & I went to it, & there hath been plenty enough to rue—though now I believe we jostle well enough together. But I rejoice Susanna is happy & like to make a good marriage.

12 JULY

I have spoke with physician Hall, as Susanna asked of me, & I confess he is all a father might wish of the man who is to marry his daughter. He is devoted to my Susanna, hath studied at Cambridge, & his father is a physician also.[20] Hall said he hath some land at Evesham where the earth springs forth medicinable plants & herbs—on which he talked much. As I departed from him, he said, "Master Shakespeare, I love Susanna truly, & I vouchsafe I shall do nothing but in care of her all her days, as well as any man living may, nay more. And I do declare marriage is a contract, an eternal bond of love." To which I might make none objection, nor might any father.

25 JULY

Oxford. I rest with the Davenants, & take much joy in my godchild. I wait upon my fellows to come here.[21]

1 AUGUST

Supped with Ben Jonson who told me how lamentable had been the performance of his masque at Theobalds.[22] The lady who played the Queen's part, forgetting the steps to the canopy (where sat their majesties), spilled her casket of gifts into the King of Denmark's lap. His Majesty then desired to dance with the Queen of Sheba, but fell down and was carried to an inner chamber. The masque proceeded apace, but not the presenters, who fell down, so much wine had they drunk. And so on—ladies falling down, spewing forth the wine and sweet meats they had consumed. I could not forbear laughing at Ben's tale, though he was ireful at what had passed. I told him such were the rewards of the Court, and that he had desired them avariciously. I doubt he will cease his royal labours. When I took my leave of Ben, his distempered anger had abated not one jot.

6 AUGUST

Today we journeyed to Hampton Court where tomorrow we play *Macbeth* for King James & the Danish King—I trust it will not be like the riotous occasion that befell Jonson at Theobalds. Yet, for what other reason I know not, I entertain some fear, yet of what I know not. Mayhap 'tis because I compliment the King, albeit in small fashion—what if he receive it ill? For an hour or more, the boy Hal [Berridge] and I rehearsed o'er his part in the Great Hall with Dick Burbage. At first, Hal was uncertain and his voice weak, but with Dick's support, he grew all the stronger, and I believe he is Lady Macbeth passing fair. Most affecting was the scene where the lady walks in her sleep. After, I passed several minutes looking at the splendours of the hall—its ceiling, the decoration, the myriad lights—I mused upon what tomorrow will be. "Tomorrow and tomorrow and tomorrow. . ." I am as unsure as a virgin bride on her wedding eve, & this ought not to be.

8 AUGUST

All my premonitions have been, most lamentably, fulfilled. An hour or so before we were to play *Macbeth* last night, poor Hal Berridge was taken grievous sick with some fever or other. We placed him in the tiring-room that he might rest & sweat out the fever. Alas, it was not to be, for the dear boy died while we were playing. I was obliged to personate Lady Macbeth (there being none else without a part to play), which was well enough, yet not what Hal had shown he could do. When we had concluded, the King expressed no pleasure in our performance, nor was I called forth by his majesty. We left Hampton Court sorrowfully bearing Hal's body with us in a cart.[23]

12 AUGUST

My mind is beset by *Macbeth* and its sad events. Yet there is much in the play that is commendable—this I think in all modesty. I must set my mind on something else, tho' what I know not. The plague abateth not, & I shall return home for awhile—my fellows need me not with them in the country.[24]

28 AUGUST

Stratford. It hath been many a month since I read Plutarch's *Lives,* but I have turned again to the book. I marvel at the felicity of the language, and the whole is a fertile soil for the imagination. I eyed the story of Coriolanus & that of Antony and Cleopatra, & I think to set about a play on one or t'other tale—mayhap both. Antony & Cleopatra might clip round the popular imagination the more, for there is love & tragedy in that tale, & their history is known well enough. I remember how the multitude flocked to *Romeo & Juliet*. 'Tis a pity poor Hal Berridge is taken from us, for I believe he could have personated Cleopatra most dexterously. Well, I must pray one of t'other young fellows hath the like dexterity.

1 SEPTEMBER

Ahead lie days of good fellowship and delight, for Tom Middleton hath come to visit us & taste the fresh country air. Anne likes him well, & I am pleased withal, for she casts a discontenting eye upon some folk when she hath a mind so to do.

2 SEPTEMBER

To my delight Middleton hath read North's Plutarch of late, & we have had deep chat on what I purpose to write. Tom thinks Coriolanus is a deep character & admires him. Such is mine own conception; though the plebeians despise him, Coriolanus *is* himself, true to himself, his country, his friends. He fails only when he is not true to himself. The irony (but no jest) is that *his mother*, who moulded him to be what he has become, asks him to be false to his nature, to his virtue. As I shall write it, Coriolanus knows all too well, in a blinking of an eye, that when he yields to his mother, he seals his own doom.[25] Coriolanus, as I write him, shall be the topless perfection of tragic man.

3 SEPTEMBER

More converse with Middleton. We walked for two or more hours by the banks of the Avon, & I did not forbear to recall those happy days when dear Hamnet and myself did likewise. I told Tom of my conception of Antony & Cleopatra. He was wise & pertinent in setting forth the difficulties of the history—time, place, action, and so on. Indeed, this historical tragedy is not easy conformable to those rules of unity that Jonson holds so dear to his heart. I told Tom that, in my mind's eye, the play shall be but a series of scenes—in Egypt, Athens, Rome, & the like, spread across the Empire—each scene, in itself, shall reveal some piece of character & so forth. Yet shall all the scenes be placed one next to another so the audience may make compare between them. Antony does this, Cleopatra that, Octavius something else besides—& therein shall their quintessential differences be exposed. I talked at much length on this, and 'twas clear Tom was enchanted, tho' I believe he holds me in too high an esteem—for what I spoke on is but the common stuff of play making—leastways in my estimation.

5 SEPTEMBER

Today, for a jest and our amusement, Tom Middleton and I wrote out some scenes on Timon of Athens whose story we had found in Plutarch. Tom said in Timon he recalled mine own *Lear*, for Timon learns he cannot purchase love, affection, or friendship. I said I thought Timon was the more complete cynic because at the last he abjures the society of men, & dies alone. I said I doubted he was the true stuff of tragedy. Howsoever, we wrote and talked together several hours. When we had done, I invited Tom to take our bits & pieces, & make of them what he would, but he declined, saying the moment being passed, he had no taste to do more. So I have set it aside—for Antony and Coriolanus are what I must give flesh & life to. Perchance I shall return to Timon in more idle days. Tom remains with us two days more, then returns to London; I sorrow for the lack of his company his return thence will bring.

10 OCTOBER

I have been returned to London some several days. There is little news. Will Sly hath buried a bastard boy child who lived but two weeks.[26] Mme Mountjoy is not well. I needs must give my time to

Antony, & when that is complete turn to *Coriolanus*. After all these years I wonder why I have set down this too fond record—for I scarce look o'er what I have writ in years gone by.

30 OCTOBER

Today we buried Mme Mountjoy; she had not been in health for some time. Mayhap I shall lodge elsewhere soon. I must ready some of my work for Christmastide; we are called to perform more times than I can give heed to. Such are the rewards of the King's Men.

20 NOVEMBER

King James hath urged the Parliament to unite Scotland with England. He hath given many reasons for this Union of the Kingdom. I shall amend the first scene of *King Lear*, which we play for the King at Christmastide, so that division of a kingdom is shown to be clean kam. Some royal favour shall not go amiss.

30 NOVEMBER

I suppose 'twas some sort of affection & remembrance for the man that took me to St. Bartholomew the less today where they buried John Lyly. I confess I owe some small debt to his plays, tho' they be nigh on twenty years old. I remember how his words seized my mind & tumbled in my imagination, tho' the sense of them was ofttimes past my comprehension. Of late he had written nothing, had become a Member of Parliament, and had desired greatly to become Master of the Revels. Master Tilney did not oblige by dying before Lyly, and besides the preferment went to Tilney's nephew.[27] Lyly was much disappointed, tho' such are life's fortunes or mis-fortunes. Thus far have the fates been kind to me, but nothing can endure eternally.

1 DECEMBER

Edmund [Shakespeare] told me today that next year he is like to be a father, though he cares little enow for the woman whom he went with it for a lusty hour or so. "But the child shall be mine, Will," he said. "It shall want for naught if I can help it." Tho' I might condemn the fault, I cannot condemn the actor, for Edmund is a dear & loving brother.

27 DECEMBER

Yester eve we played *King Lear* for the King at Whitehall. Dick Burbage, that actor sans pareil, enacted Lear to such perfection there are scarce words enow to describe him. In Lear's madness, with Cordelia dead in his arms, I marvelled at how to the very life Dick (I had almost wrote Lear) was. No dramatist can fail when Dick personates the role. Bob Armin was a wondrous affecting Fool. Me—Albany for this occasion, & passing fair enough. Condell was villainy itself, a busy and insinuating rogue, & much better than heretofore; he hath seized well Edmund's cunning. John Heminges played Kent with more ease than I had done. I could heap encomiums on all the rest of the fellows, as indeed I should, for where would my stuff be without them to flesh out my words? We have several moe plays to perform this Christmastide, & it will be a wearisome season. I have forgot to write that one of Prince Henry's titles is Duke of Cornwall, but no offence was taken. I had not known Prince Charles is also Duke of Albany, a happy coincidence.

1607

In the early months of 1607 Shakespeare finishes and polishes Antony and Cleopatra, *while in June daughter Susanna is married to the physician John Hall. Shakespeare later finds himself involved in the social unrest caused by the Levellers and the enclosure controversy (he himself is now a landowner of some note). That situation provides Shakespeare with ideas and a fresh impetus for his play on Coriolanus. Edmund Shakespeare's son is born, and then dies within two months. Despite his reservations and his distaste for the man personally, Shakespeare collaborates with George Wilkins on* Pericles, *this at the urging of his colleagues. Wilkins is a ruffian of the worst kind, and a far cry from Shakespeare's own companionable fellows. Brother Edmund falls ill and dies in December, mourned only by Shakespeare and the ever-faithful Sam Gilburne.*

10 JANUARY

This hath been a wearisome Christmastide, for we have played at Court more times than I can number.[1] When I was younger, such occasions, the Court, used to delight my eye & mind, for they were all unfamiliar. Now 'tis stale, dull, & unprofitable, for my imagination if not my purse. Yet not all hath been thus. On Twelfth Night [6 January], before we played, there was a masque by one Thomas Campion whom I had not known before. I think that Jonson hath a rival because Campion composes both his words & music.

24 JANUARY

I hear Cuthbert Burby is sick, & Nick Ling not much better. I wonder what 'tis that ails booksellers, & I fear what will become of my plays that Bert had about him.²

31 JANUARY

We rehearse *The Devil's Charter* for the Court.³ I would the cowardly braggart Barnes had stayed from us, but he would come to the Globe to observe, pester, and meddle. I rejoice I perform no role for I care little for the drama. Yet hath this rehearsal proved profitable, for Heminges' prentice, John Rice, is remarkable.⁴ His Lucretia hath quite seized my mind, & I believe that he hath all the qualities for my Cleopatra, & in sooth Macbeth's lady when next we play that piece.

5 FEBRUARY

Once more at Court for the King. We have an o'erplus of royal favour.⁵

13 FEBRUARY

I walked over to Blackfriars where Jonson hath taken him a house, & in which he doth hope his wife [Anne] will join him in reconciliation. They have undergone troublous times, but Ben thinks that she will delight in the house, which is indeed in that part of the city high in fashion. We had chat on much else, & Ben showed me a letter prefatory which he is to set before his *Volpone*. I read the letter o'er & did think that, as ever, Ben doth protest too much. I smiled when he wrote he had "ever trembled to think toward the least profaneness," tho' in truth that is no denial absolute. In my foolishness, I began to argue with him where he had written "the principal end of poesie is to inform men in the best reason of living." I should have known better; our argument continued on two hours or more until I was aweary. As I took my leave, Ben said that I should write my own defence of poetry. I forbore to reply & smiled merely. I write plays and some poems, let those suffice.

[MARCH]

Self-immur'd in my room, I have laboured mightily & long on *Antony and Cleopatra*. I confess that North's translation needs but small amendment from my hand. I thought to entitle the play the tragedy of Antony, but what of Cleopatra? Besides, I have worked with the boy [John] Rice, and he hath a capability beyond his years. He hath about him a seductive air &, to boot, his voice be not cracked. When he & Dick Burbage recited o'er some scenes, I was transported by both of 'em. For the boy to act with Dick, the magnificent actor of our age, affords him such an opportunity as will ne'er come to him again in this world. A handful of touches here & there, & I believe I shall be ready to show the play to all the fellows.

15 MARCH

To hand today a letter from goodman [Abraham] Sturley whom I had desired to send me news of affairs at home, more particularly of Susanna & physician Hall. Sturley says all's well with the world there, & enclosed a sweet note from Susanna which sayeth she desires to wed this June or July, & thinks 'tis foolish to bide her time. That I might be edified & as an exemplar, Sturley told me of what had befallen at the bawdy court. It appeareth that the god-fearing Puritan Daniel Baker (whom I have long detested because while he was bailiff [in 1603] he had some players banned from the Guild Hall) hath been accused of fornication with Anne Ward. Poor Anne, truth to tell, was great with child, and said Baker had promised to marry her. When Baker did not appear to answer her charge, he was excommunicated, and that pleases me mightily. Yet I would not that Susanna be like poor Anne, & i'faith I believe that she is possessed of more reason, and can well control those baser passions. I think she & John Hall should marry this coming June, and it may as well be settled upon now as later. Mine own Anne will rejoice.

1 APRIL

I have shown *Antony* to our company, & the fellows are well pleased. There was no need of fair persuasions or sugared words, yet did Dick Burbage & the boy Rice speak some speeches—Dick gave Enobarbus on Cleopatra in her barge [2.2.191–219]. John Rice was pert and so well spoken far beyond his years that he did not, could not, boy Cleopatra's greatness [5.2.220]. I' faith, I do believe there's not a better boy to be found in all of London who could do as well. Heminges said he was pleased because there would be no troublesome amending of it when they go into the country. "For the most part, Will," he said, "each scene is a play within itself. Indeed, we could play those last scenes after Antony's death by themselves, if we were called upon to give but a brief entertainment." I agreed but said, in jest, Dick might be unhappy unless he was resurrected as Octavius. Well, that is finished, & I think to return home soon to rest, to write, & to see my daughter wed.

5 MAY

Home & peaceful rest, save I hear of little but her wedding from Susanna. It is a blessed comfort that she will be happy. I have spoke several times with physician Hall who is a decent upright man, though peradventure given somewhat to Puritan ways, which is no great matter, I ween.

[C. 10 MAY]

Yesterday eve at the Angel, whiles I was supping a goodly ale the like of which I have not tasted in many a month, I mused whether or no I might amend & improve upon *Timon*. Lost in thought, I half-heard a man I took to be an old shepherd say to me, "You mun well've heard. 'Tis a sinful disgrace." Having now no thought in my head, I decided I would hear out the old man. His story, in brief, was that over in Hillmorton some two or three thousand men, women, & children had dug up the enclosures. He said the like had happened in other parts hereabouts as well. The old shepherd was ireful, because if it continued, he would lose his livelihood for, he said, "How can I keep my flock without them enclosures." So we talked on for some time, though I confess I do not know the rights & wrongs of the matter, for it seems all are afeard for their livelihood. I doubt not that troubles will ensue for, when all is said and done, order & degree must be maintained. But if folk are wronged, will they not revenge themselves?

15 MAY

At the Angel I fell into conversation with a morose fellow who drank his ale sullenly. For want of discourse, I asked him what ailed him, but, at first, he declined to speak, and looked downward, first at the table, then the floor. Thus I waited awhile and then repeated my question, "What is it that ails you friend? Why are ye so afflicted?" The fellow replied, "My answer depends on who you be." So I told him that I lived hereabouts on occasion, but mostly in London where I was an actor sometime & a writer of plays. He asked me if I knew Will Shakespeare, & I confessed, with a modest laugh, that I was the self-same man. "Well, if that be true, as I suppose it must," he said, " I will tell you." He said he came from Hillmorton, and had been one of the thousands that had rooted up the enclosures some days past. "We call ourselves the Diggers of Warwickshire, & I am proud to number myself with its members, for we do but resist tyrants who would grind down our flesh. You know, Master Shakespeare, there used to be many folk that laboured in the fields and for the harvest; now there be but a few shepherds that fatten the sheep for their masters, while we may go starve. Thus it is we must be disobedient and tear up the hedges. The authorities may say we be riotous & so forth, but we faint & perish. They, the ministers & such, say we should pray to heaven for bread, and have faith in God. Tell that to a poor child that hourly cries for a sop o' milk." Whiles the Digger said all this, it seemed his eyes burned with passion, and I did think his cause must be a righteous one, for he did but desire food for his family. I asked him to take some food with me, & he did so, though all unwilling.

When I departed, I pressed money upon him, which he refused. I said it was for his babes, for food for them, & then he took it, with tears in his eyes and a blessing for me. I think this must be a sorely vexed business, & many folk be harmed one way or another. It is true, too, that I have those tithes at Welcombe, so I may not stand aloof.

21 MAY

More vain and frivolous hours were ne'er wasted than I have upon *Timon*. I can improve it no more, it interests me not, & I doubt an audience would be pleased with the thing. Susanna grows ever eager, ever impatient for her wedding with each passing day (for all that Hall be a Puritan, which I must not hold against him). She is a lively daughter. Judith says little of the affair, though she hath been aidant to her sister in preparing Hall's house, the Croft, for the couple—what little there is to do. I wonder when or if Judith will marry, & each time I espy her I remember dear Hamnet. Still, I must put those thoughts to one side & rejoice in Susanna's good fortune.

3 JUNE

We are as ready for the wedding as ever we shall be. It wants but the ceremony. News that yesterday, I think, a thousand or so diggers or levellers were put to the rout in Newton by Sir Anthony Mildmay & Sir Edward Montague.[6] Many folk were hurt and, 'tis said, as many as fifty killed. I fear they must be mightily distressed to endure so much & to die in their cause.

6 JUNE

Susanna's marriage day [5 June] was everything that she, Anne, & I wished for; I rejoice in her happiness. Though not given to levity, physician Hall (or son-in-law as now I must call him) seemed well pleased, or as well pleased as any Puritan is like to be. We feasted heartily after the wedding, & I drank physician Hall's portion (though my head is sorry & sore for it today). Anne is much comforted by it all, and that is a blessing in itself.

20 JUNE

I have heard that some days past all those in Northamptonshire, who called themselves levellers and diggers, surrendered themselves to the authorities. Alas, their leaders have been executed. Some folk said the cause was religious, but this was not so—they were digging up enclosures. Yet must we endure sermons from ministers who preach that the offenders were riotous, rebellious, & grossly misled: they wanted not bread but wanted faith, and did not pray to God; they suffered but little want and buried their patience as they buried the hedges. Pah! I do but note these ministers are well-fed, corpulent, with mighty portly bellies. Yet one notion doth reside in my mind. One minister spoke of the state as a body which must have a head, limbs, a belly, & so forth, and all parts are necessary for the commonweal. This may be my study, for can it be gainsaid? And perchance the bettering of the realm may lie that way.

[JULY]

'Tis many months past sithence I read of Coriolanus in Plutarch. I had determined to write of him after *Antony*, but my mind wandered from my task, for I have, I know, lost that spark of youthfulness that drove me on. Mayhap I am become too prosperous. Indeed, I have thought this summer how life at home in Stratford beguiles me. The warm days, sweet air, some few private friends, neighbours, & above all my family & kin. Ere long I shall be a grandfather, if I know the ways of those newly wedded. Yet these recent riots, or so they are called, have turned my thoughts again to Coriolanus and the plebeians. I shall read o'er again Plutarch.

20 JULY

I had quite forgot Edmund [Shakespeare] was to be a father, & I was surprised withal to hear he hath a son.[7] The child be base-born, & I know Edmund is not given much to women. In sooth, he delights still in boys, & he and Sam Gilburne oft keep company together; they are both in either's powers.

25 JULY

Today brief news from Ben Jonson who prospers in courtly favour. He writes well of John Rice, who, "clothed like an angel of gladness with a taper of frankincense burning in his hand," spoke some of Ben's verses before the King. I am pleased for the boy and I do foretell his fame will increase far & wide. He was splendid as Cleopatra. I fear I must return to London, at least for some little while.

8 AUGUST

Today with Dick Burbage & family to share their joy in their daughter. I pray she be a healthy child, tho' these be parlous pestilent times.[8]

12 AUGUST

I should have prayed for Edmund [Shakespeare], or rather his base-born son whom we buried today.[9] Though the child was scarce two months old, my brother had taken him deep into his heart. I think Edmund hath thought always that he was an unwanted child, and he did not want his own child, base-born or no, to feel that way likewise. Sam Gilburne, who accompanied us, shed tears at the babe's obsequies.

16 AUGUST

This is a month for death and sadness. Today I helped Dick Burbage bury one of his children.[10] I know what it is to lose a son, tho' Dick bears himself better than I did. He said, "All I hope for, Will, is that gracious God opens his gate of mercy for the dear boy's soul to fly through," though his words wanted conviction. Dick says he will go to Oxford with the other fellows next month.[11]

1 SEPTEMBER

News from Susanna who be ever brimful of joy, & hath but good and kindly words for her husband. She says she takes interest in his physick, which alas mother have had need of. I fear mother's time cannot be far off. She is ripe in years, tho' she hath a cheerful disposition & hath been the fount of support and succour for Anne & all my family. On the sudden I am struck with a Roman thought—Coriolanus and his mother, who would have him be untrue to what she had him be & become. Welladay, is it all one? Nature? Nurture? I am like Coriolanus, for I have been absent, in exile, many a time & oft. But I was ne'er banished. My rumination wraps me in unfruitful foolishness. I shall write no more of these awhile.

15 OCTOBER

Some six weeks and moe have passed since last I wrote herein, and strangely, there hath been naught to write. The plague rages ever on, & takes folk of high & low degree, e'en the King's own daughter. I marvel the poor babe died far from her parents.[12] Did their majesties hold so little love for their child? I know not. Yet there is now a rumour which I overheard yester eve at the Mermaid, to wit, the King hath taken him a great favourite whose name is Robert Carr.[13] Jonson, who hath seen them together at Court, said the King pinches Carr's cheek wantonly, is forever leaning upon him, & speaks some Latin to him that he might learn it. And Ben, who hath been ever careless of his own dress, remarked upon the royal favourite's garments fashioned after the best & latest fashion. Yet his, the King's, own daughter lay afar off when she died.

17 OCTOBER

I was eating a fine piece of cheese, washed down with strong ale, at the Bel Savage Inn, when Tom Middleton entered to me. He gave me some little news, the chief of which is that two of his plays are to be published—*The Revenger's Tragedy*, which we played, and *A Trick to Catch*.[14] I did not see his *Trick*, for it was acted by the Children of Pauls, but Tom did show it to me a long time since. I enjoyed the piece e'en though it takes after Jonson's style more than any other. It is a lively play & will hold an audience, yet not a piece I would write these days. I told Tom I thought to ready *King Lear* for the printer, though I believe there will be little profit in't.[15]

29 OCTOBER

Well, our mighty Falstaff, John Lowin, bewitched at last by the wiles of female charms, today was married in St. Botolph's [Bishopsgate]. His bride is a widow, one Joan Hall, whom I knew not before this day, & she appears lusty enough, as well she might, for John *is* a weighty fellow. After their wedding, we ate and drank aplenty; I fear tomorrow will bring an ague. I had thought to stay away because of the pestilence, but I could not forgo the pleasures of fellowship with all our company.[16]

10 NOVEMBER

John Heminges tells me our company is commanded to perform many times at Court this coming Christmastide, and all shall be wanted.[17] What plays we shall perform I know not, and I have nothing new, for *Coriolanus* lives more in my head than written down. I trust my roles be small enough, for I am aweary of acting, but I must play whatever part is necessary.

11 NOVEMBER

John Heminges came to my room this morning early and carried with him a bundle of papers. John said, "Will, I know you are much occupied with your own labours, that play upon Coriolanus which we would dearly love to see ere long." I said, "The labour we delight in physics pain," whereat he laughed. Then I told him Coriolanus was keeping my mind busy, though I thought it would be some weeks after Christmas afore I might finish it well enough for our company to look o'er. "Yes, indeed," said John. "I was wondering whether with reason and discourse you might be persuaded to another task. You know we are commanded to perform at Court many times this coming Christmastide and, as yet, we want some novelty to offer their majesties. Well, by chance, after our meeting yesterday, I saw George Wilkins at the Bell Inn and we fell atalking. Well, Wilkins hath written what he calls a play, which I hold here in my hand, this bundle of papers. Now, Will, I know ye hold no affection for Wilkins, & i'faith neither do I. Howsoever, I have read o'er his piece, called *Pericles*, & there is some merit in the action, but little in the writing. Yet I do believe it could be worked over . . . ," and here I told John I could divine & surmise his plan already, to wit, that he would have me amend it in good time so that we might play it at Court early in the new year. John said it was so. I asked him if Wilkins was agreeable to such amendment (for I have no desire to converse with him), & John said the man desired but two things, to see his play upon the stage in whatever shape or form that might be, and five pounds for his troubles. So, e'en though it distracts me & I care little for Wilkins, I told John I would read the play & decide if I might fashion something from it.

12 NOVEMBER

I have read this *Pericles* by Wilkins, & Heminges' opinion is correct, by and large. The action hath interest, as do some of the characters. There's more to approve in the second half of the play than the first. The device of Gower as narrator, though quaint and awkward, serves its turn for the advancement of the action. Thus I have sent word to Heminges that I will do what I can with the piece, though it might yet remain rough & ready if our fellows must have it in time for the Christmastide festivities. Yet it might serve the occasion.

20 NOVEMBER

I have heard Harry's [Southampton's] mother died some several days past, tho' he hath not written to me of it. Not that I expect he might so do, for our days together are long since melted into thin air like a baseless vision. Yet am I reminded of mine own mother who is poorer in health than I would wish, and I fear she will die ere long. I wonder how Harry hath received his news; does he feel his mortality more than he did before? In musing on him, I think on my sonnets that, upon occasion, I look o'er to idle a pleasant hour and recall fond memories. Today, for the first time, I thought that, peradventure, one day I might publish them. Yet I would not have common minds touch them, and mayhap 'tis best that private friends only do see them.

1 DECEMBER

Pericles must be as 'tis, for it is quite beside the government of my patience. To the opening scenes I have done but little, & Wilkins' own work must suffice for the nonce. I have laboured on the latter portion &, though it could be improved, it must remain as 'tis. Mayhap I might enlarge upon some ideas & themes in another play, but not now.

9 DECEMBER

Yesterday there was a hard frost, and snow fell so abundantly that folk can scarce traverse the streets. I remain indoors, yet e'en so it is very cold and my bones are benumbed.

15 DECEMBER

Today a thaw hath set in & leastways my room is warmer. I have decided that, when once we have done playing at Court, I shall set down *Coriolanus*.

26 DECEMBER

Our company performed for the King today at Court, though I believe he saw little of what we played. For the most part the King hung about Robert Carr, or "Sir Robert" as now he is called, for he was knighted on Christmas Eve. He is indeed a handsome man, & the King kissed him before us & the assembled throng as though he were a woman. I care not, and the King may well do as he pleases as kings are wont to do, but I fear folk will mislike it. Tomorrow early I must visit Edmund [Shakespeare] in his chamber, for Sam Gilburne hath sent word he is grievous sick. I had feared for mother's health, yet 'tis likely Edmund may be taken first.

28 DECEMBER

Edmund is most grievous ill, & I fear he will not live out this day and die far from home, though not myself, nor Sam who tends him with sad devotion. The great frost, as now 'tis called, hath returned & freezes even the Thames. I have seen people walking half way across the river &, if this frost abates not, the river will be frozen entirely.

31 DECEMBER

The last day of December in this year of grace 1607. This morning afore noon I buried my brother. Sam Gilburne was with me, all tears; this week he hath been heavy, sad, and much different from the man he was.[18] I have done what I could, which is but a trifle, and should have done more. I ordered the church's great bell be rung, for poor Edmund deserved no less. I am glad we play not today for the Court. I shall remain in my room, drink deeply, and my contemplation shall be mine own mortality, and my thoughts upon dear Edmund.

❧ *Ben Jonson and his masques thrive at court (as do King James's catamites), the River Thames freezes over, and daughter Susanna gives birth to a girl. Shakespeare and the King's Men savour the prospect of opening up the Blackfriars Theatre for a more upscale audience and for winter performances. Shakespeare thinks* Coriolanus *might be an appropriate choice when performances are permitted. The bullying George Wilkins proves an ongoing thorn in Shakespeare's side, and in June John Marston finds himself imprisoned because one of his plays offends the authorities. Shakespeare encourages two new protégées, Francis Beaumont and John Fletcher, who offer the King's Men* Philaster *for when the theatres eventually reopen. Shakespeare suffers the bitter blow of his mother's death in September, but his spirits are revived somewhat when his sister Joan gives birth to a boy. Wilkins publishes his own version of* Pericles, *and the King's Men perform at Court for King James even though the theatres themselves remain closed.* ❧

2 JANUARY

This day at Court. As before, the King took less note of our presentation and more of his catamite. The Queen, so it seemed to me, affected indifference, yet surely she is much offended. I muse how the incest in *Pericles* shall be received amidst such courtly affairs. We play it shortly; ever the Prologue and Chorus, I am to personate Gower.

7 JANUARY

The Thames hath frozen around Westminster; I heard tell that the Archbishop of Canterbury hath crossed over the ice from his palace in Lambeth to Whitehall. Verily, a prelate may walk on water.

11 JANUARY

Jonson rejoices, & is overjoyed; yesterday yet another of his masques, *Of Beauty*, was played in the Banqueting House at Whitehall. Ben told me that he had written it at the especial request of Queen Anne, who was one of the masquers, with Lady Arabella Stuart, and many other ladies of the Court. Like a child with a new trifle, Ben was pleased, he said, with the cunning apparatus, the machinery, and the sumptuous jewels worn by the Queen and her attendants. I did forbear to tell Ben my opinion of such art (I did not ask Ben where now were those unusual words wherewith he was wont to spangle his speech). I think this masque can scarce be called drama, for it is the merest spectacle designed to delight but the eye and not the mind. Yet this is what is desired at Court, & is well rewarded.

18 JANUARY

Much upon the stroke of two today, Tom Dekker and I set forth to London Bridge to observe what this great frost hath done. The river was frozen o'er, and multitudes of folk were upon the ice. There were booths, a tavern in a tent, a game of bowls, and to my wonderment I saw a barber warming a pan of water by placing coals upon the ice.[1] Everywhere people disported themselves as though they were on dry land and not the frozen Thames. We saw one young man & woman go to it lustily & without shame; we lingered not, but went to drink muscadine and eggs, and mulled sack at the Bell Inn.

1 FEBRUARY

A thaw has begun, and everywhere the ice melts. I hear Susanna [Hall] is near her time, and Jonson's wife also. I ride posthaste to Stratford & trust I be not too late.

8 FEBRUARY

Today Susanna was delivered safely of a baby girl, whom she and physician Hall have named Elizabeth.[2] So I am a grandfather, possessed with all those joys when Anne gave birth to our own children. Only a boy could have made my joy the greater, but 'tis no matter.

20 FEBRUARY

Tomorrow baby Elizabeth is to be baptized in Holy Trinity; then I must return to London, for many affairs press me about.

1 MARCH

Yester eve I passed with Jonson at the Mermaid where we quaffed more ale than is good for men of our age. Yet were we both as full of spirit as any men living—me because I am become a grandfather, Ben because he is a father again.[3] I think Ben & his wife be well reconciled, leastways until Ben feels some itch or other. Peradventure I'll give Ben some latten spoons for his child, & jest that Ben can translate them for me.[4] Strange to relate, I recall naught else of our converse.

12 MARCH

Dick Burbage, Bob Armin, Will Sly, myself, & several of our company were gathered together today at the Tabard [Inn]. The news is that yesterday the Children of the Blackfriars performed again Chapman's play about Marshall Biron, which had been stayed by the authorities because the French ambassador was much offended by the piece. Why they performed it again is a mystery, & most foolish. Some of the company have been arrested, & Chapman has fled, tho' where no one knows—this from Will Sly. Dick is concerned, for he fears the Blackfriars Theatre will be closed indefinitely & so he loses money. Moreover Dick worries our own work at the Globe may be prohibited. However, Bob Armin was much more cheerful. He said to Dick that mayhap this late incident might present an opportunity to embrace. He said Dick & Cuthbert should take over the lease and manage the theatre themselves. "We can play in Blackfriars when the weather is bad & cold, as in this past winter. The audience there is higher in degree & such, and peradventure there's money in that." What Bob said set us atalking; mayhap it might fordo us, or make us quite, for ill is the wind that profits nobody.

25 MARCH

We have told Heminges to do what he may over this inhibition against playing. John thinks it may well cost us some deal of money, & we should agree not to present plays to which the authorities may take exception—histories of our realm, politics, & the like. I have said always we are safer with the Romans, and I believe no exception may be taken with *Coriolanus*. Indeed, my plebeians are a rabble which their tribunes sway like corn bending in the wind. And do I not call them Hydra, the many-headed monster? [*Coriolanus*, 3.1.93] Though the plight of the diggers & levellers is miserable, the remedy lies not in disobedience, for the disobedient cherish rebellion, & rebellion leads ever on to disorder & chaos. Of that we have had enough & plenty. Yet 'tis easy to speak thus when our bellies are stuffed full; what medicine hath the miserable when hope seems futile?[5]

20 APRIL

A salutary warning—yesterday Thomas Sackville, the Lord High Treasurer, dropped down dead. He was on trial for taking bribes, and had seemed in good health. His *Gorboduc*, which I read many years ago, was a dull thing. Will the same be said of my plays in time to come? I confess I have penned some pieces that I blush to acknowledge mine own, yet they served their turn at the time.

2 MAY

I was walking in Cheapside somewhat before noon when I met Dick Field. He told me he was newly come from Stationers' Hall, and there had seen that I had a new play entered in the register. I assured him that I had no such play, & asked him what the entry read. Dick said Tom Pavier had registered *A Yorkshire Tragedy*, & it bore my name.[6] "That profane wretch Pavier hath done it once more," I said. "It is true we played the piece some while ago, tho' we gave it out as *All's One*. It was written by George Wilkins, or so he says, tho' Tom Heywood may have had some hand in it. All I ever did was but the smallest amendment here and there—trifles, no more. But I suppose Pavier thinks my name will sell his book." Dick & I talked awhile, & Dick advised me to enter my plays in the Register e'en though I might not wish to publish them yet awhile. That might prevent others from doing so, he said. I fear nothing will prevent a mechanical salt-butter rogue.

18 MAY

I have suffered a fearful encounter with George Wilkins who showed me that he might be most violent and angry. He accosted me in the street, and demanded to know when *Pericles* would be published, for he hath need of the money. I told him that, though he had limned out the action, the greater part of the play came from my hand. "Moreover, the play remains popular with our audiences and," I said, "'tis our practice to keep a play to ourselves for a year or two. It will be printed when the company is good and ready so to do." Thereat Wilkins grew vexed, & began to threaten I know not what, save that he was determined to be even with me. He went on his way only after I persuaded him he needs must talk with the company, and determine what might be done.

19 MAY

Converse with John Heminges, to whom I made known Wilkins' threats of yesterday. John said he hath heard disquieting intelligence about Wilkins, but he does not think that he will cause me harm. "Now, if ye were a woman, it might be a different matter, for, coward and bully that he is, Wilkins will go after a woman, & kick her & so forth." John advised it would be best if we told [Edward] Blount to enter *Pericles*, &, for that matter, *Antony & Cleopatra*, in the Stationers' Register, for John believes, as did Dick Field, that might prevent publication.[7] "You know, Will, these days just your name is worth a handsome fortune, & that we must protect."

3 JUNE

Dick [Burbage] called together all our company to tell o'er what be his intent for the Blackfriars Theatre. He looks to those of us who desire a share in a new lease. The rent per annum is forty pounds, and affairs would be much as they have been with us at the Globe. Dick & his brother Cuthbert are certain sharers, as are myself, Condell, & Heminges. Of the other fellows most lack the ready money, but there may be one or two more who will join the venture. I think there is money enough to be made; e'en though our audiences will be smaller in number than at the Globe, they will pay more. I must pay heed to my old age, as well as Anne's, for, without money, old age is but misery, and I'd as lief not be acquainted with that bedfellow.

8 JUNE

Jack Marston is committed to Newgate, tho' for what cause I know not, save it is said he hath appeared before the Privy Council. So he must have offended.

9 JUNE

Jonson believes Marston is in Newgate because of some play he wrote which had in it gibes against the king—a dangerous proceeding. Marston hath much offended.

10 JUNE

I have seen Jack Marston, but briefly, & he will say nothing about his committal. He said he will never pen another play, intends to enter the Church and become a parson somewhere in the country where he may live in peace & quiet.[8]

[JULY]

John Heminges beseeched me to undertake an errand in behalf of the whole company, & I trust this may cause us some prosperity. The business began with a hint from Jonson that, if we were in need of some novelty (as is the case, for I have nothing), we might look to young Francis Beaumont, whom Ben admires this side of idolatry. I have seen Beaumont in Ben's company from time to time at the Mermaid, though I have passed but a few words with him directly. He lives on the Bankside with John Fletcher, whom I have but seen, and who comes of a good family, for his father was chaplain to our late Queen.[9] Ben had said these two bachelors together have written some plays which might serve our turn. As their lodging lay not too far from the Globe, it was but a simple task to discover them, yet it caused me some amazement. When I entered their room, they lay abed together and betwixt them was a wench whom they hold in common. I could see that the three of them had but recently satisfied their lust, & yet this was of no concern with them. When they dressed, they exchanged clothes & the like, careless of what they wore. However, they treated me in a friendly manner, & said they were honoured that such a famous poet should seek out their abode. I told them of my errand, & forthwith they produced a play they call *Philaster, or Love Lies A-bleeding*. I have told them my task now was to read their play, as would some of the other fellows, & if it suited we would play it (though I did not tell them this was like to be in our new theatre at Blackfriars). Fletcher & Beaumont were o'erjoyed, though not obsequious. I came away, my errand well fulfilled.

5 JULY

I have read *Philaster* and, though it hath faults, it will, I think, suit our purposes at Blackfriars. The characters are shallow, the action preposterous in places, & the sentiment lacks true feeling. Yet for all that, the piece hath a kind of brilliance & romance which might appeal to our courtly audience. Now we want but the theatre.

9 AUGUST

Well, 'tis done. Seven of us have taken the lease upon the Blackfriars.[10] I believe the wind be set fair for us, & we can but try. Only the authorities & the plague can meddle with our success.

13 AUGUST

Will Sly hath not lived to seize his new good fortune; he died today, though I know not if it was the plague, which daily rages, that carried him off.[11] Mayhap Will's death is a sign, & I have decided to ride to Stratford as quickly as may be. There I can find some peace, quiet, & think on a play or two.

1 SEPTEMBER

Mother is unwell, and her spirit is fast failing. Physician Hall says there is no remedy, but believes what days remain to her will be easeful & peaceful enow—a thankful blessing. She lies abed with the very life yet warm upon her lip, but she will rise no more.

10 SEPTEMBER

We buried mother yesterday.

19 SEPTEMBER

Grim news hath come from Dick Burbage, & there is nothing but death—his daughter & Fletcher.[12] I cannot think upon such tidings—we are but the stuff of dreams, our life rounded by sleep. Gentle sleep that's Nature's soft nurse.

[20 SEPTEMBER]

In the midst of death is life. My sister Joan hath been delivered of a boy child—would that mother had lived long enough to hold the babe, which she desired with fervency. I am filled with wonderment, amazed that Joan died not in the child-bearing, for she is nigh forty years old—though she hath borne all her children late. We shall see the mite baptized in a few days [23 September]; he is to be christened Michael.

SUNDAY [16 OCTOBER]

Today I stood as godfather to Henry Walker's boy; he was christened William, for me. A hearty feast after.[13] I rejoice that I may partake of the bounteous pleasures of this world, & I wish prosperity, long continuance, & blessings on my good neighbours.

1 NOVEMBER

I was glad and surprised withal when John Heminges rode up to my door this afternoon as the sun faded into dusk. He had ridden from Coventry where the company performed some days since [29 October]. His news is that we are commanded once more by the King to perform at Court this Christmastide, & John desires I should be one of their number, e'en though I act much less than heretofore. Anne spoke somewhat against his request, for it is many a long year since I passed Christmas with her and the family. And, she said, "I hath greater need of ye now that mother hath passed away." I' fecks, I am loath to go, for I fain would remain in Stratford, & write what plays I can yet devise. But the money is wanted, & I enjoy the company of my fellow actors. John sleeps here tonight; tomorrow I shall tell him he may expect me at Christmastide.[14]

2 NOVEMBER

As Heminges made ready to take his leave, he said, "Well, bless me Will, I had almost forgot to give you this book. Tom Dekker gave it to me awhile back to give to you should I pass by Stratford." I took it from John and saw it was called *The Painful Adventures of Pericles*.[15] "So I see that Wilkins hath done what he said, that he'd ne'er rest until he was evened with us," I said. "We would not let him publish the play, and so he does this. See here, John, where the title says 'as lately presented by the worthy and ancient Poet John Gower.' That is a poor kind of jest, for he knows I did personate Gower in the play. Well, much good may it do him, John. The play remains still our own." "Indeed, Will," John said, "but nothing Wilkins might do would cause me wonderment for, without doubt, he is the most disagreeable of men." So saying, John mounted his horse and rode away. I forgot to enquire of John why Dekker had wanted me to have Wilkins' book, though I suppose it was a kindly gesture.

30 NOVEMBER

London. Although the plague rages & public plays are stayed, we are to play for the King at Christmas, & now make all ready.[16]

31 DECEMBER

December's end, deep mid-winter. We have performed again at Court, &, I note, as all the world may see, the King is steadfastly enamoured with Robert Carr. The rumour is that the King hath given him some twenty thousand pounds. The Queen and the two Princes [Henry and Charles] seemed to enjoy our presentation; I know not whether the King gives them any heed. I hear that Dr. Dee, the astrologer, is dead some three days or so since.[17] I muse whether he divined his own death. Tom Middleton told me that he had heard Dee was once duped by his own assistant [Edward Kelly], who told Dee he could talk to the angels. Dee said he could transform a pot into gold, or some such thing. 'Tis all an imposture, as is much in this world.

1609

§ Troilus and Cressida *is published, and Jonson continues to produce successful masques at Court. Shakespeare begins to find peaceful Stratford more and more attractive, and withdraws there more frequently. As he muses on his own mortality, he considers it is time to put his poems in order and have them published. He is still in Stratford when his* Sonnets *are published, and he is surprised by the publisher's strange dedication that makes no sense to him. In London the plague continues unabated, emptying the city. Also during the summer a corrupt version of* Pericles *is published, an action Shakespeare attributes to George Wilkins. Later in the year, Shakespeare sets about writing* Cymbeline *as a fantastic gallimaufry of his own earlier works, and that play provokes him to think about another experiment in dramatic form he might produce to answer Jonson's gibe that he is incapable of observing the three dramatic unities.* §

20 JANUARY

A day or so ago I did recall my *Troilus* hath ne'er been published, for I prevented Master [James] Roberts from so doing some years past. I hoped our company might play it one day at the Globe, but it was performed only by desire of one of the Inns [of Court], & my fellows believed it would ne'er please the multitude. I told Heminges the thing might as well be published now & be acknowledged mine own—this because I fear what George Wilkins hath done with *Pericles*, tho' we yet keep the play close by us. So *Troilus* will now be printed.[1]

3 FEBRUARY

At the Bel Savage Inn with Jonson—he replete in triumph, for his *Masque of Queens* was enacted at Whitehall yesterday. Ben described to me both the scene and his masque in extensio (as he would say), for he enjoys his royal acclaim & favour. As before, Her Majesty and several ladies of the Court were amongst the masquers; H.M. had requested the masque from Jonson. From what he said, there was much spectacle, scenery, and machinery which gave great delight to the Court. Ben was pleased with his anti-masque of witches, hags, & such like, for the King, as all know, hath an inordinate curiosity in such affairs. Ben would have discoursed for many an hour, I believe, for his fancy is so taken with the intricacy of masques & such multiplicities in which I can but feign interest. However, I think I must turn my mind to this fashion, at least in some regard. It was fortunate that John Manningham entered the inn &, upon seeing myself & Ben, came to our table. Before Ben could recount his triumph, I told Manningham that meeting him was a curious coincidence, for I had that very day visited the booksellers who are to publish my *Troilus*, the very theme of which Manningham had suggested to me several years ago.[2] I told him Bonion (one of the booksellers) had shown me proudly the title page of *Troilus*, which declared our company had acted it at the Globe, yet this is untrue, for we did but act it for one of the Inns. Manningham said, "Indeed, for I was present that very night & was delighted thoroughly. I did not think, however, it was meat for the general multitude." Upon the sudden I was struck with a thought, & asked Manningham if he would be willing to write an epistle for the play, for there was yet time so to do, & I assured him I would deem it an honour if he would consent. "Master Shakespeare," Manningham said, "the honour & pleasure would be all mine own, & if you would be good enough as to tell me where the abode of the printer is, he shall have such an epistle forthwith." So I told him where Eld lived.[3] Then followed more deep chat, in the midst of which Ben desired to know again the booksellers of *Troilus*, for, Ben said, he was desirous to place his *Masque of Queens* as soon as might be convenient.[4] We drank a quantity of fine canary wine. Late to bed.

6 FEBRUARY

I leave for home tomorrow, for there is little enough for me in London at this present hour, & at home I may work in tranquillity awhile. John Manningham hath furnished his epistle to *Troilus*, most satisfying & laudatory. I wonder how many more plays I may yet pen.

1 MARCH

Stratford these last several weeks grows to be what most men desire in life—peaceable quietude. Though fame & fortune lie in London—leastways when there be no pestilence—yet here there is contentment of body & spirit devoutly to be wished. My work is not forgot; I mean play making, for acting hath become mere triviality, and I have ne'er been but a passing fair actor. I have fixed upon ordering my sonnets that, if they have merit after all these long years, they might be published. I had not thought so to do, for I designed them but for the eyes of dear, private friends. Yet now I sense immortal longings in me, & I would not have these poems cast heedlessly into a fire when I am dead & gone. And, for all that she is a good & kindly wife, Anne in her ignorance might commit such an act. When they are ordered, I shall dispatch them to Jonson, for I hold his good opinion is worth more than ten of some other fellows I know. Then shall I turn my mind to some two or three plays of fantasy I have thought upon.

20 MARCH

I have sent my poems to Jonson, & I pray the messenger be not careless.

15 APRIL

Heminges hath written that our company is to receive £40 from the King that we might rehearse while the plague rages. He says the fellows go into the country to perform safe from the plague.[5] In reply I have told him that, whate'er the money might be, I must remain here at home. I have new work afoot; besides they have no great need of me.

14 MAY

Today came news from Jonson, who hath read my poems & sonnets (he says). Some time past, he was taking his repast at the Mermaid & fell into conversation with George Eld (that did print his *Sejanus* and my *Troilus*) and another printer, William Hall, whom I know not, neither does Ben. Well, they fell atalking of this & that, &, says Ben, he happened to say that I had poems to publish, though why he would tell this to mere printers I know not, nor did Ben say. Howsoever, the upshot is the three of them agreed that Thomas Thorpe, who hath published Ben's plays and other books of quality, is the man for my work.[6] I do surmise Thorpe is as good as any, & I have sent him a missive that he may conclude the affair in high style, & admonished him to pay due and most careful attention to what I have writ, & that my sonnets be ordered as I did set them forth. Ben is cock o' hoop that another of his entertainments, for thus he calls them, hath been performed—this for Lord Cecil.[7]

28 JUNE

To my amazement Ned Alleyn hath sent me a copy of my *Sonnets* which, he says, he had for 5d.[8] I knew not that Thorpe had published the book. I am astonished at the dedication which Thorpe hath placed before my poems, for I did not inform him so to do &, i'faith, I know not what to make of the curious words.[9] I believe Thorpe hints at a well-placed person, perchance that thereby folk will buy the book. But it is all nonsense to me, & my sole joy is that the dear treasures, dear to me when I wrote them, are now preserved. Ned says he hath taken delight in reading them, & is rueful we did spend so little time together. The plague, he writes, hath emptied London of folk and is a solitary place.[10]

[SUMMER—JULY/AUGUST]

Naught but rain for weeks on end—forty days & forty nights—the hay harvest will be poor, other crops rot right & left. I have pondered long upon what plays to write, for I have already assayed much. I must needs entertain the multitude—this is the very purpose of plays & playing. Yet I think I shall, by subtle means, write about my art, the art of plays. Jonson is for ever preaching his way is the one to follow—humours, unities, & such like. I think I shall write something or somethings that show plays may take whate'er form an author may choose, provided the play delight the audience. And, to make clear my notions, I shall incorporate all manner of jests, allusions, satires, & the like. Folk may detect these or no; at the least I may be amused. Flights of fancy, but not of angels, & imagination are what I need.

Damn & blast George Wilkins. He hath caused *Pericles* to be published, which I authorised not, e'en though my name be upon it.[11] The thing aught never to be printed in the condition in which it lay, & why this hath come to pass I know not, save that the story is popular, & somehow Wilkins hopes to profit by it. Mayhap it is the man's vanity—to see (what he will call) his work printed, or mayhap 'tis but spite because I would not have it thus. Heminges writes that Wilkins went to his friend, one Henry Gosson (who lives in Catherine Wheel Alley near his shop on London Bridge), who hath published ballads & such,[12] & Gosson published the play. Well, 'tis done now, but I would not have my art displayed thus, in shape and form incomplete.

[5 SEPTEMBER]

Tom Greene hath asked leave to abide where he is, if it be convenient & if I desire not to retire from London yet awhile. I asked him how long he might wish to live at New Place; he said till come this time next year. All agreed friendly, though I did advise Tom that twelve months or so would see me home.[13]

[AUTUMN]

I have devised what I am pleased to call an anti-play. If Jonson can have his anti-masque, I may so term my play. This play [*Cymbeline*] observeth not those rules laid down by Jonson, for I do not believe there can be such. The play hath three plots or stories, yet one doth not begin until half the play hath passed, & another begins later yet. The jest lies in the title, *Cymbeline*, for the expectation is he, Cymbeline, hath much to do with the play, yet his part is but a jot and tittle. The stories are antique fables—a wicked queen, an innocent girl, lost sons and such—and ancient history. As a goodly measure I have writ a masque in which the great god Jupiter, sitting upon an eagle, shall descend in thunder and lightning, and he is truly the *deus ex machina* who resolves all after the fashion of the Greeks. The final scene defies all credence, yet I hope the audience will find much amusement therein. Many jests may be apprehended only, I think, by those folk in the audience (& my fellow actors) of keen discernment. For throughout the play I have woven many lines plucked from mine own plays—fictions within a fiction. Truly, there is much that is but the merest absurdity, & the jest will lie in the performance thereof, & the witnessing thereof. One subtle jape I have writ for my good old friend Dick Field.[14] This play hath set my mind awhirl on one or two more plays wherein I may play with dramatic art & poesy as suits my fancy.

17 NOVEMBER

But trifling news from Heminges, tho' the plague in London continues to rage.[15] I have sent him a letter to say I will not join the Men at Christmastide, for mine own work occupies me.[16] Yet I have promised the fellows they shall see my several novelties in the months to come.

1610

In between everyday business concerns, Shakespeare completes his work on The Winter's Tale, *which breaks Ben Jonson's dramatic rules. However, when Jonson shows him his play,* The Alchemist, *Shakespeare is full of admiration, and considers it the best thing Jonson has written apart from* Volpone. *Shakespeare enjoys a revival of* Othello *and then witnesses the various celebrations in London as Prince Henry is invested as the Prince of Wales. Less pleasant is the news of the assassination of the King of France. When the plague again breaks out in the summer and the theatres are closed, Shakespeare gladly returns to Stratford. A visit to some local friends where he hears tales of far-off places inspires Shakespeare to write* The Tempest, *which conforms to all Jonson's prescriptions and includes jests against Jonson himself. Once more, Shakespeare absents himself from the Christmas performances that the King's Men give at Court.*

10 FEBRUARY

Perforce I have returned to London, & Heminges tells me that, two days since, Robert Keysar, who had a share in the Children [of the Queen's Revels] at Blackfriars whiles they were there, hath taken suit against us all.[1] Heminges says Keysar wants our profits, tho' these be as yet few, for the Blackfriars hath cost us dearly for repairs & such—that and the plague. John says we need not worry & he has the matter well in hand. I needs must find a book of Robert Greene's *Pandosto*, that I read long since, on which I mean to fashion my next tale [*The*

Winter's Tale]. Would that Tom Nashe were yet alive, for he would possess one surely.

19 FEBRUARY

Yester night we played *Mucedorus* for the King at Whitehall, mine but a small part, for I had not purposed to play at all this season at Court. We were received fairly, & given goodly entertainment when we had done.

26 FEBRUARY

"You will remember well how [Robert] Greene called me an 'Upstart Crow, beautified with our feathers.'" This I said to Jonson & Tom Middleton at the Mermaid where we drank long & ate heartily. "Well, my latest tale, my *Winter's Tale*, will beautify Master Greene's *Pandosto* & be a grand jest. It will observe not one of your rules, Ben, for it will show the triumph of time (for such Greene also called his story) with the observation of an abyss, if I may so call it, of some sixteen years or so set square in the midst of the action." As I had surmised & intended, this declaration provoked Ben to a long, grave harangue on all those articles of dramatic art he doth espouse so dearly. I feigned attention to his words, smiled & nodded. From time to time, I told him how, in this play (as forsooth I had done in *Midsummer Night's Dream*), I provoke the audience into an awareness that they do but watch a play, a fiction—that, as it were, they might perceive *in the play* the very art we dramatists use to make a play. Tom said but little, tho' he smiled greatly, for he knew mine intent with Ben. As we were about to depart, Ben said, "Will, I do most firmly believe you write as you do because you are not capable of fashioning a play which doth observe the unities, as doth mine own." "There, Ben," I said, "I think you are wrong. If you do but attend some several months I will indeed write such a play that will reveal to you the art of the unities & such." Ben said, "I wager five pounds you cannot." "Done," I said, & we shook hands & I laughed—"there's five pounds earned swiftly & most adroitly."

3 MARCH

Alas, I do not share in £30 the company hath received for rehearsing for the King's Christmastide entertainments. Yet, 'tis a small price to pay for the liberty I enjoyed.

25 MARCH

Today I walked some ways to St. Mary Matfellon, which is the Whitechapel, to witness the baptism of Ben's daughter, named for the late queen.[2] Ben was ill at ease, & when I asked him why, he said he was happy enough for the babe, & rejoiced in her birth. "She is, forsooth, passing fair," he said. "Yet, there might be another child soon that I might have no part in lest my wife cast me aside once more."[3] After the christening, we feasted awhile at Ben's abode, & he placed into my hands the latest offspring of his pen which he calls *The Alchemist*. I promised him I would read it closely. "Aye, do that, Will," Ben said, "for I do believe you will find in it the finest exemplum of that dramatic art which I have admonished you, many a time & oft, to adopt as your own." I smiled, for I knew by heart the sermon Ben was about to preach, and I was resolved not to bandy word for word with Ben. I smiled also because I have in mind the promised play that encompasseth all of Ben's dramatic art & whose very theme & topic is art. Nonetheless I took Ben's *Alchemist* and will read it ere long, not least because our company desires to perform another piece by him. Late to bed.

2 APRIL

I confess in plainness I am full of admiration for Jonson's *Alchemist*. True, the play is much like many another of his, for his characters are but humours as he calls them, and he satirises the vices or weaknesses of sundry persons. In this play, a servant and one that professes alchemy cozen several folk who would gain riches quickly. Yet there is mirth aplenty, & Ben is not so savage in revealing folks' faults, or natural follies as he calls them. Indeed, I believe it will play well at the Globe, & I might almost wish to act in it but that I gain little pleasure in acting these days. In his Prologue Ben speaks of "these two short hours" the play requires, & I shall take up that hint in mine own play [*The Tempest*].

30 APRIL

Today *Othello* was given at the Globe. Dick Burbage was a magnificent Othello, & revealed more of the character than I thought possible by mortal man.[4] Dick hath been as much my good fortune as I his.

5 MAY

Jonson's *Alchemist* is to be performed by our company, though not myself. I did not have to persuade the fellows to present it, for each & every one found merit in the play, as I have. Dick Burbage hath laid hands on the role of Face, but the other parts are not yet settled. Though I have cast about for my next play, I have decided nothing (save the piece shall have masques, perchance an anti-masque, supernatural creatures, & shall follow those unities Jonson loves so dearly). Indeed, I think I shall do little until I return home this summer. I find no inspiration here, but I will win my wager with Ben.

25 MAY

My Cleopatra [John Rice] is in trembling ecstasy; he is to perform when Prince Henry is created Prince of Wales in a few days. Dick Burbage is to be with John.[5] I rejoice for the lad, and he is well deserving.

31 MAY

I arose late and hastened to Whitehall Stairs to see the pageant of Burbage and Rice. There was great expectation, but the crowds pressed about so greatly a finger could not be wedged in more, and I saw & heard little. Dick told me all the tale when we sat & drank ale at the Cross Keys Inn this evening, though I confess I attended little to what he said. I but recall that Dick & John rode upon two great fishes—Dick presented Wales, the boy Cornwall, all allegorical.

7 JUNE

Yester eve I walked down to the Thames to view the naval battles, for so they were called, which were staged on the river to celebrate Prince Henry's investiture. There were vasty multitudes of folk who thronged every street, alley, road, and vantage point. It seemed all of London was out and about to see such sights as might be seen. After the battles, the night was lit up by many fireworks of such brilliance, & the explosions continued nigh upon an hour. After they had done, I made my way to the Bell Inn in search of such refreshment as could be had, the hour being late. The inn was as crowded as the streets outside, but I found a small bench at the back. Next to me was a sailor newly come from France, tho' why he was in London I did not discover—he spoke some little English & I indifferent French. We talked as folk do, but most amazing was what he told me he had seen a few days past. The sailor said he had been in Paris at the time that King Henri IV was murdered by a schoolmaster of the name of François Ravaillac.[6] This happened the day after the king's wife had been crowned. The schoolmaster was, by the sailor's account, a fanatical demon in the hands of the Jesuits, & he had long desired to murder the king. Ravaillac's execution was after the French manner—his arms were pinched with red hot tongs & four horses pulled his body apart into quarters. "Mais il confess pas." At that moment I remembered how the same had occurred years and years ago.[7] 'Tis passing strange. When I returned to my chamber, I pondered o'er the sailor's tale, and I was reminded of usurpation & disorder & such— the very themes of my chronicles. All comes full circle, the wheel turns. Mayhap I shall write on this soon.

[C. 11 JULY]

As I had foretold, Jonson's *Alchemist* hath been applauded mightily, & I do not begrudge him his good fortune, for this play is the best he hath written, save his *Volpone*. Dick Burbage enacted Face as well as could be; Heminges was Subtle, Bob Armin was Drugger. Nor shall I forget [John] Lowin's Epicure Mammon, a perfect foolish hypocrite knight. Everyone else fared well.[8] Tomorrow I return to Stratford, for the pestilence increaseth and the authorities say our theatres must close again.

[AUGUST]

Idle hours, days, & weeks at home. Betimes I care not whether I write another word, for there is little enough I would write about. Yet I would still pen a play on dramatic art, but I lack a plot, some scaffold whereon I may hang what paltry thought I have. I should be thankful I am blessed with healthful, peaceful ease, & am not empoisoned by the stenches of London.

31 AUGUST

How swift this summer hath fled, & I am indolent ever. I hear tell our Master of the Revels is dead,[9] & so are his revels ended; his life is rounded with a sleep, all is now but a dream. Well, we all must come to dust like chimney-sweepers, a jest which few will comprehend in *Cymbeline*.[10] Mayhap 'tis my fault—too o'ersubtle, as is that jest about Dick Field,[11] tho' I think I have made all as plain as a pike-staff, e'en tho' the play is a gallimaufry. That is all mine intent. I maunder to no good purpose.

[AUTUMN]

Tomorrow Anne & I are to ride out to visit my good friend Tom Russell & his wife who have promised us goodly entertainment.[12]

Anne & I passed three pleasing days with Tom Russell & his Anne, together with Anne's sons by her first marriage—Dudley & Leonard [Digges]—both fine fellows who have been at Oxford University and bred well. We chatted on many a subject, but I was interested most particularly by what Dudley said of the ventures of the Virginia Company of which he is a member of the council. He told me he had seen recently a letter from one William Strachey addressed to some lady or other whom he, Dudley, knew not.[13] This is the same Strachey whom I now recall wrote some sonnet or other to commend Jonson's *Sejanus* several years ago [1605], tho' I forbear to remark there is little in that play which can be commended. But Dudley's tale, his recollection of this letter, filled me with wonder & amazement as he described the voyage, hurricano, shipwreck, the islands, Bermudas, & all the creatures that inhabit there. In one wondrous moment, the whole plot & being of the play I have mulled in my head for all these months revealed itself. It shall be called *The Tempest*, for the opening scene shall be such, & will seize the imagination of the audience straightway—though what remains of the play will have little enough to do with the title. The remainder will be enacted on an enchanted isle where a castaway magus & his daughter have been shipwrecked many years before. He is assisted by supernatural creatures (this for King James), & the storm that he hath created brings to his isle his former enemies. In due course all are forgiven & reconciled after they confess their sins, a marriage is promised for the creation of a new society, & all return to their native land whence they came. Much music, some dances, a masque or two, much to delight the eye, and all shall obey Ben's dramatic unities to the uttermost. As the magus practices his art, his magic, I will lay before my audience mine own art. Then, mayhap, I will have done with the theatre for good & all—and win the wager with Ben.

1 DECEMBER

I have fixed on a jest or two 'gainst Jonson in my *Tempest*—the chief character, the magus, called Prospero (this from Ben's *Every Man in His*

Humour), & a gibe at his childhood days.¹⁴ I doubt not that these japes will pass unnoticed; they are but small hits at Ben, his humours, unities & such. With such matters I lighten my days. I have writ to Heminges that I shall not join the company when they commence playing, nor shall I perform in the Christmastide entertainments for the Court.¹⁵ My acting days are as good as gone. However, I doubt not I shall find myself in London from time to time; for now, I am well satisfied where I am. Time is come round, and where I did begin, there shall I end. I think I am resolved to write but little & rarely in this record from now forward.

1611

❧ *Jonson continues his successful career as a writer of court masques, while Shakespeare passes the winter in Stratford. He returns to London to attend to business matters; however, he sees and is distressed by a mangled version of* Macbeth. *That is followed by a performance of* Cymbeline *that fails to fulfill his conception of the play. Fortunately,* The Winter's Tale *is staged successfully. As the year comes to a close, Shakespeare supervises a production of* The Tempest, *but declines to perform the role of Prospero. King James personally commends Shakespeare for the play, but appears to be less satisfied with a performance of* The Winter's Tale. *Shakespeare again returns home for Christmas.* ❧

15 JANUARY

The weather is cold—I keep to home & hearth. News from Jonson of his triumph at Court with another of his masques. I wonder why Ben aims no higher, though I know he glories in his fame & fortune. This last masque is called *Oberon, The Fairy Prince*,[1] which I believe is a gibe at myself, for I had sent to Ben an adumbration of my *Tempest*, & he hath perceived, rightly, I took the name Prospero from his play; so he hath returned the favour. Prince Henry enacted Oberon and entered in a splendid chariot drawn by two white bears and guarded by three sylvans on each side. Much music and songs praising the King—such stuff can be performed but once, & I see little reason for that, though only the vain seek after immortality in their works. Ben writes that he hath yet another masque to present at Court shortly—vanity thy name is Jonson![2]

15 APRIL

It hath been many a long month since I was in London, and in that time I have forgot so many of the sights, sounds and, above everything else, the stench of the city. The press of the multitudes, after the peace and quiet of Stratford, is o'erpowering; I marvel I endured this daily for so many years. I have returned to see my fellows, dear old friends, for there are several affairs of business which must be mended. I am pleased also because they are to perform several of my plays at the Globe shortly, and I have a mind to see them & the theatre again.

18 APRIL

While affairs here are well, I suffered great perturbation yesterday when the company rehearsed o'er *Macbeth* which they intend to play shortly. All went as it should until some creature, not of my creation, dared to thrust itself upon the stage and began to sing, dance, & caper about the platform with mine own weird sisters.[3] I could scarce restrain myself, but made no fuss until the rehearsal was finished. Then I accosted Heminges & the others about these additions. John said they were naught but a small novelty, & folk enjoyed such stuff. Before I could make more moan, John said it was no great matter & the stuff would be omitted if I desired. We agreed upon that.[4] Now this business hath passed, I doubt not that in years to come my plays will be minglemangled by any wasp-stung and impatient fool who chooses so to do. Pictures are not so changed, but a play may be. Such is my passing greatness.

[C. 25 APRIL]

The fellows have endeavoured bravely to perform *Cymbeline*, and did take some instruction from me when they rehearsed it. Howsoever, they would play the piece as love comedy and chronicle, and thus all my drollery ne'er came forth. The multitude liked best the roaring of Cloten, the which reminded me of those days when Kempe trod our boards. Mayhap the fault is all mine, that mine intent be not as clear as a bright frosty morn. Yet I do fault my fellows, for they would not grasp the humour of it all and would be too serious. Perhaps 'tis as well I retire altogether to Stratford.

1 MAY

I passed a pleasant evening with John Heminges—a hearty meal, passing fair wine. We talked on much, in particular what we have done together in times past. I rejoice that I have known such a man, and John said he was honoured to be my friend. For awhile we talked on *Cymbeline*, and I told John that I had been downcast a little that the piece had not been played in the manner I had wished. He said, "Well, that is true enow, Will. I believe the fellows tried and did their best, you know that." "True, enow," I said. "But do you think mine intent was perceived?" "Well, Will, if you mean all those jests about your own plays, plots, characters, & such, I believe that was plain enough. I' faith, I believe there was scarce one play you left out, one way or another." I told him that the fault must lie with me. "Mayhap, Will. But peradventure the next time we perform *Cymbeline* all will be different. Despair not." After that we had more chat long into the evening before I wished him a peaceful goodnight.

16 MAY

Yesterday was presented *The Winter's Tale* [at the Globe], which suited the company and our audience so much the better than *Cymbeline* some two or three weeks past. As is the fashion, the groundlings were well pleased with the dances, music, & songs, which enchanted every ear with sweet varied notes. They were enamoured with the statue at the close which caught their imagination. Autolycus was a hit, a proverbial hit. Jonson hath shown me his *Cataline* which our company is to perform in some weeks. I cannot be jealous of such fustian discourse, for all that it be by Ben. It will require many hired men in the performance, & whiles acts one & two are passable, the rest will, I fear, prove tiresome. The multitude will not sit entranced by speeches of some three hundred & more lines, such as Ben would have Cicero speak [4.2]. Mayhap such oration suited the Romans, or Latin writers, but it will not sit well with our groundlings, for all the attention they give us.

I have shown *The Tempest* to my fellows and 'tis, in general, well liked and thought will please the Court this coming Christmastide—for that is when Heminges thinks it will be presented. This was all mine intent, and to that end, as I told John, I included all such elements as were like to please the Court—supernatural, masques, anti-masque, songs, music, & all such. Howsoever, I do not believe they have divined my true intent, leastways not at the present. John said he thought I should return for the performance and take some role. "Why, Will," he said, "I do believe you might well act Prospero himself, for I see much of you in that character." I laughed, & with no false modesty told him the part needed a Burbage not a Shakespeare, e'en though I have played many a king in the past. Yet I did promise to consider a small part, for this might be the last occasion I might perform before the King and Queen, and there is something to be said for royal favour. Then we talked for a while on who might provide music for the songs and such, and John said he thought well of Robert Johnson. I told him I recalled that he was marvellous dexterous upon the lute, and would suit our purpose.[5] On the morrow I return home again—that I shall savour.

1 OCTOBER

With qualms & misgivings I have returned to London, leaving the blessed peace of home behind me. My task, my travail, is to o'ersee my *Tempest* which we will play before the King come Hallowmas night [1 November]. Mayhap 'tis as well, for I fear I may never write another play; we may be taken all too suddenly from this world. E'en today I heard the tale of the death of the curious Dr. Forman, who, by all account, foretold the day of his own death.[6] The Sunday afore he died, he told his wife he would die that coming Thursday, & so he did while he was in the middle of the Thames. Some say Forman's death was doubtful, that he did fordo his own life desperately that his prophecy might be fulfilled. Yet he was buried in holy ground [on 12 September], & sure he cannot have been so foolish.

30 OCTOBER

Tomorrow the company performs the first of many plays the King hath commanded for this festive season.[7] I shall be but a looker-on, tho' I play a small role in my *Tempest*. I confess some of my wonderment of old hath returned, & I recall when I first acted at Whitehall before our late queen. Much hath happened sithence.

2 NOVEMBER

With the grace and blush of modesty, I do believe yester eve was a triumph, such a triumph as e'er I have witnessed in some while. I was afeard much might go amiss with *The Tempest*, for the spectacle did depend greatly on machines & lights, what with music, songs, dancing. Yet all was as one. After we had done, His Majesty called me forth & said, as best as I could understand, "Master Shakespeare, we have been pleased to view some several of your works, but none we may say hath pleased us as well as this *Tempest*. We trust we shall see more such from your pen." I bowed low & mumbled some few words, tho' by that time his majesty had given his arm to his favourite & walked away. I shall remain in the city until *The Winter's Tale* is performed & return home afterwards.

5 NOVEMBER

Tonight the fellows presented *The Winter's Tale* at Whitehall for the King, tho' he seemed not as delighted with it as with *The Tempest*. Peradventure he was not pleased in seeing a king [Leontes] afflicted in his senses and who hath an ever-faithful wife [Hermione]. But for all that, I ne'er had the King nor Queen in mind when I penned the play—I thought more upon that wretch Robert Greene and his work. Well, 'tis no great matter to me now. Six years ago today was the Powder Treason! Home tomorrow, or mayhap two days hence.

CHRISTMAS DAY

At home with family, friends, & acquaintance. I find great content in this comforting repose which repairs my nature. I am sorry I have not passed every Christmas day thus.

Shakespeare is still in Stratford when his brother Gilbert dies and is buried early in the year. In April, Shakespeare travels reluctantly to London to testify in the Belott-Mountjoy marriage settlement trial. He is annoyed because all he ever did was to act as an emissary between the various parties. After some persuasion, Shakespeare agrees to write a piece to be performed for the marriage celebrations of Princess Elizabeth the next year. Back in Stratford, he thinks hard and long before he decides to write Henry VIII *for the celebrations. The end of the year is clouded by the news that Prince Henry is dead.*

28 JANUARY

Gilbert [Shakespeare] is not as well as he might be, tho' he knows not what ails him.

31 JANUARY

Gilbert is much the worse. Physician Hall hath administered a clyster and some potions of his own devising, but they have produced no effect in Gilbert. Hall told me that he fears Gilbert will die soon, and should make his peace. Brother Dick is grievous sad.[1]

3 FEBRUARY

We buried Gilbert today, his funeral swelled by many folk in the town. I fear the cloak of death that must clothe us all some time or another. I have written naught in many a moon, and am not like so to do.

1 MARCH

Thomas Thorpe, for what reason I know not, tho' I might well guess, hath sent me a copy of "A Funeral Elegy to Master John Peter," penned by one who calls himself "W.S." I am saddened for I knew, tho' not well, William Peter whom Thorpe tells me was murdered some five or six weeks past.[2] The poem hath some small merit and all the world may well think it mine. News from Heminges that young William Ostler is now a sharer with us, & so his marriage hath served him well.[3]

ALL FOOL'S DAY [1 APRIL]

The day is named well, & I am full of vexation. I am ordered to appear in London for some suit that [Stephen] Belott hath brought against [Christopher] Mountjoy—the marriage settlement, the dowry, & whatnot, which Belott says he hath not received or some such. Lord, I cannot recollect those matters, & yet I am obliged to leave hearth & home, go to London, & depose myself. Well, it must be done; some small comfort is I shall see again my goodly friends.

12 MAY

London. Yesterday I was deposed in Belott's suit & told what little I could recall of the affair, which was indeed but little. But blast 'em, for they want me again in June [19th], yet I'll ne'er attend again. Joan Johnson, the maid that was, was there present, & I was pleased to greet her again, for she was ever good to me whiles I lodged with the Mountjoys. She was deposed, & remembered as much as I did, which is to say but little. 'Tis curious that all is money in marriage.

16 MAY

To the Mermaid yester eve to sup ale with dear John Heminges, Dick Burbage, & many of the other fellows, even Jonson, as of yore. John told me that a marriage contract is signed between the Princess Elizabeth & Frederick V, Elector of Palatine of the Rhine (or some such thing). So the Men are commanded to perform for the revels & such, & they desire me to write some novelty for the wedding itself.[4] I did protest that I have nothing in hand, or even in mind, but Dick said it would be a great occasion, & something from my pen would be right welcome. "Why, sweet Will," he said, "is there nothing in those chronicles to take your fancy? The story's made already, as you've said so oft; but 'tis your way with the words that's the thing. Yet if you have a mind to do it, include spectacle, pageantry, & that sort of stuff, for this grand occasion calls for it." I protested again, but at the last said I would try to write something, yet they should not expect me in London to see it rehearsed or performed. John said, "Well it would be more than a pity not to see ye, Will, but if ye must hide yourself in Stratford, ye must. Yet when you write the play (for surely you will), write down all the action you conceive, so that we may know what you would tell us if you were here." Well, much more chat on this, & other affairs, more than a quantity of ale. Late to bed. I start my journey home in the morn.

[SUMMER]

I have pondered long o'er what to write for the marriage of the princess Elizabeth. My mind is but barren, quite dried up. Anne says I should write the history of King Henry VIII, for his daughter Elizabeth was our late beloved queen, & our princess is named Elizabeth too. I suppose I might do worse. I hear from Jonson that he is to travel in

France as tutor to the son of Sir Walter Ralegh. I had quite forgot Ralegh is yet immured in the Tower; he might as well be dead.

[OCTOBER]

My play on Henry VIII is finished. 'Tis little more than some scenes, though I took some delight in the fall of Wolsey. I believe it hath an abundance of spectacle & such as is called for, & they may add whatsoe'er they choose, for I care not. Heminges wrote and told me that *The Tempest* is to be performed next month [1 November], & asked me if I had any amendment, addition, or whatever. I replied I had little desire to add aught, & they should do as they please. Anne grumbles o'er everything, yet she is pleased that 'twas she said that Henry VIII was fit for a play.

CHRISTMAS

Again this Christmastide I am, happily, with family & friends with good cheer. We have been saddened by the death of Prince Henry in the midst of all the festivity for the wedding of his sister, who, they say, grieves inordinately beyond the common rate.[5] Yet the marriage will go forward in due course, for such is the way of the world. I think I may ride to London to see my play [*Henry VIII*] presented, though Anne would rather I remained at home.

Shakespeare's remaining brother, Richard, dies early in 1613. Shakespeare returns to London for the marriage celebrations of Princess Elizabeth, but discovers that his Henry VIII *has been passed over; however, several of his other plays are performed at court. He is persuaded by John Heminges to collaborate with the young John Fletcher on* The Two Noble Kinsmen. *In July Susanna Hall is the victim of false, slanderous accusations. When* Henry VIII *is finally performed at the Globe, a faulty cannon shot causes a fire and the theatre is burned to the ground. Shakespeare decides that this is a good time to leave the King's Men, and leaves the rebuilding of the theatre to his former colleagues. Shakespeare grows ever more content with life in Stratford.*

28 JANUARY

I was today with John Combe who hath writ his will, though why I know not, for he appears the very simulacrum of good health. He bequeaths me five pounds, and he hath more than plenty to give away.[1] I fear more for Richard [Shakespeare] who ails and declines. Physician Hall says his remedies are of no avail, & Richard's sole succour is prayer.

5 FEBRUARY

We buried Richard yesterday. He died peacefully in his sleep one year and one day after Gilbert died. Shall I be far behind? Tomorrow I must ride to London, for I have given my word I would see *Henry VIII* presented, e'en though there's little of my heart in't now.

14 FEBRUARY

Princess Elizabeth married Elector Frederick this day. In the midst of the preparations for our play, we caught glimpses of the royal pair, both resplendent in their silvery finery, jewels, & so forth. What might be the cost of it all dazzles the mind. The King hath a great facility to disburse the wealth of his realm.

15 FEBRUARY

My play [*Henry VIII*] is wanted no longer, for there be other entertainments afoot & more desired. But for my labours I would not complain, for my plays have been presented on seven or eight or moe occasions during these past revels. Mayhap we might have been informed sooner, yet such is the royal will. Poor John Lowin hath greater disappointment than myself, for he longed to personate King Henry, and all his labour & assiduity spent upon his role are now for naught. Heminges tells us to be cheerful, for ere long the weather will be fine enough, & the play will be presented at the Globe for all the world to see. We must be content.

10 MARCH

Busy days. Henry Walker sold to me the Blackfriars Gatehouse,[2] which I have had an eye for many a long year. It is marvellous convenient to both our theatres, when I have a mind to be in town. Besides I believe there's money can be made from it, if need be. Land & houses, they be the thing. After the deeds were signed & conveyed, I walked post-haste to see Dick Burbage that we might conclude our work together on [the Earl of] Rutland's impresa. Dick's portion of the work is more considerable than mine own, yet are we to be paid alike.[3]

24 MARCH

I had thought to view the royal tilt today, but I was prevented. John Heminges called upon me, and with him young John Fletcher. I bade them welcome & Heminges said, "Dear Will, 'tis all my pleasure, as ever 'twas, to see you. Brief shall I be, for I know you are desirous to return home to Stratford, & mayhap my errand will not be pleasing to you. The truth is our company wants some novelty which we pray you can furnish us withal, for reasons all the world can tell." I told him I had nothing in mind, that my imagination was as barren as the cornfield after scything. "Besides," I said, "I have given you *Henry VIII* which does well and like to do better." Heminges said, "I thought you might say something after that sort. However, young Fletcher here thinks that 'The Knight's Tale' by Chaucer would make a passing fair play, & would assay it, if you might give him a hand to help him along his way, as 'twere, with some hints, suggestions, & so forth. Mayhap you could spend a few days, no more than a week, to pen an act or two, such as a beginning and an ending, while John here might flesh out the scenes between, taking his cue from you." Fletcher said, "We might call it *Two Noble Knights* or some such, after Palamon & Arcite in the Tale." I thought for awhile, & I could see dear Heminges was troubled and anxious that I should accede unto his proposal. So I agreed, provided that they would not detain me beyond one week and no more. "And," I said, "I think we might call the play *The Two Noble Kinsmen*." John said, "God bless you, sweet Will," and he took my hand and grasped it heartily, shedding a tear or two as he did so.

1 APRIL

I have been as good as my word & limned two acts or so of *Noble Kinsmen*, & looked o'er some scenes Fletcher hath penned. I fear they be too stuffed with rhetoric, & I care not for his poesy, though no doubt it will suffice. I confess mine own words lack inspiration, but I can do no more, & ride home on the morrow.

15 JULY

Susanna [Hall] is brimful of vexation & ire. She hath gone to court because she hath been slandered by John Lane who hath said she had lain with Rafe Smith and John Palmer. I believe there be something else behind this slander (whose edge is sharper than a sword), and I doubt not it be religion, though Susanna says naught to me about it. I pray nothing come of this, & I marvel mightily that any folk might lay credence in this false accusation. I know not what physician Hall thinks of the business.

20 JULY

I marvelled to see John Heminges at our door yesterday evening. The weary way from London had made him almost melancholy, but he was glad & thankful to take his ease with us. After we had supped, he told me the reason for his journey. On St. Peter's Day [29 June], whiles they were playing *Henry VIII*, a peal of cannon was negligently discharged and the thatch on the roof of the Globe took fire, and, in a short space, the whole theatre was burned to the ground. "Will, everything hath been consumed, everything. Our theatre is no more. Ben Jonson was there as well, you know, and I believe he was as much moved as all our company were," Heminges said. I asked John if any folk had been hurt, and he said none. Then he smiled. "There was one fellow caught fire, but he dowsed his breeches with a bottle of ale. And, for some reason, Will, that reminds of the tale Ben told me. When he and Wat Ralegh were in Paris at Mardi Gras, young Ralegh made Ben very drunk, and then dragged him through the streets on a cart in the form of a cross. Now, why did I remember that?" I laughed & told John that Ben had in sooth written me a letter with the same intelligence. Then I asked John what the company did intend after the fire. He said that the Globe would rise out of its ashes like the Phoenix, & be built anew and more splendid than ever before. "Will," he said, "that is the purpose of my visit to you. The building will cost us dear (we know not what as yet), & the question is whether ye are willing to furnish your share & so forth." We sat in silence for several minutes, for I was pondering how

I should reply. "John, the truth is that I think my time is passed. I have thought so for some months and more, &, though I would not desert you and our fellows, mayhap now the time be ripe for someone to take my share. No doubt there's plenty as would be willing. Besides, when I come to die, I would not have my share pass into the hands of those not of our brethren. 'Tis our fellowship and goodwill together that have made us prosperous, & I would not rob you & my fellows of that." John bowed his head, and said he had thought I would say something after that fashion, tho' he was saddened grievously that it should be so. We had chat on this for more than an hour or so, but I have resolved our ways should part, and I think that all will end well thus.

22 JULY

John [Heminges] took his leave this morning with a heavy, sorrowing heart. Before he departed, he recalled upon the sudden that he owed me payment for *Cardenio*; I told him I would not take it, for he & the company had the greater need.[4] Never have I parted with a man with such heartache & melancholy. I pray we meet again e'er long.

21 OCTOBER

Autumn wanes and so do I. What was it in *Macbeth*?—"I have lived long enough: my way of life is fallen into the sere, the yellow leaf" [5.3.22–23]. Yet am I contented with family & friends. I hear the fellows perform for the King again this Christmastide, yet am I thankful I have no part in that.[5] To think, when I was young I hungered & thirsted after satisfaction, fame, & regal favour (as all hunt after fame in their lives), yet once achieved, what else remains? Mayhap contentment.

1674

Shakespeare records very little in his diary these days. The Globe is rebuilt, but Shakespeare lacks the energy to write a new play for the new building. Stratford itself is again subject to fire, and, though 50 houses are burned, Shakespeare's New Place house is spared. Once more business affairs take him to London where he passes Christmas.

1 JANUARY

Christmas hath been & gone. I sit by the hearth, listen to crickets, & think of tales sad & merry. Yet naught interests me for more than an hour, & I cannot fashion a play out of such musings, even if the desire possessed me—which it does not. From time to time I think on Hamnet, & e'en after all these years, in my mind's eye, I can see his sweet visage as 'twas when he smiled at me—ever smiling—my Mamillius.[1] That we shall meet again is all my wish.

[APRIL]

Spring. I had thought I would pen some lines, a sonnet or two, but I lack inspiration, true desire. Well, let that go.

23 APRIL

Two score & ten ago I was born; I have been happy in my lot, & think there can be no profit in regret for another life I never knew. Anne & all the family have gathered together that we may feast & rejoice, & rejoiced I am.

7 JUNE

Word from Heminges that the Globe hath risen from its ashes, & all will be complete by month's end. Alas, I cannot satisfy his fervent wish for a new play, in spite of all his pleading. Besides, the fellows have young John Fletcher who can serve them well enough, leastways as well as I did when I was of his age.

11 JULY

These two days past have been terrible and terrifying. On Saturday [9 July] in a matter of two or three hours more than fifty houses, stables, barns & I know not what else were consumed by fire. I thank God that we were spared and that New Place is as ever it was, but the grim hand of fate hath struck many neighbours & friends. Leastways we shall not have to hear the preachers tell us the fire was because we kept not the sabbath.[2] The fire proved more than poor John Combe could bear; he died yesterday, & he's to be buried on the morrow. Well, he had his will set down.

28 OCTOBER

Replingham hath today covenanted with me & Tom Greene whereby our tithes shall not suffer loss.[3] Greene doth fret himself greatly in the affair, for he fears those folk against enclosure will grow riotous.

17 NOVEMBER

Physician Hall & myself arrived in London yesterday; he rests with me at the Gatehouse, tho' he hath other affairs than mine to attend. Yet no sooner were we arrived than Tom Greene, our town-clerk, knocked upon the door. Greene is much fretted & vexed with the enclosure business, & would have me do this, that, & the other in opposition to it. I told him he need trouble himself not at all, for both Hall & I think there will be nothing done in the matter. "Why," I told him, "it will be April before they mean to survey the land." Much chat on this Welcombe enclosure business before Greene would leave us in peace. In the evening I went to the Mermaid, for Ben Jonson would have me listen to him on how his *Bartholomew Fair* had played before the common folk (those stinkards) & the Court.[4] "Nat Field & his fellows did receive ten pounds for playing at Court," Ben said, "so you know they gave satisfaction. I think, Will, you would have smiled at my Induction, for there I glance at your [*Titus*] *Andronicus* & *Tempest*."[5] I smiled & forbore to utter my thoughts, but thanked Ben for the kindly remembrance. Then we drank & talked a great deal long into the night. I fear physician Hall approves little of drink, for he but looked sourly at me this morning, scowling when I told him my head ached.

17 DECEMBER

Poor Will Ostler died yesterday. The last I saw of him he played Antonio in John Webster's *Duchess of Malfi* & did acquit himself worthily. I remember how in earnest he recited Antonio's words as he died: "In all our quest of greatness, Like wanton boys, whose pastime is their care, We follow after bubbles blown in the air, Pleasure of life, what is't? Only the good Hours of an ague; merely the preparative to rest, to endure vexation" [5.4.63–68]. Well, he hath earned his rest & i'faith mayhap "as flies to wanton boys are we to the gods; they kill us for their sport" [*King Lear*, 4.1.36–37]. Yet that is a bitter thought to lie with a man.

CHRISTMASTIDE

Tho' I would lief be at home, I have been persuaded to bide in the city so that I may witness once more my fellows perform for the King.[6] 'Tis against my judgment, tho' perchance I may never more see them thus.

§ These days there's little more than local politics in Stratford, such as the enclosure controversy, that concerns Shakespeare. He has written nothing. At year's end Shakespeare is greatly saddened by the death of Robert Armin, the comedic actor who replaced Will Kempe in the company.§

5 JANUARY

London. Blast & damn our corporation. Today from them a letter that chastiseth me, saying I do advocate enclosure at Welcombe.[1] The truth is I have said & done as little as I might, for I would offend no one, though Tom Greene vexeth me so greatly that I do begin to think Will Combe, tyke tho' he be, should do as he pleases, & enclose what he will as he will.[2] I must return home.

[FEBRUARY]

I am hounded upon all sides about this enclosure business, to which I would not be of one party or the other—tho' I am pleased my tithes are assured, for those may gird my old age.

31 MARCH

Will Combe pays no heed to Justice Coke, & scoffs at the law, the corporation, & all who would stand in his path.[3] I desire but a quiet, peaceable life, so I say nothing and will not take one part or the other. But it is a grievous wrong that Combe do assault women and children—leastways, have his men so to do.

15 DECEMBER

The months have passed quietly enough, tho' I am o'erfull of agues. I have had no thought to write as the year hath slipped by. In truth, I have nothing more to say. Today I received word from Dick Burbage that dear Bob Armin hath died,[4] & I am saddened greatly. I recall how marvellous well he personated Touchstone, Feste, the Fool to Lear—surely we shall not see his like again. How unlike Kempe he was, & for dear Bob I could fashion fools & clowns that possessed subtlety & wit. How many pleasant hours we passed together deep in chat; how I joyed in him.

1616

Despite Shakespeare's firm opinion to the contrary, his daughter Judith marries Tom Quiney, who quickly proves himself to be a reprobate by fathering a bastard child. Shakespeare amends his will accordingly shortly before his death. Shakespeare's final diary entry looks forward to a visit from two friends, Michael Drayton and Ben Jonson.

20 JANUARY

Henslowe's dead.[1] I did not know him well, but after his own fashion he served both plays and players I believe. I fear the time is short before I shall be called, & I needs must make my will.

26 JANUARY

Yesterday I made my will, which Francis Collins wrote down for me.[2] So that is done, & my mind is easier.

8 FEBRUARY

Word from Jonson that he will publish all his plays together; he lacks not temerity.[3] Ben is overjoyed also, for the King hath bestowed upon him a pension of one hundred marks [£66] a year until his death. I might feel envy for a lesser man.

10 FEBRUARY

Despite all I might do or say, Judith [Shakespeare] hath today married Tom Quiney, & the fool had not the special marriage licence—as I told him he had need of. Anne is neither sad nor happy. Well, 'tis their own bed, they must lie in it, & I may not lead other folks' lives.

12 MARCH

I said 'twould happen, but none would listen. Tom Quiney is excommunicated because he did not get the licence, nor would he answer a summons pertaining thereto.

16 MARCH

Damn & blast Tom Quiney. I have suspected long that Quiney hath some whore or another, and it hath proved true. His whore & bastard child died yesterday, which now all the world knows.[4] I have some pity for Judith, tho' I told her no good would ever come of this marriage.

24 MARCH

I must amend my will, & [Francis] Collins is to call upon me on the morrow. Though I would not punish her harshly, Judith shall have a smaller portion for her dower for, of late, she hath been more a stranger to my heart and me, and she would marry that fool Quiney. Yet if she shall have children, they shall be provided for.

20 APRIL

I rejoice that Drayton & Jonson are to visit me ere long; they be goodly company. 'Tis some while since we have met, to eat, drink, make merry, and talk of our days together. Little there is in this life that surpasseth the company of good friends.

Postmortem

Shakespeare died on 23 April 1616. Tradition (but no more than that) has it that he, Michael Drayton, and Ben Jonson got drunk together, and that Shakespeare developed a fever, from which he died. Shakespeare was buried in Holy Trinity Church, Stratford-upon-Avon, on 25 April 1616. The epitaph on his gravestone reads: "Good friend for Jesus sake forbear / To dig the dust enclosed here! / Blest be the man that spares these stones, / And curst be he that moves my bones." Later a monument of Shakespeare was placed on a nearby wall. Shakespeare left no direct descendants, although there are indirect descendants through the family line of his sister, Joan Hart.

Notes

1582
1. Wilmcote is three miles northwest of Stratford, Shottery one mile west. Shakespeare's grandfather, Robert Arden (d. 1556) lived at Wilmcote where Shakespeare's mother, Mary (d. 1608) was born, the youngest of eight daughters. Anne Hathaway (1555/56–1623) lived at Shottery before she married Shakespeare. Shakespeare's father, John (d. 1601), was a glover (or whittawer) and married Mary in about 1557.
2. Richard Hathaway was buried on September 7, 1581.
3. Richard Quiney (b. before 1557–1602) was a Stratford friend and neighbor of Shakespeare and author of the only surviving letter written to Shakespeare (October 25, 1598). Like his father, Adrian (d. 1607), he was a mercer and had married Elizabeth Phillips (d. 1632) in 1580.
4. Apparently an early version of Sonnet 145:

    > Those lips that Love's own hand did make
    > Breathed forth the sound that said "I hate"
    > To me that languished for her sake.
    > But when she saw my woeful state,
    > Straight in her heart did mercy come,
    > Chiding that tongue that ever sweet
    > Was used in giving gentle doom,
    > And taught it thus anew to greet:
    > "I hate" she altered with an end
    > That followed it as gentle day
    > Doth follow night, who, like a fiend,
    > From heaven to hell is flown away.
    >   "I hate" from hate away she threw,
    >   And saved my life, saying "not you."

    "Hate away" in line 13 is an obvious pun on Anne's maiden name.
5. Fulk Sandells (1551–1624) and John Richardson lived in Shottery; Sandells was a supervisor of Richard Hathaway's will, which Richardson had witnessed. They posted a £40 bond with the Bishop of Worcester to assure there was no impediment to the marriage.

6. Elizabeth Quiney (1582–1615) was christened on November 27, 1582.
7. A special marriage license for Shakespeare's marriage to Anne Hathaway was issued by the Bishop of Worcester on November 27, 1582. They probably married on or around December 1, 1582, perhaps at Temple Grafton, five miles due west of Stratford; however, the exact location is unknown. A special license was necessary because Anne was pregnant and marriages were not normally permitted during the period of Advent to the Epiphany (December 2, 1582–January 13, 1583). Shakespeare was 18, Anne 26.
8. Acting companies paid frequent visits to Stratford. Worcester's Men performed in 1568 when Shakespeare's father, John, was High Bailiff and Shakespeare was four years old. They returned in 1581. Other companies included Strange's and Essex's Men in 1578, Derby's in 1579, Lord Berkeley's in 1580 and 1582.

1583
1. Susanna (1583–1649) married a Stratford physician, John Hall (1575–1635), in 1607.
2. Edward Arden (1542?–83) was Sheriff of Warwickshire; his father William was Mary Shakespeare's second cousin. Edward was tried in London on December 16, 1583, and executed on December 20, 1583 (see Michael Wood, *Shakespeare*, [2003], pp. 88–94).

1584
1. Edward Alleyn (1566–1626) was born in London and became a distinguished Elizabethan actor. He had joined Worcester's Men in 1583.
2. This event took place on January 13, 1583.

1585
1. Hamnet (1585–96); Judith (1585–1662). Their godparents were probably Hamnet (d. 1624) and Judith (d. 1614) Sadler. Judith Shakespeare married Thomas Quiney (1589–c. 1655) on February 10, 1616, shortly before Shakespeare's death.
2. Edward Hall's *The Union of the Two Noble and Illustre Famelies of Lancastre and York* (1548) provided some of the source material for Shakespeare's three *Henry VI* plays.
3. Stratford-born Richard Field (1561–1624) began his seven-year apprenticeship to Thomas Vautrollier, a London printer, on September 29, 1579. On Vautrollier's death in 1587, Field married Vautrollier's widow, Jacqueline, and took over the business. Field printed Shakespeare's first published work, *Venus and Adonis*, in 1593.

4. Joan La Pucelle, Joan of Arc, appears in *Henry VI Part 1*. Shakespeare's treatment of her there is generally historically inaccurate and uncharitable, though in general accordance with Elizabethan sentiments. On the relationship between historical events and Shakespeare's history plays, see John Julius Norwich, *Shakespeare's Kings: The Great Plays and the History of England in the Middle Ages 1337–1485* (1999).
5. See the Temple Garden scene, *Henry VI Part 1* 2.4, where the Lancastrians choose red roses, the Yorkists white.
6. Sir Thomas Lucy (1532–1600), landowner in Warwickshire and Worcestershire. See also entry for March 26, 1597.

1586
1. On August 3, 1586, Mary Queen of Scots (1542–87) was arrested for her alleged part in the Babington plot on the life of Queen Elizabeth I (1533–1603).

1587
1. James VI of Scotland (1566–1625) became James I of England (1603–1625).
2. Sir Philip Sidney (1554–86), soldier, statesman, and poet, was wounded on September 22, 1586, while attacking a Spanish supply convoy near the city of Zutphen. He died three weeks later. Sidney's works were all published posthumously and influenced Shakespeare considerably.
3. Queen Elizabeth's Men received 20 shillings for their Stratford performance. They had performed the lost play *Felix and Philiomena* at Court (Greenwich) in January 1585. It was one source for *The Two Gentlemen of Verona*. The repertory of Queen Elizabeth's Men included plays on Henry V, King John, Richard III, and King Lear, all eventually subjects of Shakespeare's own plays.
4. The Angel Inn was in Henley Street, not far from the Swan Inn
5. John Heminges (1566–1630), actor and the business manager of Shakespeare's acting company. He was a shrewd businessman and frequently acted as an overseer or executor of his fellow actors' wills. He was Shakespeare's trustee when he purchased the Blackfriars Gatehouse in 1613. Heminges and fellow actor, Henry Condell (1576–1627), oversaw the publication of the First Folio edition of Shakespeare's plays (1623). Droitwich is 20 miles east-northeast of Stratford.
6. William Knell, a player with Queen Elizabeth's Men, was killed by fellow actor John Towne (d. 1617) on June 13, 1587 (see S. Schoenbaum, *Shakespeare's Lives* [1970], p. 742). John Heminges married Knell's widow, Rebecca (1571–1619), in 1588.
7. James Burbage (1530/31–97) built the Theatre in 1576 and lived in Holywell Lane, Shoreditch. The famous clown Richard Tarlton (d. 1588), who had joined Queen Elizabeth's Men when the company was formed in 1583, also lived there.

Thomas Nashe (1567–c. 1601) was a dramatist and pamphleteer, and Christopher Marlowe (1564–93) a poet and dramatist, whose plays included *Tamburlaine the Great*.

8. Shakespeare must have: a) memorized these lines instantaneously; b) had, like Hamlet, his tables or notebook with him; or c) had access to Alleyn's "sides" or part.

1588

1. William Kempe (d. after 1603) was renowned for his broad clowning and jig dancing. In 1600 he performed a morris dance all the way from London to Norwich.
2. *The Two Gentlemen of Verona*, 4.1, 5.3, 5.4.
3. *The Tragical History of Romeus and Juliet* (1562), a long rhyming poem, by Arthur Brooke (d. 1563).
4. The English fleet engaged the Spanish Armada from July 21 through August 8, 1588; a decisive turning point was the Battle of Gravelines on July 29.
5. Robert Dudley, Earl of Leicester (1532–88) was patron of Leicester's Men from 1559 until they disbanded shortly after his death on September 4, 1588.
6. Robert Greene (1558–92) was a dramatist, poet, and pamphleteer.
7. See *Henry VI Part 1*, 1.5.
8. See *Henry VI Part 1*, 2.3.6, 2.3.36, 2.3.40.
9. Shakespeare was possibly thinking of puns on Beauchamp, good field, Richard Field, Warwickshire, and the pastoral nature of the Temple Garden scene. There is a related pun in *Cymbeline*, 4.2.377, where Imogen uses the name Richard du Champ (Richard of the Field) for the headless corpse of Cloten whom she believes is her lover Posthumus.
10. See *Henry VI Part I*, 4.5.42–55. The "Talbot scenes" are 4.2–4.7.
11. It seems Shakespeare connected the deer imagery in 4.2 with Lucy and the fact that he was an ancestor of the Sir Thomas Lucy he had encountered in summer 1585. Clearly Warwickshire associations were running through Shakespeare's subconscious.
12. While he was dying, Tarlton had been nursed by Em Bull, a Shoreditch woman with a notorious reputation.
13. This was probably in 1575 when a water pageant of Phoebe courted by Arion was presented at Kenilworth, Warwickshire.
14. Elizabeth stayed with Sir Thomas Lucy at Charlecote, Warwickshire, in August 1566.

1589

1. In 1587 Philip Henslowe (c. 1555–1616), theater owner and manager, had built his famous Rose Theatre on the Bankside, the first theater south of the River

Thames. Henslowe's *Diary* provides an invaluable account of aspects of his theatrical activities from 1592–1603.
2. Shakespeare possibly recollected this incident in writing *King Lear* 2.2 and 2.4, where Kent is placed in the stocks.
3. "Martin Marprelate" was the pseudonym of a number of satirical pamphlet writers who attacked the established church's efforts to impose a uniform liturgy and royal supremacy. Nashe was one of several writers who wrote pamphlets in reply. The controversy ran 1588–90.
4. Thomas Quiney was christened in Stratford on February 26, 1589. Elizabeth was Quiney's wife.
5. Lord Burghley (1520–98) was Elizabeth's chief minister.
6. *The Arte of English Poesie* (1589) was published anonymously, but it is generally ascribed to George Puttenham (c. 1529–90).
7. See *Henry VI Part 2*, 1.4.
8. Marlowe and Thomas Watson (c. 1557–92), a minor poet, shared lodgings together. On September 18, Marlowe first duelled with William Bradley in Hog Lane, and then Watson came along and fought and killed Bradley. The cause of the fight was a quarrel between Watson and Bradley over a £14 debt that Bradley owed to Edward Alleyn's brother, John. On September 19 an inquest found that Marlowe and Watson had acted in self-defense. Marlowe was bailed on October 1, but Watson was not released until they both received the queen's pardon on February 10, 1590. See Mark Eccles, *Christopher Marlowe in London* (1934) for a full account of this incident and Marlowe's relationship with Watson.
9. These scenes are found in *Henry VI Part 2*, 4.4, 3.2, and 4.7.
10. In early November, as a result of the Martin Marprelate controversy, Sir John Harte (the newly installed Lord Mayor) ordered the London theaters to be closed. There is no record that *Henry VI Part 1* was the play performed on this occasion.
11. On November 12 the Council ordered a general cleaning up of theatrical practices, set up a censorship committee, and required prompt books to be submitted for scrutiny.
12. George Peele (1556–96), dramatist and one of the "University Wits," which comprised Marlowe, Greene, Peele, Nashe, and Thomas Lodge (1558–1625).
13. *The Old Wives' Tale* (in *Five Elizabethan Comedies*, ed. A.K. McIlwraith [1936]), lines 89, 506. These lines are echoed in: "A sad tale's best for winter. I have one / Of sprites and goblins" (*The Winter's Tale*, 2.1.25–26), and "he's a present for any emperor that ever trod on neat's leather" (*The Tempest*, 2.2.68–69).
14. On December 10 at Lowestoft.

1590

1. Shakespeare's final version in *Henry VI Part 3* reads "O tiger's heart wrapped in a woman's hide!" (1.4.137). The line was parodied by Robert Greene in his *Groats-worth of Wit* (1592) in a passage attacking Shakespeare: "for there is an upstart Crow, beautified with our feathers, that with his *Tygers hart wrapt in a Players hyde*, supposes he is as well able to bombast out a blanke verse as the best of you."
2. Watson had married Anne Swift on September 6, 1585 (Eccles, *Christopher Marlowe in London*, p. 60), though that fact does not necessarily negate Shakespeare's suspicion.
3. Sir Francis Walsingham (1532–90), Secretary of State, was notable for his intelligence service and for securing the execution of Mary Queen of Scots. He died in poverty and was buried secretly at night in St. Paul's in order to prevent his creditors from opening his coffin.
4. A stage property from another play.
5. See *Henry VI Part 3*, 3.2.168, 182.
6. Thomas Russell (1570–1634) married Katherine Bampfield (d. c. 1595) on September 7, 1590, at Bruton Church in Somerset. Shakespeare later appointed this friend as overseer of his will and bequeathed him £5.
7. John Brayne (d. 1586), James Burbage's brother-in-law, had financed the building of the Theatre in 1576. This affray was part of a long-standing feud over his wife's (Margaret, d. 1593) share of the Theatre's profits.

1591

1. *Henry VI Part 3*, 5.6.83.
2. Job Hortop's *The trauailes of an English man, containing his svndrie calamities indured by the space of twentie and odd yeres in his absence from his natiue countrie; wherein is truly decyphered the sundrie shapes of wilde beasts, birds, fishes, foules, rootes, plants, &c. With the description of a man that appeared in the sea, and also of a huge giant brought from China to the King of Spaine* was entered in the Stationers' Register on February 9, 1591, and related his voyage to the West Indies.
3. Sir John Harington (1561–1612) was a courtier and translator of *Orlando Furioso* (1591). Robert Greene wrote a play of the same name based on this translation, the title role being taken by Edward Alleyn. It was performed at Court on December 6, 1591. Alleyn's part is the only surviving example of an Elizabethan actor's part: over 500 lines written on sheets of paper pasted together to form one long "role."
4. Henry Wriothesley, third Earl of Southampton (1573–1624), Shakespeare's patron and to whom Shakespeare dedicated *Venus and Adonis* (1593) and *The Rape of Lucrece* (1594). Southampton was a supporter of the Earl of Essex

(1566–1601) and took part in the latter's rebellion against Elizabeth in 1601. His death sentence was commuted to imprisonment; he was released by James I. Exactly how and when Shakespeare met Southampton is not known. Wriothesley is pronounced "Risley."

5. John [Giovanni] Florio (c. 1553–1625), a scholar and translator, was appointed Southampton's tutor in 1591, the year *Second Fruites* was published. Among its prefatory verse is the (anonymous) sonnet attributed to Shakespeare:

Phaethon to his Friend Florio

Sweet friend, whose name agrees with thy increase,
    How fit a rival art thou of the Spring!
    For when each branch hath left his flourishing,
And green-locked Summer's shady pleasures cease,
She makes the Winter's storms repose in peace
    And spends her franchise on each living thing:
    The daisies sprout, the little birds do sing;
Herbs, gums, and plants do vaunt of their release.
So that when all our English wits lay dead
    (Except the Laurel that is ever green),
Thou with thy fruits our barrenness o'erspread
    And set thy flowery pleasance to be seen.
Such fruits, such flow'rets of morality,
Were ne'er before brought out of Italy.

6. Sir Walter Ralegh, or Raleigh (1552?–1618), courtier, soldier, and poet, was a favorite of Elizabeth, but was eclipsed when Essex arrived at Court. They became rivals.

7. The ideas noted in this paragraph are taken from Charles Gibbon, *A Work Worth the Reading* (1591), and may have provided themes for *A Midsummer Night's Dream* and *Romeo and Juliet*.

8. *Richard III*, 5.3.184, 202.

9. The three fanatical preachers were William Hacket, Henry Ardington (or Arthington), and Edmund Coppinger.

10. *Love's Labour's Lost* contains all the elements outlined here and might have been performed at Southampton's country seat of Titchfield, Hampshire, during the afternoon of September 2, 1591, as part of Elizabeth's 1591 royal progress. See the entry for September 3, 1591.

11. Hacket had been sentenced to death as a traitor on July 26 and had tried to refuse to participate in his trial.

12. Edmund Coppinger died after refusing food for seven days; Henry Arthington repented and was set free.

13. The "mask" or pageant of the Nine Worthies occurs in *Love's Labour's Lost*, 5.2. The "artifice" would include Shakespeare's extended use of sonnets in, for example, 4.2 and 4.3. Three of those sonnets were published later in *The Passionate Pilgrim* (1599), a miscellany of 20 poems attributed to Shakespeare, though only five are known to be his. 4.3.55–68 was reprinted as sonnet number III, 4.2.101–14 as number V, 4.3.96–115 as number XVI.
14. Thomas Kyd (1558–94), dramatist, best known for *The Spanish Tragedy* (written c. 1589).
15. Sir Brian O'Rourke, an Irish chieftain, had sheltered survivors of the Spanish Armada shipwrecked on the Irish coast. In 1591 he had sought assistance from James I who handed him over to the English authorities.
16. Presumably Shakespeare is being ironic. Sir Christopher Hatton (1540–91) was Lord Chancellor and one of Elizabeth's favorites. He took a leading role in the trials of Catholic conspirators.
17. See, in particular, *Titus Andronicus*, 4.1.30–58. Philomel's rape occurs in Ovid, *Metamorphoses*, book 6.
18. The alternate title of *The Spanish Tragedy*.
19. Edmund Jennings was a young Jesuit priest who said mass until the moment of his execution.
20. See Aaron's speeches in *Titus Andronicus*, 5.1. Aaron remains alive and his death is not portrayed onstage; Shakespeare handled Iago similarly at the end of *Othello*.
21. Shakespeare made use of Greene's book when writing the character of Autolycus in *The Winter's Tale*.
22. Kyd's *The Spanish Tragedy*.
23. At the conclusion of *Richard III* Lord Stanley (Earl of Derby) gives the crown to the victorious Richmond: "Lo, here this long usurpèd royalty / From the dead temples of this bloody wretch / Have I plucked off, to grace thy brows withal" (5.5.4–6). Ferdinando's great-great-grandfather, Sir Thomas Stanley (c. 1435–1504), after whom Shakespeare's character is fashioned, was a somewhat slippery figure, endeavouring to end up on the winning side in the War of the Roses. Ferdinando (c. 1559–94) was patron of the acting company known as Strange's (Derby's) Men, who performed six times during the Christmas season (possibly including the tetralogy of *Henry VI* and *Richard III*). Strange is pronounced "Strang."

1592

1. *Supposes* (1566) by George Gascoigne (1542–77).
2. Samuel Daniel (1562–1619), poet and dramatist. *Delia* (1592) was popular and ran to several editions. Daniel's *The Complaint of Rosamund* (1592) influenced

Romeo and Juliet, while his *Tragedie of Cleopatra* (1593) inspired some of the language of *Antony and Cleopatra*.
3. In 1592 Greene published a *Third Part of Conny-Catching* and *A Disputation between a He Conny-Catcher and a She Conny-Catcher*.
4. From the Prologue of Plautus's *Menaechmi*: "Now that twin, who lives in Syracuse, / comes today to Epidamnum with his slave / to look here for his twin brother."
5. On December 6, 1591.
6. *The Jew of Malta* was also performed March 18; April 4, 18; May 5, 11, 20, 30; and June 14.
7. Several hundred men were impressed at the beginning of March 1592 for service in France, where the siege of Rouen continued.
8. The first performance of whichever of the Henry VI plays was performed grossed £3 16s 8d when average takings were £1 3s 6d. There were further performances on: March 7, 28; April 5, 13, 21; May 7, 14, 19, 25; and June 12 and 19.
9. *The Spanish Tragedy* was performed March 14, 31; April 24; and May 25.
10. Barabas in Marlowe's *The Jew of Malta*.
11. Plautus, *Menaechmi*, 5.7. "Many wondrous things indeed are happening today in wondrous ways. Some deny I am I, and shut me out of doors."
12. See Richard's use of "I am" in the opening soliloquy of *Richard III*, 1.1.1–40, and his "Richard loves Richard: that is, I am I. / Is there a murderer here? No, Yes, I am" (5.3.184–85). See also Antipholus of Syracuse: "Are you a god? Would you create me new? / Transform me then, and to your power I'll yield. / But if that I am I, then well I know / Your weeping sister is no wife of mine" (*The Comedy of Errors*, 3.2.39–42).
13. *Arden of Feversham* was sold by Edward White "dwelling at the lyttle North dore of Paules Church at the sign of the gun" (title page). White was the designated seller of the first Quarto of *Titus Andronicus* (1594).
14. *Chronicles* (1577), II, 1703–08.
15. Shakespeare's mother's maiden name was Arden. During the play, Arden leaves his wife Alice to go to London. Later he is murdered by Alice, Mosbie (her lover), Black Will, and Shakebag (two hired murderers).
16. Perhaps Shakespeare recalled this event subconsciously in writing *Macbeth*. See Lady Macbeth washing her hands in 5.1.24–40.
17. See *Arden of Feversham*, 3.5.30, 4.3.17, 3.5.97, 1.1.500–02 (in *Five Elizabethan Tragedies*, ed. A.K. McIlwraith [1963]). See also "Who will not change a raven for a dove?" *A Midsummer Night's Dream*, 2.2.114.
18. The play proved popular and was also performed April 20; May 3, 8, 15, 24; and June 6.

19. Aemilia Bassano (1569–1645) is believed by some to be the "Dark Lady of the Sonnets" (see A.L. Rowse, *Sex and Society in Shakespeare's Age: Simon Forman the Astrologer* [1974], pp. 99–117). She published a volume of poetry, *Salve Deus Rex Judaeorum*, in 1611.
20. John Lyly (c. 1554–1606), writer and dramatist, best known for his prose romances, *Euphues, or the Anatomy of Wit* (1578) and *Euphues and His England* (1580). He wrote a number of comedies for performance at Court by the companies of boy actors.
21. Shakespeare's fears proved accurate: the girl was buried on August 9, 1592.
22. See the second scene of the Induction to *The Taming of the Shrew* and the numerous references in the play to Warwickshire people and places.
23. See *The Taming of the Shrew*, 4.2.8 Lucentio: "I read that I profess, the Art of Love," a reference to Ovid's *Ars Amatoria*; 1.1.33 Tranio: "As Ovid be an outcast quite abjured"; 3.1.28–29 where Lucentio quotes the Latin of *Epistolae Heroidum*. In the play there is also the general notion of metamorphosis in connection with love as reflected in Ovid's *Metamorphoses*.
24. See, for example, Lucentio: "While counterfeit supposes bleared thine eyne," *The Taming of the Shrew*, 5.1.106.
25. See entry for April 23, 1592.
26. Elizabeth Throckmorton (1565–1618).
27. Robert Cecil (1563–1612), who succeeded his father as Elizabeth's chief minister in 1598. James I, whom Cecil served as chief secretary and later lord treasurer, created him Earl of Salisbury in 1605.
28. The anonymous *A Knack to Know a Knave* (published 1594) was a popular comedy, and was performed at the Rose on June 10, 15, and 22, 1592. The reference to *Titus Andronicus* is in Osrick's speech: "My gracious Lord, as welcome shall you be . . . / As Titus was unto the Roman Senators, / When he had made a conquest on the Goths . . . / As they in Titus, we in your Grace still find, / The perfect figure of a princely mind." See also Katherine Duncan-Jones, *Ungentle Shakespeare: Scenes from his Life* (2001), p. 53.
29. Anne Brewen was burned and John Parker was hanged for the murder of Anne's husband, John Brewen. Parker and Brewen were friends, goldsmiths, and rivals for Anne's hand in marriage. Anne poisoned her husband three days after their marriage; she and Parker then conducted a secret affair for two years. When Anne became pregnant, she demanded Parker marry her; during an ensuing quarrel (overheard by a neighbor), Parker taunted Anne with her husband's murder. They were arrested and convicted. There is some similarity to aspects of the plot of *Arden of Feversham*.
30. The anonymous play, *The Troublesome Raigne of John King of England*, was published in two parts in 1591.

31. Katherine Hamlett drowned in the River Avon at Tiddington (just west of Stratford) in December 1579. It is quite likely Shakespeare recalled the event in writing Gertrude's description of Ophelia's death in *Hamlet*, 4.7.165–182.
32. Nashe's *Pierce Penniless his Supplication to the Divell* was entered in the Stationers' Register on August 8, 1592.
33. On August 7.
34. An actor, Jewell was buried August 21, 1592. Shakespeare may have intended him for a role in *The Taming of the Shrew*: a stage direction in the anonymous *The Taming of a Shrew* (published 1594) inadvertently refers to "Simon." The exact relationship between *The Taming of the Shrew* and *A Shrew* is uncertain, or which play was the source for the other.
35. Richard Field's father.
36. R.B. McKerrow, *Works of Thomas Nashe* (1958), IV, p. 7, conjectures *Pierce Penniless* was published between September 5–8, 1593. Nashe at the time was in the country because of the plague in London.
37. Robert Greene, notorious for his dissolute and licentious living, died September 3, 1592, and was buried the following day.
38. Thomas Knell (d. before 1609). In *Tarlton's Jests* (c. 1599), Knell is mentioned as playing Henry V at the Bull in Bishopsgate. The play could have been the anonymous *Famous Victories of Henry V* (published 1598), which may have been written by 1588 (the year of Tarlton's death). Tarlton, possibly the play's author, is said to have doubled the roles of the Judge and Derick at the Bull performance. See entry for November 19, 1596, for more on *Famous Victories*.
39. Nashe became involved in a long controversy with the scholar Gabriel Harvey (1545?–1630), which was conducted through a series of pamphlets. See "The Harvey-Nashe Quarrel" in McKerrow, *Works of Thomas Nashe*, V, 65–110.
40. Possibly the inspiration for the characters in *Henry IV Parts 1 & 2*, and *Henry V*.
41. John Shakespeare owed £7 to William Burbage, a Stratford resident, who had sued him in 1582. Burbage's claim was upheld in both 1589 and 1592. "[S]heriff's officers often made arrests on Sunday, when most people could be found at church" (Mark Eccles, *Shakespeare in Warwickshire* [1963], p. 33).
42. Thomas Watson was buried in St. Bartholomew-the-less, London, on September 26, 1592. Edmund Spenser (c. 1552–99) depicted him as Amyntas in *Colin Clouts Come Home Againe* (not printed until 1595). Watson's collection of 60 sonnets, *The Teares of Fancie*, was published in 1593; they had possibly been circulated in manuscript earlier. Marlowe provided a dedication (addressed to Mary, Countess of Pembroke) to Watson's *Amintae Gaudia*, entered in the Stationers' Register on November 10, 1592.
43. This entry would indicate Shakespeare returned to London in early October.

44. Aemilia Bassano, pregnant by the Lord Chamberlain, Henry Lord Hunsdon (c. 1524–96), married Alphonse Lanier, a musician, on October 18, 1592.
45. Sonnet 147, apparently reflecting Shakespeare's sentiments towards Aemilia Bassano/Lanier.
46. Robert Greene's *Groats-worth of Wit* (1592). As noted above, Greene parodies Shakespeare's "O tiger's heart wrapped in a woman's hide" in *Henry VI Part 3*, 1.4.137.
47. Joan Woodward (d. 1623) was Philip Henslowe's stepdaughter. Alleyn thus began to select and produce plays at the Rose Theatre (as well as being leading actor), while Henslowe dealt with the theater's financial aspects.
48. Plague deaths were numbering up to 200 per week.
49. John Grigg, who had recently repaired the Rose for Henslowe, was the builder and was supplied with deal boards for the construction by Henry Draper, a waterman. The house took two years to complete.
50. Henry Chettle (c. 1560–1607), printer and dramatist, published *Kind-Harts Dream* in 1592. It contains the following passage: "With neither of them that take offence [Shakespeare and Marlowe] was I acquainted, and with one of them [Marlowe] I care not if I never be: The other, whom at that time I did not so much spare, as since I wish I had, for that I have moderated the heat of living writers, and might have used my owne discretion (especially in such a case) the Author being dead, that I did not, I am as sorry, as if the original fault had been my fault, because my self have seen his demeanor no less civil than he excellent in the quality he professes [as actor or playwright]: Besides, divers of worship have reported his uprightness of dealing, which argues his honesty, and his facetious grace in writing, which aproves his Art."
51. The Alleyn-Strange company gave 26 performances at the Rose between December 29, 1592, and the end of January 1593. From March through December 1592, the plague in London accounted for 11,503 out of 25,886 deaths.

1593
1. Strange's Men also performed Marlowe's *The Jew of Malta* at the Rose on January 18 and February 1, 1593.
2. *The Comedy of Errors* was performed, apparently, on January 5, 1593, at the Rose.
3. *Titus Andronicus* (as *Titus and Vespasian*) was performed at the Rose on January 6, 15, and 25, 1593.
4. See entry for November 6, 1589. *Henry VI Part 1* was also performed at the Rose on January 31, 1593.

5. Marlowe's *The Massacre of Paris* was performed at the Rose on January 26, 1593, and took in £3 14s. Shakespeare apparently refers to two passages from *Henry VI Part 3*:

    a) And we are graced with wreaths of victory (*Henry VI Part 3*, 5.3.2).
    And we are grac'd with wreaths of victory (*Massacre*, line 953).

    b) Sweet Duke of York, our prop to lean upon,
    Now thou art gone, we have no staff, no stay (*Henry VI Part 3*, 2.1.68–69).
    Sweet Duke of Guise, our prop to lean upon,
    Now thou art dead, here is no stay for us (*Massacre*, lines 1376–77).

6. On January 28 the Privy Council issued a proclamation prohibiting play performances because of plague. There were approximately 10,000 plague deaths in 1593.
7. Through early February there were rumors of a Spanish invasion aided by some of the Scottish nobility, with the Isle of Man as a likely staging post.
8. In *The Canterbury Tales* (c. 1386–87) by Geoffrey Chaucer (c. 1340–1400).
9. *Love's Labour's Lost*, 5.2.864–66. Compare "Jack shall hath Jill, / Naught shall go ill, / The man shall have his mare again, and all shall be well" (*A Midsummer Night's Dream*, 3.2.461–63).
10. See Theseus's speech, *A Midsummer Night's Dream*, 5.1.2–22.
11. These three tales are in Book X of Ovid's *Metamorphoses*. *The Taming of the Shrew* (Induction, 2.47–51) glances at the Adonis myth: "Dost thou love pictures. We will fetch thee straight / Adonis painted by a running brook / And Cytherea all in sedges hid, / Which seem to move and wanton with her breath / Even as the waving sedges play with wind."
12. John Penry, printer and possibly part-author of the Marprelate pamphlets, was detained after a hue and cry was raised by Anthony Anderson, the Vicar of Stepney, on March 22.
13. On March 22, after a long debate, Parliament agreed to a defense subsidy of £400,000, to be collected by November 1596. Francis Bacon (1561–1626) was among those who spoke against the subsidy, arguing it would cause discontent. Ralegh was in favor because of the Spanish threat.
14. Richard Field registered *Venus and Adonis* on April 18, 1593, and Shakespeare probably supervised its printing since there are few misprints in it. The book, Shakespeare's first work to appear in print, was offered for sale at the White Greyhound in St. Paul's churchyard by John Harrison (d. 1618), bookseller. It was available for sale by June 12, 1593 (see Duncan-Jones, *Ungentle Shakespeare*, p. 63).

15. Strange's Men were at Chelmsford on May 2, 1593; the company included Edward Alleyn, Will Kempe, Thomas Pope (d. 1603), John Heminges, Augustine Phillips (d. 1605), and George Bryan (d. 1612).
16. A virulently anti-Dutch doggerel poem, signed "Tamburlaine," was placed on the wall of the Dutch Churchyard in Broad Street on May 5, 1593. The poem also contained allusions to Marlowe's *The Jew of Malta* and *The Massacre at Paris*; for example: "Since words nor threats nor any thing / Can make you avoid this certain ill, / We'll cut your throats, in your temples praying, / Not Paris massacre so much blood did spill."
17. Scadbury, near Chislehurst in Kent and about 12 miles from London, was the country estate of Sir Thomas Walsingham (1568–1630), Marlowe's close friend and a cousin of Sir Francis Walsingham. Sir Thomas had inherited the estate in 1589; prior to that, like Marlowe, he had been connected with Sir Francis's spy network. Marlowe's *Hero and Leander* remained unfinished at his death. It was completed by George Chapman (c. 1560–1634), poet and dramatist, and published in 1598.
18. Marlowe was arrested on May 18, 1593, on a charge of libel because some of his papers were found at Kyd's lodging. The papers reflected Marlowe's freethinking, atheistic beliefs, though he defended them as an interest in theology and philosophy, and a summary of Arianism. On May 20 he was ordered to remain in attendance on the Privy Council.
19. Thomas Nash (1593–1647) was the eldest son of Anthony Nash (d. 1622). Thomas married Shakespeare's granddaughter, Elizabeth Hall (1608–70), on April 22, 1626.
20. Marlowe was killed on May 30, 1593, by Ingram Frizer.
21. An inquest on Marlowe was held on June 1, 1593, by the coroner, William Danby. Nicholas Skeres and Robert Poley, associates of both Marlowe and Frizer, testified that Frizer killed Marlowe in self-defense after Marlowe grabbed Frizer's dagger and stabbed him from behind. Frizer was granted a royal pardon on June 28, 1593.
22. Nashe's *The Unfortunate Traveller* was written, in part, on the Isle of Wight during the winter of 1592–93 while he was staying at Carisbrooke Castle with his patron Sir George Carey. Both Nashe and Southampton attended St. John's College, Oxford. The first edition of *The Unfortunate Traveller* bore a dedication to Southampton, but it disappeared, somewhat mysteriously, from the second edition (see Mckerrow, *Works of Thomas Nashe*, II, 187ff, and IV, 252ff). Nashe dated his work June 27, 1593; it was entered in the Stationers' Register on September 17, 1593, and published in 1594.
23. Kyd went on to translate Robert Garnier's *Cornélie* as *Cornelia*, entered in the Stationers' Register on January 26, 1594, and dedicated to the Countess of

Sussex. Possibly Kyd was seeking Puckering's aid to regain the Earl of Sussex's patronage. Sir John Puckering (1544–96) was, variously, Keeper of the Great Seal, Speaker of the House of Commons, and Lord Chancellor.
24. Henry V stayed at Titchfield in 1415 as his invasion fleet was being readied (prior to the battle of Agincourt). Henry VI was married in the abbey to Margaret of Anjou in 1445.
25. Sir John Russell died September 13, 1593.
26. On September 25, 1593, Ferdinando, Lord Strange, succeeded to his father's title and became the fifth Earl of Derby, hence the name change for his company.
27. Presumably the anonymous *The First Part of Richard II, or, Thomas of Woodstock*.
28. Compare 1) Richard farming out his kingdom in *Woodstock*, 4.1. with Lear's division of his kingdom in *King Lear*, 1.1.36ff; 2) the conversation between Woodstock and a Courtier which includes: "*Woodstock*: But this most fashionable chain, that links as it were / the toe and knee together? *Courtier*: In a most kind coherence, so it like your grace; for these two parts, being in operation and quality different, as for example: the toe a disdainer or spurner; the knee a dutiful and most humble orator. This chain doth, as it were, so toeify the knee and so kneeify the toe, that between both it makes a most methodical coherence, or coherent method" (*Thomas of Woodstock*, 3.2.) with Osric in *Hamlet*, 5.2; 3) the ghosts who visit Woodstock in 5.1 prior to his murder that find echoes in, for example, *Julius Caesar* and *Macbeth*.
29. See *Richard II*, 4.1, especially 162–202. When *Richard II* was first printed in 1597, the abdication scene 4.1.154–318 was omitted, justifying Shakespeare's apprehensions. The scene is a good example of Richard as a self-conscious performer employing high rhetoric. For example, there is the business of Richard and Bolingbroke both holding the crown, Richard calling for a looking glass, Richard comparing himself to Christ (167–73, 237–40), his use of anaphora (207–10), and the allusion, employing anaphora, to the Helen speech in Marlowe's *Dr. Faustus* (281–86).
30. Brooke, *Tragical History of Romeus and Juliet*, p. 104.
31. See *Romeo and Juliet*, 3.3.109–13.
32. The Earl of Sussex's Men resumed playing at the Rose on December 26, 1593. It appears they performed *Richard III* there on December 30, 1593, and January 1, 10, and 27, 1594.

1594

1. *Titus Andronicus* was performed at the Rose by the Earl of Sussex's Men on January 24, 28, and February 6, 1594.
2. Roderigo Lopez (d. 1594), a Portuguese Jew who may have provided suggestions for Shylock in *The Merchant of Venice*, had been Elizabeth's physician since

1586. Although he was involved in political intrigues concerning the pretender to the Portuguese throne, he was probably innocent of attempting to poison Elizabeth. However, he incurred Essex's jealousy and ire which brought about his eventual downfall.
3. Marlowe's *The Jew of Malta* was performed at the Rose on February 4 (and on April 3 and 7), 1594. On February 3 the Privy Council had issued a prohibition on performances within five miles of London because of health concerns.
4. After being examined by Sir Robert Cecil and the Earl of Essex, Lopez was committed to the Tower on February 5, to be arraigned later in the month.
5. Danter (d. c. 1598–99) was the printer of the first quarto of *Titus Andronicus* (1594). The title page reads: "The most lamentable Romaine Tragedie of Titus Andronicus: As it was Plaide by the Right Honourable the Earle of Darbie, Earle of Pembroke, and Earle of Sussex their Seruants. London, Printed by Iohn Danter, and are to be sold by Edward White & Thomas Millington, at the little North doore of Paules at the signe of the Gunne, 1594." It is not clear what financial reward Shakespeare might have expected since dramatists sold their plays and rights in them to a given acting company, which then retained control over them.
6. Mary I (1519–58; reigned 1553–58) was called "Bloody Mary" for her persecution of Protestants, some 300 or more of whom were executed.
7. Lopez was arraigned at the Guildhall on February 28, 1594, and found guilty of undertaking to poison Elizabeth for 50,000 crowns. The judges included Essex, the Lord Mayor of London, Sir Thomas Heneage (shortly to become Southampton's stepfather), Sir John Popham, and Sir Robert Cecil.
8. Thomas Millington (fl. 1583–1603) was a publisher with a dubious reputation.
9. Perillus is a character in the anonymous *The True Chronicle History of King Leir*, performed at the Rose by Queen Elizabeth's and Sussex's Men on April 6 and 9, 1594.
10. Ferdinando, Earl of Derby, former Lord Strange, died April 16, 1594.
11. Southampton's mother, the Countess of Southampton, married Sir Thomas Heneage on May 2, 1594. The Countess was 41, Heneage (who died the following year) 60.
12. Presumably those scenes featuring Lysander, Demetrius, Helena, and Hermia, such as parts of 1.1, 2.2, 3.2, and 3.1.147–186 with Peaseblossom and other fairies.
13. The combined Chamberlain's (formerly Strange's/Derby's) and Admiral's companies performed for 10 days at Newington Butts Theatre between June 3–16, 1594. Strange's/Derby's Men had found a new patron in the Lord Chamberlain, Henry Lord Hunsdon.

14. *Lucrece* was entered in the Stationers' Register on May 9, 1594, by John Harrison, to whom Field also assigned the copyright of *Venus and Adonis* on June 25, 1594.
15. *The Jew of Malta* was performed June 4 and 13; *Titus Andronicus* on June 5; a non-Shakespearean *Hamlet*, possibly by Kyd, on June 9; *The Taming of the Shrew* on June 11. The average daily takings were only nine shillings.
16. "The loue I dedicate to your Lordship is without end: whereof this Pamphlet without beginning is but a superfluous Moity. The warrant I haue of your Honourable disposition, not the worth of my vntutord Lines, makes it assured of acceptance. What I haue done is yours, what I haue to doe is yours, being part in all I haue, deuoted yours. Were my worth greater, my duety would shew greater, meane time, as it is, it is bound to your Lordship; To whom I wish long life still lengthned with all happinesse. Your Lordships in all duety, William Shakespeare." It proved to be a popular poem.
17. The Chamberlain's Men, including Richard Burbage, Will Kempe, Shakespeare, Thomas Pope, John Heminges, Augustine Phillips, and George Bryan, went to play at James Burbage's Theatre, Shoreditch. The Admiral's Men, including Edward Alleyn, John Singer (d. 1609), Richard Jones (c. 1569–after 1624), Thomas Towne (d. 1612), Martin Slaughter (or Slater c. 1560–1625), Edward Juby (d. 1618), Thomas Downton (d. 1625), and James Tunstall (or Dunstan c. 1555–99), went to play at Henslowe's Rose.
18. Robert Gough (or Goughe, or Goffe) died in 1624 and was a member of the Chamberlain's early on, and as a boy actor played "leading lady" roles. He was listed as one of the principal actors in the First Folio.
19. The Chamberlain's Men performed in the guildhall for the mayor and aldermen of Marlborough, Wiltshire, in September 1594, for which they were paid 2s. 8d.
20. Marlowe's *Tamburlaine Part I* was performed by the Admiral's Men at the Rose on September 12, 1594.
21. Marlowe's *Dr. Faustus* was performed by the Admiral's Men at the Rose on September 30, 1594.
22. On September 22, 1594, a fire in Stratford destroyed the west side of Chapel, High, Wood, and Henley Streets.
23. Lavish celebrations for Southampton's coming of age were held at Titchfield on October 6, 1594.
24. On September 3, 1594, *Willobie his Avisa. Or the true Picture of a modest Maid and of a chast and Constant Wife* was entered in the Stationers' Register and printed later that year by John Windet. In the poem, Avisa, an innkeeper's wife, rejects the advances of several suitors, including Henrico Willobego. The

latter seeks the advice of "W.S." who had suffered similarly. Henry Willobie was born c. 1574/75.

25. See: "She is a woman, therefore may be wooed; / She is a woman, therefore may be won," *Titus Andronicus*, 2.1.82–83; "She's beautiful, and therefore to be wooed; / She is a woman, therefore to be won," *Henry VI Part 1*, 5.3.78–79.
26. Some prefatory commendatory verses in *Avisa* allude to Shakespeare: "Yet Tarquyne pluckt his glistering grape, / And Shake-speare, paints poore Lucrece rape."
27. Burghley tried repeatedly to get Southampton, his ward, to marry Lady Elizabeth Vere, daughter of the Earl of Oxford, Edward de Vere (1550–1604). On November 19, 1594, Southampton paid a £5,000 fine for refusing to do so.
28. Elizabeth Vernon (d. c. 1648) was a ward of the Earl of Essex, her cousin. Court gossip did not link her to Southampton until 1595. They married secretly in 1598 after Elizabeth became pregnant, for which Queen Elizabeth imprisoned them briefly.
29. Francis Langley (1550–1601) built the Swan Theatre in 1595 in the manor of Paris garden on the Bankside, Southwark. On November 3, 1594, the Lord Mayor had petitioned the Lord Treasurer to suppress plays.
30. The official residence of Sir John Heneage and his wife, the Countess of Southampton.
31. William Sly (d. 1608) was with the Chamberlain's Men from 1594–1605. He probably played a mixture of romantic, soldierly, and fiery roles.
32. At the Rose, the Admiral's Men performed Marlowe's *Tamburlaine Part I* on December 17, *Part II* on December 19, and *Dr. Faustus* on December 20, 1594.
33. The Chamberlain's Men performed before Elizabeth at Greenwich Palace on December 26 and 27, 1594. However, they had to wait until March 15, 1595 for their payment, which amounted to 40 marks (£13 6s 8d).
34. On December 17, 1594, Jean Chastel attempted to assassinate the king of France and Navarre, Henri IV (1553–1610), stabbing him in his cheek. Chastel was executed by having his arms and legs cut off with red-hot pincers and then his body drawn apart by four horses. The quarters were then burned.

1595

1. Thomasina Heminges was baptized at St. Mary's, Aldermanbury; she married William Ostler (c. 1585–1614), a former boy actor and one of the King's Men, in 1611. Langley married Hester Saule at St. Leonard's Church, Shoreditch.
2. On January 26, 1595, the Chamberlain's Men performed *A Midsummer Night's Dream* for the court wedding of William, 6th Earl of Derby to Lady Elizabeth Vere.
3. A hint of *The Merchant of Venice* possibly.

4. On February 15, as in previous years, orders were issued to restrain the killing and eating of flesh during Lent.
5. *Gorboduc* (1561), the first English blank-verse tragedy, was a collaboration by Thomas Sackville (1536–1608) and Thomas Norton (1532–84).
6. From June 13, 1595, there had been disturbances by apprentices in Southwark and near St. Paul's. On June 23, the apprentices discovered there was no fish to buy at Billingsgate Market. They then followed the fishwives, who had bought up all the available mackerel, to Southwark where they again created a disturbance that was subdued. On July 4, a 9 P.M. (sunset) curfew was imposed, and the posting of seditious notices was prohibited.
7. Four hundred Spanish soldiers had landed on July 26, 1595; they burned Penzance and destroyed the village of Mousehole in Cornwall.
8. The Lord Mayor had petitioned the Privy Council to suppress plays, attributing to them the recent disorders by the apprentices. He maintained plays "contain nothing but profane fables, lascivious matters, cozening devices, and other unseemly and scurrilous behaviours which are so set forth that they move wholly to imitation."
9. The Stratford fire occurred on September 21, 1595, and was concentrated in a block bounded by Sheep, High, and Bridge Streets. Sadler and Quiney (d. 1607) both lived in High Street. This and an earlier fire on September 22, 1594 destroyed 120 dwellings and 80 other buildings, causing £12,000 in damages.
10. See "the raining of corne this Summer in Wakefield" in Nashe's *Have with You to Saffron-Walden*, in *Works*, ed. McKerrow, III, 74. The phenomenon was probably caused by tornadic conditions.
11. Ralegh had returned from his voyage to Guiana on September 27, 1595. The Mermaid tavern was in Bread Street, Cheapside. It was frequented by Ralegh and his circle (including Marlowe when alive) and, later, by the dramatists Ben Jonson (1572–1637), Francis Beaumont (c. 1584–1616), John Fletcher (1579–1625), and the poet and churchman John Donne (1572–1631). Its host was William Williamson. In 1603 Williamson was succeeded by his apprentice, William Johnson (c. 1575–1616), who was one of the trustees in Shakespeare's purchase of the Blackfriars Gatehouse on March 10, 1613.
12. Anthony Munday (1560–1633) was first a child actor, then an apprentice to the printer John Allde (c. 1583–1624), and subsequently a dramatist. His *John a Kent and John a Cumber* (c. 1590) is a rare example of an extant Elizabethan holograph play. He also wrote out the original version of *Sir Thomas More*.
13. Shakespeare is thought to have written or had a hand in 1.2, 2.1, 2.2, and 4.4 of *Edward III* (see the edition by George Melchiori [Cambridge, 1998]). The line "Lilies that fester smell far worse than weeds" occurs in 2.1.452 and in

Sonnet 94, line 14. The anonymous *Edward III* was registered on December 1, 1595, and published by Cuthbert Burby (d. 1607) in 1596.
14. Presumably *John a Kent*, which *A Midsummer Night's Dream* resembles somewhat. Turnop and his rustic companions resemble Bottom and the mechanicals, while Shrimp's role resembles Puck's.
15. Book III of Munday's *Zelauto or the Fountain of Fame* (1580) includes the story of Signor Truculento, an "extorting Usurer" who "smoutched up himselfe in his Fustian slyppers." If Munday was the translator of *The Orator* (1596), he might have also shown Shakespeare the manuscript of "Declamation 95," which is entitled "Of a Jew, who would for his debt have a pound of the flesh of a Christian"—the forfeit Shylock imposes in *The Merchant of Venice*.
16. The Admiral's Men performed the anonymous play 13 times between November 28, 1595 and July 15, 1596.
17. Sir Edward Hoby (1560–1617), diplomat.
18. Helen Burbage was buried at St. Anne's, Blackfriars.

1596

1. The Chamberlain's Men performed three plays at Court on December 26–28, 1595 and another on January 6, 1596. Harington had a house at Burley, Rutland, where *Titus Andronicus* was performed on January 1, 1596. Anthony Bacon (1558–1601), Harington's neighbor in Bishopsgate, London, was a diplomat and spy, as well as the elder brother of Francis Bacon. His pageboy was Jacques Petit.
2. Burbage bought Blackfriars from Sir William More, and spent another £300 on conversion costs before the project was halted by the objections of local residents. See entry for November 25, 1596.
3. On February 19, 1596, *A Midsummer Night's Dream* was performed by the Chamberlain's Men at Sir George Carey's house, Blackfriars, for the wedding of Carey's daughter, Elizabeth, to Thomas, son of Henry Lord Berkeley.
4. The Dagger, a low-class gaming house frequented by the disreputable, was known for its Dagger ale and Dagger pies.
5. Eleanor Bull, who owned the house where Marlowe was killed, was buried March 19, 1596, at St. Nicholas's, Deptford. Marlowe was buried in the same churchyard on June 1, 1593.
6. *The Jew of Malta* was revived eight times between January 9 and June 23, 1596, by the Admiral's Men at the Rose.
7. Cardinal Albert, Archduke of Austria (1559–1621), in league with the Spanish, had in early April laid siege to Calais. The Lord Mayor and aldermen of London were required to impress 1,000 men.

8. Calais fell to the Spanish and French on April 16; Essex's expedition to Calais was countermanded on April 17, 1596.
9. See Falstaff enlisting recruits in *Henry IV Part 2*, 3.2.
10. See *The Merchant of Venice*, 4.1.182–203.
11. "... [C]onversion [by Jews to Christianity] was made more attractive in the 1280s, when converts were allowed to retain a life interest in half their property, rather than surrendering it all to the Crown, as they had previously done"(Stephen Inwood, *A History of London* [1998], p. 70). See Antonio's "mercy" speech, *The Merchant of Venice*, 4.1.378–88.
12. Presumably a reference to *The Merchant of Venice*, 3.1.106–09: "Thou torturest me, Tubal. It was my turquoise; I had it of Leah when I was a bachelor. I would not have given it for a wilderness of monkeys."
13. Essex and Lord Admiral Charles Howard (1536–1624) with more than 150 ships and 10,000 men set sail for Cadiz, where they eventually defeated the Spanish. John Donne was one of the volunteers.
14. Henry Carey, 1st Lord Hunsdon, died July 22, 1596. His son, George Carey, 2nd Lord Hunsdon (1547–1603), became patron to what were then called Hunsdon's Men until Carey became Lord Chamberlain on March 17, 1597, and the company reverted to its former title.
15. The Isle of Sheppey is nearly 40 miles east of London. The Swale is the channel of water separating the Isle from Kent.
16. See entries for April 6 and 7, 1592 above.
17. Elizabeth visited Faversham in 1572.
18. Hamnet, aged 12, was buried in Stratford on August 11, 1596.
19. Shakespeare's company performed at the Guildhall, Bristol, September 11–17, 1596.
20. See entry for November 28, 1595.
21. William Dethick (1543–1612), Garter King-of-Arms from 1586–1606, was knighted by James I in 1603.
22. John Shakespeare had apparently applied for a coat of arms earlier (see S. Schoenbaum, *William Shakespeare: A Compact Documentary Life* [1977], pp. 38–39). The coat of arms was described as: "Gold, on a bend sables, a spear of the first steeled argent, and for his crest or cognizance a falcon, his wings displayed argent, standing on a wreath of his colours, supporting a spear gold, steeled as aforesaid, set upon a helmet with mantles and tassles as hath been accustomed and doth more plainly appear depicted on this margent." The motto was *Non Sanz Droit*—"Not without Right."
23. On November 18, 1596 was held the double wedding of Lady Elizabeth and Lady Katherine Somerset, the two daughters of the Earl of Worcester, to Henry Guildford and William Petre.

24. The line ends each of the 10 verses of Edmund Spenser's *Prothalamion* (1596).
25. *The Famous Victories* was entered in the Stationers' Register on May 14, 1594, but not published until 1598. While Richard Tarlton certainly acted in the play, his authorship is conjectural (see entry for c. September 20, 1592). The play is reprinted in Maynard Mack's Signet edition of *Henry IV Part 1* (1965), pp. 179–233, and in Geoffrey Bullough, *Narrative and Dramatic Sources of Shakespeare*, vol. 4 (1962), pp. 299–343.
26. Sir John Oldcastle was the original name for Falstaff in *Henry IV Part 1*. Pope, Kempe, and Heminges have all been candidates for acting Falstaff first. On Shakespeare's use of the names "Sir John Oldcastle" and "Falstaff" see Gary Taylor, "The Fortunes of Oldcastle," *Shakespeare Survey*, 38 (1985), 85–100. See also entries for January 2 and 10, 1597 below.
27. Samuel Daniel had published *The First Fowre Bookes of the Civile Wars between the Two Houses of Lancaster and York*, a source for *Henry IV Part 1*, in 1595.
28. The historical Prince Hal was some 23 years younger than Hotspur. Like his source, Samuel Daniel, Shakespeare makes them the same age.
29. Phillips was a good, loyal colleague; he mentioned most of his fellow actors in his will, and left Shakespeare 30 shillings in gold. He made Sly one of the overseers of his will and bequeathed him a silver bowl worth £5.
30. The Boar's Head Inn or Tavern is not actually named in *Henry IV Part 1* as the setting for scenes such as 2.4, though it has often been assumed it is. The inn was located in Eastcheap, a poor, dangerous, and disreputable area of London.
31. The basis of the dispute is unknown. Earlier in 1596 Langley had sought sureties of the peace against his old adversary William Gardiner (1531–97), an unscrupulous Justice of the Peace of Southwark and his stepson, William Wayte (d. 1603). Wayte retaliated with his writ on November 29, 1596: "Be it known that William Wayte craves sureties of the peace against William Shakespeare, Francis Langley, Dorothy Soer, wife of John Soer, and Anne Lee, for fear of death, etc." According to Leslie Hotson, this dispute led to Shakespeare satirizing Gardiner as Shallow in *The Merry Wives of Windsor* and *Henry IV Part 2* (see *Shakespeare versus Shallow* [1931]). However, other scholars believe Shallow satirizes Sir Thomas Lucy.
32. Henry VIII had proscribed Welsh in 1536.
33. Feake languished until December 6, and was buried on December 7, 1596, at St. Leonard's, Shoreditch. Gabriel Spencer, an actor, was killed by Ben Jonson on September 22, 1598.
34. The Folio stage direction to *Henry VI Part 3*, 1.2.48 reads "Gabriel" for what is a messenger's role. Spencer may have played that role and possibly Gabriel the servant in *The Taming of the Shrew*, 4.1.117.

35. The Chamberlain's Men performed at Whitehall on December 26 and 27, 1596; January 1 and 6, 1597; and February 6 and 8, 1597.

1597
1. William Brooke, 7th Lord Cobham (d. 1597) and his son Henry Brooke, 8th Lord Cobham (d. 1619) were descendants of Sir John Oldcastle (c. 1377–1417), soldier and friend of Henry V. William Brooke was Lord Chamberlain from August 1596 until March 1597.
2. Henry Shakespeare was imprisoned for debt in September 1596. He was buried at Snitterfield on December 29, 1596.
3. See entry for December 8, 1594.
4. Shakespeare appears to have turned to *Henry VI Part 1* and Sir John Fastolfe as the inspiration for "Falstaff." Interestingly, the historical Fastolfe commanded someone named "Bardolph" (see next footnote).
5. In *Henry IV Part 1* "Harvey" was the original name of "Peto," and "Russell" the original of "Bardolph." Sir William Harvey or Hervey (d. 1642), soldier and courtier, married Southampton's mother in 1598.
6. She was also the wife of Sir Robert Cecil.
7. A mistress?
8. James Burbage was buried at St. Leonard's Church, Shoreditch, on February 2, 1597. Cuthbert Burbage (1566–1636), James Burbage's son, was a theater owner and connected with the Theatre, Globe, and Blackfriars theaters. He did not act, however.
9. Francis Bacon's first edition of 10 essays was on sale on February 7, 1597.
10. Margaret's husband was Henry Shakespeare (d. 1596), Shakespeare's uncle. Margaret and Henry had two children: Lettice (b. 1582) and James (1585–89).
11. In 1597 John Danter printed *An Excellent conceited Tragedie of Romeo and Juliet, As it hath been often (with great applause) plaid publiquely by the right Honourable the L. of Hunsdon his Servants.* This "bad" first quarto lacks some 800 lines found in the authoritative second quarto (1599). Shakespeare's company was known as Lord Hunsdon's Men only from July 1596 to March 1597.
12. Cobham's daughter Elizabeth had died on January 24, 1597.
13. By tradition Shakespeare's birthday has been assumed to be April 23, 1564, although only his baptism on April 26, 1564 is recorded.
14. *The Merry Wives of Windsor*, 1.1.13–25 contains possible references to Lucy's coat of arms ("the dozen white luces in their coat"), while 1.1.100–02 mentions deer poaching (see entry for Summer 1585).
15. *The Merry Wives of Windsor*, 3.1.16–19 and 22–24 is a slightly mangled version of lines 7–10 of Marlowe's "The Passionate Shepherd to his Love." An

inferior version of Marlowe's poem was published in *The Passionate Pilgrim* (1599); the full text appeared in *England's Helicon* (1600).
16. See Falstaff: "I do begin to perceive that I am made an ass" (*The Merry Wives of Windsor*, 5.5.117), and Bottom: "I see their knavery. This is to make an ass of me" (*A Midsummer Night's Dream*, 3.1.108).
17. Giles Allen (or Alleyn) had leased James Burbage a plot of land in Shoreditch on April 13, 1576. Burbage built the Theatre there with considerable financial backing from his brother-in-law, John Brayne.
18. Nicholas Tooley (c. 1575–1623) became a full member of the King's Men (previously the Lord Chamberlain's) in about 1605.
19. He was born Benjamin Johnson.
20. At the time, Pembroke's Men included William Bird (d. 1624), Thomas Downton, Richard Jones, Robert Shaw (or Shaa, d. 1603), and Gabriel Spencer. The company had leased the Swan from Francis Langley on February 21, 1597.
21. New Place was the second largest house in Stratford, for which Shakespeare paid an official £60, though the price was nominal and fictitious in order to keep its taxable value low. The house, built by Sir Hugh Clopton (d. 1496) in about 1490, sat on an acre at the corner of Chapel Street and Chapel Lane. It was three stories high (28 feet), had a 60-foot frontage, 10 fireplaces, two gardens, two orchards, and two barns. The owner, William Underhill (d. 1597), had bought New Place from a William Bott in 1567; Bott poisoned his daughter in order to possess her husband's lands. Two months after Shakespeare's purchase, on July 7, 1597, Underhill himself was poisoned by his son, Fulke (1579–99), who was eventually hanged in 1599. Thus the complete transfer of New Place to Shakespeare was not completed until 1602 when Underhill's son, Hercules (b. 1581), came of age.
22. Charles Blount, 8th Baron Mountjoy (1563–1606), soldier, friend of Essex, and Lord Deputy of Ireland 1601–03.
23. *Frederick and Basilea* was probably a new play, but is now lost. Alleyn played Sebastian, Richard Allen (d. 1601) was Frederick, Samuel Rowley (d. 1624) was Heraclius. Three boy actors named Dick, Griffin, and Will played Basilea, Athanasia, and Leonora.
24. From October 1594 to October 1597 Alleyn's company, the Admiral's Men, performed Marlowe's *Dr. Faustus* 24 times. Alleyn did retire for a time in 1597, but returned to the stage in 1600.
25. Essex's fleet tried to depart from Plymouth on June 15, 1597, but was prevented by storms. There were several more attempts in June and July; the final successful attempt came on August 14, 1597. John Donne was also part of the expedition.

26. Apparently this took place on July 6 and was designed to sooth tensions between Essex and Ralegh over their joint Spanish expedition. Ralegh reported to Cecil that *Richard II* had made Essex "wonderful merry."
27. James Burbage, son of Cuthbert Burbage, was buried at St. Leonard's, Shoreditch, on July 15, 1597.
28. Richard Topcliffe (1532–1604), notorious torturer and persecutor of Catholics.
29. In August and September 1597 Shakespeare's company travelled through Sussex and Kent, visiting towns such as Rye and Dover, as well as stopping in Bristol in late September.
30. When the first quarto of *Love's Labour's Lost* was published in 1598, the title page read: *A Pleasant Conceited Comedie Called, Loues labors lost. As it was presented before her Highnes this last Christmas, Newly corrected and augmented by W. Shakespere.* It was the first published play with Shakespeare's name on it.
31. *Richard II* was entered in the Stationers' Register by Andrew Wise on August 29, 1597. A first quarto was published later in 1597 but with the scene depicting Richard's deposition omitted (4.1.154–318). The scene was restored in the fourth quarto, published 1608.
32. Shakespeare recalled the Dover cliffs, their samphire gatherers, and seashore in *King Lear*, 4.6.
33. Philip II (1527–98), who died on September 13, 1598, had married Mary I ("Bloody Mary") in 1554.
34. The Admiral's Men and Pembroke's Men resumed playing at the Rose on October 11, 1597, performing *The Spanish Tragedy*.
35. The first quarto of *Richard III* lacks some 200 lines found in the First Folio.
36. On this same date the petty collectors for the Bishopsgate ward noted Shakespeare as one of those who had not paid an assessment of five shillings levied in October 1596.
37. Justice William Gardiner died at his house in Bermondsey Street on November 26, 1597. He was not buried until December 22, 1597. See also entry for November 29, 1596.
38. William Camden (1551–1623), scholar, antiquary, and historian, was appointed second master at Westminster School (which Jonson attended) in 1575 and headmaster in 1593. Camden was made Clarencieux King-at-arms in 1597. His written work includes *Annales* (1615).
39. Philip Henslowe gave Jonson 20 shillings on December 3, 1597, for his work on an unknown play.
40. In December 1597 the Chamberlain's Men gave a performance for the mayor and aldermen in the Guildhall, Marlborough, Wiltshire, for which they were paid 6s 4d.

41. Richard Cowley (d. 1619), listed as one of the principal actors in the First Folio, was probably an original member of the Chamberlain's Men.

1598
1. Abraham Sturley (d. 1614), another Stratfordian, wrote to Quiney on January 24, 1598 that Shakespeare was "willing to disburse some money upon some odd yardland at Shottery or near about."
2. Marlowe's *Hero and Leander*, printed by Edward Blount (1564–1632). The version completed by George Chapman was published later in 1598.
3. The first quarto of *Love's Labour's Lost*, with numerous typographical errors, was published by Cuthbert Burby on March 10, 1598, and was the first published play to bear Shakespeare's name. The play was printed by "W.W.," William White (fl. 1588–1615).
4. See 1.1.166–69, 1.1.189–209, 1.3.21–24, 1.3.36–55, 1.3.85–108, 2.3.23–45, 4.1.55–79, 4.1.103–39.
5. In *Henry V* what might have been Falstaff's role may have been switched to Pistol.
6. "The True and Lamentable Discourse of the Burning of the Town of Tiverton" (1598) by Thomas Purfoot.
7. See entry for July 29, 1597.
8. From 1594–1603 Hugh O'Neill, 2nd Earl of Tyrone (c. 1540–1616), led a revolt against the English. O'Neill ended one truce on June 7, 1598. During July 1598 2,000 men and 120 horses were ordered to be sent to Ireland. In 1599 Essex was ordered to suppress the revolt but instead merely concluded a truce with O'Neill.
9. *A Humourous Day's Mirth* was performed at the Rose on May 1, 1597, by the Admiral's Men.
10. The quarto edition of *Every Man In his Humour* was published in 1601. Jonson revised the play, possibly in 1605, changing the scene to England. The revision was published in the 1616 folio collection of Jonson's plays and listed the following as actors of the 1598 performance: Shakespeare, Richard Burbage, Augustine Phillips, John Heminges, Henry Condell, Thomas Pope, William Sly, Christopher Beeston (c. 1580–1638), Will Kempe, and John Duke (d. 1613). Shakespeare possibly picked up certain hints from *Every Man* for his own plays. In 1.1 there is a reference to a book on hawking and hunting, and Lorenzo senior's advice to Stephano resembles Polonius's advice to Laertes (cf. *Hamlet*). In 1.2 the foppish Stephano and his concern for his stockings may prefigure Osric (cf. *Hamlet*) and Malvolio (cf. *Twelfth Night*). Finally, one character is named Prospero (see *The Tempest*, one of the few Shakespeare plays to observe the unities).

11. The playhouses were the Rose and the Swan. Shakespeare was living in the Liberty of the Clink, Southwark, c. 1596–99.
12. James Roberts (fl. 1564–1608) was a printer and possibly an agent for Shakespeare's company. He entered *The Merchant of Venice* in the Stationers' Register on July 22, 1598, "provided it be not printed"—a so-called "blocking entry" preventing anyone else printing the play. Roberts printed the first quarto of *The Merchant of Venice* in 1600.
13. Burleigh's funeral was held in Westminster Abbey on August 29, 1598, with over 500 mourners in attendance, including Essex.
14. Blackwater Fort surrendered on August 29, 1598.
15. Tobie Matthew (1577–1655) was later a Member of Parliament, became a Catholic priest in 1614, translated Bacon's *Essays* into Italian, and was knighted in 1623 by James I for acting as envoy to the Spanish court in the abortive attempt to secure the marriage of Prince Charles to the Spanish Infanta.
16. Philip Henslowe commented: "I have lost one of my company, which hurteth me greatly, that is Gabriel, for he is slain in Hoxton fields by the hands of Benjamin Johnson bricklayer."
17. See entry for September 18, 1589.
18. Francis Meres (1565–1647) was a schoolmaster and clergyman. His *Palladis Tamia* was entered in the Stationers' Register on September 7, 1598, and published shortly afterwards.
19. Michael Drayton (1563–1631), poet and dramatist, was born at Hartshill, Warwickshire. Later in life he was cured of a fever by Shakespeare's son-in-law, Dr. John Hall. Falstaff in *Henry IV Part 1,* 2.4.116–17 says "There is nothing but roguery to be found in villainous man."
20. See Mercutio's speech in *Romeo and Juliet,* 3.1.94–95.
21. The neck-verse was the first verse of Psalm 51, or the "Miserere" (Miserere mei, Deus—Have mercy upon me, O God). It was so-called because a correct reading of it spared the reader's neck from the gallows.
22. Jonson apparently returned to bricklaying until January 31, 1599.
23. On October 25, 1598, Quiney wrote to Shakespeare asking for the loan of £30: "Loveinge Contreyman, I am bold of yow as of a ffrende . . . Yow shall ffrende me muche in helpeing me out of all the debettes I owe in London."
24. Born in London, Chamberlain (1553–1627) became a notable letter-writer.
25. Sir Edward Coke (1552–1634) was Elizabeth's Attorney General, noteworthy (among much else) for his prosecution of Essex in 1600, Ralegh in 1603, and the Gunpowder Plot conspirators in 1605. Coke's first wife had died on June 27, 1598. His second wife, Elizabeth Hatton, was Lord Burghley's granddaughter.
26. In Elizabethan England "nothing" and "noting" were homophones.
27. See entry for December 4, 1596.

28. Nicholas Brend (c. 1561–1601) was the son of Thomas Brend (c. 1516–98). Thomas Savage (c. 1552–1611) was a goldsmith and Heminges's landlord. Savage was the "very loving friend" of John Jackson (1576–1625), who was the overseer of Savage's will and one of the trustees in Shakespeare's purchase of the Blackfriars Gatehouse in 1613. William Leveson (d. 1621) was a churchwarden of St. Mary's, Aldermanbury, and was later involved in the development of Virginia through the Virginia Company. See entry for August 26, 1603 for Leveson's connection with Sir Dudley and Leonard Digges.

1599
1. Richard Barnfield (1574–1627), poet, published *Poems in Divers Humours* in 1598, which contained the three poems in this entry.
2. Jonson had borrowed £10 from the actor Robert Browne (d. c. 1622) in April 1598. Since he had failed to repay the debt, Jonson had been in the Marshalsea prison since late January 1599.
3. The Lord Chamberlain's Men had also performed at Court on December 26, 1598 and January 1, 1599.
4. The signatories were: Nicholas Brend, Cuthbert and Richard Burbage, Shakespeare, John Heminges, Augustine Phillips, Thomas Pope, and Will Kempe. The lease was granted for 31 years from Christmas 1598 to Christmas 1629.
5. Sir Thomas North (c. 1535–c. 1601) published his translation of a French version of Plutarch's *Lives* as *The Lives of the Noble Grecians and Romanes* in 1579. Shakespeare drew extensively on North for *Julius Caesar, Timon of Athens, Coriolanus*, and *Antony and Cleopatra*.
6. Elizabeth Condell was the first of nine children, and, since Condell and his wife married in 1599, was presumably conceived out of wedlock.
7. Thomas Dekker (c. 1572–c. 1632), dramatist and pamphleteer, wrote and adapted numerous plays, many for Henslowe and the Admiral's Men at the Rose. *The Shoemakers' Holiday* was performed at the Rose later in 1599 and given before Elizabeth on January 1, 1600.
8. Thomas Deloney (c. 1543–c. 1600) was a ballad-writer whose *The Gentle Craft* (1597–98) includes the story of the shoemaker's apprentice, Simon Eyre, who became the Lord Mayor of London, which provided the outline plot for Dekker's *The Shoemakers' Holiday.*
9. Compare "I meddle with no trademan's matters nor women's matters; but withal—I am indeed, sir, a surgeon to old shoes" (*Julius Caesar*, 1.1.21–23) with "Yes, sir, shoemakers dare stand in a woman's quarrel, I warrant you, as deep as another, and deeper too" (*The Shoemakers' Holiday*, 5.2.161–62).
10. This phrase is recalled in Jonson's *Volpone* (1606): "known patriots, / Sound lovers of their country" (4.1.95–96).

11. Interestingly, Shakespeare ascribes to both men very similar phrases: compare Antony's "Friends, Romans, countrymen, lend me your ears" (*Julius Caesar*, 3.2.73) with Henry's "And calls them brothers, friends, and countrymen" (*Henry V*, 4, Chorus, 34).
12. Shakespeare makes the parallel explicit in *Henry V*:
    > But now behold,
    > In the quick forge and working-house of thought,
    > How London doth pour out her citizens!
    > The mayor and all his brethren in best sort,
    > Like to the senators of th'antique Rome,
    > With the plebeians swarming at their heels,
    > Go forth and fetch their conquering Caesar in; (5, Chorus, 22–28).
13. Jonson satirized some of Shakespeare's techniques in the history plays in the Prologue to the First Folio edition of *Every Man In His Humour*:
    > *To make a child now swaddled, to proceed*
    > *Man, and then shoot up, in one beard and weed,*
    > *Past threescore years; or, with three rusty swords,*
    > *And help of some few foot and half-foot words,*
    > *Fight over York and Lancaster's long jars,*
    > *And in the tyring house bring wounds to scars.*
    > *He* [i.e. Jonson] *rather prays you will be pleas'd to see*
    > *One such to-day, as other plays should be;*
    > *Where neither chorus wafts you o'er the seas,*
    > *Nor creaking throne comes down the boys to please.*
14. See *Henry V*:
    > Were now the general of our gracious empress,
    > As in good time he may, from Ireland coming,
    > Bringing rebellion broachèd on his sword,
    > How many would the peaceful city quit
    > To welcome him! (5, Chorus, 30–34).
15. Henry Condell's daughter, Elizabeth (baptized February 27, 1599), was buried at St. Mary's, Aldermanbury, April 11, 1599.
16. Presumably a reference to the Prologue, lines 12–13: "Or may we cram / Within this wooden O," which is applicable equally to the Curtain and to the Globe theaters.
17. See *Henry V*, Prologue, lines 2–3.
18. While Jonson did employ conventional epilogues, the unobsequious epilogue to *Cynthia's Revels* (1600) perhaps reflects his true opinion of the convention: "Let's see: to lay the blame / Upon the children's action, that were lame. / To crave your favour, with begging knee, / Were to distrust the writer's faculty. /

To promise better at the next we bring, / Prorogues disgrace, commends not any thing. / Stiffly to stand on this, and proudly approve / The play, might tax the maker of Self-love. / I'll only speak what I have heard him say, / 'By — 'tis good, and if you like't, you may.'"

19. See Nym's repeated "that's the humour of it" in *Henry V*, 2.1. Jonson outlined his theory of the humors in the Prologue to his next play for the Lord Chamberlain's, *Every Man Out of his Humour*. "*So in every human body, / The choler, melancholy, phlegm, and blood, / By reason that they flow continually / In some one part, and are not continent, / Receive the name of humours. Now thus far / It may, by metaphor, apply itself / Unto the general disposition: / As when some one peculiar quality / Doth so possess a man, that it doth draw / All his affects, his spirits, and his powers, / In their confluctions, all to run one way, / This may be truly said to be a humour.*"
20. Edward Pearce, or Peers (c. 1560–1612) was Master from 1599 to 1612. The old Master was Thomas Gyles (d. 1600). The Children performed numerous plays between 1598 and 1606, including *Satiromastix* (1601) by John Marston (1576–1634) and Dekker.
21. Sackville had conveyed her death sentence to Mary Queen of Scots in 1586.
22. The Globe also had a Latin motto, *totus mundus agit histrionem*, to which Shakespeare alluded in *As You Like It* (see the entry for November 15, 1599).
23. Barnaby Bright, St. Barnabas' Day, was June 11 in the Julian calendar, and the "longest day." The Gospel for that day was John 15:12–17 with its well-known injunction to "love one another."
24. The book was *The First Part of the Life and Raigne of King Henrie the IIII* (1599) by Sir John Hayward (c. 1564–1627). Hayward was tried and imprisoned in 1600.
25. The Prologue and choruses in *Henry V* were omitted from the first quarto published in 1600; they were restored in the First Folio.
26. Both Day (c. 1574–1640) and Porter (d. 1599) were dramatists. Day's best known work is *The Parliament of Bees* (c. 1608). Porter's *The Two Angry Women of Abingdon* (1599) may have been inspired by *The Merry Wives of Windsor* or provided some hints to Shakespeare for *The Merry Wives of Windsor* (depending on which play was actually written first).
27. William Jaggard (1569–1623), printer and bookseller, published *The Passionate Pilgrim* in 1599, attributing all 21 poems to Shakespeare. Poems I and II are inferior versions of Shakespeare's Sonnets 138 and 144, while III, V, and XVI are taken from *Love's Labour's Lost* (see entry for September 3, 1591); the remainder are attributable to other poets. Jaggard had a history of piracy, although he and his son Isaac (1595–1627) were chosen to print the First Folio in 1623.

28. See entry for March 1, 1599.
29. *The Shoemakers' Holiday*, 5.4.57–59, in *Five Elizabethan Tragedies*, ed. A.K. McIlwraith [1963].
30. John Weever (1576–1632) published *Epigrammes in the Oldest Cut, and the Newest Fashion* in 1599. It contained the sonnet "Ad Gulielmum Shakespeare."
    Honey-tong'd *Shakespeare* when I saw thine issue
    I swore *Apollo* got them and none other,
    Their rosey-tainted features cloth'd in tissue,
    Some heaven born goddess said to be their mother:
    Rose-cheeked *Adonis* with his amber tresses,
    Fair fire-hot *Venus* charming him to love her,
    Chaste *Lucretia* virgin-like her dresses,
    Proud lust-stung *Tarquine* seeking still to prove her:
    Romea Richard; more whose names I know not,
    Their sugar'd tongues, and power attractive beauty
    Say they are Saints although that Sts they show not
    For thousands vows to them subjective duty:
    They burn in love thy children *Shakespear* let them,
    Go, woo thy Muse more Nymphish brood beget them.
    Since this is the only Shakespearean sonnet in the collection, Weever may have seen some of Shakespeare's sonnets in manuscript (see E.A.J. Honigman, *John Weever* [1987], p. 90). He also wrote epigrammes on Edward Alleyn, John Marston, and Jonson.
31. Edmund Shakespeare (1580–1607) was the youngest son of John and Mary Shakespeare.
32. Thomas Platter, a Swiss physician who visited England from September 18 to October 20, 1599, recorded his visit to the Globe and the performance of *Julius Caesar*: "After dinner on the 21st of September, at about two o'clock, I went over the river with my companions, and in the straw thatched house saw the Tragedy of the first Emperor Julius Caesar, with at least fifteen characters, which was acted very well. As is their custom, at the end of the play two actors in men's clothes and two in women's clothes danced extremely well together."
33. Robert Armin (c. 1568–1615), actor and dramatist, replaced Will Kempe as the Chamberlain's comedian sometime in 1599.
34. Essex returned to England sometime on September 27 or 28, 1599, and met with Elizabeth early on the 28th at her favorite autumn retreat, Nonsuch Palace, Surrey.
35. A play written collectively by Drayton, Richard Hathaway, Anthony Munday, and Robert Wilson (d. 1600).

36. "The doubtful Title (Gentlemen) prefixt / Upon the Argument we have in hand, / May breed suspence, and wrongfully disturb / The peaceful quiet of your settled thoughts. / To stop which scruple, let this brief suffice: / It is no pampered glutton we present, / Nor aged Counsellor to youthful sin, / But one, whose virtue shone above the rest, A valiant Martyr and a virtuous peer; / In whose true faith and loyalty expressed / Unto his sovereign, and his country's weal, / We strive to pay that tribute of our Love, / Your favours merit. Let fair Truth be graced, / Since forged invention former time defaced."
37. Some possible allusions to Shakespeare's plays in *Oldcastle* are: 1) the Welsh character Davy echoes Fluellen in *Henry V*; 2) In 3.4 Henry V says "I'll to Westminster in this disguise, / To hear what news is stirring in these brawls," which recalls Henry moving amongst his men in disguise before the Battle of Agincourt in *Henry V*; 3) Henry V is accosted in 3.4. with references to Falstaff and Poins that recall the robbery at Gadshill in *Henry IV Part 1*, 2.2; 4) in 5.1 there is a reference to Julius Caesar's assassination (cf. *Julius Caesar*, 3.1).
38. See entry for April 26, 1599.
39. In *Every Man Out*, Puntarvolo suggests Sogliardo's motto should be "Not without mustard," a play on Shakespeare's father's motto, *Non sanz droit* (see entry for October 21, 1596).
40. Some allusions to Shakespeare's plays include: 1) "let your imagination be swifter than a pair of oars" (4.6), cf. the Prologue and choruses to *Henry V*; 2) aspects of Puntarvolo and his dog are reminiscent of Launce and his dog, Crab, in *The Two Gentlemen of Verona*; 3) "this is a kinsman to justice Silence" (5.1), cf. *Henry IV Part 2*; 4) "et tu, Brute!" (5.4), cf. *Julius Caesar*; 5) the reference to Falstaff in the final words of 5.7.
41. Othello's reaction in *Othello* is diametrically opposite to Shakespeare's decision here.
42. When *Every Man Out* was published in Jonson's First Folio (1616) it carried the following postscript: "This Comicall Satyre was first acted in the yeere 1599. By the then Lord Chamberlaine his Seruants. The principall Comoedians were, Ric. Burbadge, Ioh. Hemings, Aug. Philips, Hen. Condel, Wil. Sly, Tho. Pope. With the allowance of the Master of the Revels."
43. The source for *As You Like It* was Thomas Lodge's *Rosalynde, or Euphues' Golden Legacy* (1590).
44. Thomas Morley (c. 1557–1602) was a musician and composer, particularly of madrigals.
45. See "for since the little wit that fools have was silenced" (1.2.82–83).
46. See Jaques's "All the world's a stage" (2.7.139), which echoes the Globe's motto *totus mundus agit histrionem* (all the world plays the actor).

47. See "it strikes a man more dead than a great reckoning in a little room" (3.3.11–12) and the entry for July 1, 1593. See also "Dead Shepherd [Marlowe], now I find thy saw of might, / 'Who ever loved that loved not at first sight?'" (3.5.80–81). Line 81 quotes Marlowe's *Hero and Leander*, I, 175.
48. See entry for November 3, 1599.
49. The land, on the other side of the Thames from the Globe and the Rose theaters, was between Golden Lane and Whitecross Street.
50. The Fortune, which cost £520 to build, was ready in October 1600. Alleyn acted there from 1600–05 when he again retired, although he remained a successful theater manager.
51. Jonson's son, Joseph, was baptized at St. Giles's, Cripplegate.
52. The Lord Chamberlain's Men performed at Court on December 26, 1599, January 6, and February 3, 1600.

1600
1. Thomas Heywood (1573/74–1641) was an actor and prolific dramatist who borrowed from Shakespeare's plays on several occasions. The best of his more than 200 plays is *A Woman Killed with Kindness* (1603).
2. The Admiral's Men performed Dekker's *The Shoemakers' Holiday* at Court on January 1, 1600.
3. *The Return from Parnassus* (Part I) was performed at St. John's College, Cambridge, on December 29, 1599. Nashe had been a student at St. John's from 1582–89; Heywood also attended Cambridge. In 3.1 of *The Return* the lovesick Gullio quotes from *Venus and Adonis*, while in 4.1 he says he will honour Shakespeare by placing a copy of the poem under his pillow. *Venus and Adonis* was very popular, going through 11 editions by 1620.
4. Shakespeare possibly recalled this incident in writing *Measure for Measure*. There has been some speculation that Black Luce was the "Dark Lady" of the sonnets.
5. Kempe reached Norwich on March 11, 1600. He published an account of his feat, *Kemps Nine Daies Wonder*, later in 1600.
6. William Holme (fl. 1589–1615), publisher, entered *Every Man Out of his Humour* in the Stationers' Register on April 8, 1600. The play went through three quarto editions in 1600.
7. In *Every Man Out* 3.1 Jonson probably satirizes Marston's bombastic style through the character of Clove. The virulent remarks directed towards Carlo Buffone also render that character a likely satire of Marston. Marston had earlier portrayed Jonson as Chrisoganus, a poet and philosopher, in his *Histriomastix* (1599).
8. *Antonio and Mellida* was acted by the Children of Paul's in 1599.

9. In September 1599 Henslowe paid 40 shillings to a "Mr Maxton," who was probably Marston.
10. See entries for June 5 and 9, 1594, particularly the anonymous *Hamlet*.
11. *Antonio and Mellida* contains a scene similar to the closet scene in Shakespeare's *Hamlet*.
12. Southampton carried letters from Essex to Mountjoy asking him to invade Wales as a means of forcing Essex's release. By May 7 Mountjoy had determined Essex was in no danger and that a rebellion was unnecessary.
13. Essex was examined by the Privy Council on June 5, 1600, from 9 A.M. until 8 P.M.
14. The Privy Council issued the order on June 22, 1600.
15. In fact, the Curtain survived the Council's order. It was referred to in 1627 and may have survived until 1660.
16. The Moravian Baron Waldstein (1581–1623) noted in his diary for this date that he saw an English play and that the spectators commanded a comfortable view of every part of the theater. He also noted the heads of traitors fixed on London Bridge (see *The Diary of Baron Waldstein, a Traveller in Elizabethan England* [1981]).
17. See entries for June 5 and July 12, 1599.
18. In order to try to prevent pirate editions, Roberts entered blocking registrations for *Henry V, As You Like It, Much Ado About Nothing*, as well as for Jonson's *Every Man in his Humour*.
19. Thomas Pavier (d. 1625) registered a pirated version of *Henry V* on August 14, 1600, published later in 1600 as the first "bad" quarto. He had also registered *Sir John Oldcastle Part 1* on August 11, 1600.
20. The Gowrie conspiracy took place on August 5, 1600. James VI (later James I of England) alleged he had been lured to Gowrie house in Scotland where an attempt was made on his life. The 3rd Earl of Gowrie (John Ruthven) and his brother, Alexander, were killed during the confusion. It is possible James staged the event himself in order to eliminate his enemies.
21. Nathaniel Giles (c. 1559–1634) was appointed Master of the Children of the Chapel in 1597. Giles's co-lessee and business manager was Henry Evans (c. 1543–1608). The boys' company began performing September 29, 1600, and comprised the following boy actors: Robert Baxter; John Chapel or Chappell (c. 1590–c. 1632); Thomas Day (d. 1654); Nathan Field (1587–1620), who also became a dramatist and who joined the King's Men c. 1616; John Frost (d. 1640); Thomas Grimer; Thomas Morton; John Motteram; William Ostler, who also became a King's Man in 1608; Salathiel or Salomon Pavy (c. 1588–1602); Philip Pykman (b. 1587); Alvery Trussell; John Underwood (c. 1588–1624), who also became a King's Man in 1608.

22. Shakespeare's sister, Joan (1569–1646), had married William Hart (d. 1616), a hatter. Their son, William (1600–39), was christened in Stratford on August 28, 1600. In his will Shakespeare left £5 each to William and his brothers, Thomas (1605–61) and Michael (1608–18).
23. Thomas, Lord Grey of Wilton (d. 1614). See entries for January 10, 1601; February 2, 1601; December 5, 1603; and December 15, 1603.
24. Thomas Fisher (fl. 1600–01) published the first quarto of *A Midsummer Night's Dream* in 1600, having registered it in the Stationers' Register on October 8, 1600.
25. See *Hamlet* 2.2.320–54.
26. "*Polonius*: I did enact Julius Caesar. I was killed i' th' Capitol; Brutus killed me" (*Hamlet* 3.2.99–100). The joke is that Brutus and Hamlet were played by the same actor who "killed" Julius Caesar and Polonius, both of whom were played by the same actor.
27. Richard Hooker (c. 1554–1600) was the author of *Of the Laws of Ecclesiastical Polity* (1593, 1597), which advocated the moderate position Anglicanism occupied between the two opposing extremes of Roman Catholicism and, in particular, Puritanism. He died on November 2, 1600.
28. Dekker's play is no longer extant.
29. See *Romeo and Juliet* 3.1.134.
30. See *Hamlet* 5.2.211–12
31. See *Hamlet* 3.4.2. The Lord Chamberlain's Men did perform for the Court at Whitehall on December 26, 1600 and January 6, 1601, although the plays are unrecorded.
32. Prince Charles (1600–49) was born November 19, 1600; he became Charles I in 1625.
33. The performance date of *Cynthia's Revels* is not known. Jonson's satire was directed most probably at Dekker, Lodge, Marston, and Munday. The play's subtitle, *The Fountain of Self-Love*, more than hints at Essex's behavior. Nathan Field probably played Amorphous. He became Jonson's protégée and eventually one of the era's leading actors. In *Bartholomew Fair* (5.3) Jonson alludes to Field and Richard Burbage as the best actors.
34. The Children of the Chapel may have performed *Cynthia's Revels* for Elizabeth at Whitehall on January 6, 1601, or possibly just music and songs or carols since the Lord Chamberlain's Men also performed for her on that day.
35. See the entry for November 25, 1596. Field was among those who petitioned against the use of Blackfriars by Shakespeare's company.

1601

1. Orsino may have given Shakespeare a hint for the character in *Twelfth Night*.

2. See the Induction to Marston's *Antonio and Mellida*. Shakespeare uses "personated," meaning represented, in *Twelfth Night*, 2.3.146.
3. Armin probably acted Feste in *Twelfth Night*, in which Feste sings three songs. There are also the catches and snatches in 2.3. and elsewhere.
4. John Sadler (1561–1625) was a friend of Shakespeare.
5. Sir Edward Greville (b. c. 1565) was Stratford's lord of the manor.
6. Thomas Greene (d. 1640) was a Warwick man who entered the Middle Temple in 1595 and was called to the Bar in 1602. He became Town Clerk of Stratford in 1603.
7. William Parker, 4th Baron Monteagle (1575–1622), had been with Essex on his Irish campaign. He was fined £8,000 for his part in the Essex rebellion. In 1605 he was involved in exposing the Gunpowder Plot. Sir Charles Percy (d. 1628), a descendant of the historical Hotspur (1364–1403) who appears in *Richard II* and *Henry IV Part 1*, was fined £5,000 for his role in the rebellion. Sir Gelly Meyrick (1556–1601) was Essex's household steward.
8. Blount (d. 1601) was Essex's stepfather.
9. Captain Thomas Lee (1552/3–1601). See also the entry for February 13, 1601.
10. Lee was tried at Newgate on February 15 and hanged at Tyburn on February 18, 1601.
11. These were Sir Christopher Blount, Sir Charles Danvers (1568–1601), Sir Gelly Meyrick, Sir John Davies, and Henry Cuffe (d. 1601), Essex's secretary.
12. The subtitle of *Twelfth Night* is *What You Will*.
13. The Lord Mayor had offered £100 for the names of the authors of "libels" published about Elizabeth's counsellors. One such "libel" was a contemporary rhyme about Elizabeth's chief minister, Robert Cecil: "Little Cecil trips up and down / He rules both court and crown."
14. Anne's father was Richard Hathaway (d. 1581). His shepherd, Thomas Whittington (d. 1601), left 40 shillings, which Anne owed him, to the poor of Stratford.
15. Henry Percy, 9th Earl of Northumberland (1564–1632), was Essex's brother-in-law. Sympathetic to the Catholic cause but actually innocent of treason, he was fined £30,000 and imprisoned in the Tower of London for 16 years after the 1605 Gunpowder Plot. The "Wizard Earl" was also associated with Ralegh and the supposed intellectual circle known as the "school of night," which might be alluded to in *Love's Labour's Lost* 4.3.250.
16. Bacon apparently received £1200 for writing *A Declaration of the Practices and Treasons Attempted and Committed by Robert, late Earl of Essex, and his Complices*.
17. *What You Will* was not published until 1607. It was probably acted in 1601.
18. Jonson's next play in the "War of the Theatres," or the Poetomachia, was *The Poetaster* (1601). For details of the war, see the numerous references in James P. Bednarz, *Shakespeare & The Poets' War* (2001).

19. Anthony Bacon was buried at St. Olave's church in Hart Street on May 17, 1601.
20. See entry for February 3, 1601.
21. Malvolio in *Twelfth Night* has also been thought to be modelled on the Puritan Sir William Knollys (1547–1632), the Comptroller of the Queen's Household. Knollys was notoriously infatuated with his ward, Mary Fitton (c. 1578–1647), another candidate for the "Dark Lady" of the *Sonnets*. In February 1601 Fitton had given birth to a stillborn child she had conceived with William Herbert, 3rd Earl of Pembroke (1580–1630). See Leslie Hotson, *The First Night of Twelfth Night* (1954).
22. Shakespeare inherited his father's two Henley Street houses. He rented one at a nominal charge to his sister Joan, and the other to Lewis Hiccox (d. 1627), who, in 1603, acquired a license for an inn. It was eventually called the Maidenhead Inn.
23. Sir Anthony Shirley (1565–c. 1635) and his brother Robert enjoyed several fantastic adventures, including an expedition to Persia in 1599. The latter was reported in *The True Report of Sir Anthony Shirley's Journey* (1600). This pamphlet and Kempe's return to England in September 1601 may account for the references to "the Sophy" in *Twelfth Night* 2.5.166–67 and 3.4.261–62.
24. Jonson's *The Poetaster* was performed by the Children of the Chapel at Blackfriars c. September 15, 1601.
25. The 1616 folio edition of Jonson's works listed as actors of *The Poetaster*: Nathan Field, Salathiel Pavy, Thomas Day, John Underwood, William Ostler, and Thomas Morton.
26. In Act 1 Ovid senior declares: "What! shall I have my son a stager now? an enghle [catamite] for players?" In Act 3 Tucca tells Histrio: "I will not part from them [his page boys]; you'll sell them for engles."
27. *Satiromastix* contains allusions to these three Jonsonian traits.
28. In Act 3 of *The Poetaster* Tucca talks of paying a "rhymer" 40 shillings (i.e. £2) for his work.
29. See entry for November 11, 1601.
30. Brend was owner of the Globe site; see entry for December 12, 1598. On October 7, 1601 he mortgaged his properties to his stepbrother, John Bodley (see Park Honan, *Shakespeare: A Life* [1998], pp. 268–69).
31. Samuel Crosse (1568?–1605?) was possibly Heminges's apprentice.
32. *Satiromastix* was the last play in the "War of the Theatres" or Poetomachia.
33. See *Twelfth Night*, 2.3.105–08: "*Sir Toby Belch*: Dost thou think, because thou [Malvolio] art virtuous, there shall be no more cakes and ale? *Feste*: Yes, by Saint Anne, and ginger shall be hot i' th' mouth too." Armin liked ginger washed down with ale.

34. The Chamberlain's Men performed at Court on December 26, 1601 and January 1, and February 14, 1602.
35. The subtitle of *Cynthia's Revels* is *The Fountain of Self-Love*.
36. *The Poetaster* was entered in the Stationers' Register on December 21, 1601 by the bookseller Matthew Lownes (fl. 1591–1625), who published it in 1602.
37. Cuthbert Burbage's daughter, Elizabeth, was baptized at St. Leonard's, Shoreditch, on December 30, 1601.

1602
1. Kempe and Thomas Heywood were the payees for the performance of an unknown play given on January 3, 1602. In March 1602 Worcester's Men were obliged to merge with Oxford's Men and played at the Boar's Head Inn. By the summer of 1602 they were with Henslowe at the Rose.
2. See also the entry on Shakespeare's first meeting with Heywood, January 4, 1600.
3. Nashe was 34 years old in 1601. The circumstances and exact date of his death are not known.
4. The anonymous *The Second Part of the Return From Parnassus* was performed by students of St. John's College, Cambridge, probably at Christmas 1601. The incidents recounted in this entry occur in 4.3 and 4.4 of the play.
5. In the *Parnassus* play the student Philomusus recites Richard III's opening soliloquy, "Now is the winter of our discontent."
6. The title page of the 1603 first quarto, the so-called "bad" quarto, describes *Hamlet* "As it hath beene diuerse times acted by his Highnesse seruants in the Cittie of London: as also in the two Vniuersities of Cambridge and Oxford, and else-where."
7. *The Merry Wives of Windsor* was entered in the Stationers' Register on January 18, 1602 by John Busby (fl. 1576–1619), who published the bad quarto of *Henry V*. On the same day, he transferred *The Merry Wives of Windsor* to Arthur Johnson (d. 1630), who published the bad quarto of *The Merry Wives of Windsor* in 1602.
8. Edward Curle was a law student at the Middle Temple while William Towse was a member of the Inner Temple.
9. John Manningham (c. 1575–1622) also belonged to the Middle Temple and is notable for a diary he kept in 1602–03.
10. Manningham's *Diary* for March 13, 1602 relates this story.
11. Christopher Mountjoy died in 1620, his wife died in 1606. "Tires" were women's elaborate ornamental headdresses made from gold, silver, and jewels.
12. Heminges and Condell lived in the adjacent parish of St. Mary's, Aldermanbury, where Condell was a churchwarden and Heminges a sidesman (see S. Schoenbaum, *William Shakespeare: A Compact Documentary Life* [1977], p. 260).

13. Manningham's *Diary* provides the following account of the performance: "At our feast wee had a play called 'Twelue Night, or What You Will', much like the Commedy of Errores, or Menechmi in Plautus, but most like and neere to that in Italian called *Inganni*. A good practise in it to make the Steward beleeve his Lady widdowe was in love with him, by counterfeyting a letter as from his Lady in generall termes, telling him what shee liked best in him, and prescribing his gesture in smiling, his apparaile, and then when he came to practise making him beleeue they tooke him to be mad."
14. Donne had become secretary to Sir Thomas Egerton (1540–1617), Lord Keeper of the Great Seal. He married Lady Egerton's niece, Ann More (d. 1617), secretly and without Elizabeth's permission. Donne lost his position and was imprisoned briefly.
15. See entry for January 21, 1602.
16. See *Hamlet*, 2.2.434–506.
17. In April–May 1599 Dekker and Henry Chettle were paid £5 by Philip Henslowe for *Troylles and Cresida*, a lost play. Robert Henryson (c. 1425/30?– c. 1506?) wrote the sequel to Chaucer's *Troilus and Criseyde* (c. 1385) entitled *The Testament of Cresseid*.
18. George Chapman's translation of Books I, II, VII–XI of Homer's *Iliad* was published in 1598 as *Seven Books of the Iliads*, a source for Shakespeare's *Troilus and Cressida*.
19. Worcester's Men were granted their official license to perform in London on March 31, 1602. Dekker wrote five plays for them in 1602.
20. On May 1, 1602, Shakespeare bought 107 acres of arable land and 20 acres of pasture in Old Stratford for £320. The land was owned by William Combe (1551–1610), a Warwickshire lawyer and Member of Parliament, and his nephew John Combe (c. 1560–1614), a wealthy usurer in Stratford. Shakespeare's brother, Gilbert (1566–1612), received the conveyance of the land on Shakespeare's behalf.
21. Compare Romeo's farewell in *Romeo and Juliet*, 3.5 with *Troilus and Cressida*, 4.2, where, after consummating their love, Troilus and Cressida awake to Pandarus's bawdy innuendoes and the news that Cressida is to be handed over to the Greeks.
22. Gilbert had resided in St. Bride's Parish, London, in 1597, where he was a haberdasher (see Eccles, *Shakespeare in Warwickshire*, p. 108). How long he lived in London is unknown.
23. No performance of *Troilus and Cressida* was recorded in Shakespeare's lifetime, although it may have been performed at one of the Inns of Court.
24. Richard Quiney had been elected bailiff of Stratford for the second time in September 1601, having occupied that position previously in 1592–93. On

May 3, 1602, while trying to keep the peace, he was mortally wounded during a brawl with some drunken servants employed by Sir Edward Greville, the local lord of the manor, who had opposed Quiney's election.

25. On May 22, 1602, Philip Henslowe advanced £5 to Munday, Michael Drayton, Thomas Middleton (1570–1627), and John Webster (c. 1580–c. 1634/38) for a (lost) play to be entitled *Caesar's Fall*. Henslowe's diary entry is the earliest record of Middleton and Webster as dramatists.
26. The earliest published text of *Julius Caesar* is that in the 1623 First Folio.
27. Henslowe paid Jonson £10 in advance for a play to be called "Richard Crookback" and for additions to *The Spanish Tragedy*. The former play has not survived.
28. The 1575 edition of *The Palace of Pleasure* by William Painter (c. 1540–94) contained 101 stories Painter had translated from different Latin, Italian, and French sources, including Boccaccio's *Decameron*. *The Palace of Pleasure* provided Shakespeare with sources for the plots of *Romeo and Juliet*, *All's Well That Ends Well*, and *Timon of Athens*.
29. *All's Well That Ends Well* reflects Shakespeare's earlier style; see, for example, the sonnet at 1.1.208, and the extensive use of couplets in 2.1.130–210.
30. Lavatch is the "clown role" which Armin would, presumably, have played.
31. Pavy was buried at St. Mary Somerset, London, on July 25, 1602. He had acted with the Children of the Chapel and in Jonson's plays, notably *Cynthia's Revels* and *The Poetaster*.
32. Roberts registered the first, so-called bad quarto of *Hamlet* on July 26, 1602.
33. Charles de Gontaut, Duke of Biron (1562–1602), was beheaded in the Bastille, Paris, on July 19, 1602, for conspiring with Spain against France's Henri IV.
34. Stuhlweissenburg [Székesfehérvár] was a Hungarian fortress city destroyed during the Turkish occupation of 1543–1688. The unidentified play was witnessed by Philip Julius, Duke of Stettin-Pomerania, and his secretary, Frederic Gerschow.
35. The anonymous *Thomas Lord Cromwell* was registered on August 11, 1602, and published later the same year. It was republished in 1613 and 1664, and has been attributed to Shakespeare by only a few critics.
36. On September 28, 1602, Walter Getley transferred the copyhold of a cottage and garden located at the corner of Chapel Street and Chapel Lane to Shakespeare. Covering about a quarter of an acre, the property lay across from the gardens of Shakespeare's New Place. Shakespeare paid an annual rent of two shillings and sixpence for his latest acquisition.
37. Morley died in early October 1602, probably before October 11. His position at the Chapel Royal had been taken over by a George Woodson on October 7, 1602.

38. The Admiral's Men performed Robert Greene's *Friar Bacon and Friar Bungay* on December 27, 1602. The title of the play performed by the Chamberlain's Men on December 26, 1602 was not actually recorded.

1603

1. Juliet or Julia Burbage was baptized at St. Leonard's, Shoreditch, on January 2, 1603.
2. Turner himself was murdered on May 11, 1612.
3. Thomas Pope's apprentice, Robert Gough, married Augustine Phillips's sister, Elizabeth, on February 13, 1603.
4. The play was performed in February 1603 at the Rose by Worcester's Men.
5. The subplot of *A Woman Killed with Kindness* is taken from Painter's *The Palace of Pleasure*; Shakespeare had recently used Painter's work for *All's Well That Ends Well* (see entry for July 4, 1602).
6. See Frankford's speech:

    Oh God, oh God, that it were possible
    To undo things done, to call back yesterday;
    That time could turn up his swift sandy glass,
    To untell the days, and to redeem these hours;
    Or that the sun
    Could, rising from the West, draw his coach backward,
    Take from the account of time so many minutes
    Till he had all these seasons call'd again,
    Those minutes and those actions done in them,
    Even from her first offence, that I might take her
    As spotless as an angel in my arms (*Woman Killed with Kindness*, 4.4.51–61).

7. *Dr. Faustus*, scene 19, 136–37. See also all of Faustus's final speech, scene 19, 134–90.
8. In *A Woman Killed with Kindness*, Frankford's wife, Anne, commits adultery with Wendoll. Frankford exiles Anne to live entirely alone but surrounded with every comfort and convenience. His generosity and kindness overwhelms Anne who wastes away and dies just moments after the couple are finally reconciled.
9. Inigo Jones (1573–1652) had studied in Italy. He was architect to Queen Anne, surveyor-general of royal buildings, and designer of Court masques, often collaborating with Jonson. Thomas Campion (1567–1620), poet and composer, wrote a masque in honour of the marriage of Sir James Hay which was performed in the Great Hall at Whitehall on January 6, 1607.
10. The playhouses were closed generally from March 1603–April 1604 because of the plague.

11. Drayton's poem, published before Elizabeth's funeral, failed to secure James's patronage.
12. Elizabeth died at about 2 A.M. at Richmond in Surrey. Seventy years old, she had reigned just over 44 years and five months.
13. Sir Robert Townshend (1535?–1614?) was also the patron of John Fletcher, who wrote a commendatory verse entitled "To the Perfect Gentleman Sir Robert Townshend" which prefaced Fletcher's *The Faithful Shepherdess* (c. 1609).
14. Jonson's preface to the 1605 quarto edition of *Sejanus* indicates that "a second pen had a good share" in the original version of the play. Both Chapman and Shakespeare have been suggested as that "second pen," whose work Jonson replaced with his own "weaker, and no doubt, less pleasing" version in the quarto edition.
15. On March 26, 1603, Elizabeth's body was moved from Richmond by river to lie in state at Whitehall.
16. Elizabeth Condell was buried at St. Mary's, Aldermanbury.
17. "Pro Laurentio Fletcher et Willielmo Shakespeare et aliis. James by the Grace of God, etc., to all Justices, Majors, Sheriffs, Constables, Headboroughs, and other our Officers and lovinge Subjects, Greetinge. Knowe ye that wee of our Speciall Grace, certeine knowledge, and mere motion, have licensed and authorized, and by these presentes doe license and authorise these our Servaunts, Lawrence Fletcher, William Shakespeare, Richard Burbage, Augustine Phillippes, John Hemings, Henrie Condell, William Sly, Robert Armyn, Richard Cowly, and the rest of their Associates, Freely to use and exercise the Art and Facultie of playing Comedies, Tragedies, Histories, Enterludes, Morals, Pastoralls, Stage Plaies and such others, like as these have alreadie studied or hereafter shall use or studie, as well for our Solace and Pleasure, when wee shall thincke good to see them, during our Pleasure; and the said Commedies, Tragedies, Histories, Enterludes, Moralls, Pastoralls, Stage-playes, and suche like, to shewe and exercise publiquely to their best Commoditie, when the Infection of the Plague shall decrease, as well within their nowe usual house called the Globe within our countie of Surrey, as also within anie Towne Halls, or Moote Halls, or other convenient places within the Liberties and Freedom of anie other Cittie, Universitie, Toune or Boroughe whatsoever within our saide Realmes and Dominions.
Willing and commaunding you and everie of you, as you tender our Pleasure, not onelie to permit and suffer them here-in, without anie your Letts, Hindrances, or Molestations, during our said Pleasure, but also to be aiding and assistinge to them if anie Wronge be to them offered, and to allow them such former curtesies as hath been given to men of their Place and Qualitie; and

also what further Favour you shall shewe to theise our servaunts for our sake, Wee shall take it kindly at your handes. In witnesse whereof, etc. Witnesse our selfe at Westminster the nynetenth Daye of Maye in the first year of our reign. Per Breve de Privato Sigillo."

18. Lawrence Fletcher (d. 1608) was a member of a group of English actors that visited Scotland, and apparently he became a favorite of King James. He does not appear to have been an active member of Shakespeare's company.
19. The cast of *Sejanus* included Burbage, Shakespeare, Phillips, Heminges, Sly, Condell, John Lowin (1576–1653), and Alexander Cooke (1583?–1614). *Sejanus* is the last play in which Shakespeare is known to have acted.
20. The first "bad" quarto of *Hamlet* was printed by Valentine Simes (d. 1622?) for the booksellers Nicholas Ling (d. c. 1607–10) and John Trundell (fl. 1589–26). Trundell did business in the Barbican at the Sign of Nobody.
21. During June and July 1603 plague deaths increased progressively from 30 to 1,396 per week. See F. P. Wilson, *The Plague in Shakespeare's London* (1927).
22. See the entry for July 1, 1593.
23. During the summer of 1603 some of the King's Men toured Richmond, Bath, Coventry, and Shrewsbury.
24. On June 25, 1603, Jonson presented his short masque, *The Satyr or the Entertainment at Althorp*, to Anne of Denmark (1574–1619) and her son Prince Henry (1594–1612) at Althorp, Northamptonshire, the home of Sir Robert Spencer (1570–1627). As a reward Spencer was created a baron.
25. Jonson may have lived with Esmé Stuart Aubigny (1579–1624) from 1602–07. The 1605 quarto edition of *Sejanus* was dedicated to Lord Aubigny.
26. This took place on July 21, 1603.
27. On July 14, 1603 Sir Walter Ralegh, Lord Cobham, and Lord Grey were arrested for conspiring to place Lady Arabella Stuart (1575–1615) on the throne. This was the so-called "main plot." Around the same time, Anthony Copley, Sir Griffin Markham, and two Catholic priests, William Watson and William Clarke, were arrested for plotting to kidnap King James and force him to grant religious toleration. This was the so-called "bye plot," though the two conspiracies were not actually linked to one another.
28. In July and August 1603 the weekly total of plague deaths was close to 2,000, rising occasionally to 3,000.
29. Thomas Digges (1545–95) was a mathematician and astronomer. On Leveson, see the entry for December 12, 1598.
30. Tycho Brahe (1546–1601) had studied law at various universities including Wittenburg (where Hamlet "studied") but devoted himself to astronomy. Johannes Kepler (1571–1630) was Brahe's assistant 1600–01.

31. Anne Digges (1555?–1637) and Russell were married at Rushock, Worcestershire, on August 26, 1603.
32. The sons were Dudley (1583–1639) and Leonard Digges (1588–1635). Dudley was knighted in 1607 and was involved in politics and financing colonial expeditions, as was Leveson. Leonard studied at Oxford University, became a translator and poet, and contributed a commendatory poem to the First Folio of Shakespeare's plays.
33. They were buried in Bermondsey on August 29, 1603. See also the entry for November 29, 1596.
34. Jonson and Camden stayed with one of Camden's former students, Sir Robert Cotton (1571–1631), an antiquary who accumulated a large library that went eventually to the British Museum (now the British Library).
35. For the week ending October 6, 1603, plague deaths numbered 1,641 and fell gradually week by week until the end of the year when less than 100 deaths weekly were recorded.
36. Alleyn's servant was John Bradley; he was buried at St. Leonard's, Shoreditch.
37. *Promos and Cassandra* (1578) by George Whetstone (1550–87) was a main source for *Measure for Measure*.
38. The date of Kempe's death is unknown. "Kempe a man" was buried at St. Saviour's on November 2, 1603.
39. James eventually imprisoned Lady Arabella in 1610 when she married William Seymour (1588–1660) without his permission. She died in the Tower of London.
40. See the entry for January 2, 1597.
41. Mary Herbert, Countess of Pembroke (1561–1621), was Sir Philip Sidney's sister and mother of William Herbert, 3rd Earl of Pembroke (1580–1630), who owned Wilton House.
42. Mary Herbert translated *Marc-Antoine* (1579) by Robert Garnier (1545–90) as *Antonius, A Tragoedie* (1592).
43. Grey was tried on December 7, 1603 and found guilty. The trial lasted from 8 A.M. to 8 P.M.
44. The King's Men performed at Court on December 26, 27, 28, and 30, 1603.
45. Pope's will was probated on February 13, 1604.

1604

1. In 1597 King James had published his *Daemonology*, in which he attacked *The Discovery of Witchcraft* (1584) by Reginald Scot (1538?–99). The latter book was a source for some of the supernatural elements in *A Midsummer Night's Dream*, *Macbeth*, and *The Tempest*.

2. The source for *Othello* occurs in III:7 of *Hecatommithi* (1565) by Giraldi Cinthio (1504–73).
3. Both Whetstone's *Promos and Cassandra* and Shakespeare's *Measure for Measure* are based on *Hecatommithi* VIII:5.
4. On February 2, 1604, the King's Men performed at Court before James and the ambassador from Florence.
5. *The Fair Maid of Bristow*, an anonymous comedy.
6. The patent was issued to Edward Kirkham (1550?–1617), Alexander Hawkins, Thomas Kendall (1563?–1608), and Robert Payne (d. 1622), and authorised the Children to perform in the recently renovated theater in Blackfriars.
7. See the entry for January 7, 1604.
8. John Whitgift (c. 1530–1604) had been Archbishop of Canterbury since 1583 and had opposed both Puritan and Catholic extremists.
9. An allusion to these arches might be hinted in the "pyramids" of Sonnet 123: "No, Time, thou shalt not boast that I do change. / Thy pyramids built up with newer might / To me are nothing novel, nothing strange; / They are but dressings of a former sight."
10. Stephen Belott who died c. 1646.
11. In 1612 Stephen Belott brought a lawsuit against Christopher Mountjoy claiming Mountjoy had failed to provide a promised dowry of £60 and to leave him £200 in his will.
12. Jonson's masque, *The Penates, or, The Entertainment at Highgate*, was performed on May 1, 1604, when the king and queen visited Sir William Cornwallis (1579?–1614) at his home in Highgate, London.
13. *The Malcontent* was performed by the Children of the Queen's Revels some time after February 4, 1604, at Blackfriars. It was entered in the Stationers' Register on July 5, 1604, and published later in the year.
14. See, for example: "Who cannot feign friendship can ne'er produce the effects of hatred. Honest fool Duke, subtle, lascivious Duchess, silly novice Ferneze— I do laugh at ye! My brain is in labour till it produce mischief, and I feel sudden throes, proofs sensible the issue is at hand. As bears shape young, so I'll form my device, / Which grown, proves horrid; vengeance makes men wise" (1.2.172–78).
15. Edward de Vere, Earl of Oxford, died in Hackney, London, on June 24, 1604, and was buried in the parish church of St. Augustine on July 6, 1604.
16. Augustine or Austen Phillips was buried at St. Saviour's, Southwark, on July 1, 1604.
17. Frances Burbage was baptized at St. Leonard's, Shoreditch, on September 16, 1604. She was buried on September 19, 1604.

18. Richard Bancroft (1544–1610) had been appointed Bishop of London in 1597.
19. See the entry for March 24, 1593.
20. Charles (1600–49) did not speak until he was five, and he crawled on hands and knees until he was seven.
21. *Sejanus* was entered in the Stationers' Register on November 2, 1604, by Edward Blount, and published in 1605.
22. Beeston was probably Augustine Phillips's apprentice before joining Worcester's Men in 1602; he eventually became manager of Queen Anne's Men in 1612.
23. St. Olave's was in Silver Street.
24. George Wilkins (c. 1575–1618), minor dramatist, writer and innkeeper, was author of the novel *The Painful Adventures of Pericles Prince of Tyre* (1608), apparently based upon *Pericles*. Wilkins was also a reputed brothel-keeper and generally shady character (see Roger Prior, "The Life of George Wilkins," *Shakespeare Survey*, 25 [1972], 137–52).
25. The second quarto edition of *Hamlet* was published in 1604 "according to the true and perfect Coppie." See entry for May 27, 1603.
26. Between March 27 and May 30, 1604, Shakespeare had sold several bushels of malt to the Stratford apothecary, Philip Rogers, and had also lent him two shillings. Rogers repaid only six shillings, and so Shakespeare brought a lawsuit for the remainder; William Tetherton acted as his solicitor.
27. Sometime in the first half of December 1604, the King's Men performed a tragedy on the Gowrie conspiracy (an attempt to assassinate King James by the Earl of Gowrie on August 5, 1600). The play apparently incurred some official displeasure.

1605

1. The Children of the Chapel performed Chapman's play on January 1, 1605 at Court.
2. Jonson's *Masque of Blackness* was performed in the Old Banqueting House, Whitehall, on January 6, 1605.
3. The ladies included: Lady Rich, Penelope Devereux (d. 1607), who was openly cohabiting with Lord Charles Mountjoy whom she married after divorcing her husband in 1605; Lady Frances Bevill; Elizabeth, Countess of Derby; Anne Howard, Lady Effingham (d. 1638); Lady Anne Herbert; Lady Elizabeth Howard (d. 1658); Catherine Howard, Countess of Suffolk; and Lady Audrey Walsingham.
4. See entry for December 27, 1599.
5. Sir Walter Cope (d. 1614) was a courtier and Chamberlain of the Exchequer.
6. A son was born to Southampton on March 1, 1605.

7. The baptism took place on February 11, 1605, at St. Giles's, Cripplegate.
8. On February 11, 1605 the King's Men performed an anonymous tragedy, *The Spanish Maze*, at Court for King James.
9. See entry for April 5, 1594.
10. Anne, Phillips's wife, married John Witter (fl. 1606–20) in 1606; she thereby forfeited Phillips's share in the Globe which he had left her in his will. John Heminges leased that share to the Witters in 1611, but they were unable to retain it in 1613 when they could not meet their part of the cost of rebuilding the Globe. Anne died in 1618.
11. Ratsey was hanged at Bedford on March 26, 1605, for highway robbery. Among several pamphlets on his life and exploits was *Ratsey's Ghost*, published in 1605.
12. John Stow (1525–1605) was the author of *Works of Geoffrey Chaucer* (1561), *Annales of England* (c.1580), the second edition of Holinshed's *Chronicles* (1585–7), and *Survey of London* (1598, 1603).
13. See entry for October 15, 1607.
14. Nathaniel Butter (d. 1664) was a publisher with a shop at the sign of the Pide Bull. The title page of *The London Prodigal* reads: "The London Prodigall. As it was plaide by the Kings Maiesties seruants. By William Shakespeare. London."
15. Crosse died probably in the early months of 1605 and was replaced by Nicholas Tooley as one of the sharers in the Globe.
16. Phillips left bequests to Shakespeare, Henry Condell, Christopher Beeston, Lawrence Fletcher, Robert Armin, Richard Cowley, Alexander Cook, Nicholas Tooley, Samuel Gilburne, and James Sands. Phillips died shortly afterwards; his will was probated on May 13, 1605.
17. The anonymous play was *The True Chronicle History of King Leir, and his three daughters, Gonorill, Ragan, and Cordella*, which was registered on May 8, 1605.
18. Marston's *The Dutch Courtesan* was entered in the Stationers' Register on June 26, 1605. It had been played a little earlier by the Children of the Queen's Revels at Blackfriars.
19. See entry for March 30, 1605.
20. Shakespeare's nephew, Thomas Hart (1605–61), was christened in Stratford on July 24, 1605. See also entry for September 8, 1600.
21. On July 24, 1605, Shakespeare bought a half-share interest in the Stratford tithes for £440. They brought Shakespeare a net profit of £38 a year.
22. The play was *Eastward Ho!* and the offending passage (3.3.40–47) was directed at the large number of knights King James had created and at the large number of Scotsmen who had travelled to England to make their fortunes.
23. William Peter (1582–1612) was murdered on January 25, 1612. His death was commemorated in *A Funeral Elegy* (1612) by "W.S.," which has been

attributed, largely on a computerized analysis of word patterns, to Shakespeare. John Ford (1586–c. 1639?) has also been credited with authorship of the poem. See entry for March 1, 1612.
24. Plays were restrained from October 5 to December 15, 1605.
25. John (b. 1565) and Jane or Jennet Davenant (b. 1568) kept an inn in Cornmarket Street, Oxford. They had a daughter, Jane (1602–67), and a son, William (1606–68), who became a famous dramatist and theater manager. He was knighted in 1643.
26. King James visited Oxford on August 27, 1605, and was presented with a playlet written by Matthew Gwinne (c. 1558–1627) called *Tres Sibyllae*. In it the three sibyls prophesied the same endless power to James and his heirs that they had once prophesied for Banquo, whom James believed to be his predecessor. *Macbeth* contains possible echoes of this playlet.
27. Robert Catesby (1573–1605) was an ardent Catholic who had taken a minor role in the Essex rebellion in 1601, for which he was fined heavily. He died November 8, 1605 (see entry for November 10, 1605). The others present included Lord Henry Mordaunt (d. 1608), Sir Jocelyn Percy (d. 1631), Francis Tresham (1568–1605), Thomas Wintour or Winter (1571–1606), and John Ashfield.
28. The King's Men performed 10 of the 19 plays given over the 1605–06 Christmas period, including *Mucedorus* (1598). The latter was a very popular play; it was printed numerous times and has been attributed (falsely) to Shakespeare.
29. *Volpone; or, The Fox* was first published in 1607. When it was included in Jonson's first folio (1616) Jonson added the following: "This Comoedie was first acted, in the yeere 1605. By the K. Maiesties Servants. The principall Comoedians were Ric. Burbadge, Ioh. Heminges, Hen. Condel, Ioh. Lowin, Will Sly, Alex. Cooke."
30. Edgar in *King Lear* assumes the disguise of Tom o'Bedlam whose list of devils in 3.4 is drawn from *A Declaration of Egregious Popish Impostors* (1603) by Samuel Harsnett (1561–1631). Harsnett, who was later created Archbishop of York, had been responsible for licensing Hayward's *The First Part of the Life and Raigne of King Henrie the IIII* (see entry for June 5, 1599).
31. See entry for February 5, 1601.
32. Shakespeare was to use the metaphor extensively in *Coriolanus*.
33. Catesby and others were killed on November 8, 1605 at Holbeche House near Kingswinford, near Stourbridge.

1606

1. *Hymenaei* was performed January 5 and 6, 1606. Inigo Jones designed the masque; Alfonso Ferrabosco (c. 1575–1628) was the composer and also sang in the piece.

2. The marriage was dissolved in 1613, and Jonson then tried to squelch references to this first performance.
3. The eight principal plotters—Sir Everard Digby, Robert Wintour or Winter (1568–1606), Thomas Wintour or Winter, Ambrose Rookwood, John Grant, Guido (Guy) Fawkes (1570–1606), Robert Keyes, Thomas Bates—were tried in Westminster Hall.
4. The condemned were Thomas Bates, Sir Everard Digby, John Grant, and Robert Wintour.
5. Thomas Wintour, Guy Fawkes, Ambrose Rookwood, and Robert Keyes were executed on January 31, 1606.
6. Henry Garnet, S.J. (1555–1606) had given himself up on January 30, 1606. His advocacy of equivocation at his trial is alluded to in *Macbeth*.
7. William Davenant was christened at St. Martin's, Carfax, Oxford, on March 3, 1606.
8. See entry for October 9, 1605.
9. The subsidy was approved by Parliament on March 25, 1606.
10. See *Macbeth*, 2.3.1–19, for allusions to Garnet's trial.
11. Cordell Annesley's father was Sir Brian Annesley (d. 1603). She helped thwart the attempts of her two married sisters to have Sir Brian declared insane because his will was unfavorable to them. After Southampton's mother died, Cordell married his stepfather, Sir William Harvey, in 1608.
12. Marston's *The Wonder of Women or the Tragedy of Sophonisba* was entered in the Stationers' Register on March 17, 1606. The parallels between *Sophonisba* and *Macbeth* are discussed in Kenneth Muir's Arden edition of *Macbeth* (1962), pp. xx–xxii.
13. The name of Susanna Shakespeare and 20 other people appeared on a recusancy list for failing to receive the sacrament on Easter Day (April 20) at Holy Trinity Church, Stratford. Although she could have been fined heavily, Susanna ignored the summons to attend the vicar's court. How the matter was resolved is not known, but the charges were dropped.
14. Bacon, aged 45, married the 14-year-old Alice Barnham (1592–1650).
15. *The Fleir* by Edward Sharpham (1576–1608) borrows from *Henry IV Part 1* and *King Lear*, 1.4.9–42.
16. Middleton's *The Witch* (c. 1610) reveals some influence by *Macbeth*, and two songs from *The Witch* were at some later date interpolated into *Macbeth*.
17. Both Jonson's stepfather and Middleton's father, William (d. 1586), were bricklayers.
18. *The Revenger's Tragedy* was entered in the Stationers' Register on October 7, 1607, and published shortly thereafter. The date of its first performance is not known.

19. Northumberland spent 16 years in the Tower of London; he was fined £30,000.
20. John Hall's father was William Hall (d. 1607).
21. The King's Men performed at Oxford in late July 1606, at Leicester in August, and at Dover in September.
22. Jonson's masque, *Solomon and the Queen of Sheba*, was performed at Theobalds on July 24, 1606, to entertain King James and the King of Denmark.
23. Many subsequent productions of *Macbeth* have been attended by numerous disasters, and the play is surrounded by theatrical superstitions (see Richard Huggett, *Supernatural on Stage: Ghosts and Superstitions in the Theatre* [1975], and Michael Billington, *The Guinness Book of Theatre Facts & Feats* [1982]).
24. During the last week of July 1606 there had been 66 plague deaths in London.
25. See *Coriolanus*, 5.3; in particular 5.3.182–89.
26. Sly's son John, whom he had conceived with Margaret Chambers, was buried at St. Giles's, Cripplegate, on October 4, 1606. He had been baptized on September 24, 1606.
27. Edmund Tilney or Tylney (c. 1536–1610) served as Master of the Revels from 1578 to 1610. Tilney's nephew, Sir George Buc (1560–1622), acted as deputy Master until he succeeded Tilney in 1610.

1607
1. The King's Men performed at Court on December 29, 1606, and January 4, 6, and 8, 1607. The play titles are not known.
2. On January 22, 1607, Burby, who died in 1607, transferred the copyrights of *Romeo and Juliet*, *Love's Labour's Lost*, and *The Taming of a Shrew* to Nicholas Ling. Ling, who made his will in 1607, transferred those plays and *Hamlet* to John Smethwick (d. 1641), who was also involved in issuing the First Folio in 1623.
3. The King's Men performed *The Devil's Charter, or Pope Alexander VI* by Barnabe Barnes (1571–1609) for King James on February 2, 1607.
4. John Rice (c. 1593–after 1630) joined Lady Elizabeth's Men in 1611 and returned to the King's Men by about 1619. He appears to have retired from acting by the late 1620s.
5. The King's Men performed at Court on February 5, 15, and 27, 1607. The play titles are not known.
6. Sir Anthony Mildmay (d. 1617) lived in Apethorpe, Northamptonshire (to the west of Peterborough), and Sir Edward Montague (1562–1644) was a member of Parliament for Northamptonshire. Newton, Northamptonshire, lies between present-day Corby and Kettering.

7. Edmund Shakespeare's illegitimate son, Edward, was baptized on July 12, 1607 at St. Leonard's, Shoreditch.
8. Burbage's daughter, Anne, was baptized at St. Leonard's, Shoreditch, on August 8, 1607. Plague deaths numbered 191 in July 1607, rising to 293 in August.
9. Edmund Shakespeare's illegitimate son, Edward, was buried at St. Giles's Church, Cripplegate, on August 12, 1607.
10. Burbage's son, Richard, was buried at St. Leonard's, Shoreditch, on August 16, 1607.
11. Earlier this summer the King's Men had performed in Barnstaple and Dunwich; they visited Oxford on September 7, 1607.
12. During September 1607 plague deaths reached 527, and Parliament was prorogued until February 1608. Neither King James nor Queen Anne were present when their daughter, Mary, died at Stanwell Park, Middlesex, on September 16, 1607.
13. Robert Carr (1586–1645) was created Viscount Rochester in 1611 and Earl of Somerset in 1613. By 1614 George Villiers (1592–1628) had supplanted Carr in James's affections. Carr and his wife were imprisoned in 1616 for murdering Sir Thomas Overbury (1581–1613), although they were pardoned later. Villiers also accumulated various titles, including Duke of Buckingham in 1623.
14. Both *The Revenger's Tragedy* and *A Trick to Catch the Old One* were entered in the Stationers' Register on October 7, 1607, and subsequently published anonymously. The former play has been assigned frequently to Cyril Tourneur (c. 1575–1626).
15. *King Lear* was entered in the Stationers' Register on November 26, 1607 and the first quarto, the so-called "Pied Bull" quarto, was published in 1608.
16. Plague deaths for October 1607 numbered 523.
17. The King's Men performed at Court on December 26–28, 1607; January 2, 6–7, 9, 17, 26; and February 7, 1608.
18. Edmund Shakespeare was buried at St. Saviour's, Southwark, very close to the Globe. His funeral was apparently an expensive one since the fee for ringing the great bell of the church was 20 shillings.

1608

1. *Coriolanus*, 1.1.167–69, possibly alludes to such an occurrence: "You are no surer, no, / Than is the coal of fire upon the ice, / Or hailstone in the sun." The title page of *The Great Frost: Cold Doings in London* (1608), thought to be by Thomas Dekker, depicts a scene such as is described here.

2. Elizabeth Hall (1608–70) married Thomas Nash (1593–1647) in 1626, and Sir John Bernard (1605–74) in 1649. Both marriages were childless; thus Elizabeth was the last of Shakespeare's direct descendants.
3. Jonson's son, Benjamin (and his second son to be so named, since the first had died), was baptized at St. Anne's, Blackfriars, on February 20, 1608. He was buried on November 18, 1611.
4. Latten was either a brass alloy or tin-plated iron resembling silver. Jonson prided himself on his classical learning, and chided Shakespeare for his "small Latin and less Greek" (hence the pun here on latten/Latin).
5. See entry for May 15, 1607.
6. The title page of *A Yorkshire Tragedy* (1608) reads: *A Yorkshire Tragedy. Not so New as Lamentable and true. Acted by his Maiesties Players at the Globe. Written by W. Shakespeare.*
7. Both *Antony and Cleopatra* and *Pericles* were entered in the Stationers' Register on May 20, 1608. *Antony and Cleopatra* was not published until the 1623 First Folio. A corrupt first quarto of *Pericles* was published in 1609.
8. In September 1609 Marston became a deacon, and was ordained in December 1609. He was given the living of Christchurch, Hampshire.
9. Richard Fletcher (d. 1596) was also Dean of Peterborough and later, in turn, Bishop of Bristol, Worcester, and London.
10. The seven sharers (at £5 14s 4d each) were Richard and Cuthbert Burbage, Shakespeare, John Heminges, Henry Condell, Thomas Evans, and William Sly. When Sly died five days later, his share was subdivided amongst the other six sharers. Evans was not an actor but rather an outside financial backer.
11. Sly was buried at St. Leonard's, Shoreditch, on August 16, 1608. During August plague deaths numbered 267.
12. Burbage's daughter (Julia or Juliet) was buried at St. Leonard's, Shoreditch, on September 12, 1608. The same day Lawrence Fletcher was buried at St. Saviour's "with an afternoon knell of the great bell" which cost 20 shillings (as it had for Edmund Shakespeare's burial at the same church. See entry for December 31, 1607).
13. William Walker (1608–80), to whom Shakespeare bequeathed 20 shillings, was the son of the High Bailiff of Stratford, Henry Walker (b. c. 1566?)
14. During the 1608–09 Christmas period, the King's Men performed 12 plays at Court for King James.
15. The full title of George Wilkins's book is *The Painful Adventures of Pericles Prince of Tyre. Being the True History of the Play of Pericles, and as it was lately presented by the worthy and ancient Poet John Gower* (1608). Interestingly, Wilkins dedicated his work to Henry Fermor, who was also the dedicatee of Dekker's *The Seven Deadly Sinnes of London* (1606). See Roger Prior, "The Life of George Wilkins," *Shakespeare Survey*, 25 (1972), 144.

16. The monthly plague deaths in London for September, October, and November 1608 were 653, 460, and 322, respectively. A prohibited performance on November 16, 1608 resulted in the committal of William Pollard and Rice Gwynn to Newgate.
17. Dr. John Dee (1527–1608), a Fellow of Trinity College, Cambridge, was an astrologer, mathematician, alchemist, and fraud.

1609

1. *Troilus and Cressida* was registered in the Stationers' Register by James Roberts on February 7, 1603, but not published then. Booksellers Richard Bonion and Henry Walley entered the play again on January 28, 1609.
2. See the entry for March 12, 1602.
3. George Eld (d. 1624) also printed the *Sonnets* in 1609.
4. Benion & Walley published a quarto edition of Jonson's *Masque of Queens* in 1609, the sole Jonson work they published. The printer was Nicholas Okes (fl. 1596–1639), who printed the 1622 first quarto edition of *Othello*.
5. In 1609 the King's Men visited Ipswich on May 9, Hythe on May 16, and New Romney on May 17.
6. Thomas Thorpe (1570–1635) published Jonson's *Sejanus* (1605) and *Volpone* (1607), as well as Shakespeare's *Sonnets* (1609), which he entered in the Stationers' Register on May 20, 1609.
7. Jonson's *The Key Keeper. A Masque for the Opening of Britain's Burse* was performed on April 19, 1609, for the opening of Robert Cecil's New Exchange in the Strand, London. The Exchange featured sculptural decorations by stonecutter Gerard Christmas (1576–1634) and offered luxury items for sale. It was destroyed in 1737. Jonson's masque featured a statue coming to life, which anticipates the final scene of Shakespeare's *The Winter's Tale* (see Duncan-Jones, *Ungentle Shakespeare*, p. 228).
8. Alleyn bought his copy of the *Sonnets* on June 19, 1609, the first day of publication.
9. "TO THE ONLY BEGETTER OF / THESE ENSUING SONNETS / MR. W. H. ALL HAPPINESS / AND THAT ETERNITY / PROMISED / BY / OUR EVER-LIVING POET / WISHETH / THE WELL-WISHING / ADVENTURER IN / SETTING / FORTH / T.T."
10. 1609 was the worst plague year since 1603 with 4,240 plague deaths in London.
11. The title page of the 1609 first bad quarto edition of *Pericles* reads: "The Late, And much admired Play, Called Pericles, Prince of Tyre. With the true Relation of the whole Historie, adventures, and fortunes of the said Prince: As also, The no lesse strange, and worthy accidents, in the Birth and Life, of his

Daughter Mariana. As it hath been divers and sundry times acted by His Majesties Servants, at the Globe on the Bank-side. By William Shakespeare."
12. Henry Gosson (fl. 1601–40) had published Wilkins's *The Three Miseries of Barbary* (c. 1606–07). *Pericles* proved popular; a second quarto was also published in 1609.
13. Thomas Greene, his wife, and two children had been living at New Place since 1607. Greene was unable to move into his own house, St. Mary's House, which was occupied by one George Browne, who was supposed to vacate it on March 25, 1610. Thereafter Greene hoped to renovate it and move in during September 1610 (see Eccles, *Shakespeare in Warwickshire*, pp. 131–32).
14. Imogen thinks the headless disguised corpse of Cloten is her lover Posthumus and tells the Roman general Lucius his name is "Richard du Champ" (4.2.377).
15. Plague deaths in November 1609 totalled 330.
16. During the 1609–10 Christmas season the King's Men performed 13 plays at Court.

1610
1. Robert Keysar (1576–c. 1640) was a London goldsmith who had purchased a one-sixth share in the boys' company from John Marston. The result of the lawsuit is not known.
2. Jonson's daughter, Elizabeth, was baptized March 25, 1610, at St. Mary Matfellon, Whitechapel. The church was whitewashed, after which the surrounding area was named. The church was destroyed by bombs during Word War II.
3. A Benjamin Jonson was baptized on April 6, 1610, at St. Martin's-in-the-Fields. It is not known whether this child was one of Jonson's legitimate or illegitimate children, or someone else's child altogether.
4. The performance was witnessed by Prince Frederick of Württemburg, Count of Mömpelgart.
5. On May 31, 1610, Burbage and Rice, as Amphion and Corinea, delivered speeches written by Anthony Munday. Prince Henry was invested as Prince of Wales by King James on June 4, 1610.
6. Henry IV was assassinated on May 14, 1610 by Ravaillac (1578–1610).
7. See the entry for December 28, 1594.
8. Also in the cast were William Ostler, Henry Condell, John Underwood, Alexander Cooke, Nicholas Tooley, and William Ecclestone or Eglestone (c. 1591–after 1625).
9. The Master of the Revels, Edmund Tilney, died on August 20, 1610.
10. See Guiderius's song in *Cymbeline*, 4.2.262–63.
11. See entry for Autumn 1609.

12. Russell lived at Alderminster, four miles south of Stratford-upon-Avon.
13. This letter was dated July 15, 1610, and eventually published in 1625 as *A True Repertory of the Wrack and Redemption of Sir Thomas Gates, Knight, upon and from the Islands of the Bermudas his Coming to Virginia, and the estate of that Colony* in *Purchas his Pilgrimes*.
14. As a child Jonson lived in Hartshorn Lane, London, near alleyways called the Bermudas, which were known for their aggressive criminals and other low life. In *The Tempest* Shakespeare refers to "the still-vex'd Bermoothes" [1.2.229].
15. The King's Men performed 15 plays at Court during the 1610 Christmas season.

1611

1. *Oberon, The Fairy Prince*, with music by Alfonso Ferrabosco and staged by Inigo Jones, was performed at Court on January 1, 1611, with Prince Henry as Oberon.
2. Jonson's *Love Freed from Ignorance and Folly* was performed on February 3, 1611 after being postponed for political and technical reasons.
3. The Hecate scenes in *Macbeth* (3.5, 4.1.39–43, and 4.1.125–32) are widely regarded as spurious additions.
4. *Macbeth* was performed at the Globe on April 20, 1611, where it was seen by Simon Forman (1552–1611), a physician and astrologer. Forman described the performance of *Macbeth*, together with performances of *Cymbeline* (April 1611) and *The Winter's Tale* (May 15, 1611) in his "Book of Plaies" (see Rowse, *Sex and Society*, pp. 303–07).
5. Robert Johnson (c.1583–1633) had been appointed a court lutenist in 1604. In addition to songs for *The Tempest*, he may have composed music for *Cymbeline*, *The Winter's Tale*, and *The Two Noble Kinsmen*.
6. See Rowse, *Sex and Society*, pp. 258–59.
7. The King's Men performed numerous times at Court between October 31, 1611 and April 26, 1612, including *The Tempest* on November 1, 1611, and *The Winter's Tale* on November 5, 1611, and 22 plays whose titles remain unknown.

1612

1. Richard Shakespeare (1574–1613) was Shakespeare's other surviving brother who, apparently, lived all his life in Stratford. Edmund, their other brother, had died in 1607.
2. William Peter was murdered on January 25, 1612, by Edward Drew in Exeter. See entry for October 1, 1605.
3. Ostler acquired a one-seventh share in the Globe on February 20, 1612; he had married Thomasina Heminges in 1611.

4. The wedding took place on February 14, 1613. A play, possibly *Henry VIII*, was scheduled for performance on February 16, 1613; however, it was not given because of "greater pleasures." Eight of Shakespeare's plays were performed during the preceding revels: *Henry IV Part 1, Henry IV Part 2, Julius Caesar, Much Ado About Nothing* (twice), *Othello, The Winter's Tale, The Tempest*, and the lost play, *Cardenio*, which may be by Shakespeare and John Fletcher.
5. Prince Henry fell ill after swimming in the Thames. Sir Walter Ralegh was allowed to administer a potion to him, but to no avail. Henry died on November 6, 1612, one day after the King's Men had performed *The Winter's Tale* at Court. Henry was given a state funeral on December 7, 1612.

1613

1. Combe was apparently the wealthiest man in Stratford; among his bequests were £30 for the poor, £60 for his tomb, and £1,500 in miscellaneous bequests (see Eccles, *Shakespeare in Warwickshire*, p. 119).
2. Henry Walker (d. 1616), who had bought the Gatehouse for £100 in 1604, sold it to Shakespeare for £140.
3. Shakespeare and Burbage were each paid 44 shillings for the Earl of Rutland's impresa (a pasteboard shield with emblematic devices painted upon it), which he used on March 24, 1613, at the tilt celebrating the anniversary of James's accession.
4. The lost play, *Cardenio*, was ascribed to Shakespeare and John Fletcher in a Stationers' Register entry for September 9, 1653. In May and July 1613 Heminges received payments from the Privy Council for performances of several plays including *Cardenio*. A "*Cardenna*" was performed before the Ambassador of the Savoy on June 8, 1613. Lewis Theobald (1688–1744) published *Double Falsehood* in 1728, which he claimed to have adapted from a manuscript of *Cardenio*.
5. The King's Men performed at Court for James on November 1, 4, 5, 15, and 16; and December 27, 1613; January 1, 4, and 10; February 2, 4, 8, 10, and 18; and March 6 and 8, 1614.

1614

1. The young son who dies in *The Winter's Tale*.
2. Major fires in Stratford in 1594 and 1595 had fallen on Sundays. The 1614 fire destroyed 54 houses and caused £8,000 in damage (see Eccles, *Shakespeare in Warwickshire*, p. 135).
3. William Replingham and others proposed enclosing land at Welcombe, which would affect Shakespeare and Thomas Greene, the town clerk, since their land would produce less income as pasture rather than as arable land.

4. The Lady Elizabeth's Men performed *Bartholomew Fair* at the Hope Theatre on October 31, 1614 and at Court on November 1, 1614.
5. This is a backhanded compliment since the relevant passage reads: "He that will swear *Jeronimo* or *Titus* are the best plays yet, shall pass unexcepted at here as a man whose judgment shews it is constant, and hath stood still these five and twenty or thirty years."
6. The King's Men performed eight plays at Court during the Christmas season.

1615
1. The Stratford Corporation's letter was dated December 23, 1614.
2. William Combe (1586–1667) was a forceful advocate of enclosure and had his men attack women and children who attempted to fill in his ditches at Welcombe. He ignored a March 1615 order against enclosure, and depopulated the village of Welcombe.
3. On March 27, 1615, Lord Chief Justice Coke issued an order that there should be no enclosures within the parish of Stratford.
4. Robert Armin was buried on November 30, 1615.

1616
1. Philip Henslowe died on January 6, 1616, and was buried January 10, 1616. He left £1,700 12s 8d.
2. Francis Collins (d. 1617) was a lawyer and town official. Together with Thomas Russell, Collins was named overseer of Shakespeare's will. The will made customary bequests to family and friends, though aspects of its provisions have been debated widely (see Honan, *Shakespeare: A Life*, pp. 392–98).
3. In 1616 Jonson was the first dramatist of his era to publish his plays in folio form. His publisher and printer was William Stansby (fl. 1597–1639), who two years earlier had published Sir Walter Ralegh's *History of the World*.
4. Margaret Wheeler died giving birth to Quiney's illegitimate child. Both mother and child were buried on March 15, 1616. On March 26, 1616, Quiney confessed in Stratford's Bawdy Court that he had committed carnal copulation with Margaret Wheeler and was fined five shillings.

Books Available from Santa Monica Press

www.santamonicapress.com • 1-800-784-9553

The Bad Driver's Handbook
Hundreds of Simple Maneuvers to Frustrate, Annoy, and Endanger Those Around You
by Zack Arnstein and
Larry Arnstein
192 pages $12.95

Calculated Risk
The Extraordinary Life of Jimmy Doolittle
by Jonna Doolittle Hoppes
360 pages $24.95

Captured!
Inside the World of Celebrity Trials
by Mona Shafer Edwards
176 pages $24.95

Creepy Crawls
A Horror Fiend's Travel Guide
by Leon Marcelo
384 pages $16.95

Elvis Presley Passed Here
Even More Locations of America's Pop Culture Landmarks
by Chris Epting
336 pages $16.95

The Encyclopedia of Sixties Cool
A Celebration of the Grooviest People, Events, and Artifacts of the 1960s
by Chris Strodder
336 pages $24.95

Exotic Travel Destinations for Families
by Jennifer M. Nichols and
Bill Nichols
360 pages $16.95

Footsteps in the Fog
Alfred Hitchcock's San Francisco
by Jeff Kraft and Aaron Leventhal
240 pages $24.95

French for Le Snob
Adding Panache to Your Everyday Conversations
by Yvette Reche
400 pages $16.95

Haunted Hikes
Spine-Tingling Tales and Trails from North America's National Parks
by Andrea Lankford
376 pages $16.95

How to Speak Shakespeare
by Cal Pritner and
Louis Colaianni
144 pages $16.95

Jackson Pollock
Memories Arrested in Space
by Martin Gray
216 pages $14.95

James Dean Died Here
The Locations of America's Pop Culture Landmarks
by Chris Epting
312 pages $16.95

The Keystone Kid
Tales of Early Hollywood
by Coy Watson, Jr.
312 pages $24.95

L.A. Noir
The City as Character
by Alain Silver and James Ursini
176 pages $19.95

Loving Through Bars
Children with Parents in Prison
by Cynthia Martone
216 pages $21.95

Marilyn Monroe Dyed Here
More Locations of America's Pop Culture Landmarks
by Chris Epting
312 pages $16.95

Movie Star Homes
by Judy Artunian and
Mike Oldham
312 pages $16.95

Offbeat Museums
The Collections and Curators of America's Most Unusual Museums
by Saul Rubin
240 pages $19.95

A Prayer for Burma
by Kenneth Wong
216 pages $14.95

Quack!
Tales of Medical Fraud from the Museum of Questionable Medical Devices
by Bob McCoy
240 pages $19.95

Redneck Haiku
Double-Wide Edition
by Mary K. Witte
240 pages $11.95

Route 66 Adventure Handbook
by Drew Knowles
312 pages $16.95

The Ruby Slippers, Madonna's Bra, and Einstein's Brain
The Locations of America's Pop Culture Artifacts
by Chris Epting
312 pages $16.95

School Sense: How to Help Your Child Succeed in Elementary School
by Tiffani Chin, Ph.D.
408 pages $16.95

Silent Echoes
Discovering Early Hollywood Through the Films of Buster Keaton
by John Bengtson
240 pages $24.95

Silent Traces
Discovering Early Hollywood Through the Films of Charlie Chaplin
by John Bengtson
304 pages $24.95

Tiki Road Trip
A Guide to Tiki Culture in North America
by James Teitelbaum
288 pages $16.95